Shane frowned. There seemed to be nothing out of the ordinary. No thugs lying in wait, no spirit presences that could protect or warn his enemy.

He considered calling on Legba for help. He could summon his loa-tte without resorting to the rituals required for the other spirits; a touch of his fingers on his asson, which he had brought with him, and a mental plea would be enough. Legba was the Opener of the Gate, and Shane's route lay through the shack's front door.

But it was possible Sangre would be able to detect even the subtle presence of Legba. He couldn't take that chance.

Shane tied off the boat and moved cautiously down the dock to the shack's door. He crouched down next to the window, staring in, giving his eyes time to adjust to the light.

The single room was small and bare save for a straight-backed chair in the center of the wood floor. There were a few talismans set on the floor or hanging from the walls. Anisse was tied to the chair and gagged. Sangre sat cross-legged on the floor near her. In one hand was a short-bladed knife with a black handle.

Shane pulled the gun. He knew it could not be as easy as it looked. Sangre had to have some kind of defense. But perhaps surprise would be on his side as well; his enemy would not be expecting such a straightforward assault.

It was his only hope.

Shane stood, took a deep breath and kicked in the door.

Tor Books by Michael Reaves

Street Magic
Night Hunter
Voodoo Child

VOODOO CHILD

MICHAEL REAVES

TOR®

A TOM DOHERTY ASSOCIATES BOOK
NEW YORK

VOODOO CHILD

A Tor Book
Published by Tom Doherty Associates, Inc.
175 Fifth Avenue
New York, NY 10010

Tor Books on the World Wide Web:
http://www.tor.com

Tor® is a registered trademark of Tom Doherty Associates, Inc.

ISBN: 0-812-51993-0
Library of Congress Card Catalog Number: 97-29847

First edition: March 1998
First mass market edition: April 1999

Printed in the United States of America

0 9 8 7 6 5 4 3 2 1

For Brynne, now and forever;
and for Danforth W. Comins III,
keeper of the exchequer and
cornet blower extraordinaire.

Nature, who for the perfect maintenance of the laws of her general equilibrium, has sometimes need of vices and sometimes of virtues, inspires now this impulse, now that one, in accordance with what she requires.

—Marquis de Sade

ACKNOWLEDGMENTS

As always, my thanks go first to Brynne Chandler Reaves, for encouragement, criticism, and generally putting up with my continuing to write books while producers breathe down my neck; and Steve Perry, always a fount of information about all kinds of things: in this case, Emergency Room procedure, martial arts, and Louisiana in general.

Thanks also go to Dan Comins, and a free plug: If you've any affection for Dixieland Jazz at all, check out the South Frisco Jazz Band, on the *Stomp Off* label. It's the real stuff.

Much of the research for this book was done through the Internet and the World Wide Web—more excuses for never leaving the house, unfortunately. It sure is nice to be living here in the future. . . .

1

CITY OF MAGIC

The profession of magician is one of the most perilous and arduous specialisations of the imagination. On the one hand there is the hostility of God and the police to be guarded against; on the other it is as difficult as music, as deep as poetry, as ingenious as stage-craft, as nervous as the manufacture of high explosives, and as delicate as the trade in narcotics.

—William Bolitho,
Twelve Against the Gods

French Quarter,
New Orleans,
Louisiana

February 24–25, 1998

The dead were celebrating on Bourbon Street.

It was Fat Tuesday, Mardi Gras, the last night of Carnival, and the narrow streets of the *Vieux Carré* were packed with costumed merrymakers partying themselves blind in the last hours before midnight. The night air was redolent with the smells of Cajun spices, barbecue and spilled beer. Over on St. Charles and Canal Street huge floats moved slowly through the crowds, pulled by tractors and filled with riders tossing doubloons, cups and plastic beads at delirious throngs, shouting "Throw me something, mister!" On Bourbon and Royal people leaned perilously from wrought-iron balconies, clung to street-lamp poles and danced atop parked cars. Jugglers, unicyclists, stilt walkers and acrobats found space somehow in the tightly packed crowd to demonstrate their skills. Dominatrix nuns and transvestite priests dispensed favors, while jazz from Dixieland marching bands and syncopated zydeco clashed with boombox rap and hip-hop. Legions of horsemen dressed in satin and velvet robes, feathered plumes rising over their heads, passed proudly by, flanked by clowns, masquers and mimes. On the corner of Royal and Conte an evangelist in sackcloth and ashes shouted predictions of divine doom through a bullhorn. Naphtha-fueled flambeaux carried by white-robed black men shed flickering light on the scene.

The dead blended easily into the revelry; on this last frenzied night of Carnival the sudden appearance of Satan himself would hardly raise eyebrows. Members of one of the many costumed krewes that helped stage the parades and festivities, they wore loose black robes and porcelain skull masks. They stalked through the throng, somber figures contrasting with the crowd's bright colors. Unlike the other masquers, they dispensed few party favors—only an occasional blood-red bead or baggie full of crimson powder. This did not seem to bother those filling the picturesque French Quarter. After all, the dead are not known for their generosity.

Gil Duquesne loved Mardi Gras. Every year the "City that Care Forgot" invited six million people to a month-long drunken bash, and every year Gil made out like a bandit. The other events—Festa D'Italia, the Jazz Festival, Spring Fiesta—were good too, but for sheer opportunity Carnival was the best, no question. Gil had heard it called the biggest party in the western world. He didn't know about that, but it was for damn sure the best time of year for his line of work. Sometimes he made enough of a roll to last him almost into summer.

He moved through the dense mass of humanity, sizing up marks with a practiced eye. The possibilities were so many it was almost impossible to choose. Many of the tourists wore costumes, making it hard to get through the layers of clothing to find wallets, but more than enough didn't.

He set his sights on a heavy-set tourist, standing near the brightly lit entrance of the Absinthe Bar, neck slung with a Nikon, a Rolex on one wrist and a nylon fanny pack around his ample waist. Christ, Gil thought, slipping easily through the crowd toward him, too dumb to live. If only someone else ain't shaken him down first. . . .

He stumbled against the mark, recovered his balance and grinned apologetically, like a tipsy and sheepish drunk. The other man returned the smile, clapped Gil on the back and shouted, "Happy Mardi Gras!" An instant later the surges and eddies of the crowd carried them apart.

Gil headed down Conte toward Chartres, away from the floats making their way down Bourbon Street. He slipped into the dark haven of a recessed doorway and quickly eviscerated the eelskin wallet. A nice wad of fifties and twenties, another five hundred in traveler's checks—unsigned, thank you Jesus!—plus a bit of lagniappe in the form of Visa, Discover and Amex gold cards. "Sweet charity," he murmured. This put his take so far at nearly fifteen hundred in cash alone. Amazing how much money people will carry on them in a strange city. Gil dropped the wallet and blended back into the press of revelers.

For a time he let the currents of humanity move him while he thought about the day's take. Not bad, not bad at all. He had enough to carry him solid for a couple of months and keep him well supplied with some good Southern Comfort, maybe even let him score a little coke. Life was good. *Laissez les bons temps rouler.* . . .

Of course, there were bad times as well as good. Just a few weeks ago he'd been so desperate for cash that he'd lifted a purse off a hooker, praying that she didn't belong to a certain stable that included just about every whore in the Quarter. He'd sweated that for a while, no mistake, done some serious looking over his shoulder. There were certain rules prudent men lived by: You don't pull on Superman's cape or yank the mask off the Lone Ranger and you sure as hell don't mess with Mal Sangre, the top crime lord in Louisiana, not if you don't want to wind up gator bait in some bayou.

Thank God Mardi Gras had come along, with enough easy marks to keep him from having to do that more than once. And no one had seen him and the bitch together, no one had put the finger on him. Gil knew a lot of people on the street who believed all the stories about Sangre's voodoo, how he used it to keep his people in line. Well, that was fine—let him kill all the chickens he wanted, long as he didn't know who Gil was. The only magic Gil believed in was what prestidigitation he could perform with his ten fingers. Making a pocketbook vanish out of a purse without the owner noticing—that was sorcery.

Several teenagers ran past a line of parked cars, smashing windshields with beer bottles. A biker maneuvered his Harley down the crowded street with a topless laughing woman riding pillion. Gil kept his hands in his pockets, clutching the booty he had dipped from unsuspecting victims. Let the drunks and stoners occupy the cops' attention. He looked like a citizen: thirty-something, clad in stone-washed jeans, light sweater and running shoes, his hair and mustache neatly trimmed. A face in the crowd, no more. The only thing even remotely memorable about him was a birthmark in the form of a tiny dark blemish in the white of his left eye. He wore tinted glasses to keep that from being noticed.

A black youth a few steps ahead of him cut the strap of a woman's purse and pulled it free, shoving his way through the confused crowd as she screamed. A mounted cop, wearing purple bead necklaces and gold epaulets, guided his horse adroitly through the mass of humanity and grabbed the cutpurse by the collar.

Gil watched this with the professional's contempt for the amateur. No finesse, no style. He had spent long hours practicing his craft, working on a dressmaker's dummy laced with bells until he could lift a wallet from a coat pocket without making a sound. He shook his head. Kids today didn't want to learn a trade.

He passed a few other pigeons who looked ripe for the plucking, but let them slide by. Greed could very easily land you in the House of Blue Lights, especially tonight, when the NOPD had many of its people cruising the streets as potential marks. Gil was pretty good at spotting them, but you could never be too careful. He'd done a good night's work, and now he was content to amble past the restaurants and houses ablaze with light and alive with music, their balcony railings festooned with gold, purple and green crepe paper, garlands and balloons.

He turned right on Chartres, heading toward Jackson Square. The former military parade ground was a great place to score some action, on this night in particular. Last year he'd gotten a truly amazing blow job from a drunken college girl in exchange for a handful of beads. God, he loved Mardi Gras.

The ancient bulks of the Cabildo, the St. Louis Cathedral and the Presbytere—three of the oldest buildings in the country— glowed against the night sky as he entered the square. His Nikes squeaked on the flagstones. He could smell flowering shrubs and banana trees in the small park across the court where Andrew Jackson reared his horse on a pedestal. Shouts and laughter echoed all about; a short distance down Pirate's Alley he got a glimpse of a couple backed up against the Cabildo wall, the man's pants sagging open around his hips, the woman's skirt hiked up over hers. Gil moved closer to the comforting light of one of the lamps that topped the park's iron fence. No sense tempting fate; he wasn't the only one looking for prey tonight. Some of the local skinhead gangs were cruising as well; he'd seen four of them earlier, kicking the shit out of a street person with their steel-toed Doc Martens over in Exchange Alley.

The thought was sobering. Though he was more capable than most people of avoiding danger, maybe it wasn't a bad idea to head back to his apartment. The constant partying was wearing on him. It was drawing close to midnight anyway; soon the madness would start to die down, and by morning it would be mostly over for another year. He could afford a cab, which was just as well, since his neighborhood around St. Charles was not the safest. One of the problems of not having a regular income.

Gil stared out of the square, passing one of the Civil War cannons in front of the Cabildo that had been stuffed with paper and set on fire. Its barrel glowed with embers, sending smoke twisting up into the night. He was about to stroll up St. Ann Street to hail a cab when he noticed someone standing in the shadows of Père Antoine's Alley.

An ivory skull, floating above whispering silken darkness, approached him. A white-gloved hand extended, opened. On the palm rested what seemed to be a frozen drop of blood.

Gil looked at the eye sockets of the mask. It was only a trick of the light, of course, but it looked like nothing but darkness, with perhaps faint twin gleams of red, was behind the false face. He snorted at the momentary gooseflesh the thought produced. "Thanks," he said, taking the bead from the masquer, who turned and disappeared quickly into the night. As he left, Gil glanced at his watch. It was midnight. One last gesture of *bonhomie* from a stranger before Mardi Gras ended. He felt oddly touched.

He crossed the street in front of the bakery, raising his right hand, fingers still closed about the bead, to brush hair out of his eyes. He managed to lift his arm only a few inches before it dropped down again by his side. Gil frowned; his arm felt numb, like it had gone to sleep.

He tried to raise it again, but this time the mental command had no more effect than if the limb had belonged to someone else. Gil noticed a faint tingling sensation spreading through his shoulder, leaving more numbness in its wake. He couldn't open his hand. His heart began to beat rapidly. What the hell was this? Some sort of stroke? His hands were his livelihood; who ever heard of a paralyzed dip?

He grabbed his limp right arm with his left hand; it was like seizing the cold dead limb of a corpse. Gil felt his mouth go dry. He raised the numb hand, pried it open, turned the supplicating fingers toward the moonlight and saw a fading red stain in the center of the palm.

A coffin-shaped stain.

Gil turned frantically. A block away a phalanx of mounted policemen, moving in wedge formation, ushered hard-core party animals off the street. He tried to cry out—the only time in his life he had ever called a cop for help—but all that came out was a rasping croak. The tingling was spreading across his chest and he couldn't fill his lungs. He tried to run, but his right leg buckled beneath him.

Gil lay on his back in a welter of paper cups, discarded food wrappings and other trash left by the crowd. The numbness had devoured both legs now and the tingling was advancing across his chest. He wanted to scream, but not even a whisper was possible now. His panic and terror were trapped within his skull.

He stared up at the moon riding the clear night sky. He thought his vision was beginning to blur; the single moon seemed suddenly to have divided into multiple discs bobbing uncertainly in the heavens. Then he realized that the pale shapes looking down at him were the skull faces of masquers like the one who had given him the bead. One of the forms bent down, began going through his pockets.

Then the tingling engulfed his eyes and moved toward his brain.

Mardi Gras was over. The bells had heralded the changing of the hour, the start of Ash Wednesday and forty-five days of Lent—not that very many people in New Orleans worried about atonement. A breeze from off the Mississippi stirred confetti and streamers on the streets of the *Vieux Carré*. A balloon anchored to a wrought iron railing was blown free. It rose a few feet into the air as though struggling for flight; then, the helium having seeped through its flaccid skin, drifted tiredly into the embrace of a banana tree.

The massive, ornate floats were on their way back to their dens, there to slumber until roused again for next year's citywide party. The people who had thronged the streets and parks returned reluctantly to their apartments, condos, houses and hotels, some to continue celebrating until dawn at private parties, others to sleep, exhausted. The cleaning crews moved in to clear the tons of rubbish left behind.

It has been said that even the dead party during Mardi Gras, and sleep more soundly afterward. The first part may be true—but not the second.

The dead had work to do.

VERONIQUE AND PORT-AU-PRINCE, HAITI

APRIL 9, 1988

It began in the arid austere region of the Artibonite, in the village of Veronique. In 1988 Shane LaFitte was twenty-six years old and a *houngan*, the one to whom the townspeople came with their illnesses, their fears and their prayers.

It had been a long and difficult journey for him. He had attended schools abroad, but nothing they offered in the way of career choices had appealed to him. Restless, seeking an intensity and sheen to life that his own seemed to lack, he had roamed the length and breadth of the Caribbean, working at a variety of jobs that included a stint on a Jamaican fishing trawler, a few months in Trinidad as a bodyguard for a reggae star, and even a diver for sunken treasure near the Virgin Islands. None of these adventures had calmed his restive nature, and eventually, at age twenty, he had returned to Haiti and the town of his birth.

Why he came back Shane was not sure. It was not that he felt any love for or attachment to the land of his birth; he sometimes wondered how anyone could feel anything but horror and loathing for the squalid cities, despotic officials and extreme poverty that infested the country. The village he had grown up in had little more than a hundred people in it, most of them living in shanties made of corrugated siding or gasoline cans hammered flat and nailed to wooden frameworks. His childhood memories were of constant hunger, of his father sweltering in the blazing humidity trying to earn gourds, the national currency worth hardly more than the paper it was printed on, to buy enough cassavas and yams to keep his family fed for another day. Over a hundred years of alternating foreign occupations and tyrannical dictatorships had reduced both the island and its people to thin, gaunt specters of what they once had been. The hillsides had been denuded of trees, systematically stripped for grazing land and charcoal. It was as if a vampire plague had sucked everything and everyone to a dry husk.

Shane had grown up during the reign of "Baby Doc" Duvalier, who had carried on his father's rule of paranoia, oppression, graft and feudalism. The dictator's military elite, the dreaded Ton Ton Macoutes, prowled the land, killing for the genocidal sport of it, a Caribbean *pogrom*, dumping scores of bodies in the stinking mangrove swamps and on the streets of Port-au-Prince, decaying roadblocks for the rich in their air-conditioned Mercedeses and Land Rovers. Shane had been glad to escape with his life.

And yet he had returned. It was as if the island of Hispaniola had called him back, back to that part of it that was Haiti, back to that swamp of mud and shit and human despair. When he had gotten off the plane in the summer of 1982, the young boys with purple sugar cane shucks clenched in their teeth like cigars fighting to carry his luggage; when he had found a seat on the *tap-tap* that wheezed away from the airport, bearing its crowded cargo of people, animals and merchandise; when, after the long bone-jarring ride along the coast and up through the hills, the aging Mercedes bus had at last shuddered and clattered into the town square of Veronique, Shane LaFitte knew that, for better or worse, he had come home.

It was perhaps six months later that he let Anisse, a young woman he was seeing, talk him into attending a ceremony at the local *houmfort*. Having grown up in Haiti, Shane was of course familiar with *Vondoun*, but he had never thought of its priests and practitioners as anything more than elaborate charlatans. Such beliefs belonged to a simpler age. Or so he thought until he went with Anisse to the temple that night.

The *houmfort* was a tin-roofed shanty at the edge of the village, rising starkly against the barren countryside, its dilapidated front painted with designs and epitaphs expressing the scope and strength of the *houngan*'s power. Inside the main chamber a group of townsfolk had crowded around the altar and its accumulation of candles, bottles, pottery and other devotional items. The master of the temple was a man named Ducas, who had been a *houngan* when Shane's father had been young.

At first Shane maintained his skepticism as the drummers pounded out a hypnotic, incessant beat and the dancers whirled and gyrated on the ash-strewn dirt floor. He and Anisse watched as several of them drank from wine bottles on the altar containing *clairin*, raw rum liberally spiced with hot peppers. The merest drop on one of the dancer's tongues would normally have raised a blister, but in their ecstatic states they swigged it like beer with no harmful effects.

Anisse, Shane knew, believed that this was because they were possessed by *loas* or other supernatural entities. He had tried to explain to her earlier about psychosomatic trances producing stigmata and other bizarre bodily reactions, but that idea was as absurd to her as possession was to him. "If they grow angry with you—" *Mystères*," she told him now.

Shane became impatient with all this nonsense. "You must not mock the what they will with me!" he told her, loudly enough for several of the people nearby to hear him. "If they really exist, let one of them convince me!"

The drums abruptly stopped. He looked up to see the old *houngan* staring at him, his eyes so intense they seemed almost luminous in the dimly lit room. Ducas came toward Shane, the people parting before him. He came quite near and stopped, staring at Shane with an expression that was not so much stern as reproachful. The room's silence was somehow even louder than the drums.

After a long moment, during which time Shane met the old man's gaze, Ducas finally nodded. "They have heard you, Shane LaFitte," he said. "They have heard you and they respond. Even now, one comes."

Shane started to make some disbelieving and sarcastic reply— and then the madness took him.

It was the only explanation he had, at first. When he thought and spoke later about what had happened, the only analogy he could think of was the difference between watching a movie on a big screen, in vibrant color and stereo sound, and watching it on a tiny black and white TV. Suddenly his consciousness, the awareness that normally filled his skull and his body, had been overwhelmed and shoved down into a small corner in the back of his mind. He was still aware of what was happening, but the sensations reached him as though from a great distance and muffled by layers of cotton, and he was powerless to stop what happened next.

He could sense the presence that had routed his mind from its possession of his body: a powerful entity, not malignant so much as simply and terrifyingly *alien*. He felt its cold metallic intellect peering at him, grim and distant and yet at the same time unspeakably intimate.

Then Shane was jerked away from Anisse as though some superhuman master had yanked an invisible leash. His feet left the floor; his body flew through the air the length of the temple chamber, slamming against the far wall hard enough to dislodge bits of clay. He landed on his feet next to the altar, and one hand snatched up a bottle of spicy rum. He could dimly feel his hand lift the carafe to his mouth, could sense as if from a great distance the liquid scorching down his throat as he guzzled the bottle's contents.

Then he began to dance.

The drumming began again, even more frenzied than before, and Shane's body jerked and flailed to the rhythms, feet pounding the hard red dirt. He felt himself bend backward from the waist, contorting his spine impossibly until his head was between his legs, still dancing as he did so. Others joined the dance, writhing about him in a delirious saturnalia.

His possession lasted for hours. He was being ridden by a *guédé*, a spirit of the dead, rather than by a *loa*; they were typically much more primal and physical than the latter. When it at last was over, dawn was a streak of pearl against the eastern horizon, and most of the other celebrants had left. Shane was exhausted, but, even though he had put his body through extreme contortions and tortures such as drinking pepper-laced rum,

which should have left his gullet blistered and raw, he was un-
hurt.

Anisse watched him with awe as he staggered back to her. He
collapsed against one wall of the shack, his chest heaving. He
looked up and saw Ducas smiling down at him.

"Welcome home," the old man said.

Shane LaFitte studied the ways of *Voudoun* from the age of
twenty on, serving as apprentice to Ducas. The magician per-
formed the *lavé-tête*, the ceremony of investiture that linked the
young man with the *loa* known as Legba, he who guards the
gateways and doors, including those that lead to the Invisible
World. This marked the beginning of a bond between Legba
and him that would last for the rest of Shane's life.

For three years he assisted Ducas and studied the old man's
teachings: alchemy, theosophy, the cabala and other mystic lore.
At the end of that time he had earned the right to build his own
houmfort and call himself a priest of *Voudoun*. Ducas gave him
his own *asson*, a gourd filled with rattlesnake vertebrae, a sacer-
dotal sceptre which granted him the power to call upon Legba.

For the next three years, from 1985 to 1988, Shane pursued
his calling as the servant of the gods and the people of
Veronique. Despite the grinding poverty and hardships of village
life, in years to come he would look back upon that time as one
of the most peaceful and fulfilling periods of his life.

It had not lasted long. In retrospect, he realized it began to
end when he met Jorge Arnez.

Arnez was a Cuban refugee whose family had come to Haiti
in the early 1960s. His father had taught him the ways of
Santeria, and he had gone on to become a *santero*. Although
Voudoun was, after Roman Catholicism, the "official" religion of

Haiti, practitioners of *Santeria, Macumba, Espiritism* and other beliefs were not unknown. Unlike Christians, the concept of "heathen" was unknown to them; they accepted another's faith to be as viable as their own.

Shane had first met Arnez in Port-au-Prince during a conference of *houngans* and *babalawos*. This was not long before the *Dechoukaj*, the "uprooting" that had overthrown Baby Doc's corrupt rule. Shane was making his way through the confusion and hubbub of the perpetual farmers' market on the dusty downtown streets of the city. Squawking chickens, squealing pigs and bleating goats mixed with the din of motorbikes and car horns echoing off ash-gray buildings. Compas music blared from boomboxes and open windows. The sultry air was thick with the stench of decaying refuse and the spicy scent of cooked *griot*. Street vendors sold plantains and fried fish in plastic buckets warmed by candles. Shane had stopped to buy some food when he heard a voice from behind him.

"Excusez-moi, m'sieu."

He turned to see two members of the Ton Ton Macoutes, the dreaded secret police of Haiti. Their faces were expressionless, their eyes hidden behind silvered sunglasses; Shane could almost believe they were the boogeymen of the Creole legend that gave the order its name. One held out a hand, palm up.

Shane knew what they wanted: The identification papers every Haitian citizen was required to carry. He dug the damp, folded documents out of his wallet and handed them over.

The two Macoutes looked at the papers, then at him. "You are from the Artibonite. Why have you come to Port-au-Prince?"

Shane considered his options. There didn't appear to be too many. *Houngans* and other practitioners were not particularly welcome in the nation's capital these days. If he told them the truth he would most likely find himself thrown into some miserable cell in the depths of the National Palace. If he lied and they decided to pursue the matter, the same result was inevitable. It was entirely possible that these two were trying to complete some kind of arrest quota, and if that were the case, no answer would be the right one.

His hesitation encouraged them. One stepped forward aggressively, snapping his fingers in Shane's face. "Answer the question, *m'sieu!*"

"Perhaps I can help," a new voice interjected. Both Shane and the Macoutes turned to see a short, wiry man, Hispanic in appearance, standing close by. He was well dressed in a blazer, a silk shirt and slacks. Shane knew him immediately for a fellow practitioner, one better skilled than he. Something about his attitude, his confidence, made that clear. He hoped it was not equally clear to Duvalier's thugs.

"This man is my business associate," the stranger said to the Macoutes. His voice was rich and mellifluous; the voice of someone accustomed to getting what he asked for. He produced a small white card, which he handed to one of them. Shane caught a glimpse of the printing on it; something about imports and exports. He did not see the man's name.

He waited for the Macoutes to demand the man's ID papers, but to his surprise, they nodded respectfully and stepped back. "Our apologies, *m'sieu,*" the one who had spoken before muttered to Shane. Then they strode quickly away.

Shane watched them go, then turned his attention to his savior, who was grinning at him. He showed Shane another business card. It read: *Jorge Arnez: Casilla Imports & Exports.* There was no address; only a phone number.

"I supply a great many esoteric and exotic items to governmental executives," Arnez said. Shane nodded. It was clear to him now how the man could command such respect from the secret police. Arnez traded in *Le Misère*, the private economy of Haiti's rich and influential. They had grown fat on the sympathetic outpourings of charity from other governments and private organizations by trumpeting the misery of Haiti, the poorest country in the Western Hemisphere. None of the donated funds ever reached the people for whom they were intended, of course; they were all funneled into the coffers of the Duvaliers and others whom Jean-Claude favored. A few trade merchants were granted access to some of this wealth in order to facilitate a thriving black market in contraband, drugs and other items difficult to obtain.

Something of his distaste must have shown on his face, because Arnez's smile faded slightly. "I assure you," he said as they walked along the street, "it's not as bad as it sounds. I make sure a portion of my income reaches those for whom it was originally intended. It is all very well to sneer at those who choose to work within the system, but——"

"I make no judgments," Shane interrupted. "And I am grateful for your help."

Arnez seemed somewhat mollified by this. As they returned to the hotel he told Shane something of his history. Although he was a practicing *santero*, the majority of his income came from his trade business. As Shane came to know him better, he learned that Arnez was telling the truth about investing a portion of his black market earnings into various community services about the island. It was true that in return for this he sometimes exacted exorbitant favors from the locals; still, Shane felt, on the whole there were people who were better off because of Arnez's actions. And there was no getting around the fact that he had, in all probability, saved Shane's life.

Despite their differences they found a common bond in their respective beliefs. Arnez was as accomplished a *santero* as Ducas had been a *houngan*, and Shane admired and respected him for this. He had studied chemistry and medicine in college; when Shane returned to Veronique he found that Arnez had arranged for a truckload of medical supplies to be sent to the small village, with replenishments to follow on a monthly basis.

It was the beginning of a friendship that was to last four years, and finally end in the depths of a bayou nearly a thousand miles away.

Sisters of Grace
Hospital,
New Orleans,
Louisiana

February 25, 1998

The ER was jumping when K.D. Wilcox came on shift; not at all surprising, the last night of Mardi Gras having just ended. In the first hour of the new day she saw no less than thirty-five people come through the sliding glass doors of Sisters of Grace Hospital in downtown Nola. Not all were life-or-death emergencies, true; there were cases like champagne eyeball, self-inflicted by people too drunk to remember to open the bottle pointed away from them, or boxer's fractures sustained in bar-room brawls. These sat forlornly in the waiting room until triage got around to them. One late arrival was Jimmy "Beaucoup" Davis, a homeboy who had managed to get into a fight practically every night of the festival. "Hey, Jimmy," Leonard had said, noticing the blood-soaked gauze over the knife wound in the young Cajun's ribs, "hope they didn't cut the stitches I put in last night."

Pulling on a new pair of surgical gloves, K.D. murmured "Business is good" to one of the orderlies. She hurried down the hall past a line of accident victims wearing neck collars and strapped to backboards, her lab coat billowing back from T-shirt and jeans and a stethoscope knocking against her breastbone. One thick-soled running shoe slipped in a puddle of blood on the floor; she could smell the coppery scent over the antiseptic and alcohol as she dropped to one knee to keep her balance. A janitor hurried over with a mop and disinfectant, and a nurse's aide nearly ran over her right hand, which was splayed out on the floor, with a wheelchair.

"Jesus," K.D. muttered, getting to her feet. "God keep me out of a hospital when I get sick."

She reached an exam table where a John Doe had been placed. Jerry, the nurse, was waiting for her with the chart. K.D. checked the vital signs: pulse sixty-four, respiration ten, temp 98.6, BP 122/94. Everything within normal limits, save that the breathing was a little slow. So why was he comatose?

She checked his pupils, noticing absently that the sclera of the left eye had a dark blemish. No abnormal dilation. She did a quick physical, moving his arms and legs, palpating his abdomen, looking for needle holes, stricture marks on the throat, cranial contusions. She sniffed his breath. Nothing to indicate diabetic acidosis, no whiff of bowel telling her the system was clogged. She'd order a blood workup, but she was certain he didn't have enough alcohol in him to warrant unconsciousness. His skin wasn't clammy, hot, cyanotic or unnaturally red.

Nothing out of the ordinary at first glance, then. K.D. looked at Jerry. "Any history on him?"

"Uh-uh. No wallet, nothin'."

She nodded. "Who's on tap?" She was only a third-year resident; at some point in the exam an experienced M.D. or neurologist would be needed.

Jerry shrugged. "They all busy."

"What a surprise." The hospital was understaffed at the best of times; on nights like this they really felt it. "Okay, let's get him tested; CBC, SMA, drug screen and urine."

"Want an ECG too?"

"Sure, what the hell. Maybe if he's lucky we can get a neuro to run a skull series before he croaks on the table."

"Awrite, dawlin'." Jerry moved quickly in one direction and K.D. headed off in the other, the John Doe behind her already fading in her mind under the pressure of new emergencies. This was the down side of Mardi Gras that most of New Orleans never saw. K.D. had been out celebrating as well the last few hours of the festival, knowing that it would not be long before she would be in here trying to repair some small bit of the damage that results when several million people hit the streets and party. The irony of it bothered her more than it did most of her colleagues; they were fully capable of viewing people in the real world as fascinating complex creatures, worthy of friendship, love, hate—and then, once they entered this pastel Formica labyrinth, seeing them as just bags of blood and bones. It had to be that way for them.

K.D. didn't want it to be that way for her, however. That, she felt, was renouncing a vital part of her humanity. She couldn't let herself go through the full emotional wringer each trauma case represented, of course—she'd be catatonic inside a week. But she refused to shut herself down in self-protection. As in all things, balance was constantly to be sought.

Even so, given the press of the night's work, she gave little further thought to the coma case. At one point she noticed in passing that Carl Pearson, the neurologist, was checking him out, thumping the guy's skull like a watermelon to check for lesions. Then her attention was distracted by a gunshot victim that came in on a gurney.

It wasn't until almost four A.M., when the rush had died down somewhat, that she noticed the table was empty. She checked with Carl.

"Oh yeah," he said, his voice muffled by his face mask. "Kinda interesting, actually. I gave him the deluxe: X ray, EEG, brain scan. Everything ran clean, so I sent him up for a spinal."

"Any signs of intracranial pressure?"

The neuro frowned slightly behind the mask, as though he resented having his procedure questioned. "No. But there's not much else to try. I've got him slotted into ICU. We'll see what the tap shows."

K.D. nodded. From then on until the end of her shift, probably because of the decrease in work, she found it hard to stop thinking of the coma case. There had been something odd about it in retrospect—aside from the fact that they hadn't found any trauma to explain his unconscious state. It wasn't until she was walking out to her car in the gray eastern light that she remembered.

She had opened his hands to see if there were any clues contained in the folds of the skin. Nothing, save what seemed to be a tattoo in faded red ink on the palm of the right hand. She hadn't paid much attention to it, being preoccupied with her search for symptoms, but now that she thought about it, the palm of the hand was a pretty strange place for a tattoo. And there was the tattoo itself: a square cross atop a crude coffin. It was the sort of mark they saw a lot on teenage gang members, though a bit too finely rendered to be a typical jailhouse tattoo. But this man had been middle-aged and, by the looks of him, a fairly respectable citizen.

She paused with her key in the lock of her Pathfinder. Strange. She shook her head. It was the kind of clue that a cop would be more interested in than a doctor. And in any event, he was no longer her patient.

Still, K.D. stood for a few minutes in the chill pre-dawn light, thinking about it. The memory of that tattoo reminded her that New Orleans, no matter how civilized it tried to appear, could never completely deny the dark and sinister underside of its culture. The entire city was built on swampland . . . a foundation of death and immundity, shifting and volatile. Beneath the streets, beneath the houses, beneath the mausoleums, darkness roiled: ancient, uneasy and alive.

K.D. blinked, mildly astonished at these thoughts. She was certainly capable of a mordant turn of mind on occasion; that came with the territory. But these feelings were different. She felt revulsion at having them in her head.

She unlocked the four-by-four and got in. In the east a line of nacreous light challenged the darkness. But toward the west the skyscrapers of downtown were still lit against a blue-black night.

ALGIERS,
NEW ORLEANS
AND METAIRIE,
LOUISIANA

FEBRUARY 25, 1998

Most people were sorry to see the end of Mardi Gras. The city always seemed despondent afterward as street sweepers cleaned the thoroughfares of confetti and food wrappers and people lined the curbs with garbage cans full of noisemakers and torn crepe paper. For a few days New Orleans seemed almost subdued; at least it felt that way to Lia St. Charles. And that was exactly how she liked it.

Few branches of New Orleans's law enforcement dread the festivals more than probation-parole officers. Their clients, who are not very stable at best, tend to get completely out of control during Carnival and other celebrations. Lia could always count on a number of her cases winding up back in Corrections for violating conditions. There wasn't even an up side to this for her in the form of a reduced caseload, because there were always more to take their places.

Today, twenty-four hours after Fat Tuesday, was no exception. She was across the river in Algiers at a shotgun apartment rented by one Joseph René, known to what few friends he could claim as Slow Joey. The nickname supposedly came from his lazy Cajun drawl, but a few in-depth conversations with him had convinced Lia that it applied just as well to his mental capacity. He was a parolee just out of Angola for armed robbery, and since he'd missed his last check-in and wasn't answering her knock it looked pretty damn certain he would be renewing old acquaintances upstate real soon.

She tried the door. It was unlocked; not that it mattered, since she had a key. Inside, the long narrow room was carpeted with pizza boxes, beer cans and KFC cartons. A black velvet reproduction of a Penthouse centerfold dominated one wall, and a room air conditioner vibrated like a hive of angry bees. The place smelled sour.

"Joey!" Goddamn it, she didn't have time for this. She had twenty more cases to check on today and a stack of post-sentence sheets and other paperwork as tall as the World Trade Center.

"Keep you pantyhose on, chère." Joey emerged from the hallway entrance wearing a pair of stained jeans. His accent was more pronounced and his speech more languid than she'd ever heard it. The whites of his eyes were stained red—a sure sign of Blood usage—and his pupils were the size of sub-atomic particles.

Lia studied him. He wasn't an impressive sight: skin the shade of a dead trout, arms thin and flabby and a beer belly hanging over his belt. His hair hung in lank strands down to his shoulders. He sat in a chair without bothering to remove the soft-drink cups nesting there. One foot dangled over the armrest, twitching nervously.

"You didn't come in Monday," Lia said.

"Been busy, me." He grinned at her; it might have been charming ten years earlier.

She sat on the edge of the pressed-wood coffee table, it being the cleanest spot she could find. "Busy with what? The job?"

He waved a hand in lazy dismissal. "Naw, naw . . . me, I can't hack that shit. Too hard loadin' crates, *hein?* I told 'em find som'body else."

"You saying you quit?" Her voice was steady and low now, the way it always got when she was angry. Joey became very interested in a cuticle on his left forefinger.

Lia picked up a paper cup that still had a few inches of Coke in it and threw it at him. The brown liquid soaked Joey's stringy hair and dripped down his pale chest. He leaped out of the chair, stepped on a piece of greasy wax paper, skidded and nearly landed on his ass. "*Hey!* You crazy—"

Lia looked at him calmly. "You fucked up big time, Joey. You *want* to go back to 'Gola? Back to being some lifer's personal poke? That your idea of fun?"

He chewed his lower lip, rubbed the stubble along a weak excuse for a jaw. "No way. Two years up there I was puttin' a cork in my butt, keep my pants clean. Not goin' back, no." He held up a hand, palm out, indicating his refusal, and she saw something odd there: a crimson, coffin-shaped tattoo. It looked like it had been put there fairly recently.

"What's that?" she asked, indicating it. Joey glanced at it, then clenched his fist. She saw a flicker of fear in his gaze.

Never mind; a new tattoo was the least of Joey's problems.

Lia stood. She was tall, five-ten and a half, and could lock his eyes in a level gaze. No way around it, she told herself; might as well get it over with. "You *are* going back, Joey," she said quietly. "You're cracked out, and you've been doing Blood. I can see it."

"No way, *vraiment?*"

She pulled a small plastic vial out of her purse. "Prove it."

He glanced nervously around the room. Lia put the vial back. "I don't need it, Joey. I can tell you got urine dirtier than the Big Muddy. You missed coming in, you quit your job. . . ." She shook her head. "I've given you plenty of chances. No more. I'm violating you." She started toward the phone.

He jumped across the room after her, grabbed her shoulder from behind. "Miz St. Charles, no, you *can't*—"

She let him turn her around, reached across with her other hand and took his wrist, bending it. Joey had no choice but to double over in pain. She swept her leg back against his, crouched down to keep her hold as he hit the floor. Maintaining the wrist lock, Lia picked up the receiver with her free hand and punched 911.

She tried not to feel too depressed as she opened the door to her steel gray cubicle of an office and hung her blazer on the hook. She'd lost a case today; Joey would be going back in, no question about that. Maybe his defender could swing some work release, but she doubted it.

The problem was that Joey wanted to get back in. He didn't think he did, and no doubt was sincere about not wanting to wind up some hardtimer's sweetheart once more. But the truth was that, on a deeper level, the Joeys she had to deal with day in and day out couldn't hack it on the outside. Prison represented security, an environment they could understand and cope with. Most of them found ways to get back inside those stone walls.

It would be six more days before she could spend an hour unloading all this on her shrink. The irony was that her therapist had the same professional problem that she did—maintaining an emotional distance from clients. In her line of work she had to be a combination police officer, social worker and counselor. She couldn't let herself empathize with the cases, worry about them, care about them, past a certain point. Most of them were pretty easy not to care about, but a few, like Joey, could be oddly endearing. After all, he was only twenty-three, with barely a fifth-grade education, not to mention alcoholic parents who had stranded him in a genetic *cul-de-sac* to begin with. . . . Small wonder he had low impulse control.

Lia shook her head, red curls rippling against her white blouse. It wasn't her problem.

Her next case was waiting for her: April Delaney, nineteen years old and the mother of a four-year-old girl. She came into the office bringing Soukie with her, there being no way she could afford child care working as a supermarket checker on the midnight shift. She was lucky to have a cousin who could watch the girl while April worked.

The young black woman sat gingerly in the wooden chair facing the desk while Soukie played in the corner with a Barbie missing one arm. April wore jeans that were worn and faded, but clean, and a peasant blouse. Her hair, dyed blonde when Lia had first seen her, had been cut shorter and was now its natural shade. Lia smiled at her. She considered April a success story, at least so far. A probationer, the woman used to be a streetwalker, pulling thirty or forty a trick, her sole ambition in life to be a call girl in one of Mal Sangre's escort services. A crack addict, an alcoholic at thirteen and pregnant for the first time at fifteen—twin girls she had given up for adoption. But as of today she had been clean and steadily employed for almost six months, and she was determined to get off food stamps by the summer. At Lia's recommendation the state had given Soukie, the fruit of her second pregnancy, back to her, which had done a lot for her self-esteem. One case like April, Lia thought, made up for a barge full of Slow Joeys.

"I been puttin' money away," she told Lia. "Not much; last week it was only seven dollars, but every week I put some in that savings account you helped me set up. Maybe when Soukie's old enough for college I might can send her."

"It's a good goal," Lia agreed. "You keep going the way you're going and I don't think you'll have to worry about your daughter's future."

"Oh, ain't no doubt of that," April said quickly, glancing with pride at the little girl in the faded smock who sat cross-legged on the floor, whispering to the doll and apparently unaware of being talked about. "She's been consecrated, you know. She's a *serviteur*."

Lia's smile became a bit more fixed. That was the only thing that bothered her about this case: April's fixation with voodoo. It wasn't exactly a rarity in this part of the world; still, she wished the woman could be weaned from it. It didn't look good on her sheet; some of Lia's colleagues, in fact, considered attending a ceremony at a *houmfort* grounds for violation. It was all bullshit, a primitive belief structure with no place in civilized society. Thundering drums, frenzied dancing, trance states, sacrificing goats and chickens . . . Lia suppressed an urge to roll her eyes heavenward.

"Soukie's been ridden by the *loa* more than once," April

continued. "The spirit came into her, told me my little girl was goin' to be a great *mambo* someday. Said she had the Gift."

"Let's talk about your job," Lia said.

At night downtown New Orleans looked just like any other big city: high-rise hotels, skyscrapers glowing against the darkness, illuminated billboards. Lia rolled the window of her Acura down, enjoying the relatively cool night breeze. On her way home now, exhausted as usual, hoping to put it behind her for the evening.

She was twenty-six years old and had worked for the Louisiana Department of Corrections' Probation and Parole Division for the last four years. Most of the job was paperwork: she prepared pre-sentence court reports, provided written documentation on her clients to the State Board of Pardons, and maintained case records. Some of it was a combination of field work and therapy: counseling probationers and parolees, conducting interviews and home visits with clients and family members, making sure the offender understood the parole or probation conditions. The only part that got hairy sometimes was what she had done earlier today: "Apprehend, process and transport probation and parole violators, using an intoxilizer or other drug/alcohol test as needed," was the way the job description read. That was when the Slow Joeys of her world sometimes took offense, and that was when she was often grateful for the *aikido* classes she'd been taking for the last two years—not to mention the gun she was licensed to carry. Though she hadn't had to use that yet, thank God.

Sometimes she thought about going to law school and getting a degree, maybe working in the private sector or muscling her way up in the State Attorney's office. A lot of people had told her she was overqualified for this job. But she had made no efforts in that direction so far. There were a bunch of things she didn't like about being a probation-parole officer, God knew, but it was security of a sort, and something she did well. And it was a far better job than the rest of her family could lay claim to. She had been raised in the swampy lowlands out near Lorcauville, her Pa a crawfish farmer, her three brothers all working at the rice mill in New Iberia, her sister—the one that had lived—a travel agent in Opelousas. Her inlaws could have stepped out of a Randy Newman song. Whenever she thought about them she could smell blackened catfish, jalapeño cornbread, potato muffins. She never ate Cajun these days.

When she had first started it, the job had seemed a way to help make the city and the world a slightly better place to live in. She couldn't recall feeling that way recently, though.

Lia pulled into the driveway of her house in Metairie: a one-story brick home, nothing fancy, but affordable on her salary. She had tried to buy something in Faubourg Marigny, a nineteenth-century cottage with glass doorknobs and wooden lintels, but the area was too pricey for her, and living there would have put her uncomfortably close to many of the neighborhoods she had to work. She preferred to keep some distance from her job.

Inside, she dropped her purse and overstuffed briefcase on the sofa and scooped up the mail from under the front door slot. Toulouse scampered across the floor, swarmed up her leg to her arm and then to her shoulder where he crouched, chattering happily in her ear and grooming her hair with tiny callused fingers. She rubbed a knuckle against his chin. "Miss me?" Toulouse responded by nuzzling her cheek.

Toulouse had been a gift from one of last year's admirers, a pet store owner she had dated a few times. The relationship had fizzled, but Toulouse had remained. The little capuchin monkey was affectionate and playful, and she considered him a much more desirable pet than a dog or a cat. Baby locks kept him out of cabinets and drawers, and he had been trained to use a catbox. Toulouse was the closest thing she wanted to a man in her life right now.

Lia put a few slices of grapefruit in the monkey's bowl—Toulouse hated bananas and loved Coca-Cola, two facts which never ceased to amuse her—then took a beer from the fridge and sat down at the kitchen table to sort through the mail. No surprises: the usual depressingly large percentage of bills, an advertising flyer from the local Piggly Wiggly, a mass-mailing card asking "HAVE YOU SEEN ME?" with a child's picture on it. She deposited the bills in a small wicker basket on the table; Saturday morning was set aside for such things. She started to toss the missing child information into the trash can along with the store flyer, hesitated, then stuck it to the refrigerator with a fruit magnet.

She wandered into the living room and listened to the silence, disturbed only by Toulouse's playing with his favorite toy: a rubber mouse with a bell on it. She glanced over the small collection of CDs and audiotapes near the stereo, but nothing appealed to her. There would be nothing good on TV for another couple of hours unless she cared to watch reruns of cop shows and get impatient at their inaccuracies.

This time of day was always the worst. She was still wound up from her work, a thousand and one niggling bits of information and facts about her various cases seething in her brain. The beer would barely take the edge off of that, but Lia did not allow herself more than one a night, for the same reason that she only very rarely smoked grass. She was a control freak; two years of ongoing analysis had confirmed that. How could she not be, having to move every day through lives shattered by drugs, by mental and physical abuse, by uncaring bureaucracy. Though she rarely admitted it even to herself, deep down there was a real fear of winding up the same as the human wreckage she dealt with.

Thank God for VCRs. Lia spent most of her evenings watching videotapes rented from the mini-mall down the street and not nearly enough time reading. The books by her bed were mostly potboilers, spy novels and whodunits, but at least she still made an effort. Many of her charges didn't know how to read.

This was another hazard of her trade, constantly comparing herself to her probationers and parolees. She shook her head in annoyance. It was easy to keep thinking about work, hard to leave it downtown. Lia took a hefty swig from the long-necked bottle. "I need some serious vegging out tonight, Toulouse," she told the monkey, who was chewing the tip of his tail. She tossed him a peanut and smiled as he devoured it in ecstasy. At least there was one creature in her life she could please unconditionally.

She opened the cabinet under the TV and pawed through the few movies she thought enough of to keep on tape. They were mostly comedies and musicals from the forties and fifties. She dug out one cassette with *Bringing up Baby* and *Nothing Sacred* on it, recorded off the American Movie Classics channel. While it was rewinding she put a packet of popcorn in the microwave.

It was a solitary life, but a well-ordered and satisfactory one. Enough money to get by and a job that—occasionally, at least— let her think she was making a difference. Not bad for someone who wasn't even thirty. There was still time to do something that would change the world, still time for love to sweep her away like a tsunami some day. Still time for her life to be different from others'.

Lia curled up on the couch, tossed a few pieces of popcorn at Toulouse to keep his fingers out of the bowl and watched Cary Grant struggle to complete his dinosaur skeleton.

VERONIQUE AND
SAINT-JOSEPH, HAITI
AND NEW ORLEANS,
LOUISIANA

SEPTEMBER 20, 1991–MAR 30, 1992

The change in Jorge Arnez was subtle; at first Shane did not notice it, and later he denied it. There was no single incident he could point to as the moment when it began; no discovery of some ancient and forgotten grimoire of forbidden lore, no ritual that bound his friend in some form of unholy pact. At least, not at first.

Instead he gradually became aware that Arnez had shifted the focus of his studies. No longer was he concentrating exclusively on *Santería* and its doctrines of white magic. It was not unusual, of course, for a practitioner to study or believe in more than one of the religions that had arisen from ancient African roots. But Shane had begun to hear rumors about his friend, rumors which he found unsettling. It was whispered that Jorge Arnez had become *endiosados*—self-deified, increasingly obsessed with the power that could be had from the study of the darker, necromantic arts. Supposedly he was delving deep into the secrets of *Brujeria*, witchcraft; specifically, *Palo Mayombe*.

Palo Mayombe was a phrase meaning "way of the black witch." A belief system originating in the depths of the Congo, it consisted, Shane knew, primarily of rites of malevolent sorcery. Though many aspects of it borrowed from *Voudoun*, *Santeria* and other African-Caribbean religions, its ceremonial use of sacrifice and torture and its reliance on the invocation of the spirits of the dead placed it firmly in the realm of black magic.

At first Shane did not believe the rumors, even though Arnez had dropped unsettling hints of darker discoveries in their correspondence. This was three years after he and Arnez had met on the streets of Port-au-Prince and become close friends. Arnez's black-market business had disintegrated with the fall of Jean-Claude Duvalier, but Shane had noticed no great degradation of his friend's lifestyle.

At this time Shane was still living in Veronique. He and Anisse had become man and wife a year before, and were thinking of having their first child soon. Arnez had been best man at the wedding. When Shane felt he could no longer deny the truth of what he was hearing, he left Veronique to travel to the nearby coastal village of Saint-Joseph, where Arnez was living.

His friend's house was a sprawling affair of stone and wood, set atop a bluff overlooking the Caribbean. Shane had not inquired too closely into Arnez's money sources since the *Dechonkaj*, but he felt fairly certain that his work as a *santero* was not enough to pay for such a house. Arnez worked hard at the rituals and practices of his religion, but he had a profound distaste for common labor. He was fond of quoting a Creole saying: "If work were a good thing, the rich would have grabbed it a long time ago."

It was only when he saw the fresh scars of *rayado* on Arnez's chest that Shane knew the rumors were true. They sat together that evening on the redwood deck overlooking the rocky surf forty feet below. Arnez made no attempt to deny to Shane what he had been doing; on the contrary, he boasted of it. He told his friend that he was on a path of great discovery.

"Nowhere on Earth is the underlying syncretism of various beliefs more apparent than in religions like *Santería, Voudoun, Candomblé, Shango.* Their roots lie deep in the heart of Africa, in the Yoruba, the Arada, the Congo and others. They all share a common belief in the Invisible World, the realm of the spirits.

"All things come from One, Hermes Trismegistus said. All diversity has as its base an underlying unity, a common principle. This belief holds true in both magic and science. And yet, only in science has any attempt been made to probe the depths of this unifying force. Why not in magic?

"I believe it's possible to find the fountainhead from which all we know to be true has sprung. If one penetrates deeply enough into the spirit realm, if one has the courage to face the entities that guard the path, the reward could be . . . ultimate power."

Shane found it difficult to believe what he was hearing. "You would challenge the *loas* and the *orishas* in their own domain?"

Arnez had been gazing out toward the distant horizon as he spoke; now he turned and looked at Shane. Shane found the intensity of his friend's gaze disturbing.

"I would confront Olodumare Himself if that was what was needed," he said quietly. And, though the summer day was sultry, Shane felt a chill raise the hairs on his arms.

It was from that day, that discussion, that Shane could mark the growing schism that began to separate him from his friend. Before, they had kept in touch by phone and post, sharing the occult learnings and discoveries that had been their common bond. But now Arnez became secretive, suspicious. Once Shane had made apparent his disapproval of the path Arnez had chosen, the *santero* lost whatever trust he had felt for the *houngan*. He refused to answer Shane's calls or letters, and ultimately, six months after he had first admitted the dangerous course he was pursuing, he vanished from Haiti, leaving no forwarding address.

He had been gone three weeks when the bodies were found.

There were five of them, buried in a shallow grave a few hundred yards up the road from where Arnez had lived. They had been mutilated in ways that caused even the Macoutes, most of them old hands at inflicting torture, to turn away. Little was done in the way of investigation, as the victims were only peasants from a nearby village. But when Shane heard the description of the mutilations he knew what had happened.

A devil doll and the discarded remnants of a *nganga*, the latter filled with a nauseating brew that included a skull and other human bones, had been found near the grave. Shane knew that the conjuring cauldron had belonged to Arnez, and he had a very strong suspicion that the responsibility for the murders did too. There were rituals in *Palo Mayombe* that required the use of human body parts.

Shane sensed that what he had been told was true, that Arnez had found a way to penetrate deeper into the Invisible World than anyone before him had managed. Shane knew that there were beings other than the *loas*, the *orishas* and the spirits of the dead who inhabited that mystic dimension; darker beings, entities who thrived on blood and pain. It was possible to propitiate them, but the price they exacted was high.

Apparently Arnez had chosen to pay that price.

Shane tried to tell himself that it was not his problem. Arnez was off the island and out of his life. There were rumors that he had gone to the United States, to New Orleans. Let the authorities there worry about him.

But Shane was a priest of *Voudoun*. Ducas had told him more than once that the knowledge he had gained, the abilities to summon and commune with the spirits, to ask and be granted favors, carried with it a responsibility. It was not enough to resolutely trod the right-hand path and shun the left. He was expected to correct imbalance when he saw it happening. No matter the inconvenience or danger such action caused, it was part of the job. The *loas* were always watching their *serviteurs*.

He spoke of this with Anisse. It did not take much to convince her to leave Haiti and emigrate to the U.S. Even a life lived in direst poverty there was better than what they were used to now. And both had come to feel it would be better not to have children at all than to raise them in Haiti.

They both applied for visas. It took several months for the paperwork to be processed, and during that time Shane pursued various channels of information, both magical and mundane, to learn the whereabouts of Jorge Arnez. His queries told him the rumors had been correct. His friend had relocated to New Orleans, and had changed his name as well. He now called himself "Mal Sangre," which *was* Spanish for "bad blood." The mordant theatricality surprised Shane somewhat, but after thinking about it he realized that it made sense, after a fashion. It was not uncommon for a *brujo* or a *mayombero* to take a sinister name. Showmanship worked just as well in the spirit world as in this one.

They arrived in New Orleans at the end of May. The weather was cloudy, the temperature 75 degrees Fahrenheit, the humidity noticeable but not nearly as bad as where they had come from. They had four hundred and twenty dollars in traveler's checks and eighty-six in American dollars after the currency exchange. They knew no one, had no job prospects and no place to stay. Anisse spoke English haltingly, Shane fluently.

They found a place to stay in Mid-City, a fleabag of a motel with a water bed and a broken TV, which was just as well as the sole programming seemed to be X-rated films. Fortunately, Anisse could play guitar and sing well enough to busk in the Quarter and on Canal Street, and this let them stretch their funds over the better part of two months. By that time Shane had gotten a job as a shipping and packing clerk in a sporting goods store. They found an apartment three blocks from the motel that did not require last month's rent and a security deposit.

During this time Shane's discreet inquiries on the street as to the whereabouts of Mal Sangre had borne no fruit. Seven weeks after they had arrived, however, Anisse overheard two hookers' conversation in which a pimp named Sangre was mentioned. Armed with this knowledge, Shane was able to find another hooker who was willing—for the last of the money they had brought with them—to put him in touch with his old friend.

His amateur detective work filled him with pride at the time. He was to bitterly regret it later.

vi

Less than five minutes into the first set Dave Cummings knew the goddamned head cold was going to be a real problem. Every time he went above G on the treble he started to lose it, and forget the high E and B flats; he couldn't hear a thing, his ears were so clogged. No idea if he was in tune with the rest of the band; all he could go by was the feel of the cornet's embrasure against his upper lip and the expressions of the crowd packed into the narrow darkness of the Crawfish Club. Like a blind man trying to bat clean-up. Pathetic.

If that weren't bad enough, Sharkey was about to nod off over his sax; booze or lack of sleep or both, Dave wasn't sure, but he'd already had to kick him twice and they weren't halfway through the first tune yet. Blowing cues and missing breaks like some first-year music student. Thank God you could get away with more screw-ups in a live performance than on someone's stereo. People were a lot less forgiving when they weren't distracted by watching you perform.

The atmosphere in the club was so hot and close that his glasses were fogging as he blew. It wasn't going to be one of their better nights. But most of the crowd didn't care; the two-drink minimum had long since been passed and the band might as well be playing chainsaws and power drills as far as some of the audience was concerned. The music reverberated from low rafters hung with ornamental gasoliers and walls covered with framed eight-by-tens of jazz legends from the past sixty years. The Crawfish Club had been a fixture of the French Quarter off Bourbon Street for twelve years earlier than that; it was one of the premier music halls of the city and the nation. And the Bucktown Jazz Band had been playing there every Tuesday night since 1994.

They finished their first tune—Jelly Roll Morton's "Sidewalk Blues"—and Dave took advantage of the moment's intermission to blow his nose before they began. "Sweet Lovin' Man." This one featured dual cornets, with Jeff McKenzie accompanying him; by the end of it he was envying Norm Skokes's lung power on the trombone. It was going to be a long night.

They usually played four sets at the Crawfish, each one lasting about forty-five or fifty minutes and comprising ten or twelve tunes. They left room for requests and were pretty much finished by two or three A.M. at the latest. The Bucktown was Dave's, primary band, the one he'd been with the longest: four years in May. He also played semi-regularly in the Harry Patrick Trio and the Blue Ribbon Boys, and that, along with street gigging and the occasional funeral procession and studio assignment, was barely enough to pay the rent. Although his finances weren't in bad shape at the moment—a week ago during Mardi Gras he'd made about two hundred tax-free dollars a night playing street corners with a few friends—usually it was very much a hand-to-mouth existence.

It would be different if he were in Europe. They appreciated music and art over there; he had a couple of friends who were doing quite well in Paris just playing clubs. But Dave Cummings and New Orleans were joined at the hip; it had been that way since he'd moved here, just out of his teens, in 1990, his horn in a case and everything else he owned in a knapsack on his back. This was his kind of city; one that believed in music as a primal life force. One ferry ride from Canal Street to Algiers Point, looking at Jackson Square and the rest of the Quarter lit up against the night sky, and he couldn't be pried away with a crowbar. After all, given his passion for playing, where else could he live but the home of Dixieland Jazz?

Even through his congestion he could hear Ted Saunders's clarinet soaring in vibrato and Norm's honeyed trombone flowing through and around the piece. Even feeling like shit, which he did tonight, there was no place he'd rather be.

It was worth a few inconveniences to be living your dreams.

At three-forty in the morning the last patron finally left and the Crawfish Club officially closed. Dave and Jeff McKenzie strolled back to Dave's place on Burgundy, having drunk just enough to make the short walk interesting. The whiskey had temporarily anesthetized Dave's swollen sinuses and he could almost delude himself into believing that he felt halfway decent.

He didn't remember later too much of what they talked about; mostly it was the usual shop talk, dissecting the night's performance and suggesting ways to improve their playing.

Though they both could blow just about anything made of brass, they favored the cornet; more mellow than the trumpet and more versatile, in Dave's opinion. It was good enough for King Oliver, he had said more than once, and it was good enough for him. The conversation moved on from there to more general subjects.

"So you and Katie no longer on the gossip pages, I take it," Jeff observed as they ambled past the thundering sounds of MTV echoing from the Bourbon Pub.

Dave shrugged, slightly uncomfortable. "What can I say? She had unreasonable expectations: kids, a house, a Jeep Cherokee. . . ."

Jeff chuckled. He was ten years older than Dave and had been playing in bands since 1986. "Yeah, you say that now, but sooner or later you'll let one of 'em catch you. I did."

"You didn't stay caught."

"True. Well, Satchmo was married four times; I got two more before I catch up with him."

Dave swung the cornet's case up before him and patted it with his free hand. "Who needs love when you got jazz?"

They were headed up Dumaine now, having left the shops and clubs behind for a more residential section of the Quarter. Two- and three-story homes, worn brick walls fronting the street and courtyards hidden behind wrought iron fences, were dark and silent on either side of them. Toward the west the Downtown buildings, lit by spotlights of various colors and partly shrouded by fog, looked like the towers and spires of a fantasy metropolis. Jeff shook his head. "Someone offers me the choice between love and music, I'll still take music. But these days, if someone was to offer me a choice between music and money . . ."

Dave couldn't believe he was hearing such heresy. "C'mon,

Jeff. You'll sell out when they start playing heavy metal in Preservation Hall."

Jeff was quiet for a few moments. Then: "When you're young, you think the gigs'll go on forever," he said, his tone surprisingly somber. "Hard to believe it can ever get old. But let me tell you, I wish now I'd put some money by. Just a little so I don't got to be constantly hustling. Music business is a young man's game."

Dave sneezed. "You saying you're old? You're what, thirty-seven, thirty-eight . . . ?"

"Believe me," Jeff said, more than a touch of mournfulness in his voice now, "when all you got is what's in your pockets at the end of a gig, thirty-eight can be damn old."

They turned right on Burgundy. Dave's apartment was in a ground-level rowhouse not far from the onetime slave quarters that was now a maze of swimming pools, courtyards and guest cottages called the Hotel St. Pierre. It wasn't the best area in the Quarter, but it was still safer than Treme, the neighborhood a few blocks on the uptown side past Armstrong Park, where most of the bandsmen, including Jeff, lived. The danger never seemed to worry any of the musicians, though; they routinely strolled past St. Louis Cemetery No. 1, a muggers' haven, carrying expensive horns and brass at all hours of the night, and so far no one Dave knew had paid a penalty for doing so. God loves fools and musicians.

They stopped before Dave's apartment. Jeff waved a slightly tipsy good night and was about to chance jaywalking across North Rampart when a low whistle caused them both to turn and look in the same direction.

Leaning against a parked car was a tall man, his arms folded against his chest. A streetlight backlit him, made it impossible to tell what nationality he was. There was something odd and unsettling about his utter lack of movement; he might have been carved from some dark clay or stone and propped there.

"Try somethin'?" His voice was a low, husky whisper, touched with a light rhythmic accent that Dave couldn't place. "Got dreams for sale, sweet dreams right here. . . ," and now a hand was extended, the fingers holding a small transparent bag filled with powder. Hard to tell what color it was under the street light, but it seemed to throw off glints of crimson.

The booze can really sneak up on you, was Dave's first thought. He blinked, fully expecting to see the mysterious figure gone when he opened his eyes again. It didn't happen. The dark shape was still there, along with the bag of meth or horse or whatever he was pushing.

While Dave Cummings would be the first to admit—okay, maybe the second—that he was no stranger to a good many substances listed on the DEA's Schedule One list, one cliché he'd always tried to avoid was that of the jazz-playing cokehead. He'd seen several people he knew and liked give up everything they owned for one more snort of the Devil's Dandruff, and he had no intention of traveling that road. He'd tried it once at a party in the Warehouse District, and it had been the best party he'd ever experienced. That had been enough to keep him away from cocaine ever since.

Though he wasn't sure this guy was peddling coke, he also made it a rule of thumb that any artificial joy from the street didn't make it as far as his bloodstream. That included acid, MDMA, speed and just about anything else that came to mind. His parents had come of age in the sixties, and they had told him their experiences with street shit. No, thank you.

Therefore his response to the offer was practically automatic: "Take a hike," he said as he turned back toward his door and aimed the key at the elusive lock.

He knew the other members of the band pretty well, and though a couple of them, like Sharkey, were more adventurous than he, Dave had never seen any of them buy a bag from an unknown pavement peddler either. Which is why, even in his semidrunken state, he was astonished to hear Jeff say, "Whatcha got?"

Dave turned quickly, noticing that the world had a distressing tendency to keep rocking after he finished moving. He braced himself on the black iron porch railing and watched in mild astonishment as Jeff weaved toward the mystery man. The latter still held the baggie, moving it slowly from side to side like a hypnotist swinging a watch on a chain, still crooning "Dreams for sale, sweet dreams for sale. . . ." Jeff's eyes were fixed on the baggie.

Several things were wrong with this picture, Dave told himself. He had never heard any dealer run the kind of brazen rap this one was doing, or tease a potential customer like this. And Jeff McKenzie, for all his wild man image, was as big a reader of the ingredients list as Dave was. Even drunk, he wouldn't be interested.

But interested he evidently was. He extended a palm and the dealer dropped the baggie into it. Another breach of street etiquette: Always get the money first.

"Try it, you'll like it," the silhouetted shape said, again almost singing the words. Jeff struggled for a moment with the zip lock top, then opened the baggie partway. He licked his index finger, stuck it in and brought it out with the tip covered with red powder. That's what it was—no mistaking that color, even in the harsh blue radiance. Dave saw it sparkle for an instant before Jeff stuck his finger in his mouth and sucked it clean.

He realized abruptly that the entire surface of his skin was covered in gooseflesh. The hairs of his arm and on the back of his neck were struggling erect like wheat in the wake of a strong wind.

What the fuck was going on?

Jeff's expression changed from drunken curiosity to something more like ecstatic rapture. He turned partway toward Dave, so that his face was illuminated by the light. Even at a distance of several feet, Dave could see that his friend's pupils had contracted enough to make him half blind in this dim light. Jeff took a step toward Dave, smiled lazily and said, "I know something you don't know. . . ."

His voice had the same cadence as the pusher's.

Dave, who was concentrating on Jeff, jerked his gaze back toward the car that the dealer had been leaning against. He had only taken his eyes off the man for a second; there was no way the other could have reached the haven of a doorway or window in time. Yet he had vanished like a morning mist before the sun.

"Jesus . . ." Dave felt adrenaline flooding his system, washing away any trace of alcohol; ten seconds of that kind of fear and he could pass any breathalyzer test in the country. He turned back to Jeff, only to see his friend and fellow musician stalking rapidly away, swinging his case. As Dave watched he turned the corner and was gone.

Dave took a few steps after him, then stopped. He was suddenly very afraid that if he ran around that corner he would see nobody there and no place to hide once more. And he very much did not want to see that. . . .

He fumbled his key, unlocked the door in blind haste and almost fell into his apartment. He slammed the door shut and flipped the wall switch for the lights in one movement, certain that he would see the drug-dealing stranger standing before him, no longer in shadow, nothing to prevent Dave from seeing his face. . . .

The small front room was empty.

Dave Cummings emptied his lungs in a shuddering sigh, feeling the strength go out of his legs as though they were balloons deflating. His back slid down the door until he sat on the rug.

He knew that in a few minutes he should call Jeff, make sure that his friend got home safely. A lot could happen in the few blocks between their two apartments. He glanced at his watch: four-thirty. He would call, but not for another hour or so. He didn't want to talk to Jeff just yet. He would wait.

He would wait for dawn.

On a Friday afternoon ten days after the end of Mardi Gras, Lia St. Charles was in the Criminal District Court Building on Tulane Avenue listening to the judge remand Joseph Martin René to the remainder of his DOC time back in Angola. Slow Joey looked considerably more subdued than when she had last seen him. His lank body was clad in an ill-fitting blue serge suit and his hair had been pulled back into a ponytail. It looked like he had even made a half-hearted effort at shining his shoes. It didn't help. Judge Martinelli labeled him a stain on the escutcheon of society, whacked the gavel and called for the next case. Joey didn't look at Lia as the bailiff led him out.

Quid pro quo, she thought. *Measure for measure. If you don't want the time, don't do the crime.*

In the hall she ran into Neal Rendell, a uniform cop she'd dated a few times last year. They hadn't spoken for a while but the last time they'd seen each other it had been amicable. Now he grinned at her as she stopped to say hi.

"Heard you're getting a new case."

"You heard more than me, then," Lia said. "What case?"

"Probably be on your desk. Shane LaFitte."

The name was vaguely familiar. "How do you know these things?" It wasn't the first time Neal had mentioned gossip she wouldn't have thought a uniform would have any way of knowing. He was a first class networker; two years on the force and already testing for detective, one of the few uncorrupt cops in the NOPD. Lia had thought more than once it was a shame she didn't feel a spark there.

He grinned, standing with barely a crease in his blues, his shield and shoes throwing back reflections from the ceiling fluorescents. A career man, fast track runner; ten years, she thought, he'll be Chief of Police, if not Mayor. Maybe sooner than that. "Word gets around," he said.

A real shame, but it just wasn't there between them. "LaFitte," she said, trying to call up the particulars of the case.

"Six years ago? The voodoo killing?"

"The woman that got whacked on some bayou down south?"

Neal nodded, smiling in approval at her knowledge of the case. "D.A. went for murder one, but the defense sold the jury manslaughter. Judge gave him twenty-five up at 'Gola—he served five."

Now she remembered. It had been a sensation at the time: a woman found dead in a tin-roofed cabin way out in the wetlands near Barataria. Lia remembered something about voodoo or *Santería* talismans found with the body. LaFitte had been arrested at the scene, his clothes and skin caked with her blood, his fingerprints on the knife. That was all she remembered of the case, and she only recalled that because of the voodoo tie-in. The papers had really played that part up.

And now he was out and in her care. She had known another case would be assigned to her now that Slow Joey was going back up, but she had hoped she might have a few days' grace, maybe an opportunity to make some headway on her pre-sentence investigations and other reports.

You should have known better, she told herself. After all, it wasn't like she was overworked or anything.

She bid Neal good-bye and left the building for the parking lot. It looked to be a warm day today; already the humidity was cloying, though it wasn't yet ten o'clock. She hoped LaFitte wouldn't still be high profile for the press. She had been hounded once before when one of her cases, a child molester, had been paroled. The tabloids had whipped up a public outcry that had resulted in him going back in, even though, as far as Lia could see, he had been trying his best to toe the line. She had gotten phone calls at all hours from reporters; it wasn't an ex-perience she cared to repeat. She knew there were lawyers and lawmen who sought the limelight, but she wasn't one of them. The job interested her, not the notoriety.

Well, she told herself, I'm not going to take any shit from him. Put him down and keep him down if he showed any attitude whatsoever. That was the way to do it. He was just another case.

But a quiet sense of unease, so subtle that she was barely aware of it, pulsed in the background of her consciousness.

The subtropical sun, rising over the languid Mississippi, sent a shimmering wave of indolence washing over the city. The natives, having long ago perfected the art and philosophy of *mañana*, were in no hurry to get the day started. On the wide expanse of Canal Street, discount electronic emporiums and luggage warehouses rolled back their accordion-fold storefront grids, while sidewalk vendors advertised commodities on cement squares between antique green lampposts. Derelicts roused from doorways to loudly debate screw-top vintages, and panhandlers shook paper cups at office workers heading upriver.

In the Quarter the streets were quiet, laced with the fragrance of fresh breads, baguettes and croissants baking in wood ovens. The tour buses had yet to begin their circuits. Rivulets of water pattered from balconies as residents watered plants while sipping *café au lait*. The streams mingled with sprays from hoses as shopkeepers washed away debris from the previous night's debauchery. Tourist-trap boutiques on Bourbon Street opened their doors, displaying racks of sleazy T-shirts and "authentic" voodoo dolls manufactured in China. Buskers, sketch artists, fortune tellers, magicians, mimes and various street hustlers congregated in the pedestrian mall bordering Jackson Square, setting up shop in wait for tourists from local and distant hotels.

In the Garden District the morning air was heavy with the scents of jasmine, oleander, mimosa and magnolia blossoms. Palm trees and oaks curtained with Spanish moss framed Queen Anne and Victorian mansions. The sun struck rainbow sparks from stained glass windows. Hummingbirds vibrated the stillness, hovering over azaleas and bougainvillea. The St. Charles Avenue streetcar rattled toward Tulane and Loyola carrying a full load of students. In Lafayette Cemetery family members brought flowers to loved ones and worked on restoring ornate mausoleums and vaults.

Most of the population, if asked, wouldn't live anyplace else but here in this cultural farrago, this eclectic combination of the old South, Parisian decadence and Caribbean paradise. Here every sin seemed venial, every indulgence justifiable and every occasion, including a funeral, cause for celebration. And so the day rolled on, like every day before it and every day to come. No worries; *laissez les bon temps rouler*. This was, after all, the City That Care Forgot.

Even the dead were laid back. . . .

Among other ingredients, the black iron *nganga* contained the body of a pit bull, blood from animals and men, various spices, a tarantula and a scorpion, several burnt Habana Gold Black Label cigars, a few pesos and most of a human brain. The *mayombero* squatted next to the cauldron, meditating, clearing his mind and preparing himself for the work that was to be done. He wore a pair of faded black jeans and no shirt; his lean body gleamed with sweat. The cabled muscles of his chest and upper arms were striated with *rayado*: patterned scars where years ago initiatory symbols had been cut with a razor. He rubbed ashes on his hands to purify them. Then, with a white-handled knife, he made a shallow cut in his wrist and added to the pot's grisly mixture some of his own blood. This final ritual completed, he sat back on his heels and regarded the cauldron somberly.

Over a month ago, under the light of the waxing moon, he had stolen from one of the dilapidated charnels in Pontchartrain Cemetery the skull of one Rusty Clementine, a local Yat construction worker whose favorite recreation, after downing several rum Hurricanes, was to beat the living daylights out of his wife. After enduring several years of this Mrs. Clementine finally leveled the playing field one night by vaporizing most of Rusty's midsection with a double-barreled side-by-side shotgun at close range. Fortunately for the *mayombero*'s purposes, Rusty's brain had been left intact, and even more fortunately the Yat had specified in his will, for superstitious reasons, that he was to be interred in the family crypt without embalming.

His brain had been put in the *nganga* along with the other necessary ingredients and the cauldron had been returned to the whitewashed brick tomb, there to remain over a period of three Fridays. After that it had been buried at the foot of a palm tree in the small backyard of the Creole cottage for another three Fridays. The forty-two day period had been up last night, and now the ceremony was complete. Rusty Clementine's soul, never of any particular use to anyone during his lifetime, had become a *kiyumba*—an enslaved spirit bound to the *mayombero*'s will. Whatever his master commanded of him the *kiyumba* would do.

Across the windows thick curtains had been drawn, blocking sunlight and muffling the sounds of cars and foot traffic. The front room was sparsely furnished and the only light came from candles placed on tables and chair arms. On the wall behind the cauldron the four cardinal points of the earth had been sketched in chalk. The aromatic smoke of burning incense sticks partially masked the odor of the pot as the cauldron's master stared into its noisome depths. On the floor before it were grouped twenty-one small cowrie shells in a complex pattern. The *mayombero* studied the arrangement of the shells and nodded. Then, in a soft voice, he bade that which had once been the essence of Rusty Clementine show him certain things.

The *nganga*'s dark contents swirled and subtle shifting light seemed to flicker from within, dimly illuminating the *mayombero*'s intent features. Faint sounds, like the distant babble of a badly tuned radio station, hovered at the edge of hearing. He crouched, motionless, and peered without blinking into the pot, studying the visions that roiled and wavered on the contents' surface, his face betraying no emotion save for a slight tightening of jaw muscles.

At last he nodded and swept the shells aside. He stood, feeling the pins and needles of returning circulation—he had been hunched over the *nganga* for the better part of an hour—and went to the small bathroom at the end of the hall to relieve his bladder. Over the rust-stained sink was a medicine chest with the mirrored door removed; on the shelves were small glass jars which once contained kitchen condiments and now were filled with mercury, *corojo* oil, iron filings, and other oils, herbs and incenses. He tipped a few drops from a container of almond oil into his hand, rubbed his palms together and massaged his face with the aromatic ointment, chanting a few words in Spanish as he did so.

He went to the other end of the house and got a bottle of beer from the kitchen's refrigerator, draining most of it before returning to the living room and punching a number into the phone.

When the connection was made the *mayombero* spoke swiftly and forcefully in Spanish, at one point gesturing hard enough with the bottle that a few remaining drops of beer sloshed onto his hand. He gave the person on the other end of the line no time to agree or disagree with his words. Then he hung up, and after a moment hurled the beer bottle against the wall hard enough to shatter into glass shrapnel.

S hane and Sangre met at a place called Bob's Bayou Bar, out on Highway 190. When Shane entered the dim, smoke-filled confines of the restaurant, it took his eyes a moment to adjust. Gradually details emerged out of the gloom: the ivory shine of gar and gator jawbones nailed to the wall above the bar, the knife-scarred dark wood tables, the metal signs advertising RC Cola and Bull Durham. The customers were mostly large and hulking men, many with full beards and hats laced with fish hooks and lures. In a side room a group of them crouched intently over a pool table.

He spotted Arnez—or Sangre, as he now called himself—sitting in one of the darker corners of the main room, his features dimly illuminated by a candle in a red votive glass on the table.

Shane maneuvered between the close-set chairs until he stood over his old friend. Sangre showed no particular surprise or pleasure at seeing him. He gestured for Shane to seat himself and went back to his meal. He was eating little strips of breaded meat; a picture of the dish on an appetizer menu in an acrylic table stand identified them as deep-fried baby alligator tails.

Shane sat down at the small table. Sangre regarded him for a moment while he chewed and swallowed. Then he said, "I must say I never expected to see you again. Did you come all this way to find me, or am I just flattering myself?"

Shane did not reply immediately. He looked at Sangre, trying to quantify exactly what was so different and so disturbing about the man who used to be his friend. Because he knew now that there was no longer any camaraderie between them. It was a certainty that did not have to be spoken to be recognized as truth. This man was not yet his enemy, but it would not take much to push him into that role. There was a hardness to him that Shane did not remember in Arnez. His old friend had always been manipulative and amoral to a degree, but he had been capable of kindness on many occasions, and loyalty. There was none of that in Mal Sangre.

"I think you know why I'm here," Shane said at last. "You have gone a far distance down the left-hand path, Jorge. Too far, I think, for your own safety and the safety of others."

Sangre chuckled. "And so you've taken it upon yourself to stop me."

Shane felt a flash of anger at him. He kept his voice level and low. "If it were only yourself you were endangering, I wouldn't interfere. But I know the price of your researches. I have seen the graves near your home in Haiti. I don't doubt there are more of them here in New Orleans. I can't let you continue on this course. The path you follow is a long one, and it will take much more blood to wash it clean for you."

"You know, I've missed your poetic turns of phrase, Shane. Your naive idealism. All you ever wanted to be was a simple country *houngan*, making *gris-gris* for the yokels. Admirable, in a way. But I want more; so much more that I doubt you can comprehend it all.

"You have no idea how far I've gone, my friend. I have sent my astral self further into the Invisible World than any have ever penetrated before. I have seen sights, spoken with entities, that would make your soul scream. I have passed the Gates of Creation and entered the ultimate Abyss. Listen: Did you know that beyond the Crossroads, beyond the Flaming Land, beyond the Island Below the Waters, there rises an obelisk shaped like a giant pentacle, its surface carved with *vévés* no human eye has ever seen? I have seen them. I have learned them, and for three days after memorizing their patterns my brain burned with their meanings and I raved like a madman. Would you like to see one of them?" Without waiting for an answer, Sangre dipped his finger into the sauce on his plate and began to draw a strange symbol on the wooden tabletop.

Shane watched Sangre's finger move, watched the hypnotic angles and lines take form. A wave of vertigo passed over him, and the room seemed to grow even darker. Far off, like the pounding of surf on a sunless shore, he could hear a multitude of inhuman voices chanting in no known tongue. The *vévé* seemed to shimmer and pulse with a baneful luminescence. Shane clamped his jaws against a surge of nausea and swept his hand across the table, knocking the plate to the floor and wiping the pattern clean before Sangre could finish drawing the last line. The shattering crockery brought silence to the restaurant's patrons, which neither Shane nor Sangre noticed. Shane stared at the table, sweat beaded on his face, panting as if he had just run a mile. Sangre watched him, the barest touch of a smile tugging at his lips.

"You begin to understand," he said. "And even that is barely the start of my journey."

Shane stood, somewhat unsteadily. "This is beyond blasphemy," he said. "I won't let you do this. I'll find a way to stop you."

Sangre looked up at him, his eyes hooded. There was nothing human in his gaze. "You're forcing me to take you off the board, old friend," he replied softly. "The stakes here are much too high to let anyone, even you, interfere."

Shane did not reply. The interior of the restaurant suddenly seemed intolerably close and stifling to him. He turned and pushed his way through the crowd to the door. He could still feel Sangre's gaze burning into his back.

Shane was sincere in his vow to stop Sangre; how to accomplish it was the question. He had not told Anisse of his meeting with the former *santero*, because he did not want her to worry. Had he only done so, perhaps she would have been better prepared. . . .

A week after his meeting with Sangre, while he was still puzzling over how best to put an end to the man's mad quest, he returned home in the afternoon and found Anisse missing.

There was an envelope containing a note propped on the mantle. Shane tore it open with trembling fingers and read:

"I regret this course of action, but I can't have you interfering with my purpose. Perhaps this will convince you of how serious I am. If you want to rescue Anisse, you will come to the following location in the Bayou Barataria. . . ."

There followed a detailed series of directions, including where to rent a boat. The letter concluded by cautioning him not to go to the police. There was no signature; none was needed.

Shane stood in the small, threadbare apartment, staring at the note for what seemed like centuries. Every sense seemed heightened; he could smell the gumbo being cooked and hear the sounds of zydeco from the radio in the apartment next door, could feel the slightly oily texture of the paper in his hand. But overriding all of these feelings was a single emotion: hatred.

At that moment he knew he would kill Mal Sangre. He had never harbored a desire to kill another human being in his life, but now the hunger to do so was overwhelming. He let it fill him, flood his being with strength and purpose, let it carry him out of the apartment and into his quest.

The flat-bottomed green *bateau* drifted along the surface of the sluggish bayou. In the light of the half-moon the water was as dark as India ink. Lightning bugs blinked phosphorescent green patterns in the air, a complex mating ritual. On the banks, frogs and crickets sang. A nutria, looking like a giant rat, hit the water, risking the gators in its search for food.

In the light of his miner's headlamp, Shane could see the living wall of trees that lined the waterway. He recognized some of them, even in the darkness; they were the same ones that grew in the swamps of Haiti. Live oaks, their limbs dripping with Spanish moss, gum trees, little knotty hardwoods that struggled in the shade of taller long-leaf pines and cypress. The cypress knees jutted up from the black water in gnarled, arthritic silhouettes. He remembered reading somewhere that the word "bayou" had come from an Indian word meaning "river," but unlike real rivers and streams, these waterways had no current; long, stagnant, meandering courses that stitched across the Mississippi delta and lowlands, they were perfect breeding grounds for pestilence and fever.

The swamps he had been traveling through for the last four hours were the wetlands of Barataria, the region south of New Orleans whose intricate maze of canals and waterways the famous pirate Jean LaFitte had once made his personal hideout. Now, after all this time, another LaFitte—though not a scion of the "gentleman privateer"—had come to the bayou on business just as bloody and intense as any pirate had ever attempted.

Shane wiped his face with a damp hand. The humidity had to be close to a hundred percent. Sweat ran and pooled, with nowhere to go in the saturated air. It lay on his skin like oil.

He sat in the back, near the little electric motor that filled the night air with its buzz. He used a pole to keep course, looking for the landmarks that Sangre had given him. There was one of them now: a tree stump jutting out of the water that looked, in the darkness, like a devil's pitchfork.

Shane checked his watch: three A.M. He had been on the move nonstop for over twelve hours, but he did not feel tired. His rage and his anxiety for Anisse kept him going.

His hand drifted to his belt, as it had several times during every one of the past seven hours, to the holster containing the Smith & Wesson Model .38. Also known as a Bodyguard's Airweight, it weighed less than a pound, had a shrouded hammer to eliminate possible clothing snags and could deliver five rapid-fire shots. He had gotten it from a gun shop by using a simple spell of confusion on the proprietor.

He drifted through a mass of water lilies under a hanging curtain of kudzu. Mosquitoes buzzed in living clouds and veered away from the 6-12 repellent he'd coated his head and neck and arms with. A great many of them landed on his shirt and stabbed right through the thin cotton to draw blood. He ignored them. As he emerged from beneath the kudzu a bat dipped down into the light, chasing a fat moth. A loon howled far off in the swamp, an eerie sound out of a horror movie. It seemed not at all impossible to Shane that at any moment a dinosaur might come charging out of the antediluvian darkness.

He came around a final bend in the river and saw the trapper's shack just ahead. It was immediately recognizable from Sangre's description: tar paper over plywood, with a corrugated sheet steel roof mostly gone to rust despite the zinc coating. Light from a white-gas Coleman lantern shone from the single grimy window. A dried water moccasin skin, easily eight feet long, had been nailed over the door under the porch's overhang, along with several mummified snake heads, jaws stretched wide and fangs bared. The shack was probably used as a hunting base by some old Cajun trapper who made a meager living catching snapping turtles, frogs and gators. There was a stretch of cleared land around the shack in which palmetto fans and tupelo trees had grown up and been left uncut. Somebody had planted elephant ears along the front, along with Easter lilies and a single stunted azalea bush, its waxy flowers glowing fish-belly white in the moonlight.

Shane cut the motor and poled the aluminum craft through the duckweed to the short mossy dock in front of the shack. He saw no other boat moored, but that meant nothing. They were in there, Sangre and Anisse. That he knew. Anisse would be coming with him, alive.

Sangre would not.

He remained in the boat, forcing his anxiety and fear out of him with each slow, regular breath. Closing his eyes, he sent his awareness out, trying to detect, with senses that had no name, hidden dangers in or near the building. A palmetto bug as long as a cigar buzzed abruptly out of the darkness and perched on his head for a moment before flying off. He gave no reaction; all his focus was on the tarpaper shack before him.

He frowned. There seemed to be nothing out of the ordinary. No thugs lying in wait, no spirit presences that could protect or warn his enemy.

Shane resisted the urge to leap to the dock and hurl himself against the door. Sangre was a sorcerer, and he was not a man to come to such a rendezvous without protection. Had he grown adept enough to hide his allies from Shane?

He considered calling on Legba for aid. He could summon his *loa-tête* without resorting to the rituals required for the other spirits; a touch of his fingers on his *asson*, which he had brought with him, and a mental plea would be enough. Legba was the Opener of the Gate, and Shane's route lay through the shack's front door. He could legitimately request protection and aid.

But it was possible that Sangre would be able to detect even the subtle presence of Legba. He couldn't take that chance.

Shane tied off the boat and moved cautiously down the dock to the shack's door. He crouched down next to the window, staring in, giving his eyes time to adjust to the light.

The single room was small and bare save for a straight-backed chair in the center of the wood floor. There were a few talismans—cowrie shells, skull-shaped candles, incense containers and the like—set on the floor or hanging from the walls. Anisse was tied to the chair and gagged. Sangre sat crosslegged on the floor near her, face serene, eyes closed as if in meditation. In one hand was a short-bladed knife with a black handle.

Shane pulled the gun. He knew it could not be as easy as it looked. Sangre had to have some kind of defense. But perhaps surprise would be on his side as well; his enemy would not be expecting such a straightforward assault.

It was his only hope.

Shane stood, took a deep breath and kicked in the door.

SISTERS OF GRACE
HOSPITAL,
NEW ORLEANS,
LOUISIANA

MARCH 7, 1998

It was over a week later that K.D. thought again about the coma case on the night of Fat Tuesday. She had literally been too busy to remember him before then. The hospital was always understaffed and overloaded with patients, and no department was more affected by this than the ER. On any typical night they had gunshot wounds, stabbings, automotive accidents and a host of other traumas lining the halls on stretchers. Many of the patients were Puerto Rican, Cuban and other immigrants with no insurance or medical history. The through-the-door traffic had tripled in the two years K.D. had been at Sisters of Grace, but the number of residents had stayed the same. Many of them were working hundred-hour weeks.

She was taking a brief break in one of the upstairs cafeterias, forcing down lukewarm coffee and a stale Danish and feeling guilty about being behind on her charts, when Jerry came in. He was wearing pale green scrubs with the trousers legs taped back, and looked exhausted. He dropped a couple of quarters in a vending machine and was rewarded with a candy bar which he unwrapped with his teeth as he sat across the table from her.

"Jantzen jus' fucked up big-time," he said, spitting the torn wrapper toward a wastebasket.

"Yeah?" Jantzen was the chief of medicine, an arrogant asshole who rated somewhere just under Nazi on K.D.'s popularity scale.

"F'true," Jerry said. "This guy come by a couple hours ago, said he had the grippe. Looked like shit; blue and dusky, y'know?"

K.D. nodded. This was flu season, and there were some nasty variants of the bug out there.

"Anyways, Pete checks 'im out, runs a plate on 'im, his lungs look okay. But his blood gasses're from hunger; real low oxygen level, y'know? So Pete goes, 'Maybe we should put 'im onna respirator,' but Jantzen goes, 'Just give 'im a little oxygen, he'll be fine.' Pete's like, 'Looka his skin tone,' and Jantzen's like, 'It's dese damn fluorescents—dey make ev'body look half dead.' Guy's complainin' 'bout a pain in his left side, so Jantzen prescribes morphine, sticks 'im inna bed.

"So, like a half hour later, boom"—Jerry snapped his fingers—"dis poor fuck goes into full arrest. We pump 'im, countershock 'im, give 'im ev'thing onna cart. Nuttin' . . . he's dead meat."

"What was it?"

"Influenza pneumonia. Left lung ruptured and collapsed

too. Deaf man coulda heard it, but not Jantzen." Jerry took a big bite from the candy bar. "He really called dat one good, huh? Fluorescents. Jeezus."

"What a prick," K.D. shook her head. It was a sad fact that the Peter Principle applied just as well to the medical profession as it did to most other businesses. More so, she was sometimes inclined to think. In her opinion Leonard Jantzen didn't know the difference between a saline drip and a spinal tap; it was astounding that he'd lasted for over a decade as a doctor without being hit with a ton of malpractice suits. But Jantzen was also the C.M., and so it was best to tread lightly around him. Patients' lives were not the only lives he held in his hand. This wasn't the first time he had screwed up, and everyone knew that in a perfect world he would have been tossed off the staff of Sisters of Grace long ago. But here, as everywhere else, the better you were at the game the longer you stayed on the board. Jantzen was good at playing members of the BoD off each other, and he wasn't quite enough of an embarrassment to warrant an all-out effort to get rid of him, especially since they knew he would sue for everything from restraint of trade to damage of reputation. And so he stayed on staff, and occasionally patients suffered for it.

K.D. had bumped up against him once or twice. The fact that Jantzen was a sexist of the old school didn't help matters, but in that respect he was hardly alone. K.D. doubted that male doctors would ever look on the distaff side of the profession with anything but deep distrust and hostility. Female doctors were judged inferior until they proved themselves equal, while male doctors were judged equal until they proved themselves inferior. A lousy situation, but one that didn't really surprise anyone.

She glanced at the wall clock: one-thirty P.M. "Gotta go," she said to Jerry. She gulped down the last of the coffee. It had been barely tolerable warm; cold, it tasted like it belonged in a test tube instead of a cup. Then she headed for the elevator, which had just opened its doors, and wedged herself between a young male catatonic in a wheelchair and a white-haired old woman on a gurney on her way to post-op. The only other occupant in the elevator was Pearson, the neurologist who had examined the coma case. She asked him about it.

"That one was bizarre to the end," he said. "Guy stayed comatose for nearly seventy-two hours. Then all of a sudden he opens his eyes and screams—scared the shit out of the nurse bathing him—and kicks it. Still no obvious cause. Finally had to put 'coma of unknown origin' on the death certificate."

"What about the scream? Death rattle?" Sometimes increased blood acidity in the newly dead, she knew, could cause the voice box muscles to spasm, producing a gasping screech. But Pearson shook his head.

"She says no; this was different. Says he was alive when he screamed. She was looking right at him. 'He opened his eyes,' she said, 'and he looked like he was staring straight into hell. It was a scream of pure terror, and he didn't die until after he made it.' "

The doors opened then, and Pearson headed off down the hall. K.D. followed more slowly, feeling gooseflesh prickle her arms as she walked. While she was quite aware that very few people died the way they wanted to—quickly and painlessly, in full possession of their faculties, surrounded by loved ones—this seemed a particularly unsettling way to go. But, she told herself, at least it had been over quickly for him. Most people stare into the Reaper's eyeless sockets far too long before he finally swings his scythe.

As she walked down the corridor she wondered, as she did on occasion, why she put herself through all this—the long hours, the traumatic situations, the grim realities that made up the Emergency Room of a major metropolitan hospital. Most of those who worked there felt it was a bad idea to let yourself care or get involved, or see the victims who came in as anything more than meat. Just "treat 'em and street 'em."

K.D. didn't have to toil to survive. Her great-grandfather had made a fortune in textiles, and his descendants had added to it until the net family worth was now something over thirty million. Her father had told her more than once that she could have a healthy stipend, enough to keep her well taken care of, until she "found her true calling."

It was a tempting offer, and she'd almost accepted more than once, despite their strained relationship. But the problem was that she'd already found her true calling. She was a doctor. Well, not yet, but she was working on it.

Back in the ER, K.D. saw two paramedics wheeling a recumbent form through the automatic doors. She fell in beside them. "What've we got here?"

"White male Caucasian, late twenties, altered LOC, fractured collarbone, possible cracked skull," one of them said. "Pulse one-sixty and thready, respiration thirty and shallow." Something odd in his tone made K.D. look at his face. She was surprised to see him struggling to hold back laughter. A glance at his partner showed him in the same state; both had their lips drawn tight against the smiles that kept stealing over their faces.

She looked down at the patient; he was conscious, but the painkillers had put a nice soft pink haze between him and the world. "What's so funny?" she asked, lowering her voice.

"Ask me what happened to him," the paramedic nearest her said.

K.D. rolled her eyes. She wasn't sure she was ready for this. "What happened to him?"

"He slipped on a banana peel," the other one said, and both

of them lost it. Laughter bubbled up through their noses and escaped like steam from their clenched jaws.

K.D. stopped and stared. "No, c'mon, what really happened?"

"Swear to God," the closer one said as she hurried to catch up. "Dude was shopping down at the French Market, and someone ahead of him was eating a banana and dropped the peel. Wish I'd been there to see it. One guy said it was a classic— what'd he call it, Norm?"

"Pratfall," Norm said.

"Yeah. Right out of the Three Stooges." He shook his head and laughed again.

K.D. couldn't help herself; she had to laugh as well. Sick humor was the only kind in ready supply within these walls, and after a while you couldn't help but howl at the black absurdity of it all. She remembered a time last year when a middle-aged man had gone Code Blue with ventricular fib. Rees had ordered the usual RX, and the crash cart crew had come in. The nurse who was supposed to smear the paddles with conducting fluid had grabbed the wrong bottle and doused them with rubbing alcohol instead. The 400 watt current had zapped the guy's heart back into commission, but it also set his chest hair on fire, along with the bedsheet and curtain. They hadn't let Rees and the nurse forget that one for months.

Then there had been the time, just as K.D. was going off shift, when an old lady had showed up to say she had shot herself in the heart. She had been depressed, so she had taken several Valium and her husband's gun, put the barrel against her chest and pulled the trigger. When she didn't die she decided to try it again. Still no heavenly chorus, and not even a lot of pain. K.D. had figured her for a nut case, but when the woman took off her coat and blouse, lo and behold, there were two bullet wounds, one in each of her pendulous breasts. The fatty tissue had more or less sealed itself without much blood loss, and neither of the slugs had passed through the chest wall. Needless to say, she wound up in the psycho ward.

There were others as well, so many it was hard to remember them all. The guy who had tried to commit suicide by swallowing a bottle of nitroglycerin tablets and slamming himself against the wall hard enough to break his clavicle in an attempt to detonate them. The husband whose wife had had a *grand mal* seizure while fellating him. The teenaged boy brought in naked except for a Batman mask and cape, who'd suffered a cranial contusion by jumping from a bureau and missing the bed his girlfriend was lying on.

And now this one. Holy jumping Jesus in a tow truck, she thought, as she directed one of the nurses to get the concussion case into a room. Slipped on a banana peel. And they say vaudeville's dead.

Most emergency room staffs have a rule of thumb about trauma victims: The ones bleeding the worst and screaming the loudest are often the least injured. It's the quiet ones with the little purple hole just below the belly button and the glassy look in their eyes who don't make it. K.D. had certainly found this to be true at Sisters of Grace, and tonight was no exception. In just under three hours she had dealt with a husband who'd had his scalp opened up by his wife's high heeled shoe, resulting in blood flow that had soaked his hair and shirt, a stab victim who had walked into the hospital with a switchblade embedded to the hilt in his shoulder, and a man who had managed to give himself a rather ragged circumcision when he'd drunkenly stuffed a pistol into the front of his pants with the safety off. All of these had resulted in a lot of bleeding and shouting and carrying on, but none had been particularly life-threatening; they were seen simply as more proof of the old joke that medicine would be a great profession if it weren't for the patients.

On the other hand, Jimmy "Beaucoup" Davis, the homie the nurses called a "frequent flier" because of the number of appearances he had made in the ER over the last year, would not be gracing them with his presence anymore after tonight. Jimmy had come in on a high-speed gurney with an IV in his arm and a .22 slug in his liver, the bullet having arrived at that organ by entering his upper chest at close range, ricocheting off a rib, passing through both lungs and nicking the heart's left ventricle before reaching its final resting place. Jimmy didn't make a lot of fuss when he arrived; he just moaned once or twice while they frantically worked on him and died before they could get him onto a bed.

It was a rare night that K.D. didn't wonder at least once why she wanted to be a doctor. The answer given by most of the residents had to do with a desire to help humanity, to do good. Occasionally someone would cite making over a hundred thou a year as a powerful additional incentive, but even these claimed to have a streak of altruism. The staff lived on coffee and adrenaline, putting personal needs and desires aside for the good of those in their care, trying to go that extra mile, or at least that extra inch. In short, they tried to live according to the oath sworn in the fifth century BC by Hippocrates of Kos: *I will prescribe regimen for the good of my patients according to my ability and my judgment and never do harm to anyone.*

And that was the way Kelly Diane Wilcox tried to run her life.

Many of her colleagues could point to traumatic incidents in their pasts—usually the death of a loved one—or deep-seated anxieties over death and dying that propelled them into the medical profession. They wanted to be able to wrestle with the angel of death, to tear the reins from the grasp of the Four Horsemen. K.D., on the other hand, really couldn't remember what single incident, if indeed there had been any, had convinced her to be a healer. It was just something she had always gravitated toward. As a small child she had prescribed candy medications for her dolls, had swathed them in white linen and propped them comfortably in their small makeshift beds. When she was a little older she had tried the same things on her younger brother Toby, who had not been the most cooperative of patients. Medical shows on TV and books and articles on disease and healing had always fascinated her. There had never been any question in her mind but that she would join the ranks of those who, along with police officers and firefighters, are considered the guardians of life.

And so far she hadn't regretted it. Her biggest fear was that she would, over time, grow so callous to death and suffering that she would come to find the disease processes more interesting than the patients. Most of the residents tended to view the people whom they treated as simply ways to learn more about this malady or that. What occupied them were the enigmas of treatment, the ways to exert the greatest possible control over life and death. Patients were just a means to an end. K.D. didn't want to go down that road, but she knew it was an easy route to take.

She realized she had stopped for a moment to wool-gather when Leonard yelled for her to move her ass and help him with their latest guest, a whacked-out teenager stoned on Blood, the new street drug that had been showing up in peoples' systems more and more over the past few months. K.D. hurried to comply. She peeled one eyelid back on the patient, noticing the red sclera and contracted pupils. "Give him an amp of D-50 and point eight of Narcan," she said, and had to keep from grinning as if at some private joke. Right now, at this moment, there was no place she'd rather be than here.

April stirred noodles into the skillet full of Hamburger Helper and watched Soukie through the torn screen door of the trailer. The child was playing in the small patch of ground that, together with the sixteen-foot Windflow and the concrete parking pad, made up their rental space in the Riverview Trailer Court. April had wondered more than once why it had been named that; located on the edge of bayou country in St. Barnard's Parish, the three acres of palmetto and swamp grass was probably nearer to Lake Borgne than the Mississippi. The only view from her windows was of the Chalmette Petrochemical Refinery, which was actually a pretty spectacular sight after dark, all lit up and flames shooting from various smokestacks, but by day it certainly wasn't anything you'd drag people over to see.

But then Riverview wasn't an upscale mobile home village of double-wide units populated by wealthy retirees and framed by manicured plots of grass and flower beds. This was the kind of place that gave trailer parks a bad name: untended yards and trucks pockmarked with primer, TV sets going full blast all day and all night, the aluminum and particle board boxes inhabited by people whose incomes hovered perennially at or below poverty level.

April Delaney and her daughter had been living here since May of last year, and April still considered herself pretty damn lucky. The trailer she and Soukie occupied was held together more by duct tape than rivets, the narrow foam rubber mattress they slept on was barely more comfortable than the wooden shelf beneath it, and they shared communal restrooms, showers and laundry facilities with the rest of the two dozen tenants. Even so, it was better than before, better by far than the apartment she had shared with the other women in Mal Sangre's stable, shooting up every afternoon to blitz herself out for the nights on the street. Because now she was clean and had a job, and best of all, Soukie was with her again. And nothing was ever going to change that.

Her new life wasn't easy by any means. Until she was able to scrape up enough to open a bank account April had had to pay twenty dollars out of each paycheck just to cash it. She clipped coupons from the paper with fanatical zeal. Her car needed a transmission job, and the money for that was nowhere on the horizon. But she was making it on her own. Ms. St. Charles had told her she could qualify for AFDC, but April saw welfare as a trap. She had looked into the eyes of the women living around her who got those government checks in the mail every month. If there was no other way she would do it, because Soukie came first. But as long as she could put food on the table and a roof over their heads without being beholden to anyone, she was by God going to keep on.

Dinner was done; she scraped some of it into a bowl and put it in the tiny refrigerator to cool down for Soukie. Then she turned to the door—like everything else in the trailer, it was only a couple of steps from the kitchenette—to tell her daughter to come in.

She saw the child hunched over, constructing a pattern by trailing her finger through the dirt and lining up small pebbles. April, watching, felt a slight chill. She was pretty sure that what she was seeing was only a meaningless design, the random result of a young imagination, but some deep superstitious part of her could not help wondering if Soukie was drawing a *vèvè* for the *loa* she had been consecrated to. April had no trouble believing in *Vondoun* in these modern times. Her mother had been a devout Catholic, but that had not prevented the woman from burning praise-and-hope candles or buying blood root and John the Conqueror at the hoodoo apothecary in Opelousas.

Of course, neither the Holy Trinity nor *Les Invisibles* had kept April's father from getting all over her from the age of ten until she ran away at fourteen. Though April had tried to forget everything about her life as a child—had tried to forget everything that had happened to her until she had finally started to turn her life around a few months ago—the respect and fear of the Invisible World she had learned from her mother had stayed with her.

She stepped out and scooped Soukie up from behind. Her daughter squealed with surprised glee, wriggled about and threw her arms around April's neck. She was wearing one of her mother's T-shirts that hung down to her knees. Her legs were red with chigger bites.

"What was you doin' there in the dirt, child?" she asked, to which Soukie replied, in blissful unawareness of the cliché, "Nothing."

April laughed. "Supper's ready." As she turned she saw movement out of the corner of her eye. Harris Beaumont was watching from several units down and across the dusty asphalt road. They locked eyes for a moment, and then April, her face hardening into a mask, turned and went back inside.

Harris Beaumont watched April Delaney step up into the trailer, watched the way her hips shifted beneath the pair of tight jeans. What an ass. One of these days he would find out just which way she liked to squirm and moan when he put it to her. He felt himself growing hard beneath his own jeans and slid his hand down to the bulge behind the fly, casually massaging it as he leaned in the doorway of his unit and stared at her trailer.

Lately it seemed he just couldn't get that black bitch out of his head. Partly it was lust, partly it was anger; just who the fuck did she think she was, anyway, looking down her nose at him like he was some piece of boot-scraped shit? He knew she had been a whore. He knew all about her. He had a second cousin on the NOPD pull her rap sheet for him. He had a better trailer than she did; a better job, too, working construction. Okay, so his last gig had been six weeks ago, that was how he worked, freelance. And yet when he'd tried to come on friendly to her after he'd moved into Riverview she'd given him a look that could've frozen a six-pack.

It wasn't right, Harris thought. Even putting aside the fact that he was white and she was black, once a whore, always a whore. She'd probably sucked more cocks than there were catfish in the Big Muddy, no way she had the right to look at him like that.

He realized he was rhythmically squeezing his denim-covered crotch. Might as well do something about it. He shut the door and moved quickly through the little Holiday Vagabond, closing the blinds and starting the tiny air conditioner, which wheezed asthmatically. Harris turned on the TV and picked up the remote to the VCR with one hand while he undid his belt—big bronze buckle of an American eagle holding a gun in its talons—with the other.

He sat down on the chair, the ancient Naugahyde cold against his bare butt, and aimed the remote. The tape was already in the deck; seems all he had been doing lately was spanking the monkey. On the screen appeared grainy footage of a black woman sucking off one white man while another fucked her doggy-style. Harris watched and listened to the moans coming from the screen while he stroked himself. After so many times he had the timing down pat; he came the same time both guys on the screen did, groaning his release even as he clicked off the TV with the remote.

"Shit," he muttered, staring at the dark screen. He'd had better.

He cleaned up with a towel already sticky from the day before, wrinkling his nose as he did so. Maybe he'd better pick up some Lysol down at the local stop-and-rob . . . the place was starting to smell a little gamey.

No question about it—he had to get himself some warm and wet action before he wore his pencil down to a nub. Harris leaned back in the recliner and thought again about April Delaney.

The past couple of days he'd taken to following her; not that he had anything particular in mind, as much for something to do as anything else. He knew she worked as a checker at the local

Piggly-Wiggly, and he had a pretty good idea of her hours. The lot where she parked was big and poorly lit.

Harris had boasted more than once that he'd never paid for it. He'd taken it twice, though—once in high school eight years ago and again two years ago last month. The second time had been a teenaged Cajun girl he'd picked up hitchhiking out by Westwego. That had been something for the scrapbook. He'd told her, after the two hours they'd spent parked on a deserted side road, that she should be grateful for him showing her what kind of trouble she could get into sticking her thumb out. She might have run into someone a lot meaner, someone who would have left her dead in a ditch instead of alive, her clothes torn and her twat bleeding, blubbering on the side of the highway.

He'd gotten away with it both times. Each time he'd figured he'd been lucky, and that it was better not to tempt fate again. He still looked at it that way. Pretty much.

But that April Delaney. Those tits, that ass. Who the fuck did she think she was . . . ?

One kick was enough to splinter the rotted wood around the latch and send the door slamming back against the wall. Anisse's head jerked up and she stared, her eyes wide, at the appearance of her husband. She tried to speak, but the gag muffled her words.

Sangre showed no surprise; indeed, hardly any reaction. He merely lifted his head and regarded Shane. The latter stood in the doorway, the gun pointed at Sangre's head. Shane had a momentary vivid mental image of his own appearance, almost as if he was seeing himself through Sangre's eyes: sweat-soaked, disheveled, muscles and tendons taut with rage. He looked, he knew, like a maniac fully capable of emptying the gun's chamber into the man sitting before him. And yet Sangre might have been glancing up in mild surprise at an unexpected but not unwelcome guest.

"Stand up," Shane told him. The words came out in a croak. "Stand up and die."

"You're not going to pull the trigger," Sangre said. It was the tone a parent might use to reprove an unwilling child. Anisse continued to struggle against her bonds and make desperate muffled cries.

Shane's finger tightened on the trigger. The gun was loaded with hollow points; at this range one of them would shatter Sangre's head like a gourd struck by a club. He fully intended to shoot him at that moment. But he didn't.

He couldn't.

Sangre was right—he could not pull the trigger. He stared at the gun, feeling the beginnings of panic flush through him. He tried to move his finger the quarter inch that would bring death to his enemy, tried so hard that his vision darkened to a tunnel focusing on the gun and his breath came in rattling gasps, but he might as well have been willing the muscles in Sangre's hand to constrict instead of his.

Sangre stood leisurely, tucking the knife into his belt. He stretched, then stepped forward and took the gun from Shane's hand. He broke it open and emptied the bullets out, tossed them through the open door into the humid darkness beyond. "Nice gun," he said. He threw it after the bullets; Shane heard it splash into the bayou.

Sangre stood in front of him and looked at him. He seemed almost sad. "You should never have left Haiti," he said. "You still have no idea of the stakes involved here, the scope of what I'm doing. That's what makes you dangerous, Shane—your ignorance. You're just adept enough to cause some real problems if you continue blundering about, and I can't have that."

Shane put everything he had into moving. He strained so hard that the muscles of his arms and legs began to quiver and jump. "Relax," Sangre said, and Shane felt the tension drain from his body. He stood passively, staring straight ahead. Out of the corner of his eye he could see Anisse looking at him in sorrow and despair. The thought that he had failed her was worse than anything Sangre might do to him.

"Remember the letter I left for you? I knew you'd read it. And to read it, you had to hold it in your hands."

Shane remembered the slightly greasy feeling of the paper between his fingers. The knowledge of what had happened, of how gullible he had been, slammed into him. Though he could not move, something in his eyes must have shown Sangre his realization, because he nodded.

"A little concoction of mine. Works rather well, don't you think? It's based on a drug that paralyzes the voluntary muscles. I've spiced it up a little, added a few elements—chemical and otherwise—that render the subject extremely suggestable. I could tell you to rip your own throat out right now and you'd do it without hesitating."

Shane knew it was true. His will was completely in thrall to Sangre's. The man had played him for a fool, knowing his anger would make him reckless. He had also counted on the fact that, deep down, Shane would still find it hard to believe that the man who had once been his friend could be capable of such fiendishness.

He knew now that Sangre was capable of that and more. But the knowledge had come too late. All he could do now was stand there and passively await whatever fate was in store for him.

"But I'm not going to do that," Sangre continued. "Call me a sentimental fool, but I'm going to let you live, Shane. However, I can't have you continuing to interfere with me and my work. I've got to make sure that you're out of my life for a good long time. And I think I know a way to make sure of that.

"You're going to be arrested. My men have already contacted the police—by the time they get here I'll be gone. I'm afraid they'll find a rather gruesome crime scene when they arrive. You see, you're going to murder your wife."

Shane could see the terror in Anisse's eyes and knew that it matched the horror in his own. He made his strongest effort yet to break the geas that Sangre had laid on him, but was unable to move an inch from where he stood. Nevertheless, he kept straining, hoping that perhaps the stress he was putting his body through would burst a blood vessel in his brain or rupture his heart. But he knew it was hopeless. Just as he knew, with more horror than he would have thought it possible to feel, that he would do what Sangre said.

He was going to kill Anisse.

His mind cried out to Legba, begged him and all the other *loas* for aid. But he felt no answering whisper in his mind. No gods would help him, and he could not help himself.

Sangre pulled the knife from his belt and handed it to Shane.

"Take it," he said, and Shane felt his hand grip it. "It's an autopsy knife," Sangre continued. "I believe in using the right tool for the job." He stepped away from the two of them. "Begin," he said. "And—please make a thorough job of it."

Shane screamed, but the cry of agony and despair was locked with his head—no whimper of it emerged. He fought with every fiber of his being and soul against taking that first step, but it was futile—his feet moved of their own accord, and he stalked haltingly toward Anisse, who strained against her bonds in a paroxysm of fear, finally losing her balance and falling heavily to the floor while still bound to the chair.

Shane prayed that the fall had knocked her unconscious, but

as his hands reached for her he saw her eyes still open, still staring at him in panicked disbelief and despair. He seized her, pulled the chair roughly upright. He used the knife to cut free the ropes, then dropped it. Her hands freed, she beat at his arms and chest, but he batted her blows away easily and lunged forward, wrapping his fingers around her throat.

She was still gagged; she screamed through the constraining cloth and tore at his wrists with her long fingernails, drawing blood in a dozen places. Shane did not, could not, slacken his grip. Tears began to stream from his eyes, but he maintained his relentless hold on her throat.

His enslaved body took seriously Sangre's admonition to "do a thorough job." He choked her into unconsciousness, then used the knife. By the time he had finished the walls and floor were washed with crimson and Sangre was gone. His *arson* was gone as well, taken no doubt by his enemy. Shane could hear the thrumming of a helicopter overhead, saw the white glare of the spotlight illuminating the hot darkness. . . .

xii

Tony Costanza had first heard the voice over a week ago, just after the end of Mardi Gras. He'd been walking across the Tulane campus under the shade of the giant oaks when it had whispered to him: a faint sibilant sound, like someone murmuring in his ear. So distinct had it been that he'd turned to see if anybody had come up behind him, shoes making no sound on the thick grass.

There had been no one nearby. A few other students were standing in groups talking or hurrying toward the pillared brick buildings, but none were paying any attention to him. And yet he had heard someone say, softly but quite distinctly, *"Ti bon ange."*

The words had sounded French, but Tony wasn't sure. He'd

studied Spanish in high school back in East Lansing and hadn't done particularly well in it. Anyway, what was being said didn't concern him right then so much as who was saying it.

He had looked around again. Not far away a professor was taking advantage of the mild weather to tutor his class on the lawn. A pair of joggers puffed along St. Charles Avenue in vain pursuit of the street car. Across the street in Audubon Park an old Chinese man was practicing t'ai chi, moving like an ancient mime to a slow internal rhythm.

There was no way any of those people could have spoken to him in such an intimate tone. The voice had been too soft to tell if it had come from a man or a woman. Or if it had come from anywhere outside his own head. . . .

When Tony first arrived in the Crescent City he'd thought he'd died and gone to heaven. He'd come from a Michigan winter that could have frozen the balls off a brass monkey into a balmy eighty degrees, with the smell of jasmine and honeysuckle scenting the air. His conviction that this was paradise had only been strengthened the first time he bit into a shrimp po-boy. ("Ya want dat dressed, dawlin'?" the woman behind the counter had asked, much to his confusion.) Tulane University, set in the midst of an upscale residential neighborhood, seemed light-years away from the dreary campus of East Lansing University. He had written an enthusiastic letter to his parents thanking them profusely for sending him here and promising them he would make the Dean's List to show his gratitude.

Tony was twenty years old, tall and good-looking, with hair so blond as to be almost white. He was majoring in gastro-intestinal disorders. Before he'd come to New Orleans his goal had been a residency post at UCLA or NYU Medical Center. After eight months in Louisiana, however, he was thinking seri-ously of applying to Mercy or Sisters of Grace. So far he liked everything about the city: the food, the night life in the Quarter and the Arts District; they even had a pretty good football team. What more need one ask?

And, of course, there were the drugs.

Tony was not an addictive personality. Far from it. He prided himself on knowing when to switch from cocktails to Coca-Cola, and he stayed away from the hard stuff like heroin and speed—although he'd used the latter on occasion to push through a particularly grueling day. He'd even sampled cocaine once or twice.

The best stuff he had had, though, was Blood. No question about it. It combined the crystalline rush of cocaine with the cosmic connectiveness one experienced on empathogens like acid or ecstasy, with just enough visual strangeness to make the world look fresh and new. And, though it was far too soon to tell, the addictive potential seemed to be purely psychological rather than physical. Even the experts were reluctantly admitting that there was apparently little downside to it.

Oddly enough, though it had hit the streets at least four months ago, it was still confined to the New Orleans area. A DEA man Tony saw interviewed on the news admitted to being baffled; a drug this desirable should have started showing up all over the country by now. Tony could see why. In less than a month he'd gone from his first taste of the red powder to snorting it at least three times a week. The actual high was relatively short—only a couple of hours—but the euphoric afterglow lasted most of the day. Thank God, Blood wasn't expensive; just a little more pricey than crack or ice. Still, on the strict budget his folks had given him he'd had to be a bit creative in order to make ends meet this month. He couldn't afford to do it any more often than this, that was for sure. Unless he could find a way to make some extra cash. . . .

Over the last couple of days Tony had pretty much decided the voice had been from some passerby, sounding close at hand by a trick of acoustics. He hadn't given much thought to it since then; not until he had heard it again yesterday. He'd been in class, on the verge of dozing off while old Dodgson droned on about the warning signs of incapresis, when the words once again crooned softly: *"Ti bon ange, ti bon ange . . . mon zombi as-tral . . ."*

Tony had sat bolt upright with a slight yelp, earning some surprised giggles from his fellow students and a glare from Dodgson. He had looked around suspiciously, but even in the relatively close confines of the classroom no one could have gotten that close to him without being noticed. The voice had been right in his ear . . . no, closer than that. It had been in his *head*, in stereo, like wearing an invisible Walkman.

Hearing it once he could shrug off. Hearing it twice . . . now he was worried.

No two ways about it, hearing voices was a bad sign. Tony had taken a tour of a psychiatric ward back in Michigan, had talked with a few folks in there who had to have their brains dipped daily in Thorazine to keep them from chewing their way out of their padded cells. Nearly all of them were, to use his Uncle Frank's clinical diagnosis, crazier than a shithouse rat, and nearly all of them were on a first-name basis with invisible beings that told them to do everything from bathe in their own urine to slaughter half the Eastern Seaboard's population.

It wasn't funny.

Today he'd already skipped his first two classes trying to decide what to do, and he wasn't anywhere close to a solution. Tell an on-campus counselor? Yeah, right. That would pretty much put a bullet into any chance of his eventually hanging out a shingle with a string of initials after his name. Seek private help off-campus? And how would he pay for it, with his collection of Marvel Comics pogs? His parents both subscribed to the school of thought that therapists, psychologists and others of that ilk were little better than snake-oil salesmen; no way would they shell out for it. Even if his meager supply of mad money wasn't being all sucked up his nose buying Blood, it wouldn't begin to cover it.

Tony sat up in his dorm room bed. Was it the new drug that was causing this? He couldn't see how. He'd done considerable research into the effects of psychogenics, and the bulk of the literature seemed to say that drugs like LSD, MDA and suchlike had little or no permanent effect on brain chemistry. While schizophrenia was considered to be primarily chemical in origin, and while a psychogen could theoretically push someone dancing on the edge of madness into the abyss, there was no record of drugs like that causing insanity.

That was the current theory, anyway. Of course, medical theories had a notorious habit of changing. And none of this might apply to Blood, since it was too new a substance for long-term effects to be known.

Tony shivered. He looked around the room. It was the same room it had been last night: the small wooden desk with his Powerbook atop it, the bookcase stuffed with papers and texts, the boombox with its cluster of CDs and tapes. It was the same, and yet it was different; even though the morning sun poured through the open window like liquid honey, even though the only sounds were the lazy buzzing of June bugs, the distant laughter and talk of students and the strumming of a guitar from one of the other rooms, still his nerve endings were wide open, a billion tiny sensors alert for—what?

He wasn't sure. What happens next? he asked himself. Do orders start coming from burning bushes or neighbors' dogs? Do

I climb a tower with a Winchester? Park a truckload of fertilizer and fuel oil downtown . . . ?

Tony pulled his knees up to his chest and began to rock back and forth slightly. He felt a lump of ice slowly grow in his belly. Even if the new drug wasn't responsible for whatever was happening, it seemed prudent to swear off for a while. No sense pouring gasoline on a fire, after all. It wouldn't be hard. He'd just flush what he had stashed. There had been no withdrawal symptoms, no abdominal cramps, no sweats or nausea reported by those who'd stopped taking it for a few days.

Besides, he wasn't an addictive personality. He didn't have to have the stuff. He could stop anytime. And that's what he would do. Because if there was some kind of loose chip in the old master computer between his ears, he was going to need all the help he could get.

Tony stood, dug one hand into the slash he'd made under the box spring and pulled out the baggie half-filled with crimson powder. He carried it into the small bathroom, stood over the toilet and unfastened the twist-tie. Another shiver ran through him and he waited for it to pass; not a good idea to spill it all over the floor.

Now that the baggie was open it seemed he could smell the drug: A seductive, languorous aroma that somehow made him think both of the perfume of blooming flowers and the dank mustiness of worm-turned earth. He'd never noticed that before. The scent made his head spin. The white sterile walls of the bathroom seemed to darken, becoming dim and unreal. He could still hear the sounds from the open window in his room, but they too seemed distant, like the sounds of a dream faintly reverberating beneath one's awareness. Tony stood there, swaying slightly, holding the baggie of Blood over the toilet. He seemed to be looking down at the bowl from a tremendous height. Tunnel vision, like peering through the wrong end of a telescope. He could see the baggie held between thumb and forefinger, but the hand might as well belong to someone else. He felt no sensation in his fingers; in fact, he felt no sensation at all. His body seemed disconnected from his brain. The only sense that remained was that of smell, because the odor coming from the baggie was quite strong now. Cloying, sickening, and yet somehow seductive. How come nobody else had ever mentioned it?

Tony knew he had to get rid of the stuff, get rid of it before the voice whispered in his head again. He knew it would, and soon. He could feel its presence all around him, coiling like a misty constrictor. In another moment it would speak, and he would listen. He would listen. And he would do whatever it told him to do.

Soon. But not yet. There was still time. All he had to do was empty and flush. . . .

NEW ORLEANS,
LOUISIANA

MARCH 13, 1998

L ia glanced at the clock on her desk: 2:55 P.M. Her new case was due in her office by three. If he wasn't there within the next five minutes, she thought, he would be in violation of initial report and his ass would be grass before they even met.

She wondered if that might be for the best. She had a bad feeling about this one. Maybe it was the crime he had been sent up for. Not many of her cases were homicides; most were robbery, burglary, grand theft auto and other crimes against property.

This one was different. She looked down at the case file again. According to the jury's verdict, Shane LaFitte had brutally murdered his wife in a bizarre ritualistic killing back in 1992 that had made the front pages even in this jaded city. The body had been eviscerated and the organs hung like grotesque Christmas ornaments around the shack in which she had been found. Various artifacts associated with voodoo—wax candles shaped like skulls, bottles full of incense and rum, small leather bags filled with charms—had been found on the scene. So had LaFitte, his clothes and skin soaked with the blood of his wife and scrapings of her skin under his fingernails. The knife that had been used on her had his fingerprints on it.

Lia shook her head. Her disgust was an almost palpable thing; she felt it enfold her like a cloak. How could anyone in human shape be such a conscienceless monster?

It was not the first time she'd asked herself that question.

Some cases she could try to empathize with, even feel some degree of sympathy for. But not this one. Even though he'd been a model prisoner, Lia told herself, earning an early release, LaFitte was and always will be guilty of murder. When he shows, stomp on him. *If* he shows. She almost hoped he wouldn't; then she could take him off the board without even seeing his face.

2:58. It being a Friday, she was hoping to get out of the office early. She glanced at her desk calender, and for the first time put the date together with the day.

Friday the thirteenth. How appropriate, Lia thought. Even as the thought ran through her head the door opened and Shane LaFitte entered.

He was tall and rangily built, with thick muscle sheathing his arms, shoulders and chest. Haitian by birth, according to his sheet. His skin was the color of dusky bronze. He wore an open collar shirt and a light sports jacket that did little to conceal his impressive physique. At first she thought he was bald, then realized that the black wool covering his head had been shaved very close.

Lia was surprised; this was not what she had expected.

LaFitte stood before the desk, his posture not threatening but not submissive. He seemed oddly calm; there was none of the fidgeting or nervous glancing about the room and toward her that so many of them exhibited. His presence seemed to fill the room. At five-ten and a half, Lia did not have to look up to many men. She would have to look up to Shane LaFitte, even if she were wearing heels.

The realization irritated her. She remained seated and gestured at the hardback chair near him. LaFitte moved to it and sat, never taking his eyes off her. His movements were precise, economical; he had the kind of body control that only an experienced dancer or martial artist attains. Her years of *aikido* had given her confidence that she was more than a match for most of her cases, but if it came down to it she doubted she could take LaFitte. She met his gaze. There was nothing challenging in it, but she still felt that he was taking her measure on some obscure level.

Well, that was okay. He could have a chip the size of a sequoia on his shoulder—it didn't change the facts. One of the two people in this room was a bottom-dweller, and it wasn't her.

Time to make sure LaFitte knew it.

"My name is Lia St. Charles," she said. "You can call me God."

His face betrayed no reaction; trying to read his expression was like trying to see through a masquer's porcelain visage. "Shane LaFitte," he replied. His voice was quiet, somehow melodic even in a sentence of two words—although it was devoid of Cajun or any other accent as far as she could tell.

Though he'd only spoken two words, Lia felt a sudden sense of great sadness, tragedy even, that seemed to resonate from his voice. Could it be, she found herself wondering, that he was honestly remorseful for the atrocity he had committed?

She put the thought from her mind. If it was true, well and good. But it would take a lot more than a flash of intuition to convince her of that.

According to his file he was thirty-six. He didn't look it, even after his years in 'Gola. He could have passed for her age.

"Let's get down to cases," she continued. "Specifically, your case. I want you to understand your situation, LaFitte, if you don't already. You are on parole. That means the normal rights due a law-abiding citizen are denied you. If you give me *any* cause, I will have you shipped back to Angola so fast you'll get whiplash. Are we clear on this?"

"Of course," he replied. His tone as neutral as if he were reporting the weather. She wondered where her fleeting sense of empathy had come from. The whole situation bordered on surreal. She'd never had anyone react like him before. Usually they would whine, attempt to convince her of their innocence, how the rules really shouldn't apply to them, that she should cut them some slack. The more manipulative ones would compliment her, try to clumsily ingratiate themselves in hopes that, being a woman, she would soften toward them.

For some reason she found his lack of any kind of response, and her earlier feeling of—what? pity?—for him more aggravating than a negative reaction. She wasn't going to give him the satisfaction of getting a rise out of her, though. She used her annoyance to keep her voice strong and even.

"You are to stay in this parish. If you leave it for any reason you're violated. You can't change addresses within the parish without my approval. Obviously, if I even suspect you've been involved in any kind of criminal activity or if you've been associating with anyone with a rap, even just a speeding ticket, it's up the lazy river.

"You will check in with me in this office once a week to report on your search for employment and to be urine-tested for drugs. After you land a job I'll expect to see paycheck stubs. When you find a place to live, you'll have a key made for me. Failure to report in, for any reason . . . well, you probably get the idea by now."

LaFitte nodded, polite and attentive. Lia leaned forward, looked him in the eyes, held his gaze. "You'd better have this straight, LaFitte," she said. "Because I own your sorry ass. If a cop nails you for spitting on the sidewalk, I can send you back. As far as you're concerned, I'm judge, jury and executioner. Work with me and we'll get along. Give me any shit whatsoever and I'll be your worst nightmare."

She leaned back in her chair and watched him. She hadn't delivered such a ballbuster of a speech in some time, but she felt it was warranted here. This man was powerful—not just on a physical level, but also in a way that Lia found hard to put into words. It was a subtle thing, but deep within him was trouble; she could sense it the way an ancestor from the dawn of time could sense a predator in the night.

Silence grew heavy in the air. She watched him, tried to get any indication of what was going on behind his immobile features. Not a clue, she had to admit. Superman couldn't read this guy with X-ray vision.

"Any questions?" she asked.

LaFitte was quiet for a few moments, eyes lidded slightly. He seemed to be not so much thinking as listening to some inner voice. Then he stood, so quickly and smoothly that Lia, despite reflexes honed by four nights a week in the *aikikai*, flinched slightly.

"No questions," LaFitte said. "You have made our respective positions quite clear, Ms. St. Charles. If I present you with any trouble, do not hesitate to mete out whatever punishment you deem necessary."

He paused a moment—now he was the one holding her gaze—and then asked, "May I go now?"

There was nothing the slightest bit disrespectful in his words, tone or body language. So why, Lia asked herself, did she feel she'd suddenly lost charge of the meeting?

She nodded slowly. "One week from today, LaFitte. Be here or be busted."

"One week from today," he repeated. "Thank you, Ms. St. Charles. Good afternoon."

He left the office, closing the door quietly behind him. Lia took a deep breath and blew it out. The air seemed to have cleared the way it sometimes does after a sudden summer storm.

"Jesus, what planet was I just on?" she asked herself out loud. This soft-spoken, obviously well-educated man was certainly not what she had envisioned from the crime report. Of course, she knew that murderers didn't all have to be clones of Charles Manson; they could just as easily come off like Ted Bundy. Appearance and attitude mean nothing; seems like it's always the mild-mannered innocuous ones, she thought, the pillars of the community, who can open their own organ banks. But with LaFitte Lia did not get the feeling that he had been false with her. Oh, he had obviously been playing a role, but then, so had she. Yet he had managed to do so without violating who he was on some deep level. It had been that sense of "centeredness" that had kept her off-balance. A psychopath can be a consummate actor, but peel away enough layers and he's empty at the core. Shane LaFitte, she sensed, was anything but empty at his core.

Again she wondered about that brief burst of compassion she had felt. Then she shook her head. Get a grip, St. Charles.

No matter how cultured and polished he comes across, he's still a dirtbag. According to the crime scene description he'd done everything with his wife's body short of play handball with her liver. He's a monster wearing human skin. The most dangerous psychos are the charismatic ones, the ones that can charm you straight into the slaughterhouse. A water moccasin is pretty to look at, but that doesn't make it any less deadly.

Lia closed the file and put it away. Playing back the conversation in her head, she realized that at no time had he agreed to any of the parole conditions. He had indicated his understanding but not his acquiescence. And—this part amazed her the most—he had given her permission to do her job should he transgress.

Talk about chutzpah. . . .

No question about it, Lia St. Charles told herself grimly, this Shane LaFitte would bear watching.

Very close watching.

FRENCH QUARTER,
NEW ORLEANS,
LOUISIANA

MARCH 13, 1998

Another glorious day in the Quarter, Dave Cummings thought as he sat in the courtyard of the N'Awlins Café on St. Philip Street. Water tinkled and splashed in a marble fountain marking the center of the courtyard, around which were arrayed white wrought-iron tables and chairs. The walls were draped in ivy and sculpted cherubs peeked out from the dark green growth. Dave sipped milk punch and scooped up another forkful of *étouffée*. The temperature was in the high seventies, the air somewhat muggy but by no means unbearable. His rent was paid and he had a hundred and fifty dollars in his pocket to last him through the weekend. Life could maybe get better, but it was hard to see how.

The Bucktown Jazz Band was playing at Beiderbecke's

tonight. It had been three days since their last gig at the Crawfish Club and Dave was looking forward to hitting the boards again. He hoped they would all be a bit more on their game than last time. He was feeling better, at any rate; his sinuses were no longer on the verge of meltdown and the food in front of him, for the first time in a week, didn't taste like damp cardboard.

He frowned, wondering if Jeff was okay. He'd called him the morning following that weird episode outside his apartment, not entirely sure if it hadn't all been an alcohol-induced fantasy. But Jeff had sounded fine. Yes, he'd tried some of the stuff, which Dave now realized was that new drug called Blood. It had been a spur-of-the-moment decision, Jeff had said, probably having to do with feeling old and no longer on the cutting edge.

Too strange by half, Dave told himself as he finished his meal. Time would tell. Though his band partner seemed perfectly okay over the phone, the real proof would be how he played tonight.

He paid his bill and left the restaurant, strolling past crowded stores full of antiques, bric-a-brac, handcrafted masks and jewelry. This was the older part of the Quarter, with some structures dating back well over a hundred years. It was just past noon and foot traffic was fairly heavy. Dave window-shopped, cruising along with the tourists and other Quarterites, indulging in the luxury of having nothing in particular to do and nowhere in particular to go, enjoying the sun on his face and the scents of pastry and hibiscus.

A handpainted sign on the sidewalk caught his attention: JAZZ CLASSICS, with an arrow pointing down a narrow, covered passageway between two buildings. Dave frowned. A specialty shop? He thought he knew every record store with a decent jazz and blues selection in New Orleans. Intrigued, he followed the corridor, which led him down damp cobblestones past brick walls before taking a right angle and depositing him in a tiny dimly lit shop. The city's signature tune, "When the Saints Go Marching In," played softly from hidden speakers; he recognized the performers as the South Frisco Jazz Band. The entire place was barely bigger than a walk-in closet and filled with record bins. Dave stared about in awe. There were no CDs, no tapes and very few 45s and LPs: the majority of the stock was old vinyl 78s dating back a half century or more. Labels like Blue Note, Gennett, Decca, Milestone, Columbia . . . he could hardly believe his eyes. Why had he never heard of this place? It must have just opened, although the faded posters on the walls and the general ambiance indicated otherwise.

Not surprisingly, Dave Cummings was an aficionado and collector of old and rare jazz sides. In fact, if he had anything approaching an addiction, vinyl would be it. Over the years he had amassed a collection that was the envy of many of his colleagues. It boasted rare compilations of Jelly Roll Morton, Charlie Mingus, Max Roach and Duke Ellington, to name but a few. He was always on the lookout for more treasures, and more than once he'd survived for a week on catsup soup after dropping several hundred bills on something like a 1920s recording of Clarence Williams and his Blue Five. Surely in these bins were items he couldn't live without.

He looked around for the proprietor but saw no one behind the small desk. He shrugged and started pawing through the As. The section on Louis Armstrong was satisfyingly comprehensive. Dave saw recordings from the twenties with Satchmo as sideman for the Red Onion Jazz Babies and Johnny Dodds's Black Bottom Stompers. There were bluebird discs of Armstrong and his All Stars, jam sessions with Fats Waller and Jack Teagarden, even European and Australian compilations. All of which he had, of course, but it was still nice to feel them slip past his fingers. It was like greeting old friends in a new locale.

He finished leafing through the stacks and looked about. A display case against one wall caught his attention. Within were three old albums leaning against the back of the shelf. Dave peered closer at them. One was a King Oliver collection on a French label, the other a Cotton Club bootleg from the thirties. Both were quite rare, but not so rare that he didn't already own copies of them.

The third one . . .

Dave suddenly had difficulty getting his breath. The gravelly strains of the background singing seemed to be replaced by the chorus of a heavenly host. There, right there in front of him, in near-mint condition, was the Holy Grail of jazz collectors. He'd seen pictures of it, heard tapes of it, but he'd never held a copy in his hands before.

Louis Armstrong's 1929 issue of *African Stomp* on Okeh Records.

It was one of the rarest and most sought-after discs in the history of modern music. Dave had heard of a copy being sold recently in Japan for five thousand dollars. There was a price sticker on the upper right hand corner of the cover, with a number printed on it in small neat pen strokes. For a long moment he dared not look at it directly. No matter what it is, he thought, I can't afford it. Just finding a copy was astonishing enough; finding an affordable copy would be on a par with winning the lottery.

He was almost tempted to turn away and continue his perusal of the stacks without learning how much it was. After all, one should not look into the face of the Gorgon. But who was he kidding? He didn't have that kind of will power.

He looked at the price tag. It read $1,750.00.

A good price.

Better than a good price; an incredible price. He couldn't believe his luck. And on Friday the thirteenth, to boot. A disc this rare priced this low in any other major city would be snapped up so fast it would leave scorch marks. To find it in the middle of the French Quarter, the jazz Mecca of the Western world, bordered on supernatural.

There was no way he could pass this up. He had to have it, and he had to have it *now*. If he even turned his back to look through another bin he ran the risk of someone else coming in, spotting it and grabbing it.

Dave stood there thinking furiously. He had a hundred and fifty in his wallet. He had managed to convince a local bank, a couple of years ago, to issue him a Mastercard with a fifteen-hundred-dollar limit. Even if he could charge the card to the max that still left him a hundred bucks shy. That shouldn't be a problem; surely he could have the owner hold the record long enough for him to scare up an extra hundred.

Unfortunately, it wasn't that simple. He had already put about six hundred on the card this month. Which meant the maximum he could use it for was about twelve hundred. Add the pocket money and he still lacked seven hundred.

Shit. *Shit.* There had to be *something* he could do. He couldn't let this opportunity slip through his hands. He could no more walk out of the store without that album—or at least without a guarantee of owning it—than he could have walked out without one of his lungs. For a brief, utterly insane moment Dave thought of pawning his horn. But he wouldn't be able to get enough for it. And without it, how could he make the money to get it out of hock?

"Hey!" Dave said loudly. "Anybody home?"

For a moment there was no response, and a wild impulse to smash the case, grab the record and run swept over him. Then a man stepped out of a curtained alcove behind the desk.

He was younger than Dave expected; not more than ten years older than the musician. Sandy-haired, a struggling mustache, cardigan sweater. "Can I help—" was as far as he got before Dave said, "I'm interested in the Armstrong," indicating the display case with a gesture.

"Ah, yes," the proprietor said, coming around the desk and moving toward the case while he pulled a set of keys from his pocket. "I'm told that's an extremely rare item." Dave's puzzlement must have been evident on his face, because the store owner continued: "This entire collection was my father's. He recently passed on and I opened this shop—I own the property—to sell it off." He shrugged and smiled slightly. "Gives me something to do."

That explained the sudden appearance of the shop and the ridiculously low price. Dave felt definite relief at hearing this; the whole situation had begun to seem entirely too much like something out of a Stephen King novel. It didn't solve his main problem, however, which was conjuring up seven hundred dead presidents to insure that *African Stomp* would come live under his roof. None of his musician friends were flush enough at the moment to lend him the bucks. Besides, if they knew what he wanted it for they'd just try to snatch it away for themselves.

Perhaps he could trade in some of the other, less valuable pieces in his collection . . . no. The owner had just said he was in this business to sell off his stock. And trying to peddle the records elsewhere would take too long.

There had to be some way. . . .

Then, just like that, he thought of one. And almost immediately wished he hadn't.

Playing the clubs and concerts in some of the more exotic locales of the Crescent City had, over the years, made Dave the acquaintance of a number of individuals who operated in the more outlying regions of society. Among them was a hitman named Louie whom Norm Skokes referred to (though never to his face) as Louie the Squirrel because of the man's predilection for cracking walnuts between thumb and forefinger. Another was Milo Parkes, one of Royal Street's classiest jewelers back in the fifties, now without a doubt the world's oldest gemstone fence. There were others as well, colorful personalities all; Dave had been somewhat taken aback to learn they and other shady types, including some of Mal Sangre's enforcers, made up part of the band's faithful following. He'd had a drink with one or two of them on occasion, but certainly had never considered having anything to do with any of them on a business level.

But things do change, don't they? Now it looked like he would be getting in touch with one of them: Errol Mandeville, a small-time loan shark.

Dave hesitated, then took the plunge. He told the store's owner his situation. Would it be possible to put the disc on layaway, so to speak, until he could deliver the seven hundred?

The owner hemmed and hawed, then reluctantly agreed to hold *African Stomp* for twenty-four hours, but no longer. Dave promptly handed over his Mastercard and emptied his pockets. He was quite aware that this put him in dire financial straits. The rent would soon be due again, and the only items in his refrigerator were a couple of black bananas, a tub of cream cheese so moldy it could be of interest only to the Menninger Clinic, and three bottles of beer. He would probably pick up less than a hundred bucks playing tonight if he was lucky.

But none of that mattered. All that mattered was the recording, sitting like a precious gem in the display case before him. Addiction, Dave thought ruefully, can be an ugly thing.

L ia hit the mat in a long arc, one arm leading, shoulder and upper body curved like an eggshell. She rolled and bounced to her feet just in time to face an attack from another direction. She went with her opponent's momentum, using a hip throw to send him flying, then settled into a triangular stance, center of balance low, trying to sense the other students' various positions behind and to her sides while her eyes told her who was in front. This was *randori*, freestyle, an anything-goes exercise in which one had to be constantly alert for attacks from all sides.

Jim Fontenot, a lanky, good-natured black man who had just gotten his blue belt, moved toward her for an elbow grab. He wasn't quick enough; a flurry of movement ended with Lia down on one knee, having thrown Jim over her shoulder.

Even as she felt a brief moment of smugness at the ease with which she accomplished this, Lia felt herself seized from behind and pulled down. She hit the mat hard, slapping it with both hands and blowing her breath out to absorb the impact, but even so, she had a moment's difficulty filling her lungs. Gillis Morgan, one of the second dan instructors, smiled at her and raised an eyebrow. Lia smiled back sheepishly, knowing the black belt had sensed her moment of self-absorption and taken advantage of it.

The sharp sound of Sensei's hands clapping ended the freestyle session. Lia assumed a kneeling position on the mat, *seiza*, with the other students, surreptitiously tugging her *gi* back into place and making sure the knot on her green belt was centered over her navel. She breathed deliberately and evenly, willing her pulse rate and heartbeat to slow while she focused her attention on the front of the large room.

The Agatsu *aikikai* had been a delicatessen in its former incarnation; it was a long narrow room, mostly floored with woven *tatami* mats. Mirrors lined both of the long walls. In the rear of the building were dressing rooms and showers. Above the front door was a picture of Morihei Ueshiba, the founder of *aikido*, and above that were arranged the five belts of rank that this particular school used: white, blue, green, brown and black.

The *sensei* was a diminutive Nisei woman in her late fifties named Lucy Ito, who had been teaching at this *aikikai* for the past twenty years. She was seventh *dan* and soon to be eighth, considered one of the most adept *aikido* practitioners in the United States. Those who had seen her move did not doubt it.

Lia had been studying *aikido* for nearly four years now; soon she would test for her brown belt. When she had decided to pursue a martial art she had checked out several styles before settling on this one. She had felt drawn to it, even though she knew it took much longer to gain sufficient proficiency to be able to use it for self-defense than something like *shotokan* or *tae kwon do* did. One thing she liked about it was the lack of competitiveness and macho bullshit; she had more than enough of that in her life, thank you very much. But the main reason was its emphasis on training the mind and soul as well as the body.

Sensei ordered the class to pair off in training exercises. Lia linked up with Bobby Rothstein, a man two years her senior who had just gotten his brown rank. She took the defense position, *nage*, and they bowed to each other. Then Bobby stepped in and brought a hard open-handed chop down at Lia's forehead. Lia pivoted, blocked and caught his hand, did the little half twirl with both her hands on his and bent his wrist backward. Bobby hit the mat on his back, slapping the mat to break his fall, then slapped again several times to let her know she had the technique right.

Bobby rose gracefully to his feet, bowed and they reversed positions. Lia now was *uke*, the aggressor. They both moved smoothly, their actions meshing like a well-rehearsed dance. She felt the block and pressure and went with it, slapped the *tatami* for the breakfall and then twice again to acknowledge her partner's control of the movement. She came up and they bowed. "Good one," she said.

Although she often left the *aikikai* feeling physically tired, Lia always felt mentally refreshed after a hard workout. She tried to come in at least two evenings a week and once on Saturday, though that wasn't always possible since the class was in River Ridge, a good ten miles from her house. Still, she gave it a high priority. When she had joined, Lucy Ito had explained to her the foundation of the art as she saw it. *Aikido*, she had said, was not so much a means of combat as a way of self-improvement, a method of aligning oneself with the universe. The word *"aikido"* meant "the way of spiritual harmony." Technically it was a sort of high-tech wrestling, going with your opponent's force instead of resisting it. "Flow like water, strike like iron," was how she had put it. But there was much more to it than that. One of the aspects that Lia found most intriguing was the concept of *ki.*

Ki was, according to *Sensei,* a kind of energy or power that infused all life. Once one learned to tap into it, it could be, among other things, an endless wellspring of vitalization and power. Initially this had sounded way too much like *Star Wars* for Lia to feel comfortable with it. But as she had learned more and risen in rank, her skepticism had begun to reluctantly erode.

Take Lucy Ito as an example. Lia doubted the woman weighed more than a hundred and ten pounds including the heavy cotton *hakima* and *gi* she wore. Even so, she had seen *Sensei* toss around men who weighed nearly twice as much as easily as if they were *papier mâché.* Quite a bit of this could be explained by laws of physics and momentum, of course, but some of it couldn't. Momentum had nothing to contribute when the woman stood rock still, extended one arm straight out and two burly guys using all their strength couldn't bend it at the elbow. That was almost equivalent, as far as Lia was concerned, with someone levitating off the floor and flying around the room. She didn't believe *ki* existed as a kind of mystic energy, but she couldn't deny that it embodied a physical and psychological attitude that could maximize one's performance.

She had made the mistake of mentioning some of this to April Delaney a couple of months ago, thinking that perhaps studying a martial art would give the young woman some focus and self-confidence. April had been very interested in *ki,* likening it to the *gros bon ange,* the pool of cosmic energy accessible by everyone, according to voodoo belief. Lia had quickly changed the subject; it had seemed almost heretical to her to have the precepts of *aikido* compared to such mumbo-jumbo.

In the rural lowlands where she had grown up, voodoo and *Santería* had almost as many followers as Christianity. In the small town where her family had shopped for groceries the local drug store had an extensive *botánica* section that included various herbal remedies and such exotic items as moles' forefeet, *owanga* bags, snakeskins and so on. She remembered one of her classmates in high school being taken to a "hoodoo woman" by her parents and "magicked up" to prevent any indiscreet behavior causing pregnancy. She herself had, at the age of four or five, attended a *vada*, a ceremony supposedly involving possession by *loa*. She didn't remember the why or how of her attendance; she had been given the vague impression by her parents that one of her great-aunts, who had not been quite right in the head, had taken her to the ritual without their knowledge. She remembered chaotic images: frenzied dancing, hands pounding drums, a man writhing on the ground, his eyes blank white ovals against the black skin of his face. It had been an intense, horrific experience for a young child, and Lia had resented ever since having been exposed to it and to the old witch woman in the plantation house a few years later. When April had told her that she had taken Soukie to some local temple to take part in voodoo ceremonies, Lia had seriously considered violating her for child endangerment. At its worst, she thought, such credulous worship produced madmen like Shane LaFitte, driven to sacrifice human lives in the pursuit of power or God knew what.

If she hadn't had the proof of his conviction she would have found it very hard to believe he had been guilty of such a heinous crime. She might even, she admitted to herself, have been attracted to him. A pity that the charisma LaFitte radiated came from madness, rather than from the inner peace of someone like Lucy Ito. . . .

Her attention was abruptly yanked back to the present by a subtle change in the atmosphere of the room. The students around her were suddenly charged with expectancy. She had allowed her mind to wander; thankfully, no one appeared to have noticed. What was going to happen?

She watched *Sensei* moving among the students, studying each one, and realized what it was: they were going to be given a demo. This was a treat; normally *Sensei* merely watched the senior black belts work the class. Now and then she would step in and correct a technique slightly, changing the placement of someone's foot a quarter inch or the speed of his or her turn a hair. She always seemed to know when a student could use a little fine tuning. On the rare occasions when she decided to participate, it was something to see. Only the senior students were allowed to attack her, the black belts and now and then one of the second-degree browns. Lia always watched in awe when *Sensei* took the center of the mat. Here was the difference in what she and the other students did and what one was supposed to do. *Sensei* lived in her *ki*. When she stood still, it was as if her feet were nailed to the mat by railroad spikes; when she moved, it was like watching quicksilver in human form: smooth, effortless, a study in total control. One moment she would be surrounded by eight or ten students ready to attack; the next moment the air would be full of black and white blurs as the attackers flew through space like dervishes.

Lucy Ito walked along the lines of kneeling students. "You. You. You." Lia kept her gaze averted, watching the woman peripherally. She had never been chosen, nor did she expect to be for quite some time. Her technique still left much to be desired.

Sensei paused in front of her. "And you," she said. A hint of a smile flashed.

Lia felt a momentary urge to look behind her, like a clichéd moment in a comedy. This couldn't be happening; she wasn't even a brown belt yet. *Sensei* had never chosen someone so low in rank before. She abruptly had trouble getting a full breath.

She stood and stepped up to the front of the class, her white cotton *gi* in sharp contrast with the black *hakimas* of the senior students. She felt about as inconspicuous as a nudist at an embassy ball.

Sensei stood in the center of the circle they made, a small wiry woman with iron gray hair and a remarkably unlined face. "Begin," she said.

Gillis Morgan, the senior black belt at third *dan*, launched himself at her, fingers extended to choke—and became a human missile as *Sensei* waved a seemingly negligent hand at the student, barely brushing the back of his head. Another black belt, Tom Franklin, leapt in from behind. The woman could not possibly have seen him, but she twirled nonetheless, laying a small hand on Franklin's wrist. Franklin corkscrewed up and over, hit the mat and bounced up again.

The others went in with about the same level of success they would have had jumping headlong into a buzzsaw. *Sensei* spun, pivoted, twisted, turned and whirled around her body's axis, untouchable, unstoppable.

When Lia's turn came, she hurled herself forward in an attempt to punch the older woman in the throat. She could not have said what the opposing technique was, so quick was it over. One moment she was running and then she was flying. For a brief instant she and *Sensei* had become a unit, two halves of a perfect machine, *yin* and *yang*. Then she was alone, lying dazed on the mat, and *Sensei* had already turned to face her next attacker. By the time she had rolled and come up, the exercise was over. *Sensei* stood unperturbed, as if meditating alone in a deep forest, in no more danger than one of the ancient trees.

Lia moved back to her place in the ranks and settled down again, buttocks resting on her heels. This, she told herself, was what real mastery was. This was what you could spend a lifetime seeking. Perfect equilibrium, both mental and physical. Did she for a moment believe in such things, she would have said that *Sensei* was a human vessel filled by some supernatural force, be it *loa, ki* or something utterly incomprehensible. It didn't seem possible that a mere man or woman could accomplish such things. That it was possible, and achievable, was a bigger miracle by far than anything black magic could perform.

K.D. hadn't been to the Quarter in months. This was her first day off from the hospital in nearly three weeks and she had spent most of it vegging in her apartment, listening to old Molly Severin albums and painting her toenails. But around five the place had started to seem a little cramped, so she had decided a night on the town might be what she needed.

Now, as she strolled through the dusk down the endless party that was Bourbon Street, past a pair of young black break dancers spinning and gyrating for coins, she knew she'd made the right decision. She'd been spending too much time among the sick and injured. Burnout was always a risk, especially during one's residency. It was important to recharge the batteries now and then, maybe have a conversation with someone that didn't involve blood and sutures.

She had dinner at the Crescent City Coffee House, treating herself to Bananas Foster for dessert. For the most part K.D. tried to eat healthy—lots of fruits and vegetables, lean meat, light on starches—but every once in a while her sweet tooth would not be denied. Now, the rum-based treat making a warm glow in her belly, she wandered, watching the neon lights flicker on and the mule-drawn "vis-à-vis" carriages amble by, listening to snatches of jazz, blues, honky-tonk and ragtime belting from clubs and the whiskey-voiced barkers touting salacious delights to be found within the strip joints and oil wrestling establishments. She felt little concern at being a woman alone after dark; the Quarter was actually a pretty safe place to be as long as she kept to the well-lighted and crowded streets.

No matter how many times she came here, the *Vieux Carré* still fascinated her. The first time she'd seen it she had been taken aback by how small it was—only ten blocks square, she could walk from Canal to Esplanade in twenty minutes. The number of boarded up buildings had also surprised her. Those who lived in the Quarter seemed to take perverse pride in its decadence and dilapidation. The structures were colorful, but not cheery. There was a sense of darkness, of ripe decay, to their hues: burgundy, purple, olive, brown. Despite round-the-clock partying—how do the people living on Bourbon Street ever get any sleep? she wondered—the French Quarter at times felt to her like it was on continuous life support.

Maybe it had something to do with the haunted houses that the Quarter was supposedly full of. If K.D. were to accept all the stories she had heard since moving to New Orleans, it would be easy to believe that every building in the city, and especially in the Quarter, was infested with ghosts. Most of them dated back to the 1800s, when the slave trade was alive and well, but there were more contemporary spirits supposedly roaming the alleys and streets as well. K.D. felt a slight shiver goose her spine as the thought crossed her mind. The night seemed to press down on the bright neon gaiety of the street, as if biding its time.

A gangly teenaged boy wearing jeans patched with duct tape and a ripped T-shirt displaying the Rolling Stones' *Voodoo Lounge* album cover rocketed past her on rollerblades. A pair of prostitutes stood on either side of a BMW and thrust low-cut halter tops through the driver and passenger windows. Through the wide-open doors of one of the strip clubs she glimpsed a naked woman dancer crouching on a blue-lit stage, knees wide apart and shaven mons visible in clinical detail.

K.D. stopped to admire a wooden Indian in front of a curio shop. Instead of cigars he held in his clenched fist a bouquet of plastic flowers. In the window of another shop was a four-foot-high pyramid of preserved alligator heads and two stuffed armadillos mating.

She decided to take in one of the many live band performances going on all around her. Her first choice of music was rock—her current fave rave was the Stone Temple Pilots—but one couldn't live in New Orleans and not develop some appreciation for jazz and blues. Picking a place at random, she turned into Beiderbecke's, a rustic European-style pub near St. Ann's Street.

Inside, a wave of jubilant brass washed over her. K.D. ordered a beer from a local microbrewery and sat down.

According to the sign out front, the musicians called themselves the Bucktown Jazz Band. She recognized some of the pieces they played, though none of them by name. Still, it was a toe-tapping good time, well worth the cover charge. As she sipped her drink K.D. was aware of several men eyeing her, though none approached right away. Eventually one or two probably would, and she would have to politely rebuff them. She hoped it wouldn't go any further than that. Most men figured that a woman by herself was automatically lonely, and that was reason enough to try to strike up a conversation. But K.D. had always been self-sufficient, even as a child. She didn't need anyone's company to make the evening a success.

Not that she would automatically turn down any man who happened to cast eyes her way tonight. If the right guy came along she wouldn't sneer at a little conversation and companionship. However, looking around the room, she estimated the chances of that happening as pretty slim. Most of the club's clientele were either very obviously on the make or already paired up with someone. K.D. shrugged. Life in the big city.

She turned her attention back to the band. One of the players, she noticed, was kind of interesting. He looked to be about her age, maybe a couple of years older, with short dark hair, glasses and a slight build. A bit on the thin side, but still, there was something appealing about him. He was playing a small horn instrument—she thought it was a cornet, but it could have been a tuba for all she knew—and singing backup vocal. Not exactly the sort to shatter the pent-up floodgates of passion within her, but cute nonetheless.

He took a momentary break in his playing and happened to glance her way as she was looking at him. Their gazes locked for a moment. He smiled, and she couldn't help but return it; he had that kind of infectious smile. Then the moment passed as he returned his attention to the music.

K.D. leaned back and drained the rest of her beer. The music was nice and her chair was comfortable. She just might stay awhile.

The band was flying tonight, Dave thought. They could all feel it: a synergy that made the music seem to flow smoothly and effortlessly. They hit their high point with "African Stomp," the title piece from the treasure he had just mortgaged his soul to buy, a fast-paced number that featured him as soloist while the rest of the horns blew backup. The middle section was an extensive stoptime, allowing Dave to improvise a series of rips and triplets that garnered a spontaneous burst of applause. It was, he thought, probably the best two or three minutes of blowing he'd done to date. He felt completely unfettered by limitations of breath and dexterity, able to leap over bar lines like an Olympic hurdler. It almost seemed that he, David Morris Cummings, middle-class white boy from Des Moines, had been possessed by Satchmo's spirit, channeling the master like some possessed voodoo priest. Better than sex, better than drugs. Lawsy!

It was just after his solo that he looked down and saw the young woman at a table by herself, watching him. She was drop-dead gorgeous, hair the color of dark rum, an appraising look in her hazel eyes. It was just what he needed to make the moment perfect—even if he never learned her name, never saw her again, just that smile was a memory he knew he would carry and treasure for decades.

Assuming he lived past tomorrow night . . .

The only cloud on his horizon—and admittedly, it was a pretty big and black one—was that he'd had to borrow seven hundred bills from that sleazy bookie Errol Mandeville earlier today to buy the precious piece of vinyl. The bastard had set a vigorish of fifty dollars per day, which, he had explained to Dave, was giving the musician a break because Errol liked his music. That meant that Dave would have to scare up eight hundred bucks by tomorrow, and he had no idea where it would come from. By the end of the week, Errol had intimated none too subtly, if the loan was not repaid Dave would find himself trying to explain the situation to Louie the Squirrel. Dave had no desire to speak with Louie the Squirrel. He had heard it said that Louie could press a tenpenny nail through a quarter inch of pine with the ball of his thumb. He supposedly toughened his hands by plunging them repeatedly into buckets filled with gravel and iron filings—not because it made his hands even more deadly than they already were but because he enjoyed it. No, all things considered, Dave would just as soon not have his name and address on Louie's Day-Runner list.

But that meant he needed eight Cs—already, he noted gloomily, he was starting to think in gangster parlance—by this time tomorrow. He could count on a little over a hundred for his part in tonight's performance. But where was the rest going to come from?

It was a nasty situation, no doubt about it. Short of knocking over a couple of liquor stores he had no solution in mind. But, try as he might, he couldn't remain too concerned about it tonight. Tonight the Bucktown Jazz Band was the reason music had been invented. He would worry about the money later. If he busked all night and most of tomorrow he could probably pick up another hundred in tips. Maybe he could get the other members of the band to chip in.

Somehow he would get the money. Maybe he was being young and naive, but he found it hard to believe that he could really come to harm over this. If he was a hundred or so shy by tomorrow, surely Errol would listen to reason.

As they finished their next set, he looked down and saw the woman watching him again.

Hot damn, Dave thought.

The band finished playing at just after two A.M. About two-thirds of the crowd had trickled away by then, leaving only the die-hard fans—and K.D. Wilcox.

She had wondered more than once if this really was a good idea. Oh, he was certainly cute, no question of that. And artists of any sort had always interested her, although she had seldom found them to be among the most sane and stable people on the planet. Still, there was something about him that was oddly endearing. She was long past the mothering stage in her relationships with men—at least she devoutly hoped she was—so it had nothing to do with that. K.D. decided it was best not to examine her motives too closely at this stage. Take it as it comes; after all, wasn't that what New Orleans was all about? She felt the need to connect with someone, even if it was just chatting over coffee.

As the rest of the band were packing their instruments and the waiters were putting the chairs up on the tables, he came toward her. That smile looked even better close up, she decided.

"Believe it or not, I've never done this before," he said.

"Help me out a little, would you? I need an opening line that isn't a cliché."

"It's a tough one," K.D. agreed. "After all, you don't want to look like you're just trying to pick me up."

"Exactly. I need something that'll show you I'm not like all the other guys you run into in places like this."

"Something that expresses your inner sensitivity. Your creative soul."

"That too."

They were both grinning at each other now. "How about, 'Come here often?' " K.D. suggested.

"Oh, that's good. Then you could say, 'I like the band.' "

"That works. We can wing it from there."

He stuck out his hand. "My name's Dave Cummings."

K.D. took his hand. "K.D. Wilcox." She enunciated clearly; she hated having her name mistaken for "Katie."

"I like a woman who uses initials. After we've been married twenty years will you tell me what they stand for?"

"By then I'll have forgotten."

They strolled from the club over to the Café du Monde, where, seated at one of the small tables in the all-night sidewalk coffee house, they talked. The waitress brought *café au lait* and paper plates piled high with beignets snowed under by powdered sugar. K.D. bit into one and rolled her eyes in ecstasy. "Oh, man. They should give free glucose tests with these." She sipped the coffee and milk drink. "At least I'll die happy."

"C'mon, a couple of beignets won't kill you."

She shook her head. "I'm talking about the job. The hours we work, the pressure . . . it gets to you. Residents are coolies; cheap labor for the hospital. I've gone as long as five days without sleep, working around the clock. I know people who've passed out on their feet in the middle of an operation with a scalpel in someone's spleen."

"Must be fun during Mardi Gras."

She snorted. "You've no idea. The place is always filled to the rafters with drunks, ODs, gunshot and knife wounds . . . not to mention car wreck traumas, kids with the flu and nut cases who think they've got Yellow Fever or been stung by killer bees or something. You've heard of interns?" He nodded. "We've got a guy we call an 'extern,'" K.D. continued. "All he does, during the festivals, is sit in the waiting room and sew people up. Leonard's a master at it; he can do patterns, embroidery, appliqué...."

"You're kidding."

"Swear to God. He has to do something to keep his interest up."

He looked impressed. "Sounds brutal. But you seem to be doing okay tonight."

She took a swig from her cup. "Coffee—God's gift to the medical profession. A cheap and legal stimulant. Of course, I'm probably doing severe, long-range damage to my nervous system, but why worry today about what you can put off until tomorrow?"

Dave looked a bit glum at this. "Anything wrong?" she asked.

"Hmm? No... I was just thinking about...." He chewed his lower lip for a moment. "My father," he said. "He died in a hospital when I was eleven. Alzheimer's."

"Oh, God," K.D. said, with real sympathy. "That must have been horrible to watch."

"My mom tried to keep me out of it for the most part. I just remember him gradually changing, getting angry at me for no reason, forgetting things and blaming Mom or me for it.... He would make these bizarre accusations, like once he started screaming at me that I'd wrecked the car. I was only nine, I could barely see over the steering wheel. The car was sitting out in the driveway in plain sight. He took off his belt and beat the shit out of me."

K.D. felt chills crawl over her as she listened. Of all the myriad ways there were to die, Alzheimer's was the worst. One could accept the breakdown of the body, but not the disintegration of the self. She had heard it described as a gradual peeling away of layers of personality until nothing was left but a mindless core. In medical school she had seen what had been left in the skull of an old woman who had died of the disease: the atrophied cortex and overall shrunken brain size, the shallowed convolutions, the vermicular runnels in the frontal region, almost as though some bizarre alien insect from a bad horror movie had burrowed through the tissue. K.D. thought of herself lying in some institutional bed, shrunken and flaccid, limbs thrashing in oblivious frenzy, bedsore-ridden, incontinent, intubated. . . .

She reached across the table, put her hand on his. "I'm sorry," she said.

Dave shrugged, visibly shaking off his mood. "Well, it was a long time ago. They said it was the non-genetic kind, so I don't necessarily have to worry about it."

K.D. said, "Nothing like that ever happened to me. Which is kind of odd, because that sort of trauma is what usually drives people into the pill business. I had a pretty normal childhood— as normal as it gets growing up in New Orleans. My only real complaint about my father is that he was too busy with the family business to pay much attention to me." She took a bite of beignet, chewed and swallowed. "He still is," she added. "His only way of showing affection is to throw money at me."

Dave drew patterns in the heaps of powdered sugar with one finger. "Rich family, huh?"

She nodded. "You're wearing one of their products."

He looked down at himself in mild surprise. She reached across and took his shirt collar between thumb and forefinger, tugged on it. "Canterbury Apparel. We supply most of their cotton blends."

Dave regarded the dusting of sugar on the end of his finger. "So how come you're working so hard to be a doctor?"

"What kind of a question is that? How come you're a jazz player? Real estate pays better."

"Touché."

They were quiet for a few moments; then K.D. leaned back in her chair, yawned and looked at her watch. "Jesus, it's nearly four. I should get going; busy day tomorrow."

Dave nodded. "Yeah, me too. Walk you home? You live near here?"

"Lakefront. I'll get a cab."

On the sidewalk an amateur astronomer had parked his telescope and chalked his current target—Saturn—on the sidewalk. A few drunken college students staggered along on the far side of Decatur toward Jackson Square, and foghorns bayed mournfully from far out on the river. The air was damp and smelled riparian.

"What's the hardest thing about playing in a band?" she asked him as they walked down to the taxi stand, where a couple of hopeful cabbies were parked.

"You mean besides making a living at it?" Off her smile, Dave continued: "Harmony. Making sure everyone's playing the same song at the same time. It's a lot more complicated than it looks or sounds, keeping in tune, not blowing breaks or cross-rhythms . . . it has to feel like an organic whole. Everything has to mesh, but not be static."

"Homeostasis," she said.

"Sorry, too many syllables in that one for me."

"Homeostasis. 'The ability or tendency of an organism to maintain internal equilibrium by adjusting its physiological processes,'" K.D. said, her inflection putting quotes around the phrase. "Dynamic balance. A healthy body is a homeostatic body. Disease is just an upsetting of equilibrium."

"And here I was worried we had nothing in common."

They had reached the taxi stand by now. "So," Dave said, "time for the traditional exchange of phone numbers?"

K.D. smiled and dug a pad and pen out of her purse. She scribbled her name and phone number down for him. In response he produced a business card. Under his name, address and number was a stylized silhouette of a cornet and the words "Jazz Man."

"Busy tomorrow?" he asked.

"Very. And the next day, and the next . . . but I could probably grab lunch around Friday."

He seemed subdued, she noticed. She hoped he hadn't been counting on going back to her apartment. It was a possibility she wouldn't rule out for some future date, but now was much too soon. If he thought otherwise she didn't give this potential relationship much of a chance.

But he just said, "Okay, then. I'll call you. This was fun."

"It was." One of the taxi drivers opened a door for her. K.D. kissed Dave lightly on the lips and got in the cab. As it pulled away she looked back at him standing on the curb.

She settled back and thought about it. All in all, a thoroughly pleasant evening, she decided. She had met a guy, spent some time with him, learned a little about him. He hadn't tried to induct her into a sect or rape her and leave her body floating facedown in the river. Not a bad first date for the nineties. . . .

LATIN QUARTER AND
FRENCH QUARTER,
NEW ORLEANS,
LOUISIANA

MARCH 15, 1998

The house was like many other houses on the street, which was in the Latin Quarter, one of the roughest parts of the city. Closer inspection, however, revealed certain differences. The doors and windows were heavily reinforced with steel plating and bars, and an alarm system had been installed. The reason for all of this security was simple: the dilapidated structure housed a thriving illegal business.

Inside, several of the interior walls had been knocked down in order to make more space available. On three long, narrow tables a variety of laboratory impedimenta and chemicals rested. There were beakers, retorts, scales, autoclaves, distillation columns, centrifuges . . . several thousand dollars worth of instruments and equipment. All of it devoted to a single purpose: the creation of Blood.

The *mayombero* watched as three men and two women worked. They titrated chemicals from pipettes into test tubes, heated mixtures carefully over Bunsen burners, measured dosage and toxicity. He stood by a wall cabinet containing items that seemed at odds with the rest of the equipment: apothecary jars containing various powdered herbs and plants, racks from which hung amulets and talismans, an enamel dish holding a thunderstone, and other magical paraphernalia.

As he watched, the *mayombero* reflected that it would soon be time to hire more people and increase the drug's production. It was selling very well on the street, bringing several thousand dollars a week into his pockets. But the money was not important. What was important was to make Blood available to as many people as possible.

He still thought of himself as a *mayombero*, although the truth of the matter was that he had moved far beyond such petty artificial designations. *Mayombero, santero, houngan, curandero, bokor* . . . such distinctions were meaningless to him now. He had studied *Voudoun, Santería, Palo Mayombe, Macumba* and many other disciplines. From each he had gleaned and refined an essence which he had incorporated into his grand scheme. He had moved past the arbitrary differences of these and other practices and penetrated to the underlying unity.

And, in so doing, he had glimpsed potential power beyond the wildest imaginings of those who had once been his colleagues.

The *loas* and the *orishas* were not the sole inhabitants of the spirit realm. This was common knowledge. *Les Invisibles* were composed of many different bodiless beings, most of them maleficent. There were the *baka*, evil anima who could rend one's astral form as easily as panthers and bears could lay waste to one's physical body. The *guédés*, the spirits of the dead, could also be quite dangerous unless approached via the proper ceremonies. It was possible to bend Ti' Malice, the trickster god, to one's will, but he was clever and sinister, with many ways of twisting a spell back onto the spellcaster. All of these, and many other entities, had to be assuaged in various occult fashions.

It had not been easy. The further one penetrated into the Invisible World, the larger grew the necessary sacrifices and the greater the cost, both physically and psychically. But the ultimate goal was worth any sacrifice, any cost. To appease and gain passage from the *ayaguan* had required the blood of seven children, boiled for three days and nights in a cauldron. To propitiate the *djab* he had cut a woman's throat at the moment of orgasm. He had done other, more terrible things, things that even his mind shied away from remembering. But what he stood to gain would be worth all such actions, and more.

To pierce the core of his desire, however, would require a final sacrifice—one far greater than any he had been called upon to make so far.

The *mayombero* stepped forward as one of the chemists held up a flask half-filled with crimson liquid. He moved so as to allow light from a high window to pass through the flask and nodded, approving the color and the quality.

It had taken years to perfect the *coupe poudre*, the magical formula known on the street as Blood. A combination of chemistry and conjuration, it was the sum of many varied parts: the dried skins of South American toads, datura root and yagé vine, physostigmine, tetrodotoxin, succinimides, meperidine, muscarine—the latter a potent hallucinogenic extract from the Amanita mushroom—all bound to a tailored carrier enzyme designed to easily penetrate the blood–brain barrier. It had required all his skill, both as a designer chemist and as a sorcerer, to create it. But the complex interactions of molecules were only part of what made Blood so effective. The house had to be sanctified as a *carrefour*, a crossroads between the worlds, so that the wind from the Invisible World could blow through the mix, adding a strange and indefinable essence. Each batch of Blood had to be brushed over with a branch of the sacred *mapou* tree while an adjuration to Grans Bwa, the *loa* of the forest, was chanted.

And for all the effort it took to produce, Blood was still nothing more than a means to an end. Part of it was a formula that had been known to the priests of Haiti for decades: the substance that drew people into the White Darkness, that turned one into a speechless slave with no consciousness or will. A *zombi cadavre*, what Americans usually pictured when hearing the word "zombie." But he had refined and elaborated on that formula over the years. He had found a way to control the *zombi astral*, the enslaved spirit as well as the flesh, even though separated by miles from his victim. Not all of those who became addicted to Blood heard the call, but enough would. Enough would.

Only one element of his final plan remained unaccounted for. The *mayombero* needed a vessel of power who was both strong and pure; one in whom the strength of the *loa* was mighty, but who had not lost that sense of purity and strength of purpose that attract the spirits. Such a one would be the final item on the cosmic scales that would tip the balance his way. Such vessels were few and far between, but not impossible to find.

The only thing that gave him concern now was his old nemesis. That was too strong a word, actually; at his worst he had been little more to the *mayombero* than an annoyance. The *nganga* had told him of his enemy's return, but it had not warned him of any potential trouble. At his best, LaFitte had never been a serious threat to the *mayombero*'s ambitions.

Still, the *mayombero* reflected, perhaps it would be best to have him removed from the board now. Not through the use of sorcery; his foe's astral senses were no doubt still keen enough to sense the malignancy of a spell cast against him. Sometimes the more primitive ways were the best. No sense in taking any chances, however small. . . .

Patti rung up the sale, put the black pearl necklace in its box and handed it, along with the receipt, to the customer. "Thanks," she said. "Come back soon, okay?"

The customer took the bag from her, and Patti noticed that he was staring closely at her eyes. She felt a surge of paranoia. After he had left she peered quickly into the small vanity mirror on the counter. Her face—spiky black hair, the nose ring she'd gotten last month—stared back at her. There was only a hint of redness to her eyes, no more than might be caused by a few sleepless nights. At least, that was what she hoped people would think.

In particular, she hoped that was what Georges would think, since Georges owned the Half Moon Jewelry Gallery and Patti wanted very much to keep this job. The pay was good, the location—on Royal just east of St. Louis in the French Quarter—was not far from her home in Treme, and all in all, it wasn't a bad place for someone with two years of college and a liberal arts major to be working part time. She didn't even mind working weekends occasionally, like today.

The work was fun as well, and interesting. When she had applied, she had had no idea the jewelry business could be this absorbing. She enjoyed dealing with the customers, helping men pick out engagement rings, discussing diamonds with other women, and talking to the jewelry salesmen—the latter all dressed, without exception, in cheap, scruffy suits and carrying beat-up attaché cases so as not to attract attention. The store sold fine jewelry, precious stones, gold-plated leaves and other items of a similar nature. Georges was a pleasant man to work for, full of old Continental charm gained by a lifetime spent mostly in France. Just the other day a young boy had brought in a geode he had bought at a swap meet for one dollar. Georges had cut it open with the rock saw, and Patti would always remember the thrilled look in the boy's eyes when Georges told him it was full of jewelry-grade amethyst, worth at least three hundred bucks.

All in all, it was a fine job. She sure as hell didn't want to blow it by having her boss find out she was taking Blood.

That was the one big drawback to the drug—the fact that it was immediately obvious to anyone that you'd been doing the stuff. Other drugs had symptoms, too—shrunken or dilated pupils, weight loss, that kind of thing—but they didn't immediately scream "druggie!" to the casual observer the way blood-red eyes did.

But she couldn't stop doing it. The high was so good, so pure, and without a crash at the end. As long as she kept it under control, kept it from showing, she would be okay. It wasn't affecting her physically in any way she could tell.

Unless the nightmares were part of it. . . .

Patti picked up one of the small ivory opium bottles they had recently acquired from an estate sale. She turned it over in her hands, admiring it. The opium it had once contained had, over the course of decades, reacted with the ivory in some weird chemical way and turned it a beautiful, irridescent mother-of-pearl. Not the sort of effect one usually associates with opium, she thought. Just as the dreams weren't something she'd expected to come from Blood. . . .

She'd been having them on and off for the past couple of weeks. They differed in the details, but the setting was always the same: a gray, misty, *Twilight Zone* kind of place, full of billowing clouds. At times the clouds would part and she could see, in the far distance, what seemed like a tower rising hundreds of feet high, its surface carved with strange hieroglyphics. It always seemed to Patti that she could understand their meaning, even though they were in no language she knew, if she could just get close enough. . . .

At other times she was running through the mist, and something was pursuing her. She had no idea what it was, but it was always accompanied by the insistent beat of drums, a savage, primitive rhythm. Always she woke up just as the beat reached a crescendo, woke up bathed in sweat, sometimes choking back a cry of fear.

She had no idea what the dreams meant, but she wasn't one who believed in dreams as omens. Maybe Blood was causing them—or maybe pizza. One thing she knew: They'd have to come a lot more often and be a lot scarier to convince her to swear off Blood.

Speaking of which, maybe she'd have a small snort now, just to ease her out a little. Georges was having lunch down the street at the Court of Two Sisters; she was alone in the store and there were no customers right now. What better time to slip into the back room and slip the baggie out of her purse?

After all, it wasn't like she was addicted or anything. She had it under control. She glanced at the mirror again, just to make sure her eyes hadn't gotten any redder in the past few minutes. No, it was cool. They were just a little bloodshot. Georges would never know.

xviii

The *boumfort* was in the back room of a rundown curio shop just off the main drag in downtown Chalmette. It was late—past nine—and Soukie was half-asleep, so April carried her through the beaded curtain into the dark temple.

Inside the air was close and redolent of both animal and human, almost overpowering the smell of incense. As her eyes grew accustomed to the darkness April could make out a group of men and women, mostly black, some wearing dashikis and robes, others more prosaically dressed in shirts and jeans. The taller among them had to duck and weave as they moved about to avoid hitting their heads on calabashes and bottles hanging from ceiling rafters. There were several children there as well, ranging from late childhood to early teens. Soukie was the youngest.

In one corner of the temple was the altar, a folding card table draped with black and red fabric. Its top was covered with plastic statues of various saints, a glass bowl of cornmeal, votive candles and bottles of soft drinks and liquor, some of the latter decorated with skull and crossbone outlines made from twisted white pipe cleaner stems. Surrounding the table and running up and down the legs was a strand of multicolored Christmas tree lights that blinked on and off; these provided the room's only fitful illumination.

In the center of the room was the *poteau-mitan*, a thick wooden pillar that stretched from floor to ceiling. This, April knew, represented the bridge connecting reality to the Invisible World. Lining the far wall were the drums, each a different shape and size, that summoned the *loas*. The room's walls and ceiling had been painted black. On the walls various cabalistic symbols were drawn in phosphorescent paint, and the ceiling had been dotted randomly to represent the starry heavens.

Mama Delight, the *mambo*, waddled up to welcome April and Soukie. Mama Delight easily weighed over three hundred pounds; her bulk strained the red and black robes she wore. A crimson bandanna was wrapped around her hair. "April! Child, we was worried you wasn't gonna make it tonight."

"We haven't missed a ceremony in eight months," April responded, setting down her daughter, who was fully awake now. "Even if I couldn't come I'd make sure Soukie got here somehow."

Mama Delight smiled, revealing a gold upper tooth that gleamed in the flickering light. She raised her *asson*—a gourd rattle wrapped in beaded leather—and shook it. The clattering sound of the pebbles within silenced the various conversations taking place around them. All eyes turned toward the *mambo*.

"Tonight," she said, her tone solemn and sonorous in the small chamber, "we are here to witness an investiture." She pointed at one of the older children—a boy of perhaps eleven who stood near his father, trying not to appear nervous. Unlike the other participants, he was dressed all in white: a T-shirt and loose baggy pants.

"Tonight, if the spirits think him worthy, Louis Métraux will become one with his *loa-tête*, his guardian and protector from the world of *Les Invisibles*," Mama Delight continued. "From that moment on, his life will no longer be what it was. He will have a connection to a larger world, and through that connection his soul will find a place in the afterlife."

A murmur of excitement and approval ran through the group. April watched Louis Métraux lick dry lips. It was a terrifying procedure, she knew. She had watched Soukie go through it, her maternal heart wrenched with fear and compassion. April had undergone the ceremony several times herself, but so far no *loa* had deemed her worthy of claiming. The knowledge burned shamefully within her.

As Mama Delight spoke, three young female *hounsis* filed into the room, each dressed in a simple white cotton shift and wearing red bandannas binding their hair. One began to light the votive candles, providing more light. The second one picked up the glass bowl full of cornmeal from the altar and moved to the center of the temple.

Several men positioned themselves behind the drums and started beating a slow, hypnotic tempo. The third woman began to dance, moving in a sinuous and rhythmic fashion around the room. The congregation, April and Soukie included, stamped their feet and chanted in time to the beat while the second priestess began dribbling white cornmeal from her clenched fist in patterns onto the floor beneath the *poteau-mitan*. She was drawing the *vévés*, April knew; the symmetrical emblems that reflected both the visible and invisible worlds, the signs of the various *loas*.

The drum beat grew louder, more compelling. Mama Delight began shaking the gourd rattle in time with it, adding her voice to the chant.

April could feel the forces gathering, unseen but nonetheless palpable—the *gros bon ange*, the cosmic energy that manifested itself in all living things. Looking down at Soukie, she knew the child could feel it as well; she was vibrating, and even in the dim light April could see the gooseflesh prickling her daughter's skin.

Still shaking the *asson*, Mama Delight stepped between the *poteau-mitan* and the altar. She turned toward each of the four directions, gesturing with the rattle at each compass point, as well as upward toward the heavens and downward toward the earth, marking this *bonamfort* as the center of the universe for the duration of the ritual. Lifting bottles of sanctified water and rum, she poured a few drops onto each *vévé* to greet the *loas* represented. She started with the sign for Erzulie, her *loa-tête*—the spirit of love.

One of the acolytes handed her a chicken; Mama Delight transferred the gourd rattle to her mouth, shaking her head so as not to break the rhythm, and quickly broke the fowl's wings and legs. Soukie buried her face in April's skirt during this part, and April did not stop her, even though such an action might be construed as an insult to the spirits.

The *mambo* pried the bird's beak open and expertly pinched its tongue out. This she stuck onto a carved thorn on the pillar at the temple's center. Then she seized the chicken by its neck and snapped the spine with a single flick of one strong wrist. The *manger-loa*, the feeding of the spirits, was completed. The drums continued to roar. Louis Métraux suddenly stiffened and cried out as though struck by the fangs of a cotton-mouth. His eyes rolled back in their sockets until only the whites were visible. His jaws champed spasmodically and he fell to the floor, the others moving back to make room.

No matter how many times April saw it happen, the sight of possession never failed to both thrill and terrify her. The boy was now a *cheval*, a mount to be ridden by the *loa* that had possessed him. She had seen people under the influence of the deities do impossible things. She had witnessed men walking unharmed through roaring flames, a woman chewing up and swallowing a glass goblet with no apparent harm, a child speaking in languages he could not possibly have known.

Louis writhed on the floor as if in the grip of an epileptic fit. His father, fear and uncertainty in his expression, took a step forward, but one of the *hounsis* put a hand against his chest. Louis's head snapped backward violently as though seized and pulled by invisible hands. Then his body rose to its feet, the action looking more like a huge ungainly marionette being jerked erect than a human being standing by his own volition.

The entire congregation was moaning in ecstasy now, the drums pounding out a vehement beat, the sound filling April's head, driving out all thoughts, leaving nothing but the driving relentless rhythm. Louis's body jerked spasmodically for a moment, then settled into a motionless pose. There was something disquietingly *wrong* about his stance and posture; it was nothing April could identify, but she could tell that whatever stood before them, though clothed in a human body, was not itself human. This was even more evident—terrifyingly evident—when Louis's head turned to regard them all and his mouth opened to speak. The voice that issued from him was Louis's voice, and yet it was not. Like his body, there was something—a tone, a hollowness, *something*—that said much more clearly than his words that an ancient and terrible nonhuman entity was speaking through him.

"There is a child," the voice said. April felt her blood chill as everyone turned to look at Soukie, who was the youngest one there. The drums stopped; the air crackled with tension. "A *serviteur* known to us." The voice laughed, a great lusty sound of mirth that echoed from the walls and ceiling.

"Which one of the *Mystères* speaks?" Mama Delight asked, her tone polite but firm.

There was no answer for a moment. Then Louis's hands seized the front of his shirt and ripped it open, baring his chest. All could see clearly the dark flesh rising, forming itself into lines, an image. An image of a coiled serpent.

The name passed among the worshippers in an awed whisper. "Damballah Wedo . . ."

April licked dry lips and pulled Soukie closer to her.

The eerie voice spoke again. "There is imbalance between the worlds. Strong *wanga* has been made. The child must set things right."

"She will be," Mama Delight vowed. "That we promise you."

The stigma faded after a moment. Damballah continued: "A child in knowledge, but her power is great. She must be protected."

April heard Soukie whimper and thought for a moment the girl was reacting to the voice of the *loa*, then realized she was holding Soukie's fingers in a desperately tight grip.

"Protect the child. Help the child. Or else. . . ." Damballah's voice boomed with laughter again, but there was a decidedly grim note to it this time. "Else the White Darkness take you all in a storm of blood." The last word seemed to throb in the air as Louis suddenly fell, his invisible strings severed, into a trembling heap on the floor.

Louis's father rushed forward and kneeled beside the boy. Mama Delight began to perform the rituals of closure that would bring the ceremony to an end. Her words, and the clamor of the crowd, seemed distant and unreal to April; the only sounds she could distinctly hear were Soukie's rapid, frightened breaths. She looked down at her daughter, saw that Soukie was staring across the room. April followed the child's gaze with her own and saw one of the drummers looking intently at Soukie.

April turned toward the temple's exit, not waiting for the ceremony to close, pulling Soukie with her as she ran as if from a burning building.

H arris Beaumont had followed April and her whelp into Chalmette and now sat in his parked pickup, drinking beer and waiting. He wasn't sure what they were doing in there, but they took the Lord's own sweet time going about it; it was nearly two hours later when April hurried out, a frightened look on her face, carrying her daughter in her arms as she crossed the street to her car. Harris was parked halfway down the block and was fairly sure she couldn't see him, but he scrunched down in the seat just in case. He watched as she started the car—it was an old Chevrolet that sputtered and belched black smoke—and drove off. He gave her a lead of several hundred feet before he followed.

It was late afternoon and the air was humid and heavy; hot

weather even for Louisiana this time of year. The route led them down St. Bernard Highway for a way before turning off onto a rural road that wound toward the levees and bayous. There were places where he could have pulled her over without any interference, but he decided to wait. That brat Soukie was in the car with her, and she might be a problem.

Still, Harris knew he couldn't wait much longer. Every time he saw her these days he felt the rage growing inside him. If she didn't look at him it made him angry, and when she did look at him the disgust in her eyes made him angrier still. The bitch . . . .

One of these Friday nights, he thought. Most of the park's tenants would be down the road at Rocky's Tavern or some other joint, drinking away whatever was left of the week's paycheck. Harris had no doubt that, once he gave her the high hard one, she'd be a lot more pleasant when he looked her way. But the timing had to be right. That fucking kid was a problem. This would take some thought.

He pulled a pinch of the red powder from the baggie he kept hidden under the seat, and inhaled it, feeling the rush hit him almost immediately. Great stuff, this Blood. He didn't normally go in for anything other than alcohol, but this was different, somehow. If only it didn't turn your eyes the color of a fire hydrant. . . .

His thoughts drifted back to April. Soon, now, he promised her, hands gripping the wheel tightly. Very soon. You and me, sweetheart. We are going to dance.

Dave Cummings sat on the threadbare couch across the office from Errol Mandeville's desk. Errol's office was on the third floor of a building off Canal Street. Dave thought the word "shabby" summed it up nicely. The wallpaper was faded and peeling, and there was a brown stain in one corner of the ceiling. Errol sat in a creaky office chair behind the desk, which was bare save for a phone, an ancient green blotter and a copy of yesterday's *Times-Picayune*.

Besides Dave and Errol there was one other occupant in the small room: a man of about medium height, compactly built, wearing slacks and a sports coat over a T-shirt, who sat in a corner chair reading a Captain Cobalt comic book. Dave had initially been somewhat worried that this third party was the infamous Louie the Squirrel, but Errol had introduced him as "Alfred." Alfred had glanced at Dave when he came in and then gone back to the comic book, which, judging by the speed with which he turned the pages, he was either enjoying thoroughly or having a hard time getting through.

Dave had initially been a little nervous about the meeting. He had scraped up every cent he had, and he was still a hundred and twenty bucks short. At first he'd been afraid that Errol would be pissed, but as he explained the situation and Errol had merely listened and occasionally said "Uh-huh" in an encouraging way, he had begun to relax slightly.

"I'll have the rest of it by the weekend," he finished. "No question. Thanks for being so understanding."

Errol was quiet for a moment after Dave finished. He picked up a letter opener on the desk and toyed with it. Then he asked, "What exactly did you want the dough for again?"

"A record album. Louis Armstrong's *African Stomp*."

"A record album," Errol repeated blankly.

"Yeah. An old seventy-eight put out by Okeh Records."

"A record album," Errol said again. "You mean vinyl. Not a CD."

"That's right. It's from the 1920s. Very rare."

Understanding began to wash across Errol's face. "Uh-huh. Like that whiskey."

"Whiskey." Now it was Dave's turn to repeat something blankly.

"Yeah, I read about it. Some bottle of whiskey supposed to be the only one of its kind left. Went at an auction for a couple thousand bucks."

Ah. "Something like that," David said, nodding.

"Uh-huh," Errol said again. He put the letter opener down and leaned back in the chair. "How old are you, Dave?"

Feeling that they were having some trouble staying on topic, Dave mentally shrugged and said, "Twenty-eight."

Errol shook his head and chuckled. "Jesus. Barely old enough to shave. That's your problem, right there."

"Shaving?" Dave was feeling more than a little lost now.

"Youth." Errol stood and walked around the desk, sat on the edge of it. Alfred continued to read the comic book. "See," Errol continued, "when you're that young you don't really believe anything can happen to you. You're like, bullets bounce off, you know? Gonna live forever." He grinned and shook his head ruefully again. "God, I remember. You know I'm ten years older than you, but you can learn a lot in ten years."

"I guess so," Dave said. A tiny tendril of nervousness began to work its way up his belly.

"Yeah. What happens is, someone tells you you don't do something, like pay off a loan in time, you could get in trouble, you hear them, but you don't really believe them." Errol stood up, as did Alfred, the latter putting aside the comic book. Seeing this, Dave stood up too, rather quickly.

Errol put a hand out before him, patting the air in a gesture that said "relax." "Oh, you think you believe them. But you don't. 'Cause you're gonna live forever."

Dave said "Uh . . ." as Alfred quickly crossed the room to stand behind him. He pinned Dave's arms behind his back in a single fluid movement.

Errol stood in front of him. "I know how it is. But this is a business, Dave. You understand. You go to a bank, get a loan, don't pay it back, the bank gets all over your ass. Same thing."

"Look," Dave said, feeling sweat beginning to erode the creases in his back where Alfred had his arms pinned. "Errol, I get the idea—"

"No, you don't," Errol said. "See, this is still just a movie to you. It's not real life. You got to learn the difference."

On the last word he dropped his right shoulder and shot a short, powerful jab straight into Dave's solar plexus.

It felt to Dave like his guts had been pushed up into his sinuses. Like his lungs had collapsed. He sagged in Alfred's arms, fighting for a breath, but nothing from his collar bone to his waist was working. Black spots danced before him. He gasped like a fish on a dock, feeling the pain radiating out from his center, hitting the soles of his feet and the tips of his fingers and then rebounding, doubling back on itself, multiplying in intensity. And still he couldn't breathe. He would never breathe again. He would give every jazz and blues side in his collection for one good, deep, pain-free breath. . . .

Alfred released him and Dave dropped to his knees—or someone's knees; they didn't really feel like they belonged to him anymore. As if from a great distance he heard Errol saying, "See, pain is a real good teacher. It puts you next to reality. Reminds you that you're mortal."

As Errol spoke, he walked slowly around Dave and stopped behind him. And then a fresh bolt of pain exploded through Dave from behind as Errol punched him over the right kidney. This was even worse than the jab to the gut—white-hot agony raced through every nerve ending, colliding and reverberating with the ache in his stomach. Dave tried to scream, but all he could manage was a high-pitched wheeze, like a tire losing air. A second later the agony was doubled when Errol rammed his knuckles into his left kidney.

Dave felt tears scald down his cheeks. He sagged like wet laundry onto the carpet. The only reason he didn't puke, he was sure, was because his gut was still paralyzed. It was astonishing, incredible, that so much torture could be packed into one human body. Nothing had ever hurt this bad, not even when he'd been seven years old and had jumped off a wall into a pile of lumber and driven a rusty nail completely through his foot.

He felt Alfred grab him by the arms and pull him into a semi-erect position again. Dimly he registered Errol standing in front of him. The man looked a little sad.

"Another thing about hurt—it clears the head. Opens up the thinking passageways. And that's good. Isn't it? You bet." Errol put one hand on Dave's shoulder and looked closely at him. "I just want to make sure you understand," he said, and kneed Dave in the balls.

Dave realized later that he must have momentarily passed out, because he did not recall hitting the floor. He had not thought it possible that more pain could be piled on top of what he already felt. He had been wrong. In spades.

This last attack finally caused his stomach to launch its contents. Dave lay on the floor in a sodden heap, face pressed into carpeting soaked with remnants of the shrimp po-boy he'd had for lunch, every cell in his body vibrating with pain, the sharp edge of his broken glasses frame gouging into one cheek. For a few moments he wasn't even sure where he was or what his name was. The only reality was red, pulsing pain.

Alfred pulled him back to his feet. Dave made a feeble attempt to curl himself up to try to ward off another blow, but Alfred merely pushed him back into a sitting position on the couch. Dave blinked. He could barely make out Errol leaning against his desk; his glasses were still on the floor, and without them he was as nearsighted as a baby duck.

Errol pulled a tiny packet from one of his pockets and tossed it in Dave's lap. Dave fumbled with it, recognizing it as a disposable napkin soaked in liquid soap, the kind fast food restaurants sometimes give out. He tried to pull open the foil, but his hands were shaking too badly. Errol stepped forward and tore it open, then shook out the folded square of damp paper and wiped his face for him. It tasted of astringent.

"You understand how serious this is now?" he asked gently.

Dave nodded, not trusting himself to speak, not even sure if he could speak. At least he could breathe again, though every breath seared like molten iron being poured into his chest. Hard to say what hurt worst: his stomach, his kidneys or his balls. He decided that each hurt equally bad, but there were subtle differences in the various agonies. He had perforce in the last few minutes become a connoisseur of pain.

"I didn't hit you hard," Errol continued. "Well, the gut shot was kind of strong, but believe me, the others were just love taps. Just enough to wake you up. See, you have to understand the situation. Partial payments don't cut it. This is an all or nothing kind of deal. I told you that going in, Dave. I got people I answer to, you know.

"Now you got until this time tomorrow to pay off the whole enchilada, or something *really* unpleasant is gonna happen. I tell ya, I've seen Louie pop a guy's kneecap right off. The man can be a surgeon when he wants to."

Errol pulled Dave gently to his feet. "Now go on. Go home, clean yourself up, and make me proud, okay? Don't put yourself through this shit again. No money's worth this kind of hurt. You'll be all right. I didn't mark your face. But you remember this, hear me? This is the real world, and people get hurt in the real world. I don't want to see that happen to you again. This was just for instruction. Next time, you won't be walking away from it."

Dave nodded, not trusting his ability to speak. Alfred had gone back to his chair and was perusing the letters column of the comic book. Errol stuffed Dave's broken glasses into his shirt pocket, then walked him out into the hall and pushed the elevator button for him. When the doors opened he helped Dave inside and pushed the ground floor button. Then he pointed an admonishing finger at Dave as the doors closed.

Dave staggered out of the building into the afternoon warmth. The various tortures his body had endured had faded just enough for him to manage a weaving walk. He smelled like some three-week drunk in a doorway. It would be a long, painful stagger back to his apartment.

"Oh Jesus," he mumbled as he stumbled along the sidewalk, oblivious to the tourists and others who gave him a wide berth. Errol had been right: He had had no idea what the consequences would be, even though Errol had told him not to be late with the money. It was now abundantly, agonizingly clear to him that he was hip deep in some real serious shit.

He needed a total of nine hundred bucks by tomorrow. Or he could kiss his kneecaps good-bye.

As K.D. made her rounds she found herself thinking quite a bit about Dave Cummings.

There was an attraction there, no doubt about that. The musician was fun to be around, witty, easygoing and quite talented. Cute, too. There were definite possibilities here, K.D. told herself. She hoped he would call in the next day or two. If he didn't, she would call him.

Don't get your hopes up, she warned herself. She had run into guys before who seemed together and enjoyable company, only to have them turn into Prozac puppies further down the line. Proceed with caution. Men were strange creatures: all of them desperately seeking relationships, then running screaming for the hills when one appeared on the horizon.

Still, at this point the prognosis seemed positive.

It was a relatively slow night at Sisters of Grace. They'd had an influx of what Jerry described as "DSBs and terraspheres" earlier; DSB stood for "drug-seeking behavior" and terrasphere was a more circumspect way of referring to a patient as a dirtball in his presence. K.D.'s favorite descriptive term for some of the more advanced wierdos who stumbled through the doors was "psycho-chondriacs." None of them were in evidence now, though. At this moment the ward was actually almost quiet, save for the beeps of monitors and the labored breathing of a sucking chest wound in bay three. Of course, that meant little; in the next five minutes the place could be filled with dozens of people, all requiring immediate attention. But at the moment things were still, and K.D. could feel herself starting to slow down. Time for another cup of coffee, she thought. There's too much blood in my caffeine system. . . .

She had just poured herself a cup and was stirring a spoonful of sugar into it—a double whammy for the old nervous system—when she saw a gurney come in, two grim-faced medics wheeling it. She moved quickly to meet them. "What's the story?" she asked as she paced the moving patient.

"Young black male, early twenties, extreme sinus bradycardia," one of them said. "Witnesses said he had some kind of seizure on the street."

"BP sixty over forty, respiration two per minute, pulse about twelve," the other one said.

K.D. blinked in astonishment. No one could have readings like that and still be alive; if he wasn't already dead he would be shortly. She fitted the earpieces of her stethoscope and put the receiver against the young man's chest. At first she thought there was no heartbeat, but then she heard the familiar "lub-dub." The beats were placed impossibly far apart, however. "Christ, he's beating at ten a minute." She turned to Jerry, motioned him to her. "Check his blood gases, do a drug screen. And let's get an ECG, see what's going on. Call Pearson, get him down here to run a neuro."

As they wheeled the patient toward an empty treatment bay, K.D. started running possible causes through her head. Given his age and race, the first thing that came to mind was drug overdose. She'd never heard of any depressant that could put a human body into a holding pattern like this, however. She tried to think of other possible causes: some kind of brain trauma or atypical stroke, perhaps, or a tumor involving the hypothalamus. Or it could be the final stages of a disease process: polio or cardiomyopathy, maybe even tertiary syphilis.

One of the nurses put an Ambu bag over the patient's nose and mouth and squeezed while K.D. peeled back the right eyelid, the gloves she wore making the task somewhat difficult. She saw that the sclera had turned completely blood red.

This, at least, she recognized; one of the signs of heavy Blood usage. But to the best of her knowledge Blood was a fairly benign drug; it had to be taken in great quantities, quantities far exceeding the amount needed to get high on, to reach toxicity. They had had people on Blood in here before and none of them had reacted like this; mostly they were there to be treated for panic symptoms secondary to the effects. Maybe this was some kind of synergistic interaction between Blood and another drug?

She cut open his shirt with a pair of bandage scissors. For some reason, as she taped the electrode to his bare chest, K.D. found herself thinking of the coma case that had come in the morning after Fat Tuesday. There were few or no similarities between the two; still, she was reminded of it. Perhaps because this case was as baffling in its own way as the other one had been.

"ECG's normal," Jerry said, looking at the ECG screen. K.D. looked at it also. Curiouser and curiouser: no blocks, APCs or PVCs, no flutter or fib. "What the hell is wrong with this guy?" she muttered.

One of the nurses intubated him while another got ready to administer Lorfan in case it was a narcotic overdose. Treat the symptoms, K.D. told herself, worry about the cause later. If there was a later. . . .

At that point the emergency monitor started to blare. A red light on the unit flashed urgently.

Uh-oh . . . K.D. stared at the bank of telemetry gear and the green lines jittering across the ECG screen. She peeled back an eyelid again, saw the dilated pupil.

"Ventricular fib," Jerry said. "We're losing 'im."

"No shit," K.D. muttered. She grabbed a pair of defib pad- dles from the crash cart. Jerry sprayed conducting fluid on them and K.D. quickly rubbed them together. "Two hundred watt seconds," she ordered. The wait while the unit charged stretched like taffy. At last the beeping ceased and a steady tone sounded. "*Clear!*" she shouted, ramming the paddles against the man's chest. The juice hit him and he bucked, arcing off the sheet. The line across the screen exploded in a crackle of peaks and valleys, then smoothed into a straight horizontal stripe.

"He's gone flat!" Jerry yelled.

"Three hundred!" She waited for it, waited for it. . . . "*Clear!*"

Again, no response. "Four hundred!"

The body thrashed for the third time as the current coursed through it, then settled once more, limp and unresponsive. A nurse leaned in and gave an injection of sodium bicarbonate. There was no reaction. K.D. could feel the adrenaline rush within her give way to resignation. The monitor line was flatter than Kansas. She set the paddles aside, wiped her brow. The patient had had no reason to be alive when he had entered the ER; she was surprised he had lasted as long as he had. "Call it," she said, turning away.

Jerry looked at the clock and noted the time. Another life lost, K.D. thought; the worst thing about it was how little she felt these days at each one's passing.

One of the nurses pulled a sheet over the corpse's head as K.D. and Jerry turned toward the door. "Be interesting to see what they find in the autopsy," Jerry said.

They had just reached the door when they heard a crash behind them, and then the scream of the nurse.

K.D. and Jerry spun about. The IV stand was lying on the floor, the plastic sac ruptured and spilling clear saline solution over the tiles.

The man they had just pronounced dead was sitting up.

At first K.D. felt relief. Though rare, such a return to life was by no means unheard of. Every doctor has a story about someone fighting their way back from the grave after modern medicine had given up hope of revival. But then her gaze drifted to the monitor, and what she saw there sent a wave of cold washing over her like an alcohol sponge bath.

He was still on the monitor. And the reading was still flatline.

No spikes in the luminous cardiographic line. According to the readout, the man now pulling the endotracheal tube from his throat and swinging his legs over the edge of the bed was still as dead as JFK.

He stood, the electrode tearing free of his chest. His face

was slack, expressionless, almost as if the fasciae behind the skin had dissolved. The crimson eyes seemed to burn with an unholy inner light.

"Bec mon chu," Jerry whispered . . . he had told her once it was Cajun for "kiss my ass." It wasn't said as a challenge; it sounded more like a prayer.

The corpse started toward them.

It moved swiftly, its movements fluid and purposeful. The thought flashed through K.D.'s mind that it should shamble, stiff-legged and awkward; wasn't that how zombies always walked in the movies? This one, however, obviously had somewhere to go in a hurry.

K.D. was paralyzed. She knew she should do or say something, but a hysterical voice deep within her was crying that it wouldn't do any good, because he was *dead*, dead but somehow moving, dead but somehow still alive, and all bets were off now, she was much too far down this rabbit hole ever to claw her way back to the sunlit rational world. . . .

Jerry stepped forward, put a hand out. "Say, Cap, take it easy—" he started nervously. Jerry was a large man, two-ten or thereabouts, his arms and chest heavy with musculature, whereas the dead man was thin and lanky. Nevertheless, he grabbed Jerry and easily hurled him across the length of the bay. Jerry slammed into the crash cart and fell at the feet of the other nurse, who was now flat-out hysterical, her screams echoing and re-echoing the length of the ER.

The action broke K.D.'s immobility. She stepped back out of the dead man's path and shouted *"Security!"*

The guard was already headed for them, alerted by the screams and turmoil. He raised his nightstick, but the dead man grabbed it, twisted it easily from his grasp and rammed the end of it into the guard's gut. The guard collapsed, breath wheezing from him. The dead man stepped over him and continued down the corridor.

K.D. and a crowd of nurses, surgeons, radiologists and patients watched as he marched toward the automatic doors and out into the night. No one tried to stop him.

NEW ORLEANS,
LOUISIANA

MARCH 20, 1998

ia St. Charles sat across her desk from Shane LaFitte and
looked at his papers. So far, so good; he had gotten himself a job—kitchen help at the Bienville, a Fauborg Marigny
restaurant—and a place to live. His drug screen had been negative and he was looking clean and groomed. He had also given
her a key to his new apartment. Maybe the little tirade she had
subjected him to on their first meeting was all that had been
needed.

Then again, according to the information she had received
that morning, maybe not.

"You're doing good, LaFitte," she said, slipping the report
back into the case folder. "Keep this up and you and I will get
along just fine."

She leaned back in her chair and looked at him. He was dressed in jeans and a chambray shirt, the clothes worn but clean. She found herself noticing how the fabric of the shirt stretched taut across the muscles of his chest, and twitched her mouth slightly in annoyance. She did not want to be attracted to this man.

He was sitting with fingers laced in front of him, looking introspective. Again, Lia could not help but be struck by how quiet he seemed, so at odds with the usual behavior of her clients. It would be very easy to have fantasies about him. . . .

Stop it, she told herself.

"One question," she said.

LaFitte raised his head and looked her in the eyes—again, unusual behavior in a parolee. "Yes?"

"Did you know Enriqué Hermosa, a busboy at the Bienville Restaurant?"

She watched his face; there was no shifting of his gaze as he said, "Yes. He was supposed to have been on shift last night."

"According to the officers who took the call, he scared the bejeezus out of the ER staff at Sisters of Grace Hospital a couple of nights ago. Seems he died of a drug overdose, then got up, tossed a few employees around and walked out."

"Interesting," LaFitte said mildly.

"'Interesting.' You knew nothing about this, of course."

"Are you saying I had something to do with his death?"

"You're a parolee from a manslaughter charge, LaFitte. Like it or not, that makes you look suspicious."

Another moment of silence while they gazed at each other. Lia could feel him measuring her will. She realized that she wanted him to not have any connection with the busboy's death. Of course, she didn't want any of her cases to be sent back to stir, but it seemed somehow especially important that this man remain free.

Nonsense, she thought. He's no different from any other case.

"I had nothing to do with Hermosa's death, or his addiction to Blood," LaFitte said.

"How did you know he was on Blood? I didn't tell you that."

"You didn't have to. I worked with him. I recognized the symptoms."

Lia stared at him. If they were lying, sooner or later they usually looked away. He returned her gaze, impassive.

"You can talk to me, or talk to a judge," she told him. "Your choice."

"You aren't going to revoke my parole over this," he said. "Some would, perhaps, but not you. I understand your frustration, and I sympathize. I wish I could tell you more. But you would not believe me, and it might put you in danger to know certain things."

"I can't believe I'm hearing this. You look and sound like an intelligent man, LaFitte—you should be able to realize that this kind of talk from a parolee is not a real good career move."

He nodded. He seemed genuinely sorry; the first emotion she'd sensed from him. "Believe me, I wish it could be otherwise. Let me reassure you again that I have been guilty of no wrongdoings."

"Let's pretend for a minute that I believe that," Lia replied. "What guarantee do I have, given your attitude, that you plan on keeping your nose clean?"

"You'll have to take my word for it."

"No offense, but I read what you did to your wife. I have a hard time believing anyone who's capable of that kind of savagery."

"I didn't kill my wife," LaFitte said softly.

That one didn't particularly surprise her; after all, what criminal is ever guilty in his own mind? Again the silence stretched between them. Lia knew that she should at the very least have him questioned by the cops regarding the Hermosa case. But something prevented her from picking up the phone. It wasn't some kind of supernatural power on his part—at least, she didn't think it was—it was just that, deep down inside her, it seemed very important that she should believe him, or at least give him the benefit of the doubt.

This is crazy, Lia thought. It went against everything she'd been taught in this job. Pick up the phone and get a uniform in here. See if he's this self-assured facing a room full of detectives.

She knew that's what she should do. Instead she glanced at the clock and said, "We're done for today."

She had four more cases to review after LaFitte left, and by then it was after six. She was tired; the smart thing to do, she knew, was to go home and relax. But instead Lia sat behind her desk, looking over LaFitte's files again—and wondering.

According to the information they had on him, he had been born in Haiti but educated in Great Britain on a scholarship. After graduating he had traveled around the Caribbean for a few months before returning to Haiti—this was in 1982, she noted—and information on him during the period before he surfaced in New Orleans was sketchy, although he had evidently been heavily involved in voodoo.

Many sociopaths were well educated, of course. There was nothing so atypical about LaFitte that it cried out to be noticed. Still, something deep in her gut told Lia that there was more going on here. Why did it seem so important for her to believe him?

She puzzled over it. Was this simply pheromones coming into play? Was she doing the female equivalent of a man thinking with his dick? Or did she sense something in the man that the jury had overlooked?

There was no denying he was attractive. She didn't usually go for the tall, broad-shouldered type, but there was a power in him that lured her. A quiet strength that lay not in the muscles so much as in the will.

Lia knew she couldn't afford to trust such feelings. While instinct was certainly something that let her do her job well, she always looked for concrete facts to back up her feelings before acting on them. In this case, she had none.

Just the feeling that he was telling the truth.

There was no way she could go to the District Attorney's office and ask that a case this old be reopened because her gut told her to. Though this was New Orleans, a world unto itself, it was still part of the Deep South, and women who held jobs like hers were still viewed, by and large, with all the distrust and distaste that only insecure macho men can muster. Unless she had proof she would be laughed out of the building, and maybe out of a job.

Lia sighed and ran her fingers through red ringlets. Eventually, she knew, she would have to pay a surprise visit to LaFitte, just as she had had to do with Slow Joey and many others. Sometimes, as with Joey, she would catch them in violation, and she would have to bust them. It was regrettable, but part of the job.

She knew she would find it a painful thing to bust Shane LaFitte.

More than that, some part of her whispered. A disaster.

Lia stood and put on her jacket. This was ridiculous. There was no way she was going to let herself fall for one of her cases. She had seen it happen once or twice to others in her line of work, and it had always ended in trouble. It was time to put this case and all the others out of her head, time to go home, feed Toulouse and curl up with a good book or, more likely, a video rental. She was long overdue for some quality time with herself.

Lia looked at the clock: six forty-seven. She looked down at the papers on her desk. Then, with a sigh of exasperation, she pulled out LaFitte's folder and scribbled his address on a notepad. She stuffed the piece of paper in her pocket and headed for the door. She was halfway out of her office when another thought struck her; she hesitated, then went back to her desk and unlocked the bottom right-hand drawer. From it she pulled a snub-nosed Colt .38. She was licensed to carry it, and occasionally did so when she had a bad feeling about going out in the field. She had that feeling now.

As she left the building, the .38 in her purse, Lia told herself that this was all in the line of duty; that LaFitte had been acting suspiciously and that she was perfectly justified to check him out. She kept telling herself that as she pulled out of the parking lot. With any luck, she might even come to believe it.

Carlos had been an assassin for over seven years. He had lost count of the number of people he had killed, but he knew it had to be well over a hundred. It was a lucrative occupation; his usual asking price for taking someone out was twenty grand. There were plenty around who would do it for cheaper, but in this line of work, as in all others, quality cost.

His real name was not Carlos; he'd chosen it after reading *The Day of the Jackal.* He'd also started insisting that people refer to him as an "assassin" and not as a "hitman"—the latter was much less respectable, he felt. A professional should take pride in his work. After all, on a good year he made as much money as a mid- to high-level advertising executive. He wore Armani and drove a Saab. He had tried to cultivate a taste for wine and good food, although he still had to admit deep down inside that few four-star restaurants could match a Wendy's double cheeseburger. Even so, he had distinction. The no-neck assholes he'd grown up with back in Brooklyn might have gone on to become hitmen, numbers runners, dealers and other garden-variety criminals. He had moved down to New Orleans and become an assassin. Definitely a cut above.

He was good at his job, too. So good, in fact, that he had found it was starting to bore him. There are only so many ways to shoot, stab, garrote or poison someone, and he had gotten adept at most of them. That was why Carlos had started to experiment with new and fresh methods. One had to keep creatively challenging oneself, after all. Boredom led to sloppiness, and sloppiness led, at least in his line of work, to a suite in the big stone Ramada Inn upstate. Or to the morgue. Neither was a destination Carlos had any desire or intention to visit, which was why he tried to think of different ways to perform assignments when they came his way. He had tried such exotic means of execution as using the battery pack of a camera to electrocute someone, or driving an icepick through the base of the skull. This last he had read about in a spy novel. Carlos enjoyed spy novels, although he often felt contempt for many of them, it being obvious that the authors had no real idea how to pull off a good assassination. He was seriously considering writing a book with himself as the hero. He didn't see how it could be all that hard to write a book, particularly if you had a good word processor.

His latest job had been commissioned by Mal Sangre, king of a drug cartel that was expanding through the streets of New Orleans with almost hypnotic swiftness. Carlos was pleased to handle an assassination for Sangre; it was always good to work for one of the major players. If he handled this one successfully he could probably raise his price a good two or three grand the next time out.

He had picked another unique way to dispatch his target. He had distilled the nicotine essence from a couple of expensive Cuban cigars and loaded a tranquilizer dart with it. The resulting concentrated poison should be enough, according to his research, to kill a grown man almost immediately.

A few days' surveillance had shown him that the target had a fairly regular daily schedule. The temptation was to think it would be simple, but he never counted on that. A professional covered all the angles no matter how straight ahead the job appeared.

He had carefully inspected the apartment building and the surrounding structures. The target occupied the ground floor of what had once been a large house in the Greek Revival style. The dilapidated building had been divided into a fourplex. The target's neighbors, as nearly as Carlos had been able to determine, were a couple of hookers on the top floor and a biker and his squeeze in the rooms next door. The grounds, which had no doubt once been carefully maintained, were now a jungle of bougainvillea, camellias, jacaranda and cherry trees. They provided plenty of cover for him to get close to the house.

Carlos had chosen a secluded spot perhaps twenty feet from an open rear window. He had a clear shot into the apartment's kitchen. Now he loaded the dart into a modified paintball gun and checked his watch. According to the schedule the target had been keeping to over the past three days, he would be home within the hour. Once in the apartment he usually came into the kitchen for a drink.

Carlos aimed the paintball gun, steadying his arm by gripping the wrist with his other hand. Then, satisfied that he could make the shot with no trouble, he settled down to wait.

Lia St. Charles inched across the Crescent City Connection Bridge during the last part of rush hour. In the tape deck, Stevie Ray Vaughn's blistering cover of Hendrix's *Voodoo Chile* played. As she moved slowly along Lia wondered again why she felt so strongly that Shane LaFitte was telling the truth. Though she tried not to be as cynical as the other people she knew in various fields of law enforcement, she also prided herself on not being naïve. If she had a nickel for every time one of her cases had protested his innocence to her, well, she'd have a whole lot of nickels, that was for sure.

And yet . . .

One thing Lia had developed in this job was an ability to read people. She still made mistakes, but rarely; she had become better than most shrinks at interpreting body language, at digging out the real meanings behind the words she heard. It was a skill she'd developed in self-defense, a bullshit detector that was seldom wrong.

And it hadn't been sounding earlier this evening in her office.

Be careful, she cautioned herself. There was no use lying to herself that she didn't find him attractive, but how much this was coloring her judgment of him was open to question. Looking at it as honestly as she could, Lia felt she could say she had a fair degree of objectivity. Perhaps there was a chance LaFitte was telling the truth. But she was still glad she'd brought along the gun.

Okay, let's assume he's telling the truth. Where does that put us? she asked herself.

Good question. If he had been wrongly sentenced, the case would have to be reopened. But she couldn't go to the DA's of fice on just LaFitte's word. She'd need whatever exculpatory evidence he'd amassed, if any.

Lia came off the bridge and turned north on Monroe. It would do no harm to at least listen to his side of the story. If she found him at home tonight she'd give him a chance to present his version and then go from there. Maybe she had been a little too deep in cast-iron bitch mode with him, but the fact of the matter was that he'd frightened her. Not in a sense of physical danger so much as making her afraid she'd be less than unbiased. Drawn to him, she'd overcompensated. In trying to be professional she had instead been dogmatic.

Okay, then, Lia thought as she parked two houses down from his address. You'll get your chance, LaFitte. You'd better make the most of it.

The hell of it was, she hoped he would. She wanted him to be right.

Be careful. Be very careful. . . .

It was full twilight now, the lush, unhurried dusk of the subtropics, that magical time when the world stood balanced between night and day. The light was purple and languorous, the air perfumed with the scents of azaleas and mimosa. Crickets and cicadas were beginning their strident harmonies. In the sky above her, still glowing with the last fires of sunset, she could see Venus, a pearlescent point of light. From the river came the faint whistle of a steamboat's calliope. Lia paused for just a brief moment on the steps of his apartment building to savor it all.

Then she heard a sound she recognized immediately. It came from the rear of the building: a gunshot, and then another.

S hit! Carlos couldn't believe it. He had missed! He couldn't remember the last time he'd missed. It had been a perfect setup, and yet the target had somehow managed to dodge. No one could move that fast, he had to be psychic or something.

That's what he got for trying something new and fancy. He pulled his gun—a Walther PPK; if it was good enough for 007 it was good enough for Carlos—and moved closer. He thought he saw movement within the house and capped off one shot; maybe he'd get lucky. Then there came the sound of another gun going off, and the bullet clipped the shrubbery near his shoulder.

There was no way he was getting into a shooting match.

Carlos backed hastily away, crouching and taking advantage of the cover. He was deep in the bushes when he heard a female voice shout something. He was too far away to make out the words, but the tone was unmistakable: the sound of a cop demanding compliance.

Shit, shit, *shit!* This was bad, very bad. He'd blown the sanction, at least for now. Sangre would not be at all happy with him. This has definitely been a lesson, Carlos thought glumly as he moved swiftly back through the bushes toward the street. Stick with the tried and true methods; don't experiment. A boring job was better than an angry employer, especially in his line of work.

When Lia heard the shots she immediately reached into her purse, but instead of her gun she pulled out a cellular phone. Quickly she dialed 911 and told the dispatcher the situation. There was no way she was going in; she was a probation-parole officer, not a SWAT team member. She was starting to back off the porch when the door suddenly opened.

She had returned the phone to her purse and still had her hand in the bag; quickly she grabbed her revolver and dropped into a firing stance as she had been taught. Before her stood Shane LaFitte, a gun in one hand. "Put the gun down!" she shouted, feeling her heart slamming against her ribs.

LaFitte looked astonished. He stared at her, then at the gun in his hand as though he had no idea how it had gotten there. He made no move to put it down. Lia could feel every nerve in her body vibrating at ultrasonic speed. She forced her voice to be steady. "Put the gun *down*, LaFitte, or your brains are wall-paper."

He knelt slowly and placed the gun on the porch, then stood again. In his eyes was a desperation that seemed beyond human in its intensity. "You have to let me go," he said.

Lia felt an overpowering urge to laugh, and clamped down on it. "I don't think so," she said instead. She gestured with the gun toward the far end of the porch. "Move over there and get down on your stomach. Hands behind your head."

"*Please*. If you send me back to jail I won't be able to stop him."

"Stop *who*?"

"I can't tell you that. It would put you in danger."

She felt a tiny fissure of doubt crack her resolve. She refused to let it widen. "I told you to prone out, LaFitte."

His gaze locked with hers, feverish intensity and desperation burning in his eyes. "*Please*," he whispered. "You don't understand; the *bokor* sent someone to kill me."

Lia stared at LaFitte, astonished. He was spouting the worst kind of comic book dialogue, but damned if he wasn't intense enough to almost make her swallow it.

Of course, it was all bullshit. He was in clear violation of parole—he had a *gun*, for Christ's sake!

"Listen to me," LaFitte said, his voice low and intense. "If you send me back to prison now, when I get out again—*if* I get out again—he'll be too powerful for anyone to stop him. You *must* let me go!"

For a brief moment Lia St. Charles almost believed him. She almost lowered her gun. She almost let him go.

But then she heard the rising wail of sirens in the distance, and the sound of them brought her back to reality.

"You can't send me back. I'm the only one who can—"

"Sorry, LaFitte," she said grimly, cutting him off. "You're violated."

He must have seen the truth of it in her eyes, for he said nothing in return. They stood there on the porch, a stark tableau, until the first of the squad cars arrived.

CITY
2 OF STONE

■ *The prisoner is not the one who has committed*
a crime, but the one who clings to his crime
and lives it over and over.

—Henry Miller,
Sexus

xxiv

K.D. got home early Saturday morning and found a message from Dave on her answering machine.

She was glad to hear his first words: "Hi, it's Dave Cummings. . . ." It had been two days and she was wondering if he was going to call. The memory of that first date had only grown more pleasant in the last forty-eight hours, and K.D. had decided she definitely wanted to see him again. She was well aware of the perils of trying to juggle any kind of relationship, however casual, along with her residency, but she had the optimism of youth.

Her initial delight, however, was quickly replaced by worry. Even if what he said was not enough to cause for concern, the tone of his voice was. This was the voice of someone in fear of his life.

After identifying himself, he went on to say: "Listen, I . . . I need to see you. I'm in kind of a situation and I—well, I need to talk to you about it in person. Can you meet me at the Farmer's Market first thing tomorrow morning? Please, K.D. I know it's a big imposition, but it's kind of important. It's really important."

There was a brief moment of background noise on the tape: cars, a distant riverboat whistle—which told her he had been calling from a pay phone. Then the click as he hung up. A moment later the automatic time stamp told her the call had been placed two hours earlier, at 12:40 A.M.

What the hell was this all about?

K.D. glanced at her watch, hesitated, then found the card he had given her and picked up the phone. Whatever was troubling Dave had seemed sufficiently important for him to risk her displeasure by calling after midnight. She might as well return the favor.

The phone rang four times and then gave her a recording of sprightly jazz playing under Dave's voice, which invited her to leave a message. "It's K.D.," she said. "Either you're not there or you're asleep. I can't get away from my rounds until tomorrow evening. If that's not too late for you, I guess I'll see you tomorrow at the market around six." She wondered if she should address the obvious desperation in his message, then decided not to. She would learn all about it soon enough.

She had been tired when she got in, but now all thought of sleep had been banished. She wasn't sure how to feel about this. They didn't know each other sufficiently well for him to be making demands like this on her. On the other hand, if he truly was in some kind of trouble and had no one else to go to, could she turn him down?

"Goddamn it," K.D. said out loud. This budding connection

had shown every sign of being a keeper before this happened. Now she didn't know what to think about him. She didn't want to turn down someone in need of help, but she certainly didn't want to get sucked into some kind of mind game. And there was always that possibility.

She looked out the window. Her apartment had a decent view of Lake Pontchartrain, which was impressive enough when the sun was out, but at this time of night all it showed her was blackness. Hardly conducive to peace of mind at this hour of the morning. She recalled reading somewhere that three A.M., not midnight, was actually the hour most favored by ghosts because it was the time when people are most deeply asleep, their souls only tenuously anchored to their bodies.

That would come to mind now, of course.

The quiet was beginning to get to her as well; combined with the darkness outside, K.D. could almost believe that she and her immediate surroundings had been somehow transported to the depths of the ocean or the endless night of space. She shivered despite herself. The last time she could remember being afraid of the dark she had barely been high enough to look over the sill of a window like this one.

Feeling foolish and annoyed with herself, she turned on the radio. It was set to a local rock station, and they were playing Concrete Blonde's "Bloodletting," a spooky composition about a vampire prowling New Orleans. Obviously there was a conspiracy underway to freak her out tonight.

She clicked off the radio, turned on the tube instead and set it on MTV. They were playing a video by White Zombie; that was a little better, she thought. She went through the place turning on lights. Lastly she pulled the curtains on that disturbing stygian view through the window.

When she was done K.D. felt a little less jittery, but she knew she would still be puzzling over Dave's message until dawn came. She felt a flash of resentment at him—for someone in her job sleep was more prized than gold, and he had just cheated her out of at least four precious hours of it.

Then she chided herself for being selfish. For all she knew, he might be in a life-or-death situation. Maybe he was lying in a pool of blood by the phone right now. Should she call the police? And what would she tell them? "I got this sort of distressed call from this guy I hardly know. . . ." Yeah, they'd call out the riot squad for that. She looked at his address on the business card; he lived in the Quarter. Should she call a taxi, go over there, find out if he was all right?

At this time of the morning it was all too easy to imagine various horrific scenarios. K.D. finally decided that the best course of action would be the one he had requested and she had modified: she would meet him at the Farmer's Market at six. She could probably spare a half hour for dinner around then.

That decided, she realized she was hungry. She tried to put the whole surreal situation out of her head while she fixed herself a breakfast of cereal, low-fat milk and fruit. It was nearly four; she'd spent almost an hour thinking about this. The sun would be up soon. Good, K.D. thought as she sat down at the kitchenette's pass-through. The last hour had been just a little too quiet and dark for her.

The Farmer's Market was busy with the weekend evening crunch when she got there. A huge open-air complex of sheds and stalls full of alligator pears, mirlitons and other produce, it and the adjoining weekend flea market always attracted crowds of both tourists and locals. K.D., a Dr Pepper in one hand, browsed desultorily as she looked for Dave, marveling at the diversity of items: stuffed armadillos and rattlesnakes; infinite varieties of hot sauce with names like "Bats' Brew," "Atomic Pepper" and "Religious Experience" (the latter had four varieties: mild, medium, hot and "Wrath of God"), and panoplies of tacky souvenir keychains, mugs and the like. One stall specialized in wallets, pouches and other items made from nutria hide. Ordinarily she might find herself caught up in the shopping spirit, but not now. She glanced impatiently at her watch, wondering where Dave was. She could only spare twenty more minutes. . . .

Then suddenly he was there by her elbow, wearing dark Ray-Bans and a furtive look. "Thanks for coming," he said. "You've no idea how much it means to me."

"How could I stay away?" K.D. asked. "Is this where you pass me the microfilm and then get shot?" She thought he looked faintly ridiculous in the sunglasses, since the sun had all but set.

The attempt at humor apparently flew about a foot over Dave's head. "It's nothing like that," he said, his voice low and intense, as they strolled the aisle between tables spread with discount clothing. "I know this sounds really horrible, but you mentioned your parents were rich, and . . . well, I—"

"You're trying to borrow money," K.D. said. The disappointment she felt was almost physical, like a slap in the face.

She saw him wince, as if he had felt her shock. "Just let me tell you what's going on," he said. "Then, if you want to throw your drink on me and walk out I won't blame you."

They walked out into the fading sunlight and found a black wooden bench not far from the crowd. Pigeons crowded around their feet, searching for crumbs. Dave seemed nervous; he glanced constantly about him. K.D.'s initial disappointment and the anger she had felt when she first realized what he wanted were beginning to fade; whatever was going on, he seemed genuinely fearful.

"Okay," she said. "Let's hear it."

Dave told her the story, looking around repeatedly as he spoke for anyone who gave the impression he liked to pop off peoples' kneecaps for fun and profit. He didn't try to excuse what he had done—even in the short time he had known K.D. he had realized that honesty was the best policy with her. Also, there were no excuses for what he had done. In a moment of greed and madness he had left the well-ordered and comfortable routine of his life and plunged into the jungle, and now he could not find the way back. For six hours after his meeting with Errol he had been pissing blood. The debt now stood at eleven hundred dollars. Tomorrow it would be eleven-fifty. Like a sinister financial cancer it kept metastasizing, and he was helpless to stop it. None of his friends—whom he had finally swallowed his pride and gone to—could advance him that kind of money. K.D. was his only hope.

When he had finished describing the beating administered by Errol, they both were quiet. Dave watched K.D.'s face anxiously, hoping for some sign of what she planned to say. What could she say, other than "no?" He was asking to borrow over a thousand dollars from a woman he had only met a couple of days ago; he didn't even know her first name.

At last she looked at him. "It isn't that easy," she said. "Yeah, my dad's rich, but I can't just ask him for that much money without telling him the reason. And if I tell him the truth he'll say 'no.' That I can guarantee."

"I don't suppose you'd consider lying?"

She shook her head. "For anything over a thousand bucks he's going to want paper. Something for taxes. And I don't think you can talk your bookie into giving you a receipt."

"Probably not." Dave found his heart was beating as fast or faster than it had when Errol had hit him. It was an effort to avoid hyperventilating. In short, he was terrified.

"Have you thought about going to the cops?"

He shook his head. "Are you kidding? The NOPD is the most corrupt police force going. Bank robbers hire cops to stand guard for them in this city. I can't take the chance—I might be talking to one who's working for these guys."

"Then what are you going to do?" K.D. asked.

"I guess there's only one thing to do. Leave. Get out of town before sunup." Maybe there was another alternative, but he couldn't think of it. He would have to leave New Orleans, leave the life he had made for himself, take nothing but his horn and run like a thief in the night. The painful irony was that he would have to abandon his record collection, including the album that had been the cause of all this. Although the debt had swelled to something far beyond his ability to pay, he knew he was still small potatoes to the people Errol worked for. They wouldn't spend thousands of bucks trying to bring him back here just to have Louie or some other Neanderthal yank his backbone out through his asshole. At least he hoped they wouldn't.

He said as much to K.D. "I'll have to hitchhike," he finished. "Or maybe I can scrape up bus fare as far as Baton Rouge, or—"

"I can give you a couple hundred bucks," she said. "That much I can spare. Should be enough to get you across the country by bus."

He looked at her in gratitude. "I—somehow, I'll pay you back, K.D. I'll see you again," he said. "That is, if you want me to."

"Well," she said sadly, "I won't deny this isn't the best way to start a relationship. Or finish one, for that matter. But I can't just stand by and watch this squirrel guy dismember you. Knee surgery can be rough." She stood up. "There's an ATM a couple of blocks from here." She started toward Ursulines Street.

Dave quickly followed. "If only there was some other way," he said.

"There's not. Believe me, I know. These guys want interest compounded in blood. My dad's dealt with people like them, he's told me stories."

At the automatic teller she withdrew two hundred dollars and handed the money to Dave. They stood there looking somewhat awkwardly at each other.

"Thanks," Dave said. "Well . . . I guess this isn't the best time for long good-byes."

K.D. put her hands on his shoulders and kissed him. Their first kiss, and maybe their last, he thought. Evidently she felt the same way, because she made it a kiss to remember.

Then: "Good luck," she whispered. "Let me hear from you when you can." And she turned and walked quickly down the narrow street. She turned the corner and disappeared from his view.

Dave stood there for a long moment, staring after her. This woman, whom he hardly knew, had in all probability just saved his life. He felt an unaccustomed fullness in his throat and realized he was blinking back tears.

He made himself turn and head in the other direction, toward his apartment. It certainly wouldn't do to have her sacrifice ruined by him loitering around until one of Errol's men found him. The thought of leaving the band, his friends, and the city itself was heartbreaking. But better his heart broken than his legs.

He would go back to his place and get his horn, and then he would catch a cab to the bus station. From there he would go as far as the money would take him. He thought he might be able to get to New York. There were a couple of musicians there he knew from various jazz festivals. They might be willing to put him up until he could get a gig. Maybe he might eventually make his way to Paris, see if he could make a decent living over there playing. . . .

He was starting to feel almost optimistic as he passed the Voodoo Museum on Dumaine Street. Then he saw who was standing on the building's steps.

I t was as though his short sojourn in the outer world had been something even less than a dream, more like an errant thought or memory that was gone the moment he tried to pay attention and lay claim to it. He was back in the world he had known for six years, and nothing, of course, had changed. Nothing ever changed in Angola. Unless it was for the worse.

During his term there Shane LaFitte had learned a considerable bit about the fortress that housed him and over five thousand other inmates. The Louisiana State Penitentiary, known as "Angola" after the plantation it was built on, sprawled over eighteen thousand acres sandwiched between the Tunica Hills and the Mississippi River levees. It was one of the most isolated prisons in the nation—and, he had learned by firsthand experience, one of the most brutal. From the turn of the century until the mid-1970s, time served in Angola, even for a relatively minor infraction, was tantamount to a death sentence. It was the most violent prison in the country, a lawless concrete jungle in which only the strongest and most savage survived. Wars between cliques were fought with weapons out of the Dark Ages: axes, swords, knives and shields. Men wore iron boiler plates and telephone books strapped to their chests: makeshift armor. The concrete floors, worn smooth by countless thousands of feet, were made even more slick by blood in those past decades.

It wasn't much better now, Shane reflected, lying on the thin bunk mattress in his newly assigned cell. While it was true that the Louisiana DOC had managed to institute some kind of order and power structure during the last twenty years, this was still a world ruled by fear and domination. Fortunately, his size, physique and attitude had deterred the inmates from trying to "turn him out" when he had been a new fish. Had it been otherwise he would have had to choose: either the humiliation and pain of gang rape and the subsequent near-slave status reserved for the "galboys," or fighting and probably killing whoever attempted it, which would have meant years more added to his time.

He could not afford that. He had managed to get out once without resorting to a breakout, but he could not wait for another parole. His enemy would be too powerful to take on by then; he might be so already. No, Shane decided, despite the added difficulties of trying to stop Sangre as a fugitive, this time he would have to escape.

He felt his fury at what had happened struggling to surface, but years of practice in controlling his emotions kept it at bay. *Damn* the woman! Granted she had her job to do, still it was obvious that she had been looking for an excuse to send him back.

He wondered briefly if she might have been working for Sangre, but he had sensed no controlling will overriding her own. It could be, of course, that she had simply been bribed and was doing his bidding out of choice, but he didn't get a sense of corruption from her either.

Whatever her motives, the result had been a calamity. She had no idea of the stakes involved. It wasn't merely for himself that he had to confront Sangre; other lives were at stake. Hundreds of lives, possibly thousands. Being returned to Angola was a severe reversal, but he could not—must not—let it stop him.

His bunkmate—a surprisingly soft-spoken redneck who had given his name as "Rake"—turned over on the overhead bunk, his shifting mass causing the springs and steel frame to protest. The row had been returned to their cells for the day's second lock and count just after breakfast, which had consisted of powdered eggs, grits and white-bread toast. Shane had fallen back into the routine easily—too easily. After this would come lunch, and then afternoon time in the Big Yard, weather permitting.

His cell was a typical one. It had originally been built for single occupancy, but the addition of an extra bunk had halved the living space. There was a lidless toilet at the far end—six feet from the heavy iron bars of the door—with a sink and small mirror above it. Shane could see a roach nearly two inches long exploring the rim. Having grown up in Haiti, he was no stranger to insects. It was the larger animals sometimes found within the walls of Angola one had to worry about. Rats the size of terriers had been known to crawl up sewer pipes and out of toilets, and poisonous snakes had made their way inside cellblocks more than once.

The wall over Rake's bed was decorated with pinup foldouts from hardcore magazines: women licking their lips and spreading their legs invitingly, fingers exploring labial folds. Rake began to snore, hitching glottal sounds. The mid-morning air was filled with a cacophony of music from boomboxes and tape players: rap, country, heavy metal, disco, bluegrass, even classical. Add to that the constant shouts, curses and general conversation of the inmates and the result was a constant white-noise dissonance. Shane had learned, like Rake apparently had, to sleep through it all. But he was not sleepy now.

There had been breakouts from Angola in the past, of course. Most of the escapees had made their way either through the dense undergrowth of the Tunica Hills or down the river, which could be quite treacherous along this portion of its length. Although the prison boasted high security, it could be done. Once out, if he could just maintain his freedom long enough to do what had to be done. . . .

After that, it didn't matter what happened.

The spring sunlight warmed Shane's face and arms as he paced the length of the Big Yard. The main prison exercise area was a large expanse of dirt and grass, broken by dormitories built to house overflow prisoners. There was also the infamous Red Hat cellblock, unused now, which had once contained both the death house and solitary. Cons played baseball and tossed Frisbees. Fitness freaks jogged the yard's perimeter or lifted weights at the iron pile. The omnipresent musical mélange was now composed mostly of salsa and mariachi.

A black man wearing a worn pea coat over faded denim fell into step alongside him. For perhaps a hundred yards neither of them spoke. Then his companion said softly, "Heard you were back in, brother. My condolences."

"Thanks." Graham Everett Layton was serving thirty years to life for the murder of his wife and her lover in 1977. Shane had first met him in the prison library, where Layton had been reading Dostoyevski's *House of the Dead*. He was soft-spoken and well read, and a source of intellectual companionship for which Shane was quite grateful. Layton had taught him many of the unspoken and unwritten laws governing the complex prison world: when to make eye contact and when to avoid it, where it was appropriate and safe to walk, how to hide contraband from new hacks along the inside of his belt or between the sole and inner lining of his shoes. He had also guided Shane through the medieval complexity of Angola's commerce system: dope, tobacco, candy, fuck books, even the sexual favors of someone's catamite were all legitimate means of barter in the prison black market.

"So what happened?" Layton kept his voice low, didn't look at Shane. "You were one dude I figured could keep clean, not wind up back inside."

Shane sighed. "Parole officer had it in for me." Not the entire truth, perhaps, but the easiest and simplest explanation.

"Ain't that a bitch. You be careful, you hear? Two weeks ago some longtimer in CCR shanked a guard. Warden's coming down on us for everything now. Spit on the floor, you end up in Point Look-Out."

Close Custody Restriction was the disciplinary unit where they kept the troublemakers. Point Look-Out was the prison cemetery. Layton was exaggerating; Shane knew, but not by much. This was, after all, the prison in which a group of convicts, driven to desperation, had once cut their Achilles tendons to protest management brutality. Shane tried to imagine the conditions that could make someone saw away at himself with a razor or kitchen knife until the thick fibrous band of tissue behind the ankle separated, leaving one a permanent cripple. Layton's warning was worth listening to.

"I'm not staying long," he said softly.

Layton glanced at him and raised an eyebrow as they strolled past the bleachers. "Don't have to tell you that's easier said than done. You got a plan?"

"Not yet. I'm open to suggestions."

"Nothing's impossible, 'cept maybe a fair trial. But you got to grease a few palms. Folks in here by and large ain't prone to helping others out of the goodness of their hearts. I'm not talking barter or scrip; it's got to be dollars. Enough coin can get you out of here before the ink on your fingers dries."

Shane made no reply to that. He had had no time to get to what little money he had earned in his short time of employment. New fish were thoroughly searched for contraband, but it was still possible to smuggle money into prison. Had he had the time and opportunity Shane could have brought in a hundred dollars or so tightly wrapped in a baggie and shoved up his ass. He mentally shrugged. Even had he been able to, it would not have been enough. A breakout required the cooperation of many people, including guards and administrators. Unless he could pony up bribes to the tune of a hundred apiece, at minimum, he was going nowhere.

No. Failure was not an option. It had to happen. He would make it happen.

"I hear you," he told Layton. "Maybe the gods will provide."

Layton snorted and looked up at the guards in their sentry towers. "Ain't no gods in 'Gola, man. Shit, even the devil steers clear of this place."

After busting Shane LaFitte, Lia St. Charles spent the next day going through the motions of her job. She did her interviews and fieldwork, filed her reports and carried on as though everything was business as usual. She resolutely refused to admit to herself that perhaps she had made a mistake. After all, she had gone one hundred percent by the book. She had found a parolee with a gun. What else could she have done but send him back to jail? He was lucky not to have had additional time imposed. As it was, the judge, mindful of the notoriety of the case, had had LaFitte shipped back upstate in record time.

It was the right thing to do. So Lia kept telling herself, ignoring the still, small voice deep within her whispering that she had made a mistake, a big mistake, that it was vitally important that this man remain free. Last night she had awoken with a start, bathed in sweat, from a nightmare remembered only as a fading montage of red eyes, pounding drums and a seductive voice calling to her in a language she could not understand. She had been unable to go back to sleep, and the dawn had been a long time in coming.

Today was a busy one: twenty clients coming in and several more to visit in the field. Lia yawned and took another swig of coffee; her third cup, and it wasn't even noon yet.

At the day's end she felt totally wasted and more than ready to go home. By the time she got to her house she was yawning, and for a moment seriously thought about going straight to bed. She stayed up long enough to eat dinner and sit through one boring sitcom before giving up and heading for the bedroom. Toulouse obviously sensed something wrong; he chattered anxiously and perched on the towel shelf by the sink, grooming her hair with tiny dexterous fingers while she brushed her teeth.

Her head hit the pillow at 8:40; Lia couldn't remember ever going to bed that early when she wasn't sick. She wondered if she might be having some sort of delayed reaction to the showdown with LaFitte. It had been the first time she had ever faced someone who held a gun. Even though he hadn't threatened her with it, the episode had been about a nine-point-nine on the sphincter scale, no doubt of that.

Well, it was over now and he was safely back in Angola. He'd have more gray hairs than black when he walked out of there again. Lia tried to find solace in that, but it wasn't as comforting as she'd hoped. She kept picturing the look in his eyes when she'd leveled her piece at him. There had been no fear or anger in them; only a kind of desperate pleading. He had tried to talk to her—no doubt attempting, as they all did, to convince her of his innocence—and she had cut him off. There was nothing he could say that she hadn't heard before, after all.

Was that the reason? the voice in the back of her skull asked.

Or were you afraid he'd persuade you to let him go?

Enough of this, Lia told herself. She lay on her back in bed, Toulouse curled up in his cat bed across the room, and waited for sleep to come. But she could not stop thinking about the confrontation between her and LaFitte.

What was it he had said before she shut him up? "The *bokor* sent someone to kill me." Lia frowned. The police had found some kind of dart filled with concentrated nicotine embedded in the wall. When questioned, LaFitte had claimed to know nothing about it.

She had looked up the word *bokor* and found it was a voodoo term for warlock or sorcerer; an evil magician. Had he just been frantically blue-skying to keep her from busting him? He hadn't impressed her previously as the type to panic under pressure. And there were certainly plenty of more believable tales he could have spun. It made no sense.

She yawned. Drowsiness was finally beginning to steal over her. Her eyelids drooped, her breathing deepened, and she was still mulling over those last minutes spent with LaFitte as she slid into slumber.

At first she did not know she was dreaming. She was moving slowly through billowing gray mist; it seemed to drift right through her, cold and damp, chilling her bones. The light was that of an overcast day, with no visible source. She could feel no ground beneath her feet; she couldn't feel much of anything, in fact, except the damp cold that chilled her both outside and inside. Lia looked down at herself and saw that her naked body was transparent, as though she were made of glass. She thought of that plastic model of the female body that had been on the teacher's desk in her high school biology class. But it wasn't like that, for looking at her hand she could not see bones and blood vessels beneath the skin. It was simply clear, vitreous, as though she were a sort of three-dimensional unfinished sketch.

As though she were a ghost.

She touched herself tentatively. Her flesh felt cool and solid enough, but nevertheless she could see through her hands and body. It was like looking at an X ray; that sort of gray filmy translucence. She wondered if she was dead, if her soul was wandering through some gray, cheerless limbo. But somehow she knew that wasn't the case. That left only one other explanation: she had to be dreaming.

Lia's dreams usually sorted themselves into two categories: disjointed fragmentary vignettes that coursed through her sleeping mind like psychic channel surfing, and nightmares, which thankfully were few and far between and which usually involved some kind of nameless and faceless killer pursuing her. This dream was different, unique. She ran her hands over herself. She felt no repugnance at her state; even the damp coldness was not unpleasant. She had certainly experienced enough of this kind of weather living in New Orleans.

The mist seemed thicker now, coiling and lapping about her. Its touch, though cold and damp, was oddly seductive. Lia closed her eyes and put her head back, felt the mist caressing her. It seemed almost a living thing, its tendrils stroking her, cupping her breasts and questing tenderly through her pubic hair. She altered her stance, letting the sensation move freely between her legs. The touch of the damp mist against the sensitive folds of skin there was electrifying. It entered her, rose within her. Her breathing became sharper, faster, and a moment later the sensation exploded within her, a full-body orgasm, reverberating from crown to feet.

Lia opened her eyes and looked down at herself, feeling half-stunned from the intensity of the climax. The mist now curled and eddied within her abdomen, a small gray ball of cloud. Her nipples were stiff and hard and her breasts were swollen. She saw fog seeping from the nipples like pale ectoplasmic lactation.

There was no landscape, no sign of anything except the rolling mist. She could not decide if she were floating in it or actually standing on it as if in some child's nursery tale. There was no sense of fear and confusion; on the contrary, she felt very much at peace. Within her the fog thickened, growing white and opaque. Again she thought of bones within an X ray's veiled flesh.

Her stroking fingers passed over her stomach again, and she realized that it was growing larger.

Her belly was swelling, rounding out in the unmistakable bulge of pregnancy. Within she could see the mist solidifying even more, taking on the shape of a developing fetus. Lia felt no amazement at this, but rather a sense of great joy and accomplishment. Why she should feel this way puzzled her; she had never particularly wanted children before. But it suddenly seemed extremely important that this child swiftly forming within her be born.

She was now as gravid as a woman in her ninth month; the gestation had taken place in a matter of moments. But instead of labor beginning, the accelerated pregnancy seemed to slow and stop. Lia could plainly see within her a fully formed unborn child, milk-white and luminescent. It floated upside down, its head pointing downward, tiny legs crossed and bent, making it impossible to determine its sex. By bending over she could plainly see its composed and serene features.

As she stared at it, it opened its eyes and looked at her.

Lia gasped, but did not look away from the gaze of her unborn child. All the wisdom of the ages seemed to lie behind those bright eyes. She felt an overpowering love for it. After only a moment of this, however, the feeling of love and happiness was abruptly washed away by a dark and compelling sense of dread.

Faintly, in the distance, she could hear drums beating.

She looked up, turned to scan the cloudscape all about her. She was still surrounded by drifting mist. But something was different. Something had changed.

Something was coming.

Something evil.

The drumbeat, savage and insistent, grew louder. Lia knew she should run, but in what direction? She could not tell from which way the nameless horror was approaching. All she knew was that it was coming, and coming fast—the fear was like an icicle stabbing through her heart. She had to run, run *now*, before—

There! Ahead of her, in the mist: a darker shape, growing larger and darker still as it approached. With each step the sound of the drums increased. The thing's outline was vaguely manlike, but somehow she knew that was a deception. It might have been human once, but no longer.

Lia turned to run but, as in so many dreams, she found she could move only with the greatest difficulty. It was as though the mist impeded her now, held her back. Though she poured every ounce of strength into her legs, it was like trying to run through clinging tar.

And then the horror was upon her.

A hand like burning obsidian grasped her shoulder and pulled her roughly around. The drums were deafening now, their tempo growing. She stood no more than a few inches away from the thing, yet it was still somehow indistinct, formless, its outline rippling like a cloud of ink, retaining only a basic humanoid shape. It had no facial features save two blank eyes that glowed like embers. The hand hurled her roughly backward. The mist cushioned her fall, but once down she could not get up.

The thing stood over her, silent, menacing. Terrified, Lia wondered if it planned to rape her; its blurry, volatile shape made it impossible to tell whether it was equipped to do so.

The drums roared, building toward a crescendo.

It knelt on one knee and reached for her. Hands that looked insubstantial but were instead strong and solid seized her swollen belly. Nails like talons dug into skin, tearing it. She had felt no pain during the rapid growth of the mist-baby within her, but now it felt as though she were being split apart by red-hot knives. With one huge surge of strength the thing ripped her open from crotch to sternum. There was no blood, no outgushing of viscera; there was only the pain, so intense that Lia wondered why she did not awaken or die from it.

It reached in, pulled the mist-baby from within her like some nightmarish caricature of cesarean delivery. The mist-baby writhed feebly in the thing's grip and then dissipated as those taloned hands tore it apart. The vapors that formed it became once more part of the cloudscape. As they did so the mist all about her, as far as she could see, flushed crimson as though washed with gore. The drums thundered a final, deafening refrain and then were silent. The thing stood again, spreading its arms apart and leaning back. It roared, a primal and savage scream, louder than the drums at their height—she could not tell if the sound was made in anger or triumph. Then it leaned down toward her again, those burning eyes coming closer, filling her field of vision—

She screamed.

Lia awoke, gasping, covered with sweat. She sat up in bed, thinking at first she still heard the echoes of the thing's roar in her head, then realizing it was a peal of thunder. Outside her windows lightning flashed, strobe-bright, and wind-driven rain lashed the house. Toulouse, always terrified of thunder, leaped into the bed to cower in her lap.

Lia turned on the bedside lamp, then sat cross-legged on the bed, cuddling the frightened monkey, trying to will her own fear to vanish. Most of her dreams, even the most vivid nightmares, usually faded from her mind within a few minutes of waking up. But the memories of this one stayed fresh and clear—all except one thing. In the final moment, when the thing had leaned down to glare at her, its indistinct features had suddenly sharpened into focus and she had recognized its face. But now she could not remember who it had been. She only knew that the recognition had been the nightmare's crowning horror.

She had never experienced anything like that before. It had been so vivid, so *real*. It seemed to Lia that she could still feel an echo of the searing pain she had experienced when the thing ripped her open.

Feeling a sudden renewed sense of dread, Lia pushed Toulouse to one side, ignoring the monkey's indignant protests. She pulled up the oversized T-shirt she slept in—the little Martian from the old Warner Bros. cartoons on it aiming a blaster and demanding "Take me to your coffee!"—and looked at her stomach.

On her skin, fading but still faintly visible, was a thin red line—a line that marked exactly where the thing had torn open her womb.

"Oh, *shit*," Lia whispered. The words were drowned out by another crash of thunder.

xxvii

W hen Dave saw the man standing on the steps of the Voodoo Museum his first reaction was one of disbelief.

He had almost come to think of that strange night in front of his flat when Jeff scored the Blood from the dealer as no more than a disturbing dream. Yet there the dealer was, apparently having just come out of the building. He was putting his wallet away in the inside pocket of his windbreaker. Even from across the street Dave could see that the billfold was bulging at its seams.

Without thinking, he backed into the shadow of a recessed doorway and kept watching.

The dealer, having evidently just finished buying something inside, came down the steps and moved quickly down the street, heading toward the river. Dave let him get a half block ahead before he followed.

The dealer continued down Dumaine to Decatur and turned right, through Jackson Square, past the Millhouse complex and the Hard Rock Cafe. The sun had set fully by now and the antique streetlamps and storefront gas and neon lights were coming on. Clouds were beginning to gather—black ominous ones that said thunderstorm. Foot traffic was fairly light down here, but Dave was able to keep the dealer in sight. The man never looked back. When he reached Bienville he turned east, toward the Mississippi again.

Dave had no idea why he was following the dealer. He should be back at his apartment, packing hastily so as to catch the next bus out of town. Instead he was tailing a criminal, probably a dangerous one, into an area of the Quarter that was not the safest place to be after sundown. The region below Decatur and north of Canal was a rundown industrial center, full of warehouses and deserted storefronts. There was nothing here to attract the tourist trade, so it was largely a hangout for druggies, derelicts and other human debris. Dave followed his quarry as the latter made his way down an alley. Overflowing dumpsters lined the walls and fire escapes hung like giant rusting cobwebs. The cracked pavement was littered with trash.

The dealer had money—that he had seen. Was that why he was following him? Did he honestly think he could somehow rob this guy without suffering major mayhem? This is insane, Dave told himself. But he could not make his feet turn about and carry him back to the relative safety of the streets he had left. He was desperate, and though he wasn't even sure what his motives were, he kept going, hiding behind the dumpsters to avoid being seen. The alley was dimly lit by the yellow glow of a few rear entrance lights. A rat scurried through the garbage by Dave's feet as he crouched behind an overflowing bin.

The dealer's footsteps were quiet. Dave risked a quick look around the dumpster, saw the man sitting, facing away from him, on a plastic milk crate about fifty feet ahead. He was dialing a number on a cell phone. There was a rumble of distant thunder as he put the phone to his ear.

He's a criminal, Dave told himself. He made that money selling death to addicts. But that same money could save Dave's life. Poetic justice. So his thoughts ran along the surface of his mind, while deeper down the slower currents whispered that all this was bullshit, that assault and robbery were the same no matter who the victim was, that if he did this he would be no better than the hitman he was trying so desperately to avoid meeting. But he didn't listen. He couldn't listen. Because this, he knew, was his last chance.

"All right," the dealer said into the phone, by way of greeting. "'S up, man? . . . Yeah, it s'posed to happen, soon as Sangre finds him some poor dumb fuck to cut . . ." Another growl of thunder drowned out the next sentence. " . . . How t'hell should I know? . . . Yeah, Pontchartrain be the place. . . . No, fool, you can't bring y'woman, this is serious shit! Leave th' bitch home. . . ."

Dave had no idea what the man was talking about, but he recognized the name Sangre. Mal Sangre was the top drug lord in New Orleans, the man whom the police were sure was behind the spread of Blood through the streets. Not a man, in short, whom you wanted to fuck with, unless you harbored a serious death wish.

There was one more dumpster between him and the dealer. He picked up a brick that lay nearby. If he could just get close enough to throw it, knock the guy out. . . .

Get serious, the voice he was rapidly coming to hate whispered in his head. That only works in the movies. Even if you can hit him with the brick, it'll probably kill him. And then you'll be a murderer, and that's not exactly the best direction for your career to take, is it?

Dave gripped the brick hard enough to hurt. Whatever decision he made, he knew he had to make it soon, before whoever his quarry was waiting for showed up. He stared around the dumpster again for a long moment—then put the brick down. Face it, he told himself, you've got as much chance of taking this guy out as you do of blowing a duet with Satchmo himself. There was only one sensible course to follow, and that was to sneak quietly out of the alley, go back to his apartment and start packing. If he could make it to the dumpster behind him he had a good chance of reaching the street without being seen.

Dave moved away slowly in a sideways crouch so as to keep an eye on the dealer. Traversing the fifty or so feet between the garbage bins was one of the longest trips he'd ever made—or so it seemed by the time he finally reached the shadowed security behind the far one. Once there, he breathed a quiet sigh of relief. From here he could easily make the street without risking being seen by the other man.

He stood, took a step backwards—

And his shoe came down on an empty beer bottle.

He might still have kept his balance had the other shoe not slipped on a greasy taco wrapper. As it was, both feet shot out from under him and he landed flat on his back hard enough to knock the wind from his lungs and cause stars to wheel before his eyes.

Dazed, Dave tried to struggle to his feet. He didn't hear footsteps, but suddenly the dealer was looming over him, his face contorted in rage. "What the fuck you doin', man?" He grabbed Dave by the shirt and pulled him to his feet. "Huh? You spyin' on me, asshole?" He slammed Dave against the side of the dumpster, causing a shower of filth to rain down about them both. Dave could see that the glaring eyes were exceedingly bloodshot; one was entirely rimmed in red.

Dave struggled to reply, but no air coming in meant no words going out. Though this wasn't as bad as being gut-punched by Errol, it was by no means pleasant. The dealer shoved him hard against the ribbed metal wall again, loosening more debris. Dave groped up and back with both arms, trying to grab the side of the dumpster, and felt the fingers of his left hand close about something heavy and cylindrical in the bin. He didn't stop to think; he just gripped it hard and pulled.

At first it resisted his effort to move it, and the despairing thought that it was too big or too wedged under trash hit him. Then it came free and he swung it at the dealer's head. It was an awkward left-handed blow, but the dealer didn't see it coming until too late. The object—in a flash of lightning Dave saw it was a nine-inch length of iron pipe—struck his assailant on the back of the head just above the neck. Dave saw the man's eyes go wide in pain and his jaw drop in surprise and shock. Momentarily stunned, he fell forward against Dave, releasing his grip as he did so. Dave shoved him away with frantic strength and the dealer dropped to his hands and knees.

The blow hadn't been hard enough to do more than take the fight out of him for an instant, Dave knew. He slid to one side against the dumpster's surface, his brain keening like a smoke alarm. He lifted the pipe and struck again with all his strength just as the dealer raised his head to look at him. The pipe hit full against the man's forehead. The dealer collapsed as though shot, and at the same moment the storm broke, a drenching torrent accompanied by another thunderclap.

Dave dropped the pipe and stared at the dealer. The dead man—there was no doubt that's what he was, Dave could see brains and blood leaking into one of the rapidly forming puddles at his feet—lay before him, eyes staring with sightless accusation. Dave turned away, dropped to his hands and knees and vomited onto the filthy pavement.

After perhaps five minutes, during which time the alley became a swamp of offal and refuse, he managed to get to his feet and stagger away from the scene of his crime. He had reached the mouth of the alley when he suddenly remembered the reason he had followed the dealer in the first place: the bulging wallet.

Dave turned and stared back at the body . . . the body of the man he had killed, but he would not, could not let himself think about that. Not if he wanted to do what he had to do. Not if he wanted to keep his sanity while doing it.

Self defense, he kept repeating to himself, over and over as he began the long walk back to where it lay. A mantra of denial. Self-defense, self-defense, self-defense. . . .

The head wound had bled quite a bit, even with the torrential rain the area around the head was still a fading crimson pool. And what he'd read in paperback thrillers was true, he realized with the calm of heavy shock: Spilled brains do look like gray toothpaste.

He crouched down beside the body. The wallet had gone in an inside pocket on the jacket's right side, which was, of course, the side the corpse was mostly lying on. Dave swallowed, put out his hand and pushed on the left shoulder, trying to roll the body over on its back. Its waterlogged weight resisted him, and when he let go it sagged back into its former position. The movement caused more brains to ooze like mulched paper. Dave closed his eyes as nausea surged again.

He used both hands to push harder; it almost felt as if the corpse were fighting back, refusing to be moved. Jesus, he thought, what if he's not dead? Even worse, what if he *is* dead and it doesn't matter? He remembered how spooky and surreal the dealer had seemed when he had first encountered him.

Another peal of thunder boomed and Dave cried out in shock and fear. The fear gave him the burst of adrenaline he needed to roll the body over on its back. The dealer sprawled in the noxious flood, arms outstretched as if inviting crucifixion, dead eyes unblinking in the rain. Dave found the jacket's zipper and tugged at it; it slid down a quarter of the way before jamming on the nylon material. There was just enough room for him to slide his hand between windbreaker and shirt, and this he did, groping between the two layers of clothing as gingerly as if he expected to find a cottonmouth hiding there. A moment later he had the billfold in his hands.

He didn't take the time to pull the money out here. Instead he took off at a stumbling run out of the alley and up the street, the rain lashing at him, driving him on. After two blocks he stopped and clung to a lamppost, gasping for air and waiting for the stitch in his side to diminish. His gorge was threatening to rise again, but he clenched his teeth and fought it back down. He realized that he still had the wallet clutched in one hand and stuffed it in one of his front pockets. Then, at last, exhausted and nauseated, he headed for home.

Back in his apartment he stripped out of his wet clothes and bundled up in a bathrobe, standing in front of the wall heater until most of the shivering subsided. He had a feeling that the shakes wouldn't be completely gone for a long time. A good thing you can't really go gray overnight, he thought, looking at himself in the mirror over the fireplace. Still, the face that looked back at him was that of a stranger, one whose eyes he couldn't meet.

After a stiff shot of Wild Turkey, Dave felt calm enough to examine the wallet. He did not look at the driver's license; he didn't want to know the man's name. He opened the money pocket, fully expecting to find only a hundred or so—God was fully capable of such a cruel joke, he knew. But instead there was over three thousand dollars stuffed between the leather folds. Enough to pay Errol back and have some left over.

Dave stared at the money in his hands. The nightmare was not quite over yet, he knew; he still had to call Errol and arrange payment. It would be the crowning touch if Louie the Squirrel or someone equally deadly kicked in his door now. But for the moment he couldn't pony up even the small amount of effort it would take to dial a phone. He just sat on the couch, staring at the money. Blood money, he thought. A strange balance of scales. He had found a way to save his life—by taking another's.

Carlos glanced about the small windowless waiting room. He was in the reception area of one of the many legitimate businesses Sangre owned primarily as covers for laundering his drug money, this particular one being a night club in Bridge City. The place was decorated cheaply: wood veneer paneling, orange shag carpet, a blatantly artificial ficus and a landscape painting over the threadbare couch. A secretary chewed gum in time to her hunt-and-peck typing on the keyboard of an ancient IBM Selectric. He'd heard Sangre was rich, but you couldn't tell it by looking at this place.

Carlos sighed. He'd been sitting there for twenty minutes and the inactivity had done nothing good for his anxiety level. He'd already glanced through the ancient copies of *Louisiana*

Life and *New Orleans Magazine* that adorned the end table. Now there was nothing left to do but brood.

Of course he would be honest and upfront with Mr. Sangre. He had fucked up, after all. He had blown the sanction, and he would make good on his mistake. Even if Sangre decided not to pay him he would still take out Shane LaFitte. It was a matter of professional pride.

The thought had occurred to him—foolish to pretend otherwise—that Sangre's expression of displeasure with him might be somewhat more extreme than withholding payment. Carlos had heard quite a few stories of Sangre's temper and of what had happened to those on the receiving end of it. Though he'd talked to a lot of otherwise intelligent people who swore that Sangre was a sorcerer who could kill someone with a look, Carlos did not believe in black magic. Sangre did not have to be a magician to frighten him, however. The man was powerful enough without having to resort to sorcery. Maybe he couldn't kill with a look, but he certainly could with a gesture to one of his hirelings.

Though he doubted Sangre would be that extreme—it's hard to hire freelance help when word gets around that mistakes are capital offenses—some kind of physical punishment could well be expected. What would he do then, Carlos asked himself. Stand there and take it, or resist and maybe wind up modeling concrete wingtips to catfish in the Mississippi?

He wasn't sure how he would react, and he devoutly hoped the situation wouldn't come to that. Probably it wouldn't. Mr. Sangre was a businessman, after all. He knew that the way to hurt a man most was to hit him in his wallet.

The secretary stopped typing and listened to her headset, then looked at him. "Y'all can go in now." Her southern accent was as thick as blackstrap molasses.

The office beyond the narrow door—hollow-core, an easy break-in, the professional within him noticed—was no more impressive than the waiting room. More prints adorned the walls, these of duck and fox hunting. A small refrigerator, the size and shape of a safe, purred in one corner. Sangre stood behind the desk, gazing out the window as though the view was an impressive cityscape rather than the wall of the Cajun fast food place next door. He waited a moment before turning to face Carlos.

Carlos had only met Sangre once before, when he had been given the job. He had been slightly surprised at how short the drug lord was; surely no more than five-seven or -eight. Height notwithstanding, Sangre was obviously not a man to fuck with. He was lean and compact; his upper body, dimly visible through the light cotton shirt, was banded with wiry strips of muscle that seemed to have no softening fat at all. Carlos could see the faint tracings of scars that laced his chest and upper arms. His face was gaunt and had the glow of polished mahogany, as though lit from within by the intensity of his gaze. He was sweating, Carlos realized; though the air conditioning in the room was keeping the temperature quite cool, Sangre's skin was covered with a fine sheen of perspiration.

His gaze held Carlos for a moment, almost as headlights can pin a rabbit or squirrel to asphalt. Then Sangre smiled slightly—almost shyly, Carlos noted in disbelief, a smile very much at odds with the rest of the man's body language—and gestured for Carlos to sit in the single chair facing the desk. Carlos did so, trying not to appear nervous. Did Sangre look so tense because he was angry? Or was there some other reason?

"So good of you to come." Despite his strained demeanor, the drug lord spoke quietly, his Cuban accent giving the words a slight lilt. "I thought it important that we discuss this matter face to face."

"Sure," Carlos said. "I promise you, Mr. Sangre, that it won't—"

"Happen again?" As Sangre spoke he opened a desk drawer and took an eight-by-ten photograph out. He placed it on the green desk blotter. Carlos saw with some surprise that the photo was a picture of himself. "No," Sangre continued, "it most definitely will not."

"I was tryin' something new," Carlos continued. "I'm always lookin' for ways to improve, y'know. I don't know how he dodged that dart, but he can't dodge a bullet. This time I'll take 'im out, Mr. Sangre."

Sangre smiled again. He picked up a silver letter opener and toyed with it. Carlos noticed a strange scent, barely detectible, in the air: some kind of incense or burning herb. For some reason it added to the uneasiness he already felt.

Still playing with the letter opener, Sangre said, "LaFitte's parole was revoked. He has been returned to prison."

Shit. Carlos didn't like the direction this was heading. There was no way he could hit LaFitte up in Angola, so he would have to discharge his debt in some different way. And he had the feeling that Sangre was going to lay some real nasty assignment on him as punishment.

Well, it was no more than he deserved. "I'm sorry, Mr. Sangre. Whatever you want me to do to make up for this, consider it done." He straightened his shoulders and looked the other man in the eyes. After all, his honor as an assassin was at stake.

Sangre returned his gaze for a moment, then nodded in apparent satisfaction. "Thank you, Carlos. So few people take responsibility for their actions anymore." He was holding the letter opener by the blade; now he flipped it and caught it by the hilt, holding it tightly in his closed fist. "Since you have made such a generous offer, what I would like for you to do—is die."

He stabbed the letter opener down at Carlos's picture, burying the blade's tip in the image's forehead. Simultaneously Carlos felt an agonizing pain burst within his brain. The sound of a gigantic waterfall, deafening and yet somehow also silent, seemed to fill his ears. He saw Sangre look up at him, and the man, the room, everything, was tinged in red. The crimson hue intensified, washing out everything—

And carried him away.

Sangre felt a wave of dizziness and nausea sweep over him as the assassin collapsed. A drop of sweat fell from his face onto the photograph. Despite the nausea, he was smiling.

He looked at the dead body of Carlos, sprawled in the middle of the room. No need to check pulse or breath to know that the man was dead; Sangre had felt him die, had been, for the briefest of moments, connected soul-to-soul with him. Which was not surprising, since he had killed him by sheer force of will.

He sat down in the squeaky office chair. Once again he had proven conclusively that he was on the right track—that the power he sought was attainable, even though the cost was high. He had struck the bungling assassin down with the power of a *loa* or an *orisha*—he, who had once been a mere *mayombero*. No need for supplications or rituals designed to entreat gods to aid him—*he* had been the god.

True, it had not been easy; to keep the lines of occult force open from the Invisible World had taken sustained effort, both mental and physical. Deep within the spirit realm there were sources of power independent of spiritual entities, capable of being tapped, provided one had the strength and courage.

Sangre opened the refrigerator and took out a bottle of Gatorade. He swigged a few swallows. He had often found it helpful, after such intense efforts of sorcery, to replenish electrolytes just as an athlete would after running a marathon. The first time he had killed in this manner he had almost passed out from the effort and pain. But, just as an athlete becomes conditioned to grueling training and effort, so he was slowly growing more and more accustomed to the physical price that had to be paid for the use of such power. He was close to achieving the ultimate goal of every practitioner of the black arts: mystic power that could be wielded spontaneously and independently of deities or demons.

But, though he had made remarkable progress in the years since he had left Haiti, he was not there yet. Though the assassin had provided a convenient test case to gauge the extent of his strength and control, Sangre knew that it would be days before he would be up to trying something like this again. And this was merely to accomplish the death of one man standing before him. What he wanted—needed—was the ability to smite hundreds, thousands, at a distance of many miles. To have that kind of power would require one last invocation and sacrifice—one far greater than any he had made to date.

He would have to do something about LaFitte as well. This time he would not assume that prison would put an end to the man's ability to cause trouble. He would have to take the risk of offending the man's *loa-tête.* It would not be difficult. It did not require a sorcerer to insure that someone die up in Angola. LaFitte was the least of his worries.

Sangre felt his head clear as the sweet liquid raised his blood sugar level. He could be patient. Once he found the one who would serve as a conduit, everything would come together for the final ritual. Soon—in just a week, in fact—he would have power to rival that of the most powerful sorcerers since the dawn of time. The price would be high—very high.

Fortunately, he was not the one who would have to pay it.

The mess hall was always crowded. Shane had no particular affiliation with any group or gang, so finding a place to set his tray down was like looking for a place to park in a downtown garage. After about ten minutes of cruising the big room, passing tables full of prisoners shouting and handing food back and forth, he found a place to sit between an old Chinese man, who mumbled the scrapple and soft white bread between mostly toothless jaws, and a white male who looked to be in his mid-twenties. The latter wore his hair pulled back in an oily ponytail.

He said nothing to either of them, concentrating on the food, trying not to wonder what the scrapple was made of. He was halfway through it when his plastic fork broke and he decided he wasn't hungry enough to get another one. Instead he sat there, fingers laced and supporting his chin, and brooded. He thought about escape.

It wouldn't be easy. Angola had long been known, for good reason, as the Alcatraz of the South. It boasted over twenty towers manned by guards who were certified marksmen. The sewers and storm drains were too small to crawl through and the water table too high to permit tunneling out. On rare occasions someone would attempt a breakout by clinging to the undercarriage of a bus or truck or hiding in a delivery vehicle, but these potential routes to freedom were checked carefully by the prison staff. There had been escapes in the past, of course, but they were mostly accomplished by trustees or convicts outside the prison walls on work gangs, court trips or other business. In one case that Shane recalled, a guard had been bribed to doctor a log book, covering up the fact that the prisoner had been improperly placed on a jail work crew reserved for misdemeanor offenders. Once outside the gate the prisoner had bolted at the first opportunity. Another man had simply stabbed a guard and managed to climb the two fences topped with razor wire without being shot.

Once beyond Angola's grounds the road to liberty was hardly a smooth paved blacktop. The escape routes usually took two directions: through the forbidding wilderness of the Tunica Hills or down the Mississippi by stolen boats. Those who made it past the fences had to contend with gator-infested swamps, severe heat or cold, clouds of mosquitos and other hardships. Nearly all escapees were recaptured or gave themselves up after only a few days.

It was obvious that if he wanted to make a successful escape from Angola he would need help. More help than any human being could provide.

He would need the aid of his *loa-tête.*

And that could be more dangerous than seeking aid from the most homicidal prisoner within these walls.

"You goin' eat that banana?"

The question had come from Ponytail, who offered a disarming grin when Shane looked his way. Shane could smell the prison-brewed liquor they called "pruno" on his breath. He handed him the banana without speaking, then got up to scrape his tray.

Ponytail—his accent said he was Cajun—left as well, trailing along behind Shane as he exited the hall. It was gate time, when prisoners had limited freedom to roam the grounds and buildings. As Shane made his way through the maze of corridors Ponytail stayed close, but not too close. Shane tolerated this until they reached the library. The small room, its walls lined with wooden bookshelves, was deserted save for two inmates who did not look up when Shane turned, grabbed Ponytail and shoved him against the door.

"Is there something I can do for you?" he asked softly.

The young Cajun squirmed in his grip, unable to break the hold Shane had on his upper arms. "Hey, hey, lighten up . . . me, I wasn't followin'—"

Shane tightened his grip and pushed the smaller man's back up the wall, lifting his feet an inch or more off the floor. He was surprised to find himself grimly enjoying the knowledge of how easily he could hurt Ponytail. "Lying is only going to bring you pain. Now, once more—what do you want?"

Ponytail avoided meeting his eyes. "Heard you got sent back by that bitch St. Charles. She on my case too . . . me, I was mindin' my own business, stayin' clean, *hein?* And she bust me anyway. . . ."

"Shut up," Shane said. It was obvious that Ponytail had gotten a fix on him for some reason; perhaps it was no more than the desire most of the weaker prisoners had to hook up with someone stronger for protection and company. He didn't come off to Shane as a galboy, but that didn't mean it wasn't so. In any event, the question was what to do with him. He could not afford to make unnecessary enemies; on the other hand, he didn't want to be perceived as easily manipulated.

Ponytail, evidently taking Shane's silence as encouraging, rattled on: "Me, I'm Joey René; they call me 'Slow Joey' on account of my accent, you know? Doin' an armed robbery beef, four years. Been in two already."

Shane released him and patted him down expertly to make sure he wasn't carrying a shank. "I'm going to ask you again: What do you want?" he said. "I'd better hear an answer this time."

René fussed with his shirt for a moment and smoothed a few dangling strands of hair behind his ears, as if anything could possibly improve his looks. "Heard somethin' you might want to know, me." He gave Shane a sly look. "Word is someone's down on you."

Shane felt his gut tighten. He stared at René, pinning the smaller man to the door with his gaze. The news wasn't unexpected. The last time Sangre had been satisfied with having him imprisoned and out of the way—possibly a sentimental gesture based on the friendship they once had, more likely to avoid offending Legba. Now, judging by the assassination attempt at his apartment, that wasn't enough. It would be very easy for a man of Sangre's connections to engineer someone's death within these walls.

"Thought you could use a friend, maybe," René continued.

"Me, I got *beaucoup* connections inside. Maybe we work together, save you ass, *hein?*"

"And what's in it for you?"

René glanced nervously about and lowered his voice. "They say you a magic man, LaFitte. A *serviteur*. I figure, maybe we help each other. Maybe you teach me some things, make my life easier inside. I help keep you alive. Sound good?"

Shane turned away. "I don't think so." René struck him as a classic cell soldier——one who talked tough when the doors were locked, but was of little use in a situation.

René tried to follow him and continue the conversation but another look from Shane made him back off.

Shane returned to his tier and found his cell empty; Rake was no doubt still in the mess hall. The man's life consisted mostly of sleeping and eating. Shane sat in the empty cell and thought about his options.

He could not perform the rituals required to contact his *loa-tête* while sharing a cell. Private cells were scarce and much in demand. It would require far more money than he had to buy one from a convict lucky enough to have one, and he did not have the necessary pull with the Assistant Warden to be assigned one. He could ask to be reassigned to protective custody, citing his fear that someone was out to kill him, but even that would not give him the necessary privacy. No, there was only one way to find the seclusion he needed.

The Hole.

He would have to get himself assigned to an isolation cell, what used to be called "solitary confinement." In Angola solitary was known as the Intensive Management Unit, a polite euphemism that masked the brutal reality. He had never been down there, but he had heard the units described: windowless cavities in stone, ten feet long and seven feet wide, each equipped with a single bunk and an iron toilet and sink combination. A place that most prisoners dreaded, but which would be perfect for Shane LaFitte's needs.

As for getting assigned there, that would be easy enough. All he had to do was attack a guard or another prisoner. It would be dangerous, but he had no choice. And the danger of getting assigned to the Hole was nothing compared to the danger he would face once he was in there.

Because once inside that bubble of granite, he would have to call up his own personal demon.

There was no other way. He had to escape, had to find Sangre and kill him. Not just for revenge; not even to quiet the pain and self-loathing that had lived in his heart for six long years, because he knew nothing short of death could do that. He had to kill Mal Sangre before the latter unleashed an evil on the world that no one could stand against.

And perhaps not even Sangre's death would be enough.

Sangre had known what he was doing, oh, yes. He had not wanted to risk Legba's wrath by killing Shane, but he had judged his one-time friend well. He had known that the horror of what Shane had done would paralyze him, destroy his strength of will, keep him from trying to escape from prison and seek revenge. And he had been right. For more than half a decade, Shane LaFitte had languished in Angola, unable to escape the feeling that on some deep level he deserved the sentence. He had neglected his duties to his *lou-tête* and fallen out of favor with Legba. Sangre had taken him out of the game most effectively.

But he had been released, eventually. And the strength to resume the fight had started to seep back into him. And then had come this latest reversal.

Shane balled his hands into fists, stared up at the urine-stained mattress above him. He could not afford to wait passively for his sentence to run its course again. Everything he had managed to glean about the nature of Sangre's plan indicated that it would come to fruition very soon. He had to be stopped *now*, before he became unstoppable.

It was up to Shane, and him alone, to do it.

METAIRIE, LOUISIANA
MARCH 25, 1998;

BELVEDERE PLANTATION,
HIGHWAY 81,
LOUISIANA
OCTOBER 2, 1976

Lia had not gone to her office for the past couple of days, ever since the nightmare; it was the first time she had missed work in at least a year. Instead she stayed inside, listening to the monotonous drumming of the rain, which continued all that day, and trying to forget those glaring red eyes and the pain of the thing's talons ripping into her dream body.

She tried to read, and when she couldn't keep her mind on the mystery novel she had started, she tried to watch some old movies she had videotaped. When she couldn't concentrate even to that extent, she gave up and simply lay on the couch, watching the rain sheet down in ever-changing patterns on the front windows.

Toulouse could sense that something was wrong. He curled

up in the warm space between her body and the back of the couch and lay quietly, occasionally raising his head to peer intently into her eyes. Lia had never appreciated the little monkey's company as much as she did that day. She stroked his fur and talked to him, and Toulouse shivered with pleasure and groomed her hair between tiny fingers barely the length of her little toe.

She had not been able to remember after waking up what the final terrifying image of the nightmare had been. It had been a face, that she knew, but nothing remained of it except the burning eyes. The entire dream had seemed so incredibly real. She could still feel faint reverberations of the orgasm she had experienced, as well as the pain of the savage cesarean.

Only a dream, Lia told herself for the fiftieth time that day. "Only a dream, Toulouse," she said out loud, hugging the monkey to her.

Toulouse looked solemnly at her. *Oh, yeah?* his gaze seemed to be saying. *What about those scratches on your belly, lady? How do you explain those?*

That was what she had been asking herself all day. The red welts had faded after a couple of hours, but the area still remained tender to the touch. The best explanation she'd been able to come up with was psychosomatic trauma—stigmata, in other words. The dream had been so vivid, so real, that her body had responded to its images by echoing the wounds in her flesh. But that raised a whole other set of disturbing questions. Was she losing her mind—should she check herself into the nearest looney bin? Would the dream—or another, equally intense one—come to her again tonight? Was it possible to be so terrified by a dream that she could die of shock?

Lia had never experienced anything like this before. In the past her nightmares, frightening though they were at the time, were still just dreams, and on some deep level she had always been aware of that even during the dream. She had assumed she was dreaming at the beginning of this one, but as it had continued it had seemed somehow to assume its own reality—not a waking reality, but just as authentic. It was hard to convince herself, even now, that the amorphous dream demon was not lurking somewhere in the house, waiting for her to fall asleep again. This was New Orleans, after all, a city whose people had once attempted to oust street dealers in the Bywater District by hiring a voodoo priestess and a crew of dancers and drummers to make bad ju-ju on their asses.

"Don't be ridiculous," she said out loud. Such things were impossible. They didn't happen—at least, not to people she knew.

She pulled a comforter off the back of the couch and wrapped it around her to quell a sudden attack of the shivers, because she knew she was fooling herself. Such things *did* happen to people she knew. But to admit that required going to a place in her mind that she had not visited in a long, long time. She most definitely did not want to go there, but as she lay watching the rippling image of reality through the rain-streaked glass, it was hard to resist. . . .

At eight years old, what had impressed her the most was the *size* of the house. Great-Aunt Jeanne had told her it was one of the biggest plantation houses in the parish, but that meant nothing to Lia then—she wasn't even sure what a plantation house or a parish was. When they drove up the oak-lined drive her aunt had talked about how Belvedere House was a combination of "Greek Revival and Italianate architecture," but Lia's first thought, when they came around the bend and she beheld the huge tumbledown structure, was that this was what Heaven must look like. True, it was a somewhat rundown vision of Heaven, but compared to the house she and her family lived in near Loreauville, it wasn't much of a stretch for Lia to imagine St. Peter, clad in immaculate white robes and wings, a halo floating over his balding head, waiting to interrogate them on that big porch behind a row of white fluted columns. The fantasy made Lia smile as Aunt Jeanne parked the car and they walked up the marble steps.

Inside, however, was not what she had expected to find beyond the Pearly Gates. Not at all. Inside were cavernous chambers, one opening upon another, each made shadowy and sinister by heavy curtains that filtered the sunlight down to a perpetual glowing. Each was filled to bursting with dark, heavy oaken furniture: massive chests of drawers, overstuffed chairs with dingy gray antimacassars, four-poster beds. Most of the furnishings had leering leonine and demonic faces carved into them, along with friezes of troubling visions that haunted Lia's mind long after she passed them by. Some of the rooms were so stuffed with tables, chairs and the like that they had to make their way through them single file. Dead hornets crackled, paper-dry, underfoot. A ripe scent of mildew and decay filled the air, and dust rose in clouds from their passage, making Lia sneeze repeatedly.

"Where are we going?" It was the question she had asked repeatedly during the drive from her house, and Great-Aunt Jeanne had not yet answered it, not really. "Someplace wonderful," she had said at one point. "You'll find out when we get there," another time. Well, Lia thought, someplace wonderful might describe the outside of this old mansion, but the wonderfulness had all stopped at the door. And now they were here, and she wasn't finding out any more than she knew before.

On the other hand, she thought, as another mummified insect corpse crunched like fresh popcorn beneath her foot, I don't think I *want* to find out.

They ascended a narrow staircase to a second floor that consisted of a mezzanine hallway lined with alternating doors and huge oil paintings. The grim-faced men and women in the paintings seemed to be sternly evaluating Lia. She hurried along behind her aunt, sure that the eyes in the picture were shifting to follow her, like she had seen them do once in a spooky cartoon. In a matter of moments the trip had changed from an adventure to an ordeal. She had been nervous being left in Great-Aunt Jeanne's charge ever since the old woman had taken her to that voodoo ceremony three years ago. She didn't remember too much of it—mostly she just remembered being scared and crying. Her parents had not let Great-Aunt Jeanne babysit her since that time, but this had been an emergency: One of Mama's sisters had taken sick down in Jeanerette, and there had been no one else to watch Lia.

Lia lagged behind, watching her aunt move ponderously and determinedly down the open hallway. Most of the time the old woman was sweet to her grand-niece, and always had a piece of hard rock candy in one of the pockets of her shapeless patterned dress when she came to visit. Ever since being taken to the *rada*, however, Lia had on occasion seen Great-Aunt Jeanne watching her with a frightening intensity. On this day her parents had hardly driven out of sight before the old woman had put Lia in the old rattletrap Ford and brought her here. The promise of a sno-ball cone at the end of the day had been enough to quell any misgivings Lia had had about the trip, at least up to now. But as she followed her aunt's enormous *derrière* down the hall, listening to the stentorian breathing that sounded far too loud in the quiet old house, she was beginning to suspect that it would take more than a sno-cone to make her feel good about whatever was about to happen. A *lot* more.

They passed three or four closed doors, huge portals made of dark wood, surrounded by massive lintels and jambs. The doors seemed twelve feet high at least, massive barriers protecting the world from whatever unnameable horrors might lurk in those rooms.

It seemed to take forever to get to the door at the end of the hall. This one was not closed—a gap of about six inches showed nothing but hungry darkness within. As Great-Aunt Jeanne slowly pushed the door open—Lia was surprised that it did not creak, but instead swung silently and smoothly on oiled hinges—the air in the room puffed out, and Lia wrinkled her nose. It was oddly dry, given the humidity outside, and laced with the scent of sour milk. And it was *cold*, colder than it had any right to be in an un-air-conditioned house in Louisiana in September.

Great-Aunt Jeanne took her hand. "Come, child," she said in that reedy voice of hers, "you'll thank me for this one day." She pulled her niece forward.

That settled it, as far as Lia was concerned. Every child knows that "you'll thank me for this one day" is Parentese for "This will hurt you *so* much more than it hurts me." Lia put every bit of willpower she had into somehow welding her dirty canvas sneakers to the floor, feeling the downy hair on her arms and the back of her neck rise. Another cool zephyr, like a monstrous exhalation, washed over her. She could taste fear in her mouth—hot as blood, sharp as copper. There was *something* in that room, something not quite alive but not entirely dead either. Lia didn't question how that knowledge came to her, just as she didn't question its clear and simple truth. She could feel her spine icing up, just like the air conditioner in Papa's car when he ran it too long, and she tried to pull free of her aunt's hand, a thin inarticulate sound of protest bubbling from her throat. If she could just break Great-Aunt Jeanne's hold, if she could somehow flee this dark and spooky maze of a house, back out to the hot open air full of the whir of June bugs and the scent of red dirt. . . .

But that didn't happen, of course. For Lia was only a child, and Great-Aunt Jeanne was a grown-up, and the grown-ups *always* won. If she had learned nothing else in her eight years on this planet, she had learned that.

The door swung wide, and Great-Aunt Jeanne entered the dark chamber with Lia in tow.

The room was dark with more than night. It was the darkness of the grave, seen from inside while you scream and scratch frantically at the lid, driving wooden splinters deep under your fingernails. The darkness inside one of those old refrigerators that parents were always afraid their kids would suffocate in, back when Lia's mom had been a little girl. The darkness of the lowest, bottommost unexplored levels of Injun Joe's cave. The faint light from the hallway behind her didn't even think about trying to encroach.

Lia was beyond horror now. She no longer made any whines of protest, and her feet moved forward in jerky, mechanized steps without any discussion with her brain. The smell of clotted milk made her stomach roil, and the clammy air seemed to enfold her. I'm in the old refrigerator, she thought, trapped in the old refrigerator, and guess what, Mom? The little light doesn't stay on.

If Great-Aunt Jeanne noticed the smell or the chill in the air she gave no sign of it. She leaned forward, still holding onto Lia's hand, and fumbled with her free hand. Lia heard a *click* and light appeared—not much light, only the dim yellow illumination of a table lamp beside a bed—but enough.

Enough to make Lia wish for the dark again.

She and Great-Aunt Jeanne were standing on one side of an imposing four-poster bed, piled high with quilts and a thread-bare chenille spread. Lying in the bed, propped slightly up by a multitude of pillows, was an old black woman.

"Old" did not do her justice. She could easily be the oldest living thing in the world, Lia thought. And probably the fattest, too. She was enormously, grotesquely fat, her bulk pushing up the mound of quilts almost higher than Lia's head. Her arms lay on the covers, each as big around and about the same color as the two dachshunds Great-Aunt Jeanne kept back in her house in Loreauville. Her big hands were gnarled, arthritic, with knuckles like pecans.

Her face. . . .

Lia didn't want to look at her face, but something about it drew her gaze. The old woman's head lay on the topmost pillow (the pillowcase was of a flowered pattern, so faded that Lia was unsure if she was imagining the blossoms and stems or not). It was the color of an old tobacco stain, bloated and flabby and somehow sunken as well, like a jack-o'-lantern that has gone to rot. Her lips and cheeks sloped in around toothless gums.

Her eyes were the worst. The lids were open, and Lia could see the opalescent cataracts that covered them, barely revealing the dark pupils beneath. She *had* to be blind, even an eight-year-old girl could tell that, but her eyes did not stare, unseeing, in one direction—instead they roved, like restless cameras, swinging this way and that independently of each other. Sometimes one or both of them would roll up and back under the lid, and Lia had the awful feeling that the old woman was somehow staring into her own head when this happened.

Her adult self, looking back on this memory, relying on the training she'd had as an officer of the law, recognized this now as a sign of stroke or other traumatic brain damage. As a child she had only known that the old woman's eyes were terrifying. She was so frightened at this point that she had not even noticed Great-Aunt Jeanne releasing her hand. She could run now if she wanted to. But at the moment of this realization one of those awful eyes, filmy and streaked like a half-cooked egg, turned in her direction, and its sightless gaze held Lia in place more securely than chains.

Dimly, as from a great distance, she felt warm wetness run down her leg and puddle around her shoe. The knowledge that she had peed herself did not cause her even faint embarrassment.

The old woman's sightless gaze ran over her, hot as a laser in the otherwise cold room. When she spoke, it was not to Lia but to her aunt. Her voice came with difficulty, like bubbles bursting in a miasmal swamp.

"C'est l'enfant dont tu m'as parlé?"

"Oui," Great-Aunt Jeanne replied. "Je l'ai amené pour votre bénédiction. Elle a une forte volonté, bien qu'elle ne le sache pas encore."

Lia did not understand the words; she only knew they were in French. Her parents could speak it, but she had heard them do so only rarely. Her mother had told her how the teachers in public school would punish her for not using English, making her write "I will not speak French" a hundred times on the blackboard. She knew Great-Aunt Jeanne and the old woman were talking about her, but that was all.

Then the old colored woman grabbed her wrist in one cold, arthritic hand.

Lia shrieked in raw terror. She struggled to free herself, but the ancient crone held her firmly. She drew the young girl closer. The sour milk smell washed over Lia, causing her stomach to churn. Great-Aunt Jeanne watched impassively as the old woman reached over with her other hand and touched Lia's forehead, lightly sketching a sign on it. A blessing or a curse; no way to tell.

"*Manassia*," she whispered, and those blind eyes seemed to burn behind their translucent film. And with that, eight-year-old Lia reached her limit. The waiting darkness rushed in, and the room, Great-Aunt Jeanne and the horrible old woman mercifully faded away. . . .

xxxi

POYDRAS,
RIVERVIEW
TRAILER COURT
AND METAIRIE,
LOUISIANA

MARCH 26, 1998

April Delaney drove carefully through the rain, hoping, as she did every day during the four-mile drive between the Piggly-Wiggly in Poydras and the Riverview Trailer Court, that her car would make the trip without breaking down. One of the wipers had quit working yesterday; thank God it was the one on the passenger side. The other one squeaked with every pass of its blade over the glass, a grating, fingernails-down-a-blackboard sound that set her teeth on edge. There was never any money to fix things like these. One of these days the car would refuse to start, and April didn't know what she would do then.

Though still afternoon, it was dark enough from the storm that she switched on the headlights. One was out of alignment and shone more toward the sky than the road, but by putting them on high beam she was able to see well enough through the rain.

She looked at her watch and increased her speed a little. Her cousin Meg was watching Soukie at the trailer, and Dennis, Meg's husband, expected her to be home and have dinner on the table by seven at the latest.

A glare of headlights in the rear view mirror attracted her attention. A car had come up behind her and was following close enough to make her a little nervous. April thought about pulling over and letting the car pass, but the turn onto the dirt road leading out to Riverview was coming up. Whoever was behind her could wait until she turned off.

She put on her blinker, slowed and turned. To her slight surprise the car behind her turned too. Probably Old Man Rubideaux coming back from a beer run, April told herself.

The muddy road forced her to slow down even more; soon she and the other car were barely doing fifteen miles an hour. Ten minutes down the road the car behind her abruptly sped up, pulling alongside her. She had just enough time to realize it was Harris Beaumont's pickup when it slammed into the rear panel of the driver's side, forcing her off the road.

April screamed as she lost her grip on the wheel. The car slewed sideways through the mud and came to a stop, half on the road and half in the tall, lank palmetto grass. The pickup stopped as well, blocking her car. April grabbed the collar shift and rammed it into reverse, trying to back up, but the tires spun helplessly in the mud and grass. Through the rain-streaked windshield she could see Harris getting out of the truck's cab. He tossed an empty beer bottle away as he tottered toward her.

She opened the door to run, but it was too late—he was there. He grabbed the door and pulled it the rest of the way open, then half-bent, half-fell into the front seat on top of her.

April screamed again, trying to kick at him with both feet, but the steering wheel was in the way. Then his weight was on top of her, crushing her into the threadbare fabric of the car seat.

He said nothing. His breath, reeking of beer and cheap whiskey, nauseated her. He held her down with one forearm across her upper chest while he pulled clumsily at the snap of her pants with the other. She kept screaming, hoping desperately that someone might hear her, all the while knowing that they were a good mile and a half from the trailer park, with no one closer than that. She fought him as best she could with one arm, the other arm being pinned under him. Harris managed to rip her pants open and raised himself up slightly so as to have room to pull them down. She tried to arch her back and throw him off her, but there was no place for him to go. He ripped at her blouse, tearing it and the brassiere beneath it partly away, exposing one breast.

She screamed again, louder. He stopped tearing at her clothes long enough to hit her with his closed fist on the side of her head. "Shut up, bitch," he muttered thickly. April saw stars and her vision darkened. While she was momentarily stunned he tore savagely at her pants, ripping them along one side and pulling them down around her ankles. Then he fumbled at his belt.

April knew she only had a few seconds left to do something. His forearm still rested across her collarbone. She arched her upper back, causing his arm to slip toward her face. She thrust her head forward and sank her teeth into the grimy flesh. It tasted of sweat and machine oil.

Harris howled and reared back, freeing both of April's arms for a second. She shoved at him with all the strength she could muster, pushing him out the partly open door. He sprawled in the rain, his pants open and sagging around his hips.

April turned and clawed for the door handle on the passenger side. The door swung open and she slid out into a morass of mud and soaking wet grass. Her pants were bunched up around her ankles; rather than try to pull them back on, she simply kicked them the rest of the way off, along with her shoes. Naked except for her torn blouse, she ran around the front of the car toward Harris's truck.

She heard him bellow with rage behind her, heard him struggling to get to his feet, but the combination of the booze and his sagging pants was making that difficult. April could see white clouds of exhaust puffing from the truck's tailpipe—he'd left the engine running, no doubt for a quick getaway.

She slid in behind the wheel, put it in gear and stomped on the gas. The wheels spun for a moment in the wet earth, causing her heart to surge toward her throat. In the driver's side mirror she saw Harris coming slowly toward her. He put a hand against the left rear fender, steadying himself; then he spun around and fell to his knees as the truck roared forward, fishtailing wildly, so quickly that April almost lost control of it as it sped up the narrow muddy lane.

Lia lay on her couch, sipping hot tea and watching the rain. Her trip down memory lane had left her as exhausted as a fifty-mile hike. Even now she could feel the helpless rage and resentment at her aunt for taking her there. She had been hysterical for two days after the ordeal, and neither her parents nor she had ever spoken to Great-Aunt Jeanne again.

Quit being such a baby, Lia told herself sternly. Okay, the visit to Belvedere Plantation had been a horrible thing to endure as a child, but it was far in the past now. She was a grown woman, and she had no business staying at home if she wasn't sick; there were people depending on her. She felt guilty at canceling her appointments.

The guilt galvanized her. She had to check on April, at least; the woman was working so hard to turn her life around. She deserved better from her probation officer than this. Lia got up, the movement bringing a sleepy protest from Toulouse. She wasn't even dressed yet. She pulled off her nightgown and stood before the bedroom closet mirror, checking her stomach to make sure that the marks hadn't come back. Then she put on jeans and a light sweater.

She called April's number and hung up after the ninth ring. It was entirely possible that the woman was at work; April worked varied hours at the supermarket, she knew. Lia opened her briefcase and checked April's schedule for this week. Today she worked ten to three.

Abruptly she decided to take a chance and drive out to April's trailer park. It was as much to get out of the house as to check on her case; she had over the past few hours developed a raging case of cabin fever.

As she prepared to leave the house Toulouse leaped on her shoulder and clung to her hair, whimpering slightly. "Want to come along?" she asked the little monkey. She sometimes took her pet with her on outings; he was well-behaved in the car. Soukie would love to see him again, Lia knew. And, she admitted to herself, his company was comforting today.

It was more than twenty miles as the crow flies from Metairie to Eastern St. Bernard Parish; it would be getting dark by the time she got there, given the traffic at this time of day. If they weren't there, Lia told herself, she would leave a note on April's door.

It wasn't the most relaxing of drives, what with the rain beating down and the congested roads, but she still felt better being out and doing something. She didn't want to admit it to herself, but a big part of her decision to go had to do with a growing uneasiness at being in the house as daylight waned.

She drove through Bywater and the funky "Lower Nine" netherworld east of Faubourg Marigny, past miles of cheap shotgun houses, Creole cottages and post-war bungalows. Most of them were rundown and dilapidated from years of neglect, but now and then she would see a house freshly painted or tricked out with gleaming aluminum siding, the yards behind the chain link fences green and freshly mown. Her route took her southeast on St. Claude Avenue, past redneck bars and cheap seafood joints, to the blue-collar bedroom community of Chalmette, where the street name changed to St. Bernard Highway. Buildings and houses began to thin out after that, and she drove past riverside grazing land and tiny fishing communities seen dimly through a gray haze of rain.

The trailer park where April and Soukie lived was out near the Chalmette Petrochemical Refinery—a huge, intricate construction of pipes, cracking machinery, smokestacks and slurry tanks that sat in the swamplands northeast of Poydras. It was evening by the time Lia got there, and the refinery was illuminated by blazing halogen lights and frequent eruptions of smoke and fire. It looked, through the curtain of rain, like some bizarre alien mother ship squatting on several acres out in the middle of nowhere.

She pulled off the county road and into the muddy oval lined with trailers. April's was one of the best-looking; even so, Lia thought, it wasn't likely to grace the cover of *Mobile Home Monthly*. It was raining harder now than it had all day. Lia saw that April's battered old Chevy wasn't parked on her lot, and sighed. Toulouse stood on his hind legs and peered over the dashboard, nose twitching. Lia scratched the back of his neck. "Looks like we came a long way for nothing," she told the monkey.

She had intended to leave a note, but there was no awning over the door, and the rain was coming down hard enough to turn any scribbled message left there to illegible pulp in a matter of minutes. "Well, shit," Lia murmured. She ran a hand through her hair, fingers tugging with difficulty through the snarled red ringlets—her hair always turned into an unmanageable thicket of curls in weather like this. Mostly because she didn't feel like turning around and driving back just yet, Lia took a brush from her purse and made an attempt to work its bristles through her tangled locks. Toulouse, fascinated as always by her hair, scrambled up on one shoulder to help.

There was another car parked in front of the power pole, she noticed; an old green Volkswagen. Lia remembered that April's cousin usually baby-sat Soukie while April worked. Perhaps this was her car. As it grew darker she noticed there were lights on in the trailer. She absently plucked at the brush until it was clean, then opened the door a crack to drop the handful of hair on the ground.

It was at that moment, before she could close the door, that she heard, faint but unmistakable over the drumming of the rain on the car roof, a woman's scream.

xxxii

RIVERVIEW
TRAILER COURT AND
SISTERS OF GRACE
HOSPITAL,
NEW ORLEANS,
LOUISIANA

MARCH 26, 1998

April was in sight of the trailer park sign when the truck went into a skid that she couldn't pull out of. The front end hit the sign post, catapulting her forward and slamming her forehead against the steering wheel. For the second time within the hour she saw stars. She slumped back in the seat, staring with unfocused eyes at the twinkling lights in the rear view mirror, and might have passed out completely had she not been revived by a surge of adrenalin when she realized she was seeing the lights of a car approaching from behind. She recognized the askew beam of the right headlight.

He had followed her in her own car.

April slid out of the cab, sinking to her ankles in the cold mud. She ran, heedless of the pebbles that bruised her soles, toward the first row of trailers. But her car was alongside her in moments, blocking her escape before she could reach them.

Harris slammed out of the Chevrolet, weaving toward her with murder in his expression. She realized it didn't matter that they were no longer isolated; he meant to kill her and in his drunken rage he didn't care who saw it happen. Naked and defenseless as she was, she didn't have a chance of survival.

She did the only thing she could do. She screamed, as loud as she could, before he reached her.

Lia heard the scream, heard the desperation in the voice, and was out of the car and running toward its source before she was even fully aware of her actions. She moved so quickly that Toulouse had no time to leap back into the dry safety of the car, and instead clung to her shoulder, chattering and scolding indignantly as she ran.

Through the rain she could dimly see a car parked sideways across the road just beyond the court's entrance, and two figures—a man and a woman—struggling. She heard shouting from behind her, but did not look back to see who it was. Her purse was back in the car—not that it mattered, since she hadn't brought her gun this time. A routine visit to one of her best cases was not a situation one normally packed heat for.

She glanced desperately around for something to use as a weapon. There was nothing; just a gray expanse of mud and scraggly grass. No one had come from any of the trailers to help; either the park was deserted, or—more likely—no one wanted to get involved.

Well, she was involved now, Lia thought grimly, like it or not. She was within ten feet of the two by now and could recognize the woman, even though her face was bloody and she was almost naked—it was April. The man—dark greasy hair, stocky build, stubble—had one hand around her throat and was trying to get a grip with the other. As Lia ran up he saw her, hurled April to the ground and turned toward her. She saw the scarlet rims to his eyes. Blood and booze; a real bad combination.

She couldn't have asked for a worse set of circumstances—slippery ground, rain, an opponent easily twice her strength. She needed all the help she could get. And so she did the only thing she could think of to gain a bit of an edge: She plucked Toulouse from her shoulder and hurled him at the man.

The little monkey seemed to understand what was expected of him. He wrapped arms and legs around the man's head, fastening his teeth into an ear. The man screamed and struck at Toulouse with both fists. Toulouse quickly sprang free before one of those blows broke some bones.

Another figure flashed past Lia; she saw a black woman who had to be April's cousin run to the fallen woman and grab her by the shoulders, pulling her away from danger. By this time Lia was directly in front of April's attacker.

He lunged at her, right hand outstretched. She pivoted to her left, then blocked and seized his wrist with her left hand. At the same time she grabbed the back of his neck with her other hand and pushed down while yanking his arm up.

It worked just the way it was supposed to; he pinwheeled in a half flip, landing on his back with a splat of mud and water.

She had hoped it would knock the wind out of him, but no such luck. He was down, but not out. The move had turned Lia so that she was facing away from April, looking back the way she had come. And she saw, standing in the road, staring in shock and horror, April's daughter Soukie. She must have followed when April's cousin ran out to help.

She was less than three feet from April's attacker.

He looked up and saw her. Lunged up on his knees with an inarticulate cry of rage, reaching with one hand to grab her arm—

Lia heard herself screaming *"No!"*—a long drawn out cry that seemed to reverberate. She tried to move forward, to grab the guy, but suddenly the air was the same viscous consistency as the mud beneath her feet. She felt blood pounding in her head as she strained with all her might—

It seemed then that someone had fired a flare gun nearby. The air was suddenly charged with a bright actinic glare: she could see millions of raindrops, each one separate and distinct, frozen on their fall from heaven to earth. Lightning, she thought . . . and surely it was thunder that followed immediately, even though the groundshaking rumble sounded eerily like the laughter of some grimly amused giant or elemental. It had to be thunder, because if it were laughter, that would surely mean she had lost her mind. . . .

But a thunderbolt didn't explain the vision Lia saw against the clouds, stark in the bright light, frozen like those myriad drops of rain: the vision of a gigantic gaunt man, towering as high as the clouds themselves, wearing black vestments, a stovepipe hat and small round dark glasses. She could see the clouds dimly through him, and it seemed, as he moved, that his tattered coat was full of stars. Over his right shoulder he bore a short, massive cross carved from black wood, and with his left hand he seemed to be reaching down, down from the very heavens . . . Lia felt a sudden surge of vertigo. Was he reaching *down* from above or *up* from a pit of infinite depth? He seemed to shift perspective bizarrely, as though he somehow existed *outside* the three dimensions she knew.

His fingers, black as a bog at midnight, each as round as a barrel, moved with strange gentleness toward the man, who cowered down with a cry of fear, pressing his face into the mud in a blind and futile effort of escape. But there was no escape. The index finger, translucent yet heavy as fate, caressed his back. A shudder ran through him, and then all movement ceased.

And then the rain was falling again, pounding down on them harder than ever, and Lia found herself looking into the eyes of the child, April's daughter, whose eyes were round with solemnity and knowledge, and no sign whatsoever of fear. . . .

April's cousin stayed back at the trailer and put Soukie to bed—the child had gone to sleep surprisingly easily, considering what she had seen. Lia had left Toulouse crouched on the kitchenette counter, lapping at a bowl of Coke and pausing only to glare at Lia as she left; he had apparently not yet forgiven her for throwing him at Beaumont.

Lia accompanied April to Sisters of Grace Hospital, where the resident on call, a woman a couple of years younger than Lia, examined her. Save for cuts and bruises, April was unharmed. The story they had given the police was that Harris Beaumont had assaulted April Delaney and then dropped dead in his tracks, no doubt due to heart failure or some other natural cause to be determined.

On the way to the hospital in the ambulance, April had spoken of what they had seen. "It was Baron Samedi, *Guédé Nimbo* himself, come to save my child and me," she said. She looked at Lia as though challenging her to dispute the statement. Baron Samedi, she had said, was the lord of the graveyard, ruler of the *guédés*, one of the most powerful of all the *loas*. The keeper of the dead, the ferryman who controls the passage of souls to the afterlife.

Lia had said nothing. She didn't want to believe what she had seen, but there was no way she could deny it—the memory was too vivid, too *real*. A voodoo god had stretched out his hand and saved their lives by taking Harris Beaumont's. Either that, or she was ready for a Thorazine sponge bath.

"I *told* you my Soukie was special," April went on. "She got the power within her, the power to call the *loa*. She their chosen one."

Lia listened to the words, unwilling to believe them, but unable to see any other choice. If she alone had seen the apparition, then it would be obvious that she needed a long rest in a butterfly net. But April and her cousin had seen it as well, and neither of them seemed to have doubts about their sanity.

She thought of the nightmare, the fading welts on her skin where the dream demon had torn the child of mist from her. Had she somehow, in the dream, sensed the power of the child—April's child?

She didn't know. She didn't know anything anymore. In the space of an instant she had slipped sideways out of the rational world and into an entirely different one, a world in which ancient pagan gods came at the call of a little child. A world in which everything she knew, everything she believed in, was now suspect.

A world in which she most definitely did not belong. And how, Lia wondered, was she ever going to get back to the world she knew?

For two days after the incident in the alley Dave kept to himself, venturing out, with only a couple of exceptions, no further than the nearest convenience store to buy food. He was convinced that at any moment the police would be pounding his door down and arresting him for murder. His imagination alternated that vision with an even worse one: some of Sangre's men, associates of the one he had killed, torturing him with household appliances for revenge. But the worst scenario by far was one that came to him only in nightmares: the dead man looming over his bed in the midnight hour, red-rimmed eyes glowing like coals in Hell, brains still oozing from his splintered skull. . . .

The first trip he had made was on the day after what had happened (he still had a hard time, even in his own mind, using words like "killing" or "murder"). He had gone over to Errol Mandeville's office to pay off the "vig," as Errol termed it, Errol had accepted the money, patted Dave on the cheek and told him he was a good boy. "My advice—stick to music from now on," he had added. "You ain't really cut out for a life of crime."

You'd be surprised, Dave had thought.

The second excursion had been down to the river's edge around three in the morning. He had stuffed the dead man's wallet into a large mayonnaise jar and filled the glass container with gravel and rocks, then hurled it as far as he could into the muddy depths. It would stay down there until the end of time. There was no way he could be linked with the crime now, he told himself.

There had been nothing on the news or in the paper concerning the discovery of the body; evidently the death of a drug dealer was not notable news in the Quarter. Despite all this, Dave still couldn't bring himself to venture outside. He even missed a gig at a local club, much to the baffled annoyance of his fellow band members.

He didn't call K.D. because he didn't know how to explain his continued presence in New Orleans. When he finally came up with a plausible lie to tell her—that he'd sold some of his other rare jazz albums to pony up the cash—he realized that the probably could have done that for real if he'd only thought of it soon enough. The irony was both stunning and depressing.

Finally, after four days, he called K.D., catching her on her way out the door for the hospital. She seemed genuinely glad to hear from him, and suggested he come over to Sisters of Grace so that they could grab a cup of coffee and he could tell her all about it.

The last place on earth Dave wanted to be at this point was

a hospital—well, maybe the second to last place if the list included a cemetery. But he wanted to see K.D. again. The only subject that had been on his mind as much as—maybe even more than—the murder had been her. When he had been ready to run for his life, the thought of leaving her had been as painful as leaving his companions in the band and the city itself. He didn't know if how he felt qualified as love, but it obviously rated higher than just friendship.

And so, a couple of hours after dark, he took a cab over to the hospital to see her.

The last time Dave had been in an emergency room was over seven years ago, up in Albany. He had poured a cold drink into a glass just taken from a dishwasher and the change in temperature had caused it to shatter, leaving a cut that ran the length of his palm and required numerous stitches. He remembered the place as very similar to this one. Walking through the entrance, the glass doors hissing open with startling quickness, he could feel the tension of the people within, both patients and practitioners. It was like the highest pitch of a tuning fork, more felt than heard.

Dave told the clerk he was here to see K.D. Wilcox, then sat down in the waiting room between a man with a bloodstained handkerchief pressed against his forehead and a woman who stared vacantly at the wall and occasionally produced a deep, phlegmy cough that sounded like there was industrial waste in her lungs. She made no attempt to cover her mouth when she did this, and after a few minutes Dave prudently moved to another seat near the Coke machine.

K.D. came and got him after about ten minutes. She led him into the trauma ward, past the gleaming bays, some with people lying on gurneys, others empty, to a small nurses' station at the end of the hall. "Want some coffee? Tastes lousy, but it's hot."

"That'd be great." He watched her move down the hall, her stethoscope slung back over her shoulder and her long dark hair, pulled into a topknot ponytail, tickling her collar. It wasn't hard to be the best-looking person in a room full of gunshot and knife victims, but K.D., in Dave's opinion, would outshine the competition in any arena. Just seeing her made him realize how lonely and frightened he'd been in the last few days.

When she came back, she would have to lie to her. How could he do that? Dave asked himself. If he really was falling in love with this woman, and if she felt even slightly the same about him, how could he embark on what might be a long and intense relationship based on a lie? And not just a trivial lie. Let's face facts here, he told himself. He wasn't fibbing about something relatively innocuous such as going out with someone else. He was lying because he had murdered someone.

Take the long view, he thought. You and K.D. fall in love, get married, have kids. Forty years from now you're still waking up in a cold sweat because your family might learn that you took a human life. Never mind self defense, never mind the guy was an asshole who no doubt would have killed you. Probably a good lawyer could plead it down to manslaughter. It doesn't matter. The bottom line is, a man is worm food because of you.

There's always a balance to things, Dave thought. In music, in health, in everything. You're in severe karmic receivership, boy, and soon—maybe not today, maybe not tomorrow, as Bogie said, but soon—that wheel's going to come trundling back and roll right over you.

He felt himself growing angry. All right, he challenged himself silently, what's the alternative? Confess? Get serious. She forgave you for borrowing money to pay off a stupid debt, to a bookie . . . does that mean she's willing to overlook the fact that you literally bashed someone's brains out? Not likely. You've got most of your life still ahead of you, you've got a career doing what you love, you've got—maybe—a beautiful woman who, let's face it, stands to inherit more money than you could carry with a forklift . . . you're going to throw all that away because some jagoff pusher is dead? It's not like you're ever going to kill anyone again. You probably wouldn't step on a spider at this point. Why in God's name would you trash all that?

Just because it's the right thing to do?

At this point he saw K.D. coming back with two Dixie cups of steaming coffee. With her was a woman who looked closer to his own age, tall and striking, with flaming red hair kinked in a mass of curls. She looked like she'd been out in the rain recently, and she'd done some trekking in the mud as well, to judge by her shoes. The two were deep in conversation.

"I don't see any reason why she can't go," K.D. was saying as they came within earshot. "Though you might want to make sure someone stays with her tonight; she's still pretty shocky."

"I was planning to," the other one said. She looked tired and wrung out, Dave thought. K.D. evidently thought so too, because she said, "Make sure you get some rest. You had a pretty hard time too."

"Thanks," the redhead said. "It was pretty . . . unsettling."

"Tackling someone on Blood can be hairy. We had a guy here last week. . . ." She shuddered. "You wouldn't believe me if I told you."

"That's him. Dead man walking. How'd you know about it?"

"Enriqué Hermosa?"

"It was related to one of my cases."

K.D. took a gulp of coffee, seemingly not minding the heat.

"That fucking Sangre and his street shit. We've been getting a ton of Blood cases in here over the last two weeks."

By this time they'd reached Dave. K.D. handed him his coffee. "Lia, this is Dave Cummings; he's a musician. Dave, Lia St. Charles," she said. "She's a police officer."

Dave felt his stomach fall into a bottomless pit. He barely avoided spilling scalding coffee on his shoes.

"Probation-parole," Lia St. Charles corrected her. "I'm with the Department of Corrections, not the police."

"Right, sorry." K.D. squinted at Dave. "You okay? You look like your blood pressure just dropped ten points."

Dave sipped at his coffee, holding it with both hands. "I'm fine," he said. "Low blood sugar, I guess."

K.D. shook St. Charles's hand. "Good luck with her. They'll sign her out up front." She dug a business card out of her pocket and gave it to St. Charles. "That's my pager. Call me if you've got any questions about her."

St. Charles nodded, took the card and handed K.D. one of her own. "If you think of anything else we need to know about April." Then she moved off down the corridor.

"I don't know who was more shook up," K.D. said, watching her go, "the assault case she brought in or her." She took another drink of coffee, glanced at the business card and tucked it into her pocket. Then she sat down on the desk and looked expectantly at Dave. "So, tell me all about it. How'd you get out of this mess with your kneecaps intact?"

Dave was quiet for a long moment. He looked at her eyes, saw the curiosity and expectancy in them, and the obvious relief that everything had worked out okay for him. The care that was evident, care for him.

"I don't know why I didn't think of it earlier," he said. "I just sold off some of my other albums to collectors I know. . . ."

V isitor for you, LaFitte."

Shane rolled over and sat up on his bunk, staring in surprise at the guard standing outside the cell door. Who would come all the way up to Angola to visit him? His first thought was that it was Sangre, but he could see no reason for that. The man was too practical to waste time coming to gloat, and if he wanted to have Shane assassinated he certainly wouldn't do it in person.

But who else could it be? He had made no friends and few acquaintances during his brief time outside. Well, there was only one way to find out.

When they led him into the conference room his surprise

turned to astonishment, for sitting on the other side of the thick wire-mesh-and-glass partition was Lia St. Charles.

For one of the very few times in his life, Shane LaFitte was completely taken aback. The guard had to nudge him forward to take his seat opposite her. He did so slowly, watching the woman. She looked like she'd gone through a recent and considerable shock, he thought. There were dark circles under her eyes and a haggard, haunted look in them.

She hesitated for a moment, then leaned close to the speaker plate. "What really happened, LaFitte?"

"What do you mean?"

She slammed a hand down on the formica tabletop. "You know what I mean," she said, her voice low and intense. "Did you kill your wife? Yes or no?"

Shane held her gaze with his own, and something in it made him decide to tell her the whole truth. "Yes—and no. Mal Sangre held my *ti bon ange*—my will, my conscience—in his control. I had no choice but to obey him."

"What are you saying? That he made you some kind of zombie?"

"In a sense. If it helps your understanding to think of it that way, then yes."

She looked steadily into his eyes for a long moment, then leaned back as though suddenly drained. "I must be nuts," she said, half to herself. "I must be out of my fucking mind."

Shane said nothing; he merely waited. Waited, and tried not to hope.

"The whole drive up here," she continued, "I kept asking myself why I was doing this. I still don't know. But I had to look you in the face again, to find out why it seems so goddamn important that I believe you."

"It's important because it's the truth."

"I know," St. Charles said dully. "God help me, I believe you now."

His throat was dry. "Can you get me out of here?"

She gave a single bark of laughter. "How? Tell the DA's office that the case should be reopened because you were under an evil spell? I'd wind up on the front page of the *Enquirer* or the *Midnight Star*."

He said, "You've been touched by one of *Les Invisibles*."

She leaned forward again and leveled a finger at him. "LaFitte, if you're somehow responsible for this, if you're fucking with my head some way, I swear to God I'll—"

"No. But I can sense that they've been present for you. And nothing less than a visitation could have changed your mind about me."

She was quiet again, this time for well over a minute. Then, speaking in a voice that was almost a monotone, she told him what had happened to her over the past week—the nightmare, the attempted rape of April Delaney and the subsequent appearance of the Lord of the Dead, who had apparently been summoned by April's daughter.

"I don't have any other explanation for it," she said. "April always said her child was special, was favored by the gods. I never believed her, of course. Now I don't know what to believe."

Shane glanced at the clock; there were only a few minutes left of their time together. "This girl—is she an only child?"

St. Charles frowned. "I don't think so—no, she's not. April had two other children—twins, I think. She gave them up for adoption."

He nodded. "That explains much. She is a *dossu*—a child of power. Twins possess great strength in the Spirit World, and on occasion the child born after them shares that gift."

She took a deep breath, blew it out slowly. "That makes about as much sense as anything else I've heard recently. I wish to God I could convince myself that I was hallucinating somehow, but. . ."

He nodded, remembering his own initial experience with the *loa*. "It's a tremendous shock to see fantasy become reality."

"Look . . I'm sorry, LaFitte. I was just doing what they pay me to do. I guess that doesn't help a lot now. . . ."

"It may not," he told her, "but it means something."

St. Charles raised her gaze to his again. "What the hell is Sangre doing? This new drug. . . ."

"Blood, yes. It's a part of his plan." Before he could say any more the guard approached.

"Time, LaFitte."

He leaned forward and said in a quick, low voice, "I'll contact you."

"Let me give you my number . . . it's—"

The guard clapped a hand on his shoulder. "No," he said to her. "Tonight—when you sleep. I'll be there." The guard slid his hand under Shane's arm and pulled him roughly from the chair. "I said time. You deaf?"

He watched her staring at him in open-mouthed astonishment as he was led back to the sally port. Even with her recent experience he knew she was finding what he'd said hard to believe.

As a matter of fact, so did he. He had nothing with which to work the magic of sending; his *asson* had been taken from him long ago. But he had to reach her through the Invisible World. It was essential that she understand.

Even though she could do nothing to help him.

* * *

Yard time; the inmates milled, aimlessly for the most part, around the expanse of hard-packed red dirt and scraggly Bermuda grass. It was surprisingly cool for this late into spring, but Shane enjoyed the crisp breeze against his skin. Layton had said to him once that only the air was free, moving where it would, when it would. He was a prisoner, but as long as he could feel the air caressing him, a small part of him could share that freedom.

He thought about his surprise visit. So Lia St. Charles had finally understood and accepted the truth. Now he had to convince her of the danger that Sangre posed. In his quest for power, the man had delved deeper into the Invisible World than anyone else had dared to do; even a *houngan* of Ducas's skill and power would not expose his mind and soul to the blasphemous knowledge that the *loas*, *guédés*, *seguns* and other entities so jealously protected.

What Sangre did not realize, or more likely, what he refused to accept, was the danger inherent in his quest. The power he sought demanded a steep price. The further he ventured into the abyss, the further behind he left his soul and his sanity. It was a subtle process, one he would not be aware of until, in all probability, it would be too late to remedy.

There was little or no chance that he would have the self-awareness and strength to stop himself. Therefore he had to be stopped, before—

Shane was not sure what warned him, what pulled him from his reverie barely in time to stop the vicious short thrust of the shank—a four-inch blade, he learned later, made from the metal strip off a mattress frame, honed to razor sharpness, the handle wrapped in electrical tape for a firm grip—that lanced toward his belly. He twisted, not quite fast enough to avoid a long shallow cut across his lower ribs, and swung his elbow at the same time toward the face so close to his own. He had no idea who had come at him, got only a blurred impression of features as his arm impacted hard against his attacker's jaw, driving a grunt from the man and throwing him off balance.

Then they were both down, rolling in the iron-rich dirt, Shane grabbing the other man's wrist and stopping the shank's descent just before it ripped into his throat. For a long moment he struggled to hold the blade away from him—and then there was the whine and crack of a bullet striking the ground not three feet away, and then another and another . . . the guards in the nearest tower were firing at them to separate them.

His attacker dropped the makeshift knife and scrambled away from Shane, but not quickly enough—the con screamed in agony as one of the bullets shattered the lower part of the arm that had held the shank. Two guards appeared from nowhere and hauled him to his feet, ignoring his pain-filled curses. Shane recognized him then, with some surprise; René, the ponytailed geek who had tried to cozy up to him earlier.

Another pair of guards turned toward him. He managed to dig his fingers into the dirt and scoop up a fistful of earth before they yanked him roughly upright, one of them twisting his wrist in a painful come-along grip.

"CCR, asswipe," one of the guards grunted in his ear. They shoved him toward the Reception Center building, which also housed Death Row and Close Custody Restriction.

Despite what had happened, Shane found it difficult to repress a grim smile. The guards made no distinction between attacker and attacked; he would be thrown into solitary, and the only reason Sangre's man would not was because he would be in the infirmary.

It was what he wanted, though the way it was accomplished

was not his first choice. Still, this would get him the privacy he so desperately needed. Ironic to think that, in his zeal to finish the job this time, his enemy might have inadvertently given Shane instead the means to gain his freedom.

XXXV

**GARDEN DISTRICT
AND METAIRIE,
NEW ORLEANS,
LOUISIANA**

MARCH 27, 1998

It was dawn when K.D. finished her shift. Dave hung around, keeping out of her way and reading magazines in the waiting room. For a guy who had just survived a brush with the underworld, he seemed rather subdued to her, but she had seen so many different ways that people react under stress that she didn't give it too much thought.

They had breakfast at a bistro not far from her apartment. Dave paid her loan back, thanking her profusely, but seemed otherwise not real big on conversation.

Well, that was okay, she thought. She was just as glad he didn't feel the need to regale her with sparkling, effervescent wit after a long stint in the ER. The assault case that St. Charles had brought in had somewhat depressed her. Obviously below poverty level, working hard to provide as good a life as she could for her daughter, all the odds against her, and if all that weren't bad enough, now she had to be assaulted by some redneck Blood-sucking asshole who couldn't keep his dick in his pants.

Men, K.D. thought sourly. Talk about your necessary evil. Sometimes parthenogenesis seemed like a real workable concept.

Of course, they weren't all bad. One of the ones that wasn't sat across the table from her at this moment. True, he had gotten himself into a rather dangerous situation, but he'd had the sense to get out pretty much on his own, thank God. K.D. felt a wave of affection wash over her as she looked at Dave, who was picking at a crawfish *étouffée*. She felt a familiar tingling deep down in her abdomen. My, my, she thought. Well, it wasn't like she hadn't been toying with the idea since their first date. . . .

He must have felt her gaze; he glanced up. He seemed slightly bewildered by her smile. "Long night," he said.

"I'm used to 'em. I'm not tired."

"Me neither. Hard to believe, after the past couple of days."

He made a gesture with his fork that took in the surroundings. "Nice place."

"I eat here a lot. It's right around the corner from my apartment."

He nodded and took another bite, and K.D. felt a flash of mingled amusement and irritation. Jesus, men could be dense.

"Yep, just a hop, skip and a jump from here," she said. "Nice place; got it all to myself. No roommate. Daddy pays for it." He glanced up at her; she let the smile widen into a grin. "Did I mention that I'm not tired?"

*   *   *

"I guess I was a little slow on the uptake back in the café," he said. The noonday light filled the bedroom with a warm glow. Most of the covers were on the floor, along with their clothes. He was admiring the buttery sheen of the light on the perspiration that coated her thigh.

"You might say that. My next line was going to be, 'Let's go back to my place and fuck.'"

Dave chuckled. "That would've made the old lady at the next table choke on a hush puppy."

"I know. I was glad to avoid having to Heimlich her."

Dave stretched and yawned. It wasn't a particularly original observation, he knew, but—life was funny. A few days ago he had been contemplating running from the mob with only his horn and the clothes on his back; now he was lying in bed beside a beautiful woman, his debts paid, and no worries.

Except, of course, for the small matter of his having committed murder.

He was aware that K.D. was looking at him. "You okay?"

"Me? Yeah . . . why?"

"You just withdrew at warp speed."

"I'm fine. Just . . . thinking."

"I hope you're not upset that I asked you to wear a condom. It's just, you know . . . a little paranoia slops over from the work place."

"Don't be silly. It's not that. . . ." *It's just that I killed a man and stole his wallet, and that's why I'm lying here beside you instead of huddled in some bus depot out in the middle of nowhere. . . .*

"Dave," K.D. said, raising up on one elbow and looking semi-serious, "let me draw your attention to the fact that we just had carnal knowledge of each other. Several times, in fact. I've got the sheet burns to prove it. In most cultures this is considered an intimate thing, so long as money doesn't change hands. People have been known to share their thoughts on occasions like these. What I'm saying is, if there's something on your mind, now is not the time to feel shy."

He grinned uncomfortably. "It's nothing to do with you—"

"Did I say it had to do with me? I wasn't being paranoid, I was being friendly. Concerned." When he didn't reply, she continued, "Think about it for a minute while I go do womanly things." She got up and moved across the bedroom to the bathroom. He watched her pass through a shaft of sunlight from the window, body taut and firm, breasts high, hair spilling down over the muscles in her back. K.D. Wilcox was beautiful, smart, funny, and, if not in love with him, certainly from all indications willing to have a serious affair with him.

But it was very obvious that she was a woman who demanded honesty, who would not be satisfied with anything less than his complete candor. How could he tell her what he had done?

How could he not?

Dave balled a fist and smacked it against the bedsheet. The longer he put it off, the harder it would be to tell her, the more he would live in fear of having her learn the truth by him talking in his sleep or through some inadvertent slip of the tongue. This wasn't the sort of secret burden he could keep to himself forever. That much, at least, he knew about himself.

An image of the man he killed rose up before him, dead eyes staring in sightless accusation through rain that gave the illusion of tears. Dave blinked back tears of his own. Oh Jesus, he thought, what am I gonna do?

As night approached, Lia St. Charles felt herself growing increasingly nervous. During the long drive back from Angola she had tried a thousand times, unsuccessfully, to convince herself that the events of the past two days had been nothing more than some strange fever dream, a hallucination brought on by too much work and stress. But she knew, deep within her gut, that truth was in the experience. Even if April and her cousin had not been there to substantiate what had happened, Lia would know, on some undeniable level, that she had not been imagining things.

Soukie had summoned the *lou*. And the *lou* had killed Harris Beaumont.

And Shane LaFitte was somehow intimately connected to it all.

What had he said before the guard had taken him away? "Tonight—when you sleep. I'll be there."

As evening drew on she felt more and more nervous at the promise in those words. Had LaFitte somehow been responsible for the nightmare she had had, that terrifying dream of mists and blood? Lia knew that a big part of voodoo lore was the priests' supposed ability to project themselves into the Dream World, or the Spirit World, or whatever it was called. Just as the *lous* and the spirits of the dead supposedly could, they could visit someone in their dreams.

Had he done this?

Would he do it tonight?

The outside light grew purple as dusk fell. Lia paced nervously through her house, compulsively checking locks and peering through windows, as though she expected to see LaFitte somehow miraculously appear on her lawn. Toulouse seemed to share her skittishness; the little monkey scampered anxiously about the house, making shrill noises that did nothing to ease her mind.

In addition to her apprehension, Lia felt betrayed. She had

never put the slightest credence in voodoo. To her, all of that harked back to her childhood in Cajun country, to her great-aunt and various other relatives who implicitly believed in such bullshit. She had repudiated all that, moved on, and to have it now rise up before her with undeniable proof of its existence was offensive and disturbing on a very deep level. Even her brothers and her sister at times resorted to charms and hoodoos, on the principle that it couldn't hurt and might help. She remembered her Great-Aunt Jeanne once, when Lia was seven, trying to contact Lia's "other half"—her other sister, who had died at birth—through occult means. Even with the gullibility of a child she had not believed such things could be done.

Now, however, it appeared that she was wrong.

She tried to take her mind off it all by watching some video-tapes. *Arsenic and Old Lace*, *Sullivan's Travels*, *Singing in the Rain*, she couldn't make it through the first ten minutes of any of them. She tried a mystery novel, but after reading the same page three times she gave up on that too.

The clock over the mantle said twenty after nine. Lia usually went to bed before midnight, as she tried to get to her office by eight. Tonight, however, she was seriously thinking of staying up until dawn. But what good would that do? She couldn't go without sleep indefinitely. Sooner or later she would drift off, and then. . . .

She yawned. No matter how fearful of sleep she was, she knew she wasn't going to be able to stay awake much longer. The long drive to and from the prison, coupled with the traumatic events of April's attack, had taken their toll; her body needed rest.

She put it off as long as she could, but eventually she found herself in her bedroom, getting ready for bed as though this were any normal night. A sort of fatalism came over her as she brushed her teeth and turned down the covers; the mundane preparations were somewhat soothing. But she could not forget the red marks on her stomach that marked where her dream body had been ripped open by the dark, nebulous creature of her nightmare. She had heard it was possible to die of shock from a sufficiently vivid nightmare. Would she prove that tonight?

Lia turned out the light and pulled the covers up to her chin, staring wide-eyed at the dark ceiling. The house seemed to echo and pulse with silence, a sense of waiting. Curled on his bed across the room, Toulouse whimpered slightly in his sleep. Supposedly animals could sense occult presences far more easily than people could. . . .

The only thing that was keeping her from full-blown hysteria was a sense, unsupported but no less solid, that Shane LaFitte was not her enemy. That somehow they were on the same side, that he was her ally against a foe much more dangerous than anything she had ever imagined.

It was cold comfort.

Ridiculous, she told herself, to be afraid of dreams, afraid of the dark. She was a grown woman, whose job often put her into danger. She was not the sort to be fearful of phantoms.

But she did not feel like a grown woman. As she slipped into sleep, Lia St. Charles felt very much like a child, a small child lost and frightened, with no one to show her the way home.

The CCR cell was windowless, lit by a grid-protected hundred-watt bulb that was constantly on. The walls measured ten feet by seven feet. That meant seventy square feet of floor space, which might sound like a lot, Shane reflected, to someone not incarcerated there. But the bunk was just over three feet wide and six and a half feet long, and the iron toilet-and-sink combination took up at least three feet by two feet. That, plus the spaces between the end of the bunk and the wall and behind the commode, left a pathway about seven feet long and three feet wide. Some men, Shane knew, had been confined in that narrow space for months at a time. It was illegal to cage an animal in a zoo that tightly.

He was sentenced to be in these cramped quarters for a week.

With luck it would not take that long to plan some kind of escape. It couldn't, he told himself grimly; if he had figured Sangre's plan right, the next two days were crucial.

The first thing to do was to use his privacy to contact Lia St. Charles again. He doubted there was anything she could do to help him, but he had to try. If nothing else, contacting her in her dreams would give her the final proof that he was telling the truth. It would make her his ally, and once he escaped he would need all the help he could get.

What he was attempting was dangerous. He was no longer under the protection of Legba, and so could easily be prey for the demons and spirits that roamed the Invisible World. But there was nothing he could do about that. He closed his eyes and sat with his back straight, breathing deeply, feeling his muscles relax as he entered the trance state.

Bodily sensations faded, became remote and distant, as he concentrated on sending his *namm*, his spirit self, into the Invisible World. The darkness behind his eyelids was gradually replaced by a roiling gray mist, lit by no discernible source. He looked down at himself and beheld his dream body—a translucent, naked, spectral version of his corporeal self.

He felt pleased. It had been a long time since he had attempted the art of astral projection, and it was gratifying to know that he had not lost his ability to do so. But achieving the Invisible World was only the beginning.

Shane began to walk, striding through the landscape of clouds and mists. He could not feel his feet striking firm ground, and the gray fog about him seemed unchanging, but nevertheless he knew he was making progress. Just as he knew he would eventually find the one he sought.

After an unmeasurable amount of time had passed, he saw her, a dimly shining form ahead in the mists. She turned, sensing his approach by some subtle sense that operated on this plane. She seemed frightened at first, and although she relaxed somewhat when she recognized him, the fear did not leave her eyes entirely. She seemed unconcerned about her astral form's nudity, no doubt due to the surreal, dream-like surroundings.

"You don't seem surprised to see me," Shane said. He knew she could hear him, though his insubstantial form could not speak as his fleshly body could.

"At this point, not much of anything surprises me," St. Charles replied. She looked around nervously. "I've been here before."

"Yes. I can feel the reverberations of it. You were attacked by a *guédé se rouge.*" At her puzzled look, he continued: "A red-eyed devil, the old *papaloi* call them. A vengeful spirit of the dead."

"Vengeful? For what? I've never killed anybody." She shuddered. "Its face—I don't remember what it was, but it looked like—someone I *knew.* . . ."

"It could very well have been. Or not; sometimes they take the images of those close to their victims."

"But *why?* Why single out me?"

"Many of them hate all living beings simply because they are alive. They are drawn to powerful people; they crave that power as the living might crave drugs."

She looked confused. "Powerful? Me? What are you talking about? I'm no witch or sorceress or whatever you call it . . . until a couple of days ago I didn't believe in any of this."

"It's not just mystical power that attracts them. The power of a strong personality, courage, strength of will . . . all these traits are magnets, although the power of magic pulls them the strongest. These spirits are vampires; by draining you of your vitality they can, for a brief time, feel alive again themselves."

"But why *me?*" she asked again. "There are plenty of strong-willed people around who don't get sucked into some weird parallel world every night. I'm not going to wind up here every time I go to sleep, am I?"

Shane did not have an answer for that. He did not know for certain why Lia St. Charles had been claimed by the Invisible World, or why the *guédé* had attacked her, though he strongly suspected it had to do with him. By seeking her aid, he was putting her in danger.

He told her as much. "Sangre will not stop this time until I'm dead. I'm too much a threat to his plans."

"And just exactly what are his plans?"

He didn't answer immediately. A wavering moan, its origin impossible to locate due to the echoing quality of the sound, came faintly out of the mists. St. Charles gasped as she saw, hidden deep within a far-off cloud, a huge, hulking shape, dark and bestial, that slouched momentarily into view. "What the hell is *that?*"

"I don't know." Shane watched the form turn and disappear once more into the mist.

"You don't *know?* I thought you were the tour guide for this theme park!"

"The Invisible World is big—too big to imagine. No priest, no shaman, has explored more than a tiny bit of it. Even Mal Sangre does not know all its secrets, though he may think he does."

Another sound—a gelatinous oozing, as of something huge and plastic—reached them. St. Charles moved closer to Shane.

"Is it safe to be out in the—open—like this?"

"Probably not. Come." He took her hand—the dream-flesh felt cool and oddly insubstantial—and they moved quickly away from the noise.

After a time they stopped. All was silent again, save for the almost inaudible stirring of the mist. St. Charles looked around her. "Is it all like this?"

"Only to the uninitiated. For those who know where and how to look, the Invisible World is a rich and fascinating landscape."

"So glad to hear it. Sounds like the perfect place for a resort, maybe some time-share condos."

"Listen carefully," Shane said. "I don't know how much time we have, and I want you to understand the danger Sangre represents. He has created the drug called Blood for one purpose—to recruit slaves. Once someone is hooked on the drug, his spirit is enslaved to Sangre's will. There are varying degrees of susceptibility—everyone's body chemistry is different—but for the most part, the Blood addicts will perform unquestioningly any task Sangre sets for them."

"So what's his purpose? Is he putting together an army?"

"In a sense. He doesn't plan to physically overpower anyone or any place, as I understand it—at least, not yet. His quest is for magical power. He wants to be on a level with the gods. There are those deep within this plane who will grant him that, but their services are not easily or cheaply bought. Most of the entities who exist on those far levels are what we call *Petro*—of the dark side. They desire pain, fear, and blood in payment for their secrets. And the greater the prize, the greater must be the sacrifice."

"I've done some research since I was paroled, and communed with beings on this plane who have told me much. Sangre, after years of study and work, is close to reaching his goal. But it will require two final blood gifts: a mass sacrifice and an individual one. Those who will make up the mass sacrifice are not important to him; no doubt he will rely on his Blood zombies for fodder. But the individual must be very special. One who is innocent, both physically and spiritually, yet of great untapped power."

He was quiet. She looked at him, and he saw the horror grow in her expression as she realized what he meant. "Soukie. Oh my god, it has to be Soukie!"

He nodded grimly. "It makes perfect sense. From what you've told me, she has the potential for great power within her. And she is a child—an innocent. He could not ask for a better victim."

"What can we do? We've got to stop him!"

"I can do very little," he told her, "as long as I'm incarcerated. And the law is helpless—if they could have arrested him, they would have done so long before now. Sangre is very careful—he makes sure no taint of crime touches him. And his own people are too terrified of his power to betray him."

"I can't just ask the D.A. to release you," St. Charles said. "I need exculpatory evidence—something admissible that either proves your innocence or makes a strong case for it. Magic spells, voodoo gods and so on just don't stand up in court."

"We don't have time to do it within the system. I expect Sangre has everything he needs now for the ceremony that will invest him with the power of the gods. It will take place, I'm almost certain, in the dark of the moon, which is less than forty-eight hours from now."

"Jesus Chri—" she started, but stopped when Shane held up a cautionary hand. "Be careful. What is no more than a minor bit of blasphemy in the real world can have powerful repercussions in this one. You don't want to call us to someone's or something's attention."

She glanced about nervously. "What if he already has Soukie? What can we—?"

"She's in no danger until the time of the ceremony. The sooner I get out of here, the sooner I can do something to stop him."

"Why not just use your magic? Why haven't you done that already? What kept you in Angola for six years when you knew you were innocent, and you knew what Sangre was up to?"

He did not answer for a moment. When he spoke, the words came hard. "Guilt. Not the law's concept of it, but the guilt I felt in my own soul. I . . . killed my wife—killed her with my bare hands." He could not meet her eyes as he spoke. "It's true that Sangre forced me to do it, but still . . . it's not an easy thing to accept about oneself."

There was silence for a moment; Shane could see her thinking about his words. Then he said, "It's not that easy to 'use my magic,' as you put it. I have little of the materials I need in prison. My *asson*—the symbol and repository of much of my power—was taken from me. I can bewilder a guard or two so that they do not see me pass, but I can't fool a roomful of people that way. I intend, when I'm through talking to you, to petition Legba, my *loa-tête*—my patron saint, in other words—to aid me. Legba is the Lord of Crossings, the Opener of the Gate. He may grant my plea to leave this prison for the outside. But all the *loas* are temperamental. I have not propitiated Legba for many years. The gods require attention; failing to get it, they grow dissatisfied, even angry, with their servants."

"Okay," St. Charles said. "All you can do is try. What can I do in the meantime?"

"Nothing. Stay out of Sangre's way. This doesn't concern you—"

"Forget it. You dragged me into this. If Soukie's in danger there's no way I'm not seeing it through."

He knew he would not be able to dissuade her. "I'll contact you when I've escaped."

"I hope you've got a plan that goes beyond escaping. When I wake up, how am I going to know this wasn't just a dream?"

Shane reached out and, with his thumb, quickly sketched a *vévé* on her skin between her breasts: two Xs, side by side. A simplified form of the sign of Aïzan, the First Priestess—an aspect of Legba. They glowed blood red; the only color anywhere to be seen. "That will be there when you wake up," he told her. "May it protect you until I see you next."

He stepped back from her. The mist was beginning to darken around them. Lia St. Charles crossed her arms over her breasts, hugging herself, shivering against a sudden chill in the dampness.

"Be careful, LaFitte," she said. Her voice sounded hollow and far away. "There's too much riding on this for either of us to make a mistake."

"I know," he replied, and realized that he had spoken out loud—he was back in his corporeal body again. He was drenched in sweat and trembling——to remain in the Invisible World for so long had taken a great deal of energy. He needed to rest—but there was one more trial he had to undergo first.

Shane pulled from his pocket a handful of the red yard dirt he had scooped up before the guards had hauled him away. Sitting crosslegged on the cold concrete, he dribbled from his closed fist a tiny stream of dirt, forming a circle about a foot wide. It was preferable to make the *vévé* out of chalk, ashes or flour, but this would suffice. Within the circle, manipulating the trickle of earth with the ease of long practice, Shane inscribed the complex sign of Legba: a cross representing the intersection of the material and spiritual worlds, adorned with arabesques and smaller crosses.

Again he composed himself, breathing evenly, and sent his mind out into the void once more. But this was a different sort of effort—this was a plea, an entreaty. A call to he whom Shane LaFitte had served for so long.

The light overhead grew dim. The walls, so close a moment ago, now seemed infinitely far removed: towering mountains glimpsed dimly at the edges of a darkling plain. Above him iron-gray clouds parted, revealing a firmament of strange stars. A gigantic shape took form against them: an old, stooped man with a *maconte* slung over one shoulder and a walking stick in one hand. Eyes that burned like twin suns peered down at Shane.

Papa Legba—*Maît' Carrefour*, the Gatekeeper—had come.

xxxvii

CHALMETTE AND
LOUISIANA STATE
PENITENTIARY,
LOUISIANA

MARCH 27, 1998

April slept with the lights on and a chair wedged under the door the first night after the attack. It hadn't been an easy time. She had had several episodes of spontaneous crying and semi-hysteria, as well as nightmares in which a mountainous Harris Beaumont did titanic battle with Baron Samedi while she crouched, a pitiful human insect, at their feet.

Soukie, oddly enough, seemed pretty much unaffected. April worried that she might be suppressing her fear and upset, but Soukie seemed on the whole to be more concerned about her mother's well-being than herself. This eerie calm April attributed to the child's magical ability to call on the *loa* for aid. She asked Soukie several times if this was in fact what she had done, but her daughter claimed not to remember much of what had happened.

April figured this was just as well. She wished she could forget as easily.

She had not taken Soukie to the *boumfort* for the last meeting. The past few times they had gone, one of the drummers had shown an intense interest in her daughter, staring at her in a way that made April nervous. It would only be worse now, because she knew word had gotten out about what had happened; her cousin was also a member of the *boumfort* and wasn't the best at keeping secrets.

She wouldn't be out of the trailer today, most likely, save that she needed to cash her check and buy some groceries. The supermarket she checked for gave a small discount to its employes, which was why April was there on her day off; pushing a shopping cart down the crowded aisles. Another advantage to shopping where she worked was that she knew the cheapest and best value items by heart.

Soukie sat in the cart's fold-down seat; she was too old to be riding in it, but she still liked to occasionally, and today April was just as happy to have her daughter as close to her as possible. If they made a Snugli big enough to fit a child that size, she'd probably be carrying Soukie around strapped to her chest all day.

It was strange to be doing so commonplace a thing as shopping after what had happened. April wondered if, for the rest of her life, she would be comparing her day-to-day experiences with the sight of Baron Samedi towering over her, his stovepipe hat seeming to brush the very stars, his enormous finger crushing the life from Harris Beaumont as Harris might once have crushed a June bug. . . .

She took a deep breath and gripped the cart's handle as the white floor and shelves seemed to grow momentarily gray. It was still too overwhelming to remember all at once; amazing that she could remember it at all, that she hadn't blocked it out entirely like Soukie apparently had. She could only allow momentary flashes of it in her head without growing dizzy and faint.

She made her way through the checkout line, chatting for a moment with Lynette, the checker, while Jerry Horton bagged her groceries. Then she wheeled the loaded cart and Soukie out into the bright, humid afternoon.

Thank God the car hadn't been wrecked when Harris forced it off the road. Ms. St. Charles had paid for the tow truck. The front end now shimmied a bit more than usual when she went over forty-five, but April could live with that for the time being. Far worse was the fact that she could still smell Harris's bull-rut scent in the front seat's upholstery. It seemed impossible, was probably just her imagination, yet when she drove the car, even with all the windows down, that strong male smell all but gagged her. She'd used an entire bottle of Fantastik on it, and still it stank.

She opened the trunk and lifted the first of the three bags of groceries from the cart, noting absently a car cruising slowly down the parking lane. She turned away from the cart and Soukie to deposit the bag in the trunk. As she did so she heard a car door slam.

An instant later Soukie screamed *"Mommy!"*

April spun around to see a tall black man pulling her daughter roughly from the cart. Soukie kicked her legs and continued to scream as April lunged forward. The man kicked the cart forward, directly into her path; she hit it and fell to one knee. By the time she had gotten to her feet the man had gotten Soukie into the car and the driver had floored it. The car rocketed down the parking lane, narrowly missing several shoppers, and screeched out of the lot and onto the street.

Soukie was gone, but April could still hear her screaming.

Then she realized that it was she who was screaming—raw, desperate cries of horror and helplessness that were drawing people from all directions. But none of them could help. None of them could change what had happened. None of them could bring Soukie back. . . .

Legba looked down upon his *serviteur*: "Been a long time since you address me, *cheval*," he said. His voice reverberated over Shane like an earthquake.

Shane bowed his head. "Your pardon, *Maître*," he said. "I have been derelict, and I ask your forgiveness."

"It will take more than that," Legba rumbled. "You ignore your patron for this long, then crawl back seeking, not to serve, but to ask favors." The apparition took a massive corncob pipe from his mouth, its bowl glowing like a volcanic crater. He upturned it and tapped it, and a shower of fiery meteors streaked the dark sky.

"I ask a boon not for myself, but to make reparation for an old evil and to prevent a greater one. I must escape this prison, *Maître*. Only the Gatekeeper can show me the way, that I may stop my enemy's plans."

"You speak of the one who calls himself Mal Sangre."

"Yes, *Maître*."

Legba seemed to brood in thought for a moment. "He has overstepped his bounds," the *loa* said eventually. "Made a pact with the Nameless, seeking the power of the Gods."

Shane felt his spine grow cold. Ducas had alluded vaguely to the Nameless on occasion: beings of power so far removed from the affairs of humankind, buried so deep within the Invisible World, that no religion had ever ventured to name or understand them. They were entities so utterly and abysmally *alien* that mortal minds risked madness probing too close to their domain.

"Your purpose is worthy," the Gatekeeper said. "How will you stop him?"

Here it was, Shane thought; the crucial request. If the *loas* did not accede to his petition, he might as well stay in Angola until he rotted. It was impossible to tell how they would react; they might find the concept of what he wanted to do heretical and offensive. There was only one way to find out.

He explained his plan and made his entreaty. Legba drew back, straightening until his head was like a black planet among the stars. Shane thought he saw other titanic forms behind Legba: an enormous snake, large enough to swallow the world; a dark silhouette in top hat and dark glasses; a shadow wearing some form of military uniform and carrying a colossal machete. These forms, and others that appeared and melted like mist, conferred with Legba. Echoes of their discussion vibrated the ground beneath his feet.

At last the Gatekeeper turned back toward Shane, while the forms of the other *loas* faded away. "Your request is granted. A way will be shown. But the price will be high."

Shane felt mingled relief and trepidation. He had hoped for the former and expected the latter. Offenses to the gods were not easily forgiven. "Whatever it is, I will pay it."

Legba raised his staff and brought it down. The tip of it, as big in circumference as a redwood, struck the ground with the impact of a bomb. Shane had difficulty keeping his balance. "This will be the way: You shall journey in the flesh through the Invisible World. And this will be the price: You shall have a guide."

The *loa*, supporting himself with his staff, bent down on one knee. He laid the corncob pipe on the ground before Shane. A blast of heat enveloped him—the pipe's bowl was a cavernous arch, within which glowed coals and embers the size of boulders. It was like standing before a blast furnace.

"Enter, Shane LaFitte." Legba's voice was full of grim humor.

Shane felt himself retreat a step, involuntarily, before the intense heat. For a moment he wondered if Legba meant him to die. Though the gigantic pipe before him was not exactly "real," the heat coming from it was real enough. He would burn like a feather if he was foolhardy enough to walk into that hellish interior.

But Legba was his patron. He had agreed to grant Shane a way out of Angola. And he had said the price would be high.

Shane walked forward.

He had to use his hands to help him climb the thick wall of the bowl. He grabbed the curved lip, fully expecting the flesh of his palms to blister and slide away from his bones. That did not happen, though the pain as he gripped the red-hot surface was agonizing. Biting down on a scream, he pulled himself up and stood, reeling for a moment from the heat and pain.

Then he stepped into the bowl.

It was like walking into a gigantic lava tube. Sweat burst from Shane's pores, only to be instantly evaporated upon contact with the superheated air. His lungs were scorched as he inhaled. The pain was unimaginable, unendurable—yet somehow he endured it.

He struggled forward. To his dim astonishment his body showed no physical injury, though it was hot enough to roast and peel his skin away. He stumbled on, his vision a red haze as he tried to pick his way safely among the incandescent debris.

As he walked, one agonizing step after another, Shane cursed the cruel inventiveness of the gods. A high price, indeed. He was literally walking through hell to escape Angola.

But wait—what had Legba said? The price was not this torment. The price, the *loa* had told him, was that he would have a guide....

He tried to peer ahead through the dancing, glowing air. Apparently he was no longer in Legba's pipe—ahead of him was a labyrinth of tunnels, all filled with fire. How could he find his way through this maze? It was so hard to think with his nerve endings on fire....

Then he saw, coming toward him through the smoke and glare, the one Legba had said would be his guide. His price.

Shane reeled back. A scream of pure horror burst from him.

He turned to run, to flee back into Angola, but there was no escape. No matter which way he turned, she was there before him.

His guide. His price.

His wife, Anisse.

She was as he had last seen her, as he had left her in the bayou shack. Her belly had been slashed open, and her intestines hung in ropy tangles about her feet as she walked. Both of her eyes had been stabbed with the autopsy knife; one of the flaccid orbs hung on her cheek, dangling by its optic nerve. The nipples and skin had been flayed from her breasts. Her throat had been slashed; blood still dripped from it, slow and clotted. The drops sizzled when they struck the coals.

Shane staggered back until his back was pressed, unfeelingly, against the molten wall of the tunnel. There was no escape from this, no retreat, not even into madness. He sobbed harshly, and the tears that flowed from his eyes were instantly snatched away by the heat.

Anisse stepped closer. She held out one hand. She did not speak. Of course not, Shane's mind gibbered; she *can't* speak. She can't speak because I cut out her tongue.

He took her hand. There was no other choice.

Her silence more terrible than any accusation, Anisse turned and led him deeper into hell.

3 CITY OF THE DEAD

Wisdom we know is the knowledge of good and evil—not the strength to choose between the two.

—John Cheever,
John Cheever: The Journals

FRENCH QUARTER
AND METAIRIE,
NEW ORLEANS,
LOUISIANA

MARCH 27, 1998

Dave knew he wasn't playing worth shit tonight, but there didn't seem to be anything he could do about it. His timing was off, as was his tone; he was blowing like someone who'd never clamped lips to a horn in his life. That was how he felt, anyway. The audience at the Crescent City Room didn't seem terribly unhappy with the band, thank God, and Sharkey, Jeff, Norm and Ted were covering well enough for him. They'd sold about a dozen copies of their latest CD, stacks of which were sitting in view behind the bar, and they were only halfway through their third set. Certainly nothing to complain about.

Still, there was no magic in the music for Dave tonight. He was just going through the motions. He was a good enough musician that, even playing by rote, he could keep time and not embarrass himself and the rest of the band. But for the first time he could remember, it wasn't fun. It felt like—horror of horrors—a job.

Their current number was "Blue Dog Rag," another selection from the *African Stomp* LP. Before he had come down to the club, Dave had sat for nearly half an hour staring at the large square of cardboard displayed atop his record cabinet. Satchmo, dressed in a suit and a tribal headdress of feathers and bones—black pride had meant something different back then—was there on the cover, blowing his horn, cheeks puffed out, each looking capable of holding a pound of walnuts. The title was spelled out in bones above him.

An innocuous-looking item, all in all, considering it had caused a man's death.

If it was any consolation, he wasn't the only one whose playing was less than inspired tonight. Jeff MacKenzie's performance was lackluster as well. Maybe it was just an off night for the band; that happened, more often than anyone cared to admit. Jeff's playing wouldn't be so noticeable. Dave thought, if he hadn't decided for God knew what reason to wear those dark Ray-Bans. He looked like he was doing a bad Ray Charles imitation.

Dave had a solo coming up. He wished K.D. could be here, but she was over at Sisters of Grace, as usual. Hard to have a relationship with a woman who worked a seventy-hour week. Having her here might have inspired him to play better.

He swung into the solo hard and fast, stepping forward to the edge of the stage as he blew. The small room was packed, the audience mostly silhouettes due to the lights directed at the band. He idly scanned the crowd as he made the cornet sing, wondering if there was anyone here he recognized.

He had decided that the best thing to do was continue with

his life as usual. He was still terrified that he would be awakened by the pounding of a nightstick on the door at three A.M., accompanied by a bullhorn voice telling him to come out with his hands up. His nightmares were the stuff of old Warner Bros. gangster movies, *dream noir* in stark blacks and whites, always ending with a rattle of machine gun fire and him clutching his chest and falling down a flight of stairs.

But he couldn't let the fear rule him. Dave had given it a lot of long, hard thought, and had come to the conclusion that his life simply did not in any way equate with that of a scumbag drug dealer's. To say he had robbed and murdered a man was only one way of looking at it. Another way was that he had taken money made off of the pain and suffering of junkies and used it to buy and preserve a work of art. You could even say he'd done the world a favor by ridding it of one more parasite. For that he should go to jail?

Of course, it was likely the cops wouldn't see it that way. But as each day went by, his sense of danger lessened. He had read somewhere that if a crime is not solved within the first forty-eight hours, the chances are overwhelming that it won't be solved at all, and he clung to that. Every day that passed put him further and further away from discovery. He would never feel truly safe again, Dave knew, but he hoped that someday he might once again have some peace of mind.

He was almost done with the solo. He let his eyes drift slowly back across the room once more as he built toward a climax—

And then fear seized his lungs in a vise.

There, standing in the back—hard to see, with the lights glaring—but it was *him*, no doubt about it, the man he had killed, good as new, staring directly at him, eyes full of hate and a desire for revenge, the bastard had somehow stepped out of the cemetery and into the Crescent City Room. It was impossible, it couldn't be, but he was looking right *at* the son of a bitch, holy fucking shit, what was he going to *do*—?

Dave became aware that he had stopped playing. Silence hung as heavy as the thick pall of smoke in the air. Everyone, the band and the audience, was looking at him. He blinked, shook his head, and stared again at the face that had stopped his breath and nearly his heart.

It wasn't him.

He could see that clearly now. It was a superficial resemblance, a similar haircut and face, that was all. It wasn't him. It wasn't him.

It wasn't him.

"You okay, Dave?" Norm asked him, putting a concerned hand on his shoulder. Dave managed a nod. There was no way he could keep playing, though; he felt like he'd been kicked in the stomach by a mule. He turned away, moving like an old man toward a chair near the edge of the stage as Sharkey grabbed his mike and announced the band's intention to take a short break.

Dave sat down, holding onto his horn to keep his hands from trembling. So much for composure and equanimity. So much for peace of mind. He knew now that he would never be free of the fear and guilt—it would haunt him for the rest of his life.

Jeff sat down in the chair next to his. "What's the matter, man? Little too much gumbo at dinner?" His voice seemed strangely listless.

"Yeah, maybe that was it." Dave looked up at Jeff and felt a surge of annoyance at the ludicrous shades the man was wearing. "Christ, Jeff, you need a tin cup and pencils. Take those off," and before Jeff could stop him he reached up and pulled the shades off his friend's face.

Then he got his second shock of the evening. Jeff quickly

turned his head away and grabbed the glasses back, but not before Dave had seen his eyes. All it took was one glimpse to tell him what was going on.

The pupils of Jeff's eyes were completely rimmed in red.

When Lia St. Charles awoke there was a robin singing outside her window. The sun was a handsbreadth above the horizon, and the world looked fresh and new and clean.

It was tempting to just lie there and enjoy the sunlight slanting in through the windows and the sounds of the morning. But it was already late; she had to get to work. She had other cases to keep abreast of, after all. She couldn't just drop everything else while she waited for Shane LaFitte to escape from Angola. Using his voodoo powers. To battle a sorcerer bent on gaining ultimate power.

With her help.

God Almighty, she thought. I'm so far out of my mind I can't even see it from here.

She sat up and pulled her T-shirt away from her chest, peering down through the stretched neck. The angle was awkward, but she could easily see the mark that LaFitte had put there between her breasts, bright as blood. It faded as she looked at it, leaving only a pale remnant.

Feeling as though she moved in a dream, she brewed chicory coffee and had an almond croissant, feeding Toulouse a piece of it. Then she got dressed. Which really was the dream—this world, or the gray fogbank in which she and LaFitte had talked last night?

She wished she could believe that the latter had been a dream, that she had awakened into reality. But she wasn't so sure, because on her chest was the *vévé*.

"So," she said out loud as she sipped her coffee, "what happens now?"

She knew the answer to that, although she wasn't happy about it. Now she waited. Waited for Shane LaFitte to escape. Waited for him to contact her. Waited to do what she could to help him against Mal Sangre.

Lia was painfully aware that in doing so she would probably put an end to her career, not to mention winding up in jail herself if the cops found her with LaFitte. Why was she involved in this? Granted that all he had told her was true, granted that he was some kind of modern-day voodoo priest who was involved in a larger-than-life battle with some evil sorcerer, why was it her problem? She was convinced now that LaFitte was not a danger to her. Let him escape—she would say nothing, do nothing, to prevent it—but why couldn't she just walk away from it?

Because of Soukie, of course. If there really was the slightest threat to the child, she had to do all in her power to prevent it. That wasn't even open to discussion.

Lia was still brooding over it all when she got to her office. Once there, she decided that the best thing to do was just bury herself in paperwork for a while. Nothing like bureaucracy to make you forget there's such a thing as magic in the world.

After two hours of processing case files, just when she was about to chuck the entire filing cabinet out the window, the phone rang. The voice on the other end was sobbing, hysterical; it took her a moment to recognize it as April Delaney's.

NEW ORLEANS
CITY PARK AND
CENTRAL BUSINESS
DISTRICT,
NEW ORLEANS,
LOUISIANA
MARCH 28, 1998

When Shane came to his senses he found himself lying in the shade of a massive oak tree, its spreading branches draped with Spanish moss. It took a minute for the memory of his horrendous journey to come back to him; when it did it was with the effect of a physical blow. His entire body stiffened; his fingers clutched, digging through grass into deep, loamy soil. A high, keening sound came from between his set teeth.

Gradually he began to regain control over himself. He managed to sit up and look around. At first all he could see were the huge oaks. In the distance, however, he could glimpse buildings, and suddenly he knew where he was—in New Orleans City Park. Legba had been true to his word. A way had been provided, though the price had been high.

Very high.

The *loa* had not been completely unpitying, however. Lying on the grass beside him was a hollowed-out calabash gourd, painted with mystic symbols of the *loa* and containing within it what sounded like dried rattlesnake tails. Legba had given him a new *asson*, consecrated as he had requested it be.

Shane got to his feet, leaning against the tree for support, the *asson* clutched in one hand. In the distance he could see pedestrians, bicyclers and rollerbladers enjoying the warm spring air. He was wearing the usual Angola uniform—blue jeans and a denim work shirt. There was nothing about it that would immediately mark him as an escapee. More important was his lack of identification and cash. Something would have to be done about that.

Shane focused on that problem as he found his way out of the park. Concentrate on the moment at hand. Think of nothing else, especially not your wife's ruined face, her eyeless gaze mutely accusing you, her cold dead hand in yours, leading you through a conflagration no less painful than the sight of what you did to her. . . .

He reeled, seized his head in both hands as if to wrench the vision from it. A couple walking past him watched in mingled concern and disgust as he staggered toward them, and gave him a wide berth.

Shane sat down on a park bench, breathing slowly and deeply, until the world steadied once more. Coming toward him was a young man who looked to be in his mid-twenties and exuded the confidence and aplomb that only a moneyed yuppie can. Perfect, Shane thought.

He marshaled his faculties, concentrating on the yuppie. It was the same power of persuasion Sangre, when he was Jorge Arnez, had used on the Macoutes. Shane had used it more than once himself. It was not easy, particularly as hungry and tired as he was. But his desperation gave him inner strength. He *had* to make this work.

As the yuppie started to pass Shane he paused and frowned in mild perplexity, as if realizing he had just forgotten something. One hand slipped as if by its own volition into the pocket of his Dockers and pulled out a wallet.

Shane kept staring at him, focusing his will, hoping that no other pedestrian or cyclist would choose this moment to come by. The yuppie's frown deepened. He looked at the wallet as if he'd never seen it before; then, ignoring Shane completely, stepped over to the bench and put the billfold down on it. His brow cleared and, smiling as if he had just disposed of a trivial but annoying obligation, he headed on down the walk.

When he was out of sight Shane quickly pulled what money there was—sixty-two dollars, less than he had hoped, but better than nothing——from the wallet and left the leather billfold lying on the bench. In a few minutes the yuppie would realize he had lost it and would come back to look for it. Shane moved quickly in the opposite direction, toward the edge of the park.

He spent ten of the sixty-two at a nearby deli. When he had finished eating he felt renewed—physically, at least. A few doors down was a used clothing store where he picked up a long, duster-style coat for half the remainder of the money. It was ragged and torn, but it had deep pockets, in one of which he could hide the *assom.*

The next step was to find Lia St. Charles. She would be surprised to see him at her office the day after their rendezvous in the Invisible World, but not as surprised as the prison officials up at 'Gola would be when they opened the CCR cell and found it empty.

It was already past noon. He caught a bus for the Central Business District.

Time was running out.

Once again Mal Sangre peered into his *nganga*. Once again the vile brew within stirred and coalesced into images, images that only he could read.

The portents looked good. Very good. At last he had the final link in the chain that would bind him to his heart's desire. The girl was *dassn*, a child of power, one of great strength and great innocence—exactly what was called for as a sacrifice. When his agent had reported her presence at one of the local *houmgforts* he had hardly believed it could be so easy.

All the elements for the sacrifice were in place. Tonight, in the dark of the moon, he would breech the final barrier and bathe within the fountainhead of ultimate power. The spirits who guarded it, who demanded the sacrifice, lurked so deeply within the Invisible World that no religion had names for them. But the Nameless were no less powerful for being unrecognized. They demanded blood, innocent blood, blood that stank of fear and pain, as the key to the final door.

And they would have it.

It was all proceeding perfectly. According to reports, Shane LaFitte, while not dead as Sangre had intended he be, was languishing in solitary confinement up in Louisiana State Prison. There would be time enough to deal with him after he was released from the restricted cell. There was no way he could get out. Sangre had taken LaFitte's *asson* himself, and he knew that LaFitte had fallen out of favor with Legba.

Sangre nodded, satisfied, and passed a hand over the *nganga*. The swirling images subsided. He was not done yet, however.

There was another matter to be dealt with, a small and incidental one, but best not to leave any loose ends in his organization, not on the eve of what he had worked toward for so long. One of his distributors had been killed last week, his head broken open in a French Quarter alley. The murderer had gone unpunished. This could cause possible resentment and dissension among his other employees, and he could not have that. It was a trivial thing, but attention to such things is what makes good leadership. He would deal with it personally, the same way he had dealt with that pickpocket weeks ago.

Sangre leaned over the cauldron again. The *kyanga* within should have no problem communing with the soul of the dead distributor and learning from him his killer. Then there remained only the matter of punishment. He had something suitable in mind. An old-fashioned primitive bit of hoodoo, but sometimes the old ways were the best.

April had called her instead of the police. Lia had immediately called Neal Rendell and reported the kidnapping. That done, she grabbed her coat and her gun and headed for the door, only to open it and find Shane LaFitte standing before it, fist upraised to knock.

Surprise paralyzed her for a moment. He took one look at her face and said, "It's happened already."

"Soukie's been kidnapped."

"Yes. Tonight is the dark of the moon."

"What can we do? How do we find her?"

They continued down the stairs together. "He'll perform the ceremony in a place of power," Shane said. "A cemetery, most likely—they are crossroads, junctions between the living world and the spirit world."

"But which one? There're dozens of cemeteries in New Orleans."

He didn't answer. He doesn't know, she thought, feeling a pang of hopelessness shoot through her. It would be impossible to check each one of them before the night was over.

Which meant only one thing: They had lost, Lia thought bitterly. They had lost before they had even begun.

GARDEN DISTRICT
AND CENTRAL
BUSINESS DISTRICT,
NEW ORLEANS,
LOUISIANA

MARCH 28, 1998

W hat's wrong?"

"Nothing."

"I'm a doctor, you know. I could trepan your skull and look inside."

Dave didn't reply, didn't even crack a smile. Jesus, K.D. thought, something's really eating him. She hadn't seen him this disturbed since he was trying to borrow money from her to ward off impromptu knee surgery.

"Doesn't have anything to do with that trouble you were in, does it?"

He was quiet for a moment; then, much to her surprise and shock, he looked at her and burst into tears. It had been some time since she'd seen a grown man cry—the last was on shift, when she'd had to tell a teenager's dad that his son hadn't survived a head-on with an embankment—and the sight of tears rolling down cheeks covered with stubble was upsetting in the extreme. She raised up on her elbows in the bed, just in time for him to roll over and bury his face in her shoulder.

He sobbed for quite some time, while she patted his shoulder and whispered ineffectual comforting phrases. At last he seemed to regain control. He sat up and looked at her, and she thought that she had never in her life—not even in life-and-death situations at Sisters of Grace—seen a face more haunted. She could see the clock over his shoulder; the luminous digital readout told her it was just after eight P.M. She was working a late shift today, and so they had both slept at his place, spending the day mostly in bed.

She took him by the shoulders and looked in his eyes.

"Dave," she said, "What the hell is wrong?"

He took a deep breath, and told her.

He wasn't sure why he told her. He had lain awake for most of the night thinking; thinking about his buddy Jeff, hooked on Blood; thinking about the horror stories K.D. had told him of addicts who came through those sliding glass doors, their veins full of poison and their eyes empty of hope; thinking about the dead man in the rain, eyes forever open. When she had asked him what was wrong it all just came pouring out, first in tears and then in words.

Her reaction was what he had feared and expected it would be.

"You *killed* a man?" She said it softly, wonderingly, unbelievingly. "You killed him *and* robbed him?"

"I didn't mean to. . . ."

She slid away from him toward the edge of the bed. "Maybe you didn't mean to kill him, but you meant to rob him. And you covered it up. You *lied* to me."

Dave reached a hand toward her; she shrank away from it as if it were a rattler. "I don't fucking *believe* this! I'm calling the police." She reached for the phone on the bedside table, but he moved quicker, grabbing it and pulling it out of her reach.

"You *can't!* I told you before—what if one of them's on the take from Sangre? I wouldn't last the night!"

"That's just bullshit! You *killed* somebody! Jesus, I've been sleeping with a murderer!" K.D. slid out from under the covers and moved quickly across the room, grabbed her purse and pulled a cell phone from it. Dave leaped out of bed and tried to take it from her; she shrank back, and with a jolt of despair he realized that she was afraid of him.

They both stood there for a moment: she cowering, naked, from him, he feeling absurdly foolish and vulnerable, standing there just as naked. "K.D.," he said helplessly, "K.D., I love you."

"You don't love me," she said. "You don't kill someone and then lie about it to the one you love!"

She started to dial the phone again. He moved forward to take it from her; she lashed out with one leg, the ball of her foot impacting against his groin with devastating force. Dave gasped in agony, felt his legs turn to sponge rubber and sank down on the floor, holding himself and concentrating on not throwing up. It wasn't as bad as being kicked in the balls by Errol, but it was by no means pleasant.

K.D. dropped the phone and stared helplessly at Dave. "Oh, God," she said in a small voice, and then sank to the floor as well. She wrapped her arms around her knees and began to cry.

He managed to crawl over to her and put his arm around her;

she didn't shrink from his touch this time. That was something, at least.

"I wouldn't hurt you," he said. "It's *me*, K.D. You know I wouldn't hurt you."

"I *don't* know it," she said, the words broken up with hitching breaths and tears. "I don't know *you*. It seems like you haven't told the truth once since I've met you."

He didn't know what to say to that. "This is the truth. I couldn't spend the rest of my life with you, knowing I'd lied about this."

She dried her eyes with the palms of her hands and looked at him. "What're we going to do? I can't live with you, knowing you killed someone."

"What do you want me to do? Tell the cops? Turn myself in? They'll put me in *jail*, K.D."

"Wouldn't it be self-defense?"

"Following a guy into an alley, getting into a fight, knocking his brains out and stealing his wallet to pay off a loanshark? Perry Mason couldn't get me out of this."

"There's got to be someone we can go to for advice," she said. "I don't know any lawyers or cops. . . ."

An idea occurred to him. "What about that woman who brought the assault case in? What was her name? St. Something . . ."

"St. Charles? She's a parole officer, not a cop."

"Yeah, but she'd know about this stuff. Just ask her, you know, hypothetically—"

"No," K.D. said, and there was a tone to her voice that he hadn't heard before. "*You* ask her hypothetically. It's your responsibility." She got up and found the pants she was wearing last night, draped over a nearby chair. She fished St. Charles's business card out of the pocket and gave it to Dave. The pager number on it was followed by a parenthetical: *Emergencies Only.*

He was pretty sure this qualified as an emergency.

Sangre stood by his office window, staring out at the night. All the pieces of the game were his, now——it remained only to put them in their proper positions. Tonight would be the culmination of all his work. Tonight he would join the pantheon of the all-powerful.

Before the sun rose again he would possess the power to create and destroy with a thought. To control men and use them as puppets, by the power of his mind alone. No more having to truckle to the gods and appease them through intermediaries. No more having to peer into a cauldron that held a dead man's soul, or seek foretellings from the arrangement of cowrie shells or seeds or chalk marks on cement.

No more worrying about the ravages of age, the inevitable slowing and stilling of his heart. He would be of the flesh, and yet beyond the flesh. The best of both worlds.

Gathering himself, he sent out the Call. Of all those who had become addicted to Blood, only a very few were worthy of this summons. They were out there, waiting, as they had waited for the past year and more. The majority of them would not hear, were not needed——their purpose had been to provide him with the money needed to finance his studies and research. A means to an end, no more. In the weeks to come the supply of Blood would dwindle and vanish. It was no longer needed.

He touched their minds, one by one——the medical student, the musician, the jewelry store clerk and many others——and bade them come. They would congregate at the gates of Pontchartrain Cemetery, one of the oldest "cities of the dead" in New Orleans. There, aided by the residual power of the dead, he would use their blood to open the Gate and attract the Nameless.

And then the blood of the child would satiate Them.

He turned and looked at her. She sat, bound and gagged, only her eyes betraying her fear, in a chair by the door. Sangre crossed to her and stroked her hair lightly; she shrank back from his touch.

"So cold and afraid," he murmured. "Tonight you will beg for my caress, when you meet Those who will claim you."

CENTRAL BUSINESS
DISTRICT AND
FRENCH QUARTER,
NEW ORLEANS,
LOUISIANA

MARCH 28, 1998

Lia's beeper went off as she and Shane were crossing the parking lot to her car. At first she didn't recognize the number—but then she reconsidered. It might have something to do with Soukie.

She pulled out her cell phone and returned the call. She didn't at first recognize the male voice that answered.

"I'm Dave Cummings," he said. "We met the other night at the hospital? When you came in with the woman who'd been attacked?"

After a moment she recalled a face—vaguely, at least. "I'm afraid I don't have time to talk right now, Mr. Cummings. I'm in the middle of a crisis—"

"Aren't we all," he interrupted. "I just need a few minutes of your time. I've got a problem I'm afraid to go to the cops with. It's about that guy who was selling the Blood drug—"

She and Shane had reached her car, and Lia had been about to hang up on Cummings when this last sentence got her attention. "Who? Sangre?" She noticed Shane watching her in puzzlement and held up a hand indicating for him to wait.

"Well, he's the guy behind it all, isn't he? I, um—I killed one of his pushers."

Lia came to a quick decision. This might not have anything to do with finding Sangre or Soukie—but then again, it might. It was a faint possibility of a clue, which was more than they had now. Something deep within her said she needed to hear what this guy had to say.

"I think we'd better talk," she said. "But not over the phone—I'm on a cellular, and they're not secure. Let me meet you—the sooner the better."

Dave hung up and looked at K.D. "She wants to meet me. In the Quarter. The Bayou Lounge; it's over on Dauphine."

K.D. said nothing. While he had talked to St. Charles she had gotten dressed, and he now felt at a distinct disadvantage being still naked. He pulled on a pair of pants, then asked with considerable trepidation, "Will you come with me?"

She took her time answering. Dave waited, feeling each second stretch longer than the last. At last she sighed and said, "God, I'm such an idiot."

The Bayou Lounge was a small Parisian-style bistro, filled with mirrored panels and red leather banquettes. It was crowded, but Lia spotted Cummings sitting at a table near the back. With him was the doctor from Sisters of Grace. There was a palpable air of tension between the two.

She and Shane slid in the booth beside the two. Cummings eyed Shane with surprise and a little alarm. "I thought this was going to be a private conversation," he said.

Lia correctly interpreted his concern. "Don't worry; he's not with the police." Cummings looked somewhat relieved. "Now," she continued, "tell me what you know about Mal Sangre. Quickly; we haven't got much time."

The musician took a deep breath and began his tale. He was hesitant at first and required some prompting to keep the story on track, but as he continued he grew more concise. The doctor—Wilcox was her name, Lia remembered—said nothing during it. The reason for her reserve soon became apparent when Cummings revealed how he'd lied to her.

As he continued talking, Lia's disappointment and impatience grew. It was becoming obvious that nothing Cummings knew would help them. She and Shane needed to get out of there and resume their search. At the same time, she had agreed to give this man advice, and judging from his story he desperately needed it.

She glanced at Shane. She knew he was feeling the same impatience that she was, but no trace of it showed in his face or body language. He was listening closely to Cummings's story. She glanced at her watch. It was after nine P.M. already.

She had asked Shane if he could not seek help in their search from the voodoo gods he served. He had admitted that was a possibility, but he was reserving doing so as a last resort. He would be, no doubt, petitioning them heavily during the confrontation with Sangre; he didn't want to draw from that particular well too often.

"That's the situation," Cummings said, and Lia realized that she had let her thoughts wander for the last few moments. "I made a mistake," he continued. "A bad mistake, I know, but I keep thinking there have to be some kind of mitigating circumstances. I don't want to go to jail, but I also don't want this on my conscience."

"So you've had no involvement with Sangre directly," Lia said.

He looked slightly confused. "That's right. I wouldn't know him if he sat on me. What's that got to do with—?"

"I'm sorry," Lia said. "I thought your story would have more bearing on what we're investigating." As she spoke she started to rise from her seat, but Shane's hand on her arm pulled her down again. Cummings and Dr. Wilcox both looked at her in astonishment.

"Wait a minute," Dr. Wilcox said. "That's all you've got to offer? What should he do? Turn himself in? Do we try to pretend the whole thing never happened?"

Lia sighed. "If you'd asked me a couple of weeks ago, I'd have told you to tell the police what you told me. Now—I don't know. Life doesn't look quite that simple to me anymore. You seem like a good man," she said to the musician. "You two have obviously got something good together. This goes against everything I've been taught, but—the guy you killed was a scumbag. Fuck him. He's better off dead.

"Now, if you'll excuse us, we've got our own problems to deal with," she continued, starting to rise again—and once again Shane restrained her.

Speaking for the first time, he said to Cummings, "The man you killed—you said he was talking on a phone in the alley." When Cummings nodded, he continued, "Did he say anything at all about Sangre or any plans he might have had? Please try to remember. It's vitally important."

Cummings frowned in thought. Lia felt Shane's fingers dig slightly into her arm, and realized that his intuition was telling him that there was yet something that could be learned from this man, even as hers had earlier.

Cummings sighed and shook his head. "I'm sorry. I can't remember."

Lia realized she'd been holding her breath; now she released it in disappointment. She could sense that Shane was frustrated as well. "Thanks anyway," she said. She looked at her watch, then at Shane. "We'd better—"

"Wait a minute," Dr. Wilcox said to Cummings. "You told me earlier he said something about 'Pontchartrain.'"

"Oh, yeah," Cummings said slowly.

Lia felt her heart begin to hammer. "Pontchartrain?" she asked. "As in Pontchartrain Cemetery?"

"Maybe. I remember now; he said something like, 'Pontchartrain's the place.' He also said that Sangre was going to do it as soon as he found someone to cut." He looked back and forth between Lia and Shane. "Does that help?"

"It does," Lia said. "Immensely. Thank you—you may have just saved a child's life." She stood up, and this time Shane rose along with her. "We've got to go. Thanks again." She shook hands with Cummings and Dr. Wilcox. "And good luck—whatever you decide."

"Shouldn't you be going to the police with this—" Dr. Wilcox started to say, but she stopped when Shane leaned over the table and looked down at Cummings. His expression intense, he said, "Be very careful. Sangre is not a man to accept affront without retribution. After tonight, if all goes well, you may breathe a little easier. But if I were you, I would go to a *houngan* and ask for protection. I would help you myself, if I had the time."

"A *houngan*?" Cummings asked incredulously. "You mean like a witch doctor? What, are we talking magic here?"

"No," Shane replied. "We're talking sorcery—the blackest kind. The kind that could strike you down anywhere, at any time. *Please* believe me—and get help."

With those words he turned and left the restaurant. Lia followed. She spared a backward glance at the other two; they were still sitting there, staring after her with expressions of mingled confusion and astonishment.

There was a time when I would have felt the same way, she thought. I wish I still did.

But there was no time to reflect on that. She looked at her watch again as she reached the street. Nine-thirty. Two and a half hours to go.

It would be enough time, she told herself. It had to be.

xlii

FRENCH QUARTER
AND PONTCHARTRAIN
CEMETERY,
NEW ORLEANS,
LOUISIANA

MARCH 28, 1998

After St. Charles and her companion had left, Dave sat for a few minutes in silence, toying with a plastic olive spear. He had no idea what to make of the black man's cryptic warning, but he wasn't giving it a whole lot of thought—he was much more preoccupied with the parole officer's opinion that he and K.D. should put this behind them and get on with their lives.

Could he do it? Even more importantly, could K.D. do it? Could they stay together, build a relationship, with the knowledge of his crime hanging over them both? It occurred to him, rather belatedly, that by telling her he had made her—what was the term? An accessory after the fact? That problem seemed to him easily solved, however. If he was ever found out, he would simply swear that he had never told K.D., that she had no knowledge of what he had done.

Could he live with what he had done? He thought he could. As the days and weeks went by, that night in the French Quarter alley became more and more unreal to him. The nightmares came less often now, and when they did they were not so vivid. He knew he would never forget what had happened, but maybe, just maybe, he could forgive himself.

If K.D. would forgive him.

Dave risked a glance at her. She was staring off into space, obviously lost in thought as well. A waitress came by and asked her if she wanted another drink; she shook her head. Then she looked at Dave.

"What are you going to do?" she asked him.

"What are *you* going to do? Leave me? Turn me in?" He took her hand in his. "If you leave me, K.D., it doesn't matter if I go to prison or not. I used to think the most important thing in my life was my music—it's not anymore. Now it's you. I think I can live with what I did. The question is, can you?"

She didn't answer for some time. Dave forced himself to sit still, forced himself not to speak, forced himself to ignore the twisting in his gut as he waited for her verdict.

At last she looked up and met his eyes. "I can try," she said. "I can't promise you that I'll feel this way for the rest of my life, or even next week. But I'm willing to try, Dave. That's all I can do."

He felt a wave of relief that left him as exhausted as blowing a four-hour set. "That's all I ask." He looked into her eyes, and she smiled, and he remembered how he'd felt when he first saw her in the club, only two weeks ago, though it seemed an eternity. How he'd thought to himself that, even if he never spoke to her, never learned her name, never saw her again, that one simple moment of her beauty would be enough. That was how he felt now. He wanted this moment to go on forever, and he promised himself that, no matter what happened next, he would always remember it, always treasure it. He let go of her hand, raised his drink and saluted her.

K.D. smiled at him, taking joy in the joy he so obviously felt. Maybe she was crazy, but she loved him—that much was obvious to her now. She was sure her decision was going to give her some sleepless nights, but right now she intended to stand by it. She had always been a law-abiding person, but in this case she felt the law was wrong. Dave Cummings was no more a murderer than she was.

He had his drink raised halfway to his mouth and was smiling at her when he collapsed. He dropped the drink with a shriek of pain and fell sideways out of his chair onto the floor with shocking abruptness, curling into a fetal position, rigid with agony.

She leaped up, knocking her own chair over, vaguely aware of the concerned reactions of the restaurant's other patrons as she dropped down on her knees next to him. "Dave! Dave, can you hear me?"

His face was pale and he was diaphoretic—the sweat was so heavy he looked as if a waiter had poured a pitcher of water over him—and when she grabbed his wrist the pulse rate was too fast and thready to count. He tried to scream again, but it came out a dry, rattling wheeze, his face contorted, his mouth stretched down, revealing his teeth. His limbs jerked and quivered, waves of tetanic spasms passing over him.

K.D. twisted around, shouted at an anxiously hovering waiter, "911! *Now!*" As he ran to the phone she pulled a penlight out of her purse, shined it into his eyes. Dave's pupils were equal and reactive. Her mind quickly ran through the possibilities: Seizure? Stroke? MI? Aneurysm? Anaphylaxis? DIC? He wasn't clutching his chest, and he didn't seem to be reacting like any stroke or MI she'd ever seen. Nor was he bloating up like it was an allergy.

A psychosis of some kind? She didn't know, she didn't *know*—!

Behind her the waiter said, "The paramedics are on the way."

Dave let out another strangled scream. He looked up at her and what she saw in his face wasn't the usual fear a dying man had.

What she saw was pure terror.

.

Pontchartrain Cemetery was built in the 1700s for the same reasons that had required the other fifty-odd necropoli in the city to be constructed: With much of New Orleans below sea level, and drainage for the most part nonexistent, conventional burial was usually less than permanent. A six-foot-deep grave could fill with five feet of water before the gravediggers had finished their excavations. Coffins were at first forced into the water and mud with poles, or ventilated to allow water to seep in and fill them. But even if people could manage to inter someone, there was no guarantee the deceased would stay buried. After a heavy rain the contents of fresh gravesites would sometimes erupt out of the muck like a cut-rate version of Judgment Day, and it was a common sight to see decomposed bodies floating down storm-flooded streets.

Finally a solution was found, inspired by European burial customs: the creation of freestanding tombs and mausoleums aboveground. Such was Pontchartrain. At its time it was meant to be a place for the upper crust of society to repose for all eternity, and the city's elite lavished considerable money and imagination on it. Small-scale replicas of many of the world's great sepulchers and crypts arose within the white marble walls, among them a miniature Taj Mahal and an Egyptian pyramid and sphinx. There was a dolmen-like edifice vaguely resembling Stonehenge, a Grecian temple bedecked with Doric columns, a Chinese pagoda and dozens more eclectic structures. The gradual degeneration of the inner city neighborhood that surrounded it, however, had taken its toll upon Pontchartrain; over the decades most of the tombs had become overgrown and dilapidated, their whitewashed plaster crumbling away and exposing the bricks or stone beneath, much as their tenants' mortal beauty had long since sloughed away from the bone.

No one had been buried in Pontchartrain in at least thirty years, and the city fathers occasionally made noises about having the entire five acres razed, as every year several foolish tourists wandered in alone among the maze of its narrow avenues and fell prey to the muggers and rapists who prowled there. But even the patience of the dead would be tried by the glacial progress of modern bureaucracy, and so Pontchartrain Cemetery continued to brood, ancient and alone, a canker in the heart of New Orleans.

Lia parked two blocks away, in front of a huge warehouse where Mardi Gras floats were stored. The area that faced the east entrance to Pontchartrain was primarily industrial, and the street was silent and deserted. Only one streetlight worked, at the far end of the avenue, and the abandoned buildings loomed over them as they approached the cemetery. The silence was absolute; not even the sound of nearby traffic reached them. A river fog was beginning to blanket the area, diffusing the lights of the downtown towers into soft auroral glows. Lia felt that she and Shane might be the last living people on a dying planet, walking into the city of the dead to mingle their dust and bones with the rest of long-departed humanity.

The air was swiftly growing cold. The darkness was almost palpable; in addition to the lack of moonlight, storm clouds were moving swiftly in from the Gulf, blotting out the stars. She heard the distant rumble of thunder and wondered uneasily if this were a natural storm or one somehow summoned by Sangre's impending appeal to the forces of darkness.

It was difficult to take a deep breath; the fear seemed to fill her lungs and wrap itself around her heart, slowing its beat, thickening the blood in her veins. She glanced at the man who walked beside her. Hard to read his expression in the deepening gloom, but if he was afraid, she could find no sign of it in his face. She hoped he had a reason to appear so confident.

She remembered that when he had first come into her office—it seemed decades ago, now—she had warned herself against the physical attraction she had felt for him. There had been no time for those feelings since he had escaped from Angola, but now, all of a sudden, she recalled standing with him in her dream, the two of them naked in their translucent astral forms. She had not given it much thought at the time—after all, it had been a dream, albeit a dream shared with another. But now the memory of it swept through her with a rush. Its intensity astonished her.

Maybe, Lia thought, maybe, if we got out of this alive. . . .

She had asked him if he had a plan, and he had said he did, although he hadn't gone into details. As they prepared to cross the street to where the cemetery walls, white as leprosy even in the murky night, awaited them, Lia stopped and put a hand on his arm. "Now would be a good time to tell me your plan," she whispered, "and what I can do to help."

He nodded, and pulled from one of his coat pockets a small gourd, decorated with primitive drawings. It rattled slightly as he lifted it. "Legba created this *asson* for me," he told her, "at my request. Notice how it is painted with different *vévés*—the symbols of the *loa*. Usually an *asson* can draw upon the power of only one of the gods. With this one I can call upon them all if need be."

"Okay, you can call them," she said. "But does that mean they'll come?"

Shane shrugged, his expression impassive. "The *loas* do as they will. We can but hope for the best."

"So that's all we've got to face down someone you're saying is one of the most powerful sorcerers on Earth?"

"Someone who has the *potential* to be one of the most powerful sorcerers on Earth. Until he makes this final sacrifice to the Nameless, he is vulnerable." Shane looked at the luminous dial of his watch. "It's almost midnight. If we're going to stop him, it must be now. Are you with me?"

She wanted to say no. She wanted very badly to run back to her car and drive away from here, away from New Orleans, away from all this madness that her life had become. But where would she go? If Mal Sangre did attain this ultimate power, how far would his influence extend? How much would the world change?

Would it be a world worth living in?

She took a deep breath and drew her gun. "I'm with you. Let's go."

PONTCHARTRAIN
CEMETERY AND
SISTERS OF GRACE
HOSPITAL,
NEW ORLEANS,
LOUISIANA

MARCH 28–29, 1998

K.D. rode with Dave in the ambulance, the sirens scream-ing. The paramedics were efficient and quick, but with all their gear they had no more idea of what was wrong with him than she did.

"BP sixty over forty," one of them said. "Respiration forty and shallow, pulse one-ninety—he's white as a jug of milk, Jesus, we got full blown shock here. What'd he do, pop his aorta?"

K.D. ignored the question. "Start a big bore IV, TKO, nor-mal saline," she said. "Put the shock trousers on him." As they complied she huddled close beside him, holding his hand, which was clammy and cold. "Goddamn it, Dave," she whispered to him, "Don't you fucking die, you hear me? Not now!"

It was a long ride to the hospital.

* * *

As they entered the cemetery Shane opened wide his senses, extending his awareness and perception to the maximum of his ability. To do so left himself vulnerable, he knew, but he could not chance being taken by surprise. Even without the final boon that Sangre sought from the Nameless, the *bokor* was a formidable opponent.

The black wrought-iron gate was unchained and ajar. There was no one guarding the entrance. He and Lia moved cautiously down a narrow aisle flanked by ornate burial vaults bedecked with pediments, porticoes and cast iron grillwork. Weeds, grass and brambles grew thick and tall around the tombs' foundations, which were becoming obscured from view as the ground fog thickened.

Still there was no sound save the occasional faint reverberation of thunder. Heat lightning flickered eerily in the clouds massing overhead.

He hoped that Legba and the other *loas* would be there for him. Like all gods, they were mercurial, prone to follow whims beyond the comprehension of mortals. He could only pray that they would consider Sangre's presumptuousness in contacting the Nameless enough to warrant action.

Shane hoped he would not regret bringing Lia St. Charles along—not that there had been much chance of persuading her to let him go without her. On the face of it, it seemed madness to allow her to accompany him—and yet something in his gut had moved him to do so. He wasn't sure why, but the feeling was as strong as it was mysterious.

They reached the intersection of another avenue. Directly across from them rose a miniature chapel, complete with a broken Tiffany window and a three-foot-tall marble angel mounted on the roof, wings rampant. Some vandalism in years past had resulted in the angel's head having been broken off, and it had subsequently been placed like an infant in the crook of the statue's left arm, where it stared, with an expression of vague longing, at its former position.

And now, at last, a new sound began, welling up as though from the ground itself. At first Shane thought it was another grumble of thunder, but it was too regular for that. Almost immediately he knew what it was, and knew what it portended.

The drums. The hypnotizing beat that signaled the beginning of a ceremony. Shane had heard them many times over the years, but this time he did not recognize the cadence. It was a darker, more ominous percussion than anything he had ever heard before. These drums spoke of blood and fire, of dark madness, of a world where no sun shone and no flower bloomed. They spoke of pain and suffering and death.

They spoke of the heart's desire of Mal Sangre.

Shane felt Lia's fingers dig into his arm. She felt it too: it was a rhythm that made the stomach clench and the head spin. It was coming from the center of the graveyard.

Her hand slid down his arm and found his.

Together they advanced toward the sound of the drums. Somewhere in the distance a church began to toll the midnight hour.

The Sisters of Grace trauma team rolled, drawing blood, hooking up an ECG and a portable chest fluoroscope. Dave moaned softly throughout the procedure.

"What d'hell's dat?" Jerry said, staring at the X-ray image. K.D. looked at the picture and caught her breath. There appeared to be some kind of . . . *growth* . . . inside his chest and abdomen. She couldn't see the internal organs for it, whatever it was. Was it slowly pulsating, or did she imagine that? "Jesus," she whispered, her mouth dry. "Get a surgical set. I'm going in."

Gowns, gloves and a sterile kit were quickly produced. Jerry swabbed Dave's abdomen with betadine. "Who's the gas passer on call?" K.D. shouted, only to find the anesthesiologist at her elbow, gloved, gowned, masked and shielded.

"Put him to sleep, Tom. Do it fast." Her voice was shaking.

He nodded as he pushed a syringe into Dave's IV line. "Give him twenty seconds."

She had the scalpel on his abdomen when the clock's sweep hand hit twenty seconds. She pushed the blade in and started the cut. Somebody—not Jerry—leaned in and mopped the incision with a sponge. K.D. concentrated, cursing her trembling hand. She sliced through skin and muscle, into the peritoneum and the cavity—

A stench assailed her even through the mask. It was all she could do not to recoil. The crew around her began gagging.

Once, about eight months ago, a bag lady had walked into the ER complaining that her left leg wouldn't support her weight. K.D. had been there when Jerry and some of the other nurses had started unwrapping the thick layers of clothing and newspaper the woman had swathed herself in, even though the temperature outside was in the eighties, with equal humidity. As they continued to undress her they had begun to notice the smell—the sickly sweet, overpowering odor of putrescence. Jerry had pulled the final layer of newspaper away, revealing her upper leg: A writhing mass of maggots had eaten away the flesh until the white gleam of bone shone through in spots. The stench had been incredible, overpowering.

This was worse.

She set her teeth against nausea and called for retractors.

Two of the nurses applied them almost hesitantly, and K.D. understood why. There was something terribly wrong here; this was like no pathology she had ever seen before. Something that went beyond medicine, beyond science. The warning words of St. Charles's companion seemed to echo in her head: *We're talking sorcery—the blackest kind. The kind that could strike you down anywhere, at any time. . . .*

The normal din of the ER seemed to fade away, to be replaced by a breathless silence. She swallowed dryly and said, her voice a half-whisper, "Open him up."

They pulled back on the retractors, spreading the incision wide. Jerry swung the overhead light closer, shining it into the cut.

And K.D. screamed—

PONTCHARTRAIN
CEMETERY AND
SISTERS OF GRACE
HOSPITAL,
NEW ORLEANS

MARCH 29, 1998

Lia gripped the .38 in one hand and Shane's fingers in the other as they made their way through the cemetery. The ground fog was quite thick now; it undulated lazily about their feet, reminding her of the gray realm of dreams.

They edged around a large tomb thickly overlaid with ivy—and beheld the ceremony. In the cemetery's center was a small open square and a tomb in the shape of an obelisk nearly twenty feet tall. It was, according to legend, the resting place of Anna Gautreau, the nineteenth-century voodoo priestess who had used her influence on the wealthy and superstitious to claim the cemetery's most prestigious plot. The base of the burial house was decorated with various fetishes and scrawled symbols left by contemporary acolytes. A young magnolia tree had taken root to one side. Before the tomb's entrance was a large granite block nearly three feet tall; the ground mist lapped at it. To one side of it were the three drums and their players, and a large carved post that Lia dimly recognized from pictures of voodoo ceremonies. A brazier set on the other side illuminated the scene with flickering orange light.

Between the block and the tomb stood Mal Sangre. He wore a black cotton T-shirt and black jeans, apparently immune to the night's damp chill. Surrounding him in a rough semicircle were two dozen or more people, ranging from the itinerant to the well-to-do. Though she could not see their eyes to judge the degree of Blood addiction, Lia had no doubt that she was looking at Sangre's "zombies."

But where was Soukie?

Sangre was chanting words in a harsh voice, using a combination of English, Spanish and several other languages, one of which she thought might be Latin. Lia wasn't sure what other tongues he was speaking, but they seemed somehow to be far older than Latin. The English words she could barely make out over the thunder of the drums:

"I conjure thee, Creatures of the Wastes, by the rites of the Wastes! I summon thee, Dwellers in Darkness, by the powers of Darkness! I abjure thee, Beasts of the Abyss, by the strength of the Abyss! I evoke thee, Nameless of the Gods, by that which cannot be spoken! Iä kengu! Iä kengu! Iä knbbnr! Iä vastnr!"

The syllables, the rhythm of the chant, were mesmerizing. Lia listened, not understanding most of the words but gleaning from the intonations and the cadences of Sangre's voice a kind of dim understanding of what the ritual was about. And that understanding, faint and imperfect though it was, was enough to horrify her almost to the point of madness. Her gun hung, forgotten, at her side. She felt herself swaying slightly, as were the zombies, to the disturbing litany.

Though her eyes were fixed on Sangre, she could sense Shane at her side, and knew he was similarly fascinated.

"Thou who art before all Gods, before all men and all legends of men, before all things, Ancient of Days, receive thou these offerings and grow strong!"

At the apex of the obelisk, something was forming.

It was hard for Lia to make out what it was—it seemed to be a slowly writhing clot of blackness, darker than the night which surrounded it. It expanded, growing not in a smooth progression, but fitfully, in starts and stops. After a moment Lia realized that its growth was tied to Sangre's chant and to the strange atonal beat of the drums.

As it grew larger it seemed to take on depth somehow, although the perspective kept changing; at one moment she seemed to be peering into a well of infinite depth, and the next, looking up at the summit of an impossibly tall mountain. And now its Stygian shade was leavened by streaks of color: dark reds and oranges and purples. They dimly illuminated the roiling clouds of blackness.

Sangre's voice became harsher; the words that crashed from his lips seemed to cut her like flung shards of stone. She saw that, despite the cold, he was sweating, and the veins were standing out in his arms and neck, showing intense mental and physical strain.

The drums changed their cadence, settling into a steady, heartbeat-like pace that still seemed, somehow, subtly *wrong*. And the darkness above the obelisk began to throb in time with the drums. Each time it throbbed, the variegated flashes within grew brighter. Lia felt her own heart stuttering within her chest, trying in vain to match the off-tempo beat.

Then, abruptly, one of the drummers struck his instrument a quick, sharp blow, louder than all the rest. And simultaneously with that blow a beam of crimson light lanced from the heart of the black cloud and arrowed down, striking one of the zombies who stood patiently waiting. Like a laser it sliced through his chest, leaving a smoking hole that Lia could momentarily see through before the victim jerked like a hooked fish and fell bonelessly. A sharp smell, like ozone and brimstone combined, filled the air.

None of the other zombies took notice of the action, nor did Sangre. If anything, the sorcerer's concentration upon his litany seemed more intense than ever. The drumming continued without a break. Lia stared at the dead body lying twisted on the ground, half hidden by the mist, and wondered why she felt no more shocked than she did. It was as if the drumming had anesthetized her emotions.

A few moments later the drummer hit another sharp note, and another beam burst from within the cloud and felled another of the passive victims. Again and again it happened. There seemed to be no pattern to it; two or three would fall with no more than a second's time between, and then minutes might go by before the cloud would strike again. Nor did the beam progress in any orderly manner among the ranks—it seemed to pick its victims out at random, cutting down one here, another over there. . . .

And with each death, the black cloud grew bigger, pulsing more and more strongly.

All but two of the victims had fallen when Sangre left off his chant abruptly and turned to vanish within the tomb's dark interior. He emerged a moment later, bearing in his arms a small bundle wrapped in a blanket. This he laid on the altar, then pulled the folds of the blanket apart, revealing a small child, bound and gagged.

It was Soukie.

At the sight of the helpless girl Lia at last found the inner strength to fight against the mesmerization that had held her. She looked at her watch. It was almost midnight. Panic blossomed within her at the thought of what the hungry cloud might do to the girl. She could not let this continue; she had to do something!

Lia raised her gun and fired.

K.D. screamed again and threw herself backward, slamming into Jerry, jostled by the other nurses who were also trying to get away. In a matter of seconds the operating bay became a scene of horrified panic as seasoned professionals, men and women who had faced within these walls some of the most blood-chilling sights the mind could conceive, pushed and shoved and fell over each other in their attempt to get clear of the operating table on which Dave Cummings lay.

The incision in his abdomen had narrowed again when the nurses released the retractors, but it was still wide enough. Out of it poured a tide of scorpions, spiders, beetles, and vermin. K.D. looked down at her gloved hand and saw a fat black widow spider scuttling up it, dark as ink against the pale gray Lycra. She flicked her wrist, shuddering in revulsion as the spider fell to the floor where Jerry stepped on it.

But it was only one of what had to be dozens, perhaps hundreds; they were still writhing out of the open cut, crawling along the table, dropping to the floor where they quickly disappeared under equipment stands. One of the orderlies, who had fallen to his hands and knees during the initial panic, shrieked in pain as a scorpion stung him on the wrist.

K.D. backed against the operating bay wall, staring in disbelieving terror. No wonder the X ray had shown some kind of occluding, writhing mass within the body cavity. In medical school she had heard of a man snorkeling in a lake who had aspirated a wasp that landed on the lip of his air tube. The insect had stung him repeatedly, and he had died when the inside of his airpipe swelled shut. This had to be a thousand times worse. Dave should have swollen up like a balloon from anaphylaxis. The wonder was that he had stayed alive as long as he had; the ultimate horror was that he was still alive now. The monitor showed the jagged lines of tachycardia; his heart was still beating.

All about him the chaos and panic continued as members of the staff stomped on and swatted at the hordes of insects and arachnids. They had finally stopped erupting from his viscera. K.D. looked from the incision up to Dave's face—and saw his eyes snap open.

PONTCHARTRAIN
CEMETERY AND
SISTERS OF GRACE
HOSPITAL,
NEW ORLEANS
MARCH 29, 1998

Lia could have sworn she had aimed right for Sangre. She was a decent shot; she tried to practice at least once a week at the indoor range near her office. She knew enough to go for a trunk shot at this distance. But the bullet struck the edge of the tomb, missing Sangre by two feet.

The sound of the gunshot was staggeringly loud to her. The drums stopped immediately, and the drummers leaped up and fled into the darkness of the cemetery with cries of fear. Evidently they were not enslaved to Sangre's will as the zombies were.

Sangre whipped his head around in her direction, and she had never seen such livid rage and hate on any living being's face. He spoke no word, made no gesture, but the two remaining zombies turned toward them. They did not shamble slowly; they ran, leaping nimbly over clumps of tall grass and broken stones, arms outstretched.

Oh, *shit*, Lia thought.

Shane had never seen a ritual like this before. It combined aspects of *Vouvdoun*, *Santéria* and many other practices, as well as things he had never seen or heard of. It was a rite designed to penetrate deeper into the Invisible World than any he had seen before.

He had not been as captivated by the arcane patterns of the ceremony as Lia had been. Rather, he had been waiting for the preliminary sacrifices to be disposed of. It was a decision, he knew, that would cost him many sleepless nights if he survived—each time one of Sangre's zombies fell before the fire of the Nameless, Shane seemed to feel the searing beam strike through his own heart. But it was the only way. If he let Sangre know now that he was here, his enemy would turn his slaves on them and there would be no chance of stopping the ceremony. It was a calculated risk, because with each sacrifice the Nameless grew stronger. But now Lia had interrupted the ritual and forced his hand.

Fortunately, there were only two of Sangre's slaves left. One of them, a young man with prematurely white hair, leaped toward him. A single uppercut to the jaw felled him, but only momentarily—it was obvious that Sangre's mental domination was keeping his slave going. Shane put the boy on the ground again and broke his ankle with a quick, sharp thrust of his heel; a trick Ducas had taught him years ago as a last resort for subduing unruly acolytes. Out of the corner of his eye he saw Lia sidestep the female slave—a woman with spiky hair and a ring in her nose—

then hook her leg behind her attacker's and drop the woman to the ground with a palm thrust to her chest. Shane felt a sharp surge of admiration.

His attention was brought back to more immediate matters when the boy he had crippled grabbed him around the legs. Shane wrestled himself free, only to see the slave pull himself to his feet with the help of a nearby marble cross and hobble toward him again.

With a pang of regret he realized that nothing short of unconsciousness or death would stop the boy's attack. There was no way around it. He seized a broken chunk of stone from the ground and swung it against his attacker's head. The slave dropped as if shot.

He turned to help Lia, only to find that she had apparently come to the same conclusion and had choked the woman out.

Now only Sangre was left.

He turned his attention again toward his old enemy—and felt his heart leap to his throat.

When Sangre saw LaFitte and the woman standing at the edge of the brazier's light, his astonishment threatened to overwhelm his rage. He had been so certain that his enemy was still locked in one of Angola's windowless cells that for an instant he wondered if all his work and study had left him deranged.

He could not stop to wonder how LaFitte had escaped, or how he had found him. The invocation was almost complete. A rift had been opened between the two worlds, a crack that bridged the gulf to the Nameless. And the Nameless had come, eager for blood and pain. It was the child They were interested in—the others were merely to gain Their attention and whet Their appetites. To deny Them the child's soul and power would be catastrophic—not only would They hold back from him what he had sought for so long, but They would demand . . . *reparation*.

Above him the cloud pulsed darkly, angrily, red and purple stitching through it like malevolent sparks.

There was no time left. Sangre looked down at the bound and gagged form of the child. She had been drugged just enough to prevent her from calling to the *loa* for aid, but not enough to dull her sensitivities—it was important that she feel the maximum amount of pain and terror. Quickly he took up the dagger. It had been fashioned when the house of Mars was ascendant, tempered in a fire of laurel and yew boughs and quenched in blood and brine. Once he drew it across her skin and anointed it in her blood, it would neutralize whatever protection she might be under and give the Nameless free access to her soul.

The fivefold scoring across her breast would bring the sacrifice to its climax. Sangre prepared for the cut—

Shane saw his enemy, with the dagger poised over Soukie's breast. He lifted his *asson* high and shouted, "Grans Bwa! Spirit of the forest, aid me now!"

One of the *vévés* on the *assom* glowed as though phosphorescent. Though there was no wind, a branch of the magnolia tree suddenly whipped across the altar, striking Sangre's arm and sending the dagger sailing away, to be lost in the darkness and ground mist. Sangre screamed in shock and rage. He pointed his other hand at Shane, muscles rigid as wire cables, and Shane felt an invisible blow strike him with the strength of a roundhouse punch. He staggered back, almost dropping the *assom*.

Lia caught his shoulders, steadying him, then stepped around him. She held the gun in a two-handed grip, aiming it at Sangre, but before she could fire, the same unseen force struck her hand and the gun went spinning away in the opposite direction from the dagger.

Shane raised the *assōn* again. "Shango! Lord of lightning, I call upon you!"

Another *vévé* gleamed with radiance. Down from the clouds hurtled a thunderbolt that struck Anna Gautreau's mausoleum, shattering the century-old edifice. Marble shards and fragments flew in all directions; both Shane and Lia dropped to the ground to avoid the stone shrapnel. Shane saw the brown upper half of a skull hit the ground before him and tumble to a stop, the eyeless sockets staring at him with what seemed a secret and terrible amusement. He caught his breath, looking up quickly to make sure that the child had not been harmed by the blast.

Apparently no fragment had touched her. The same could not be said for Sangre, however. The *bokor* stood, swaying slightly, staring down in shock at his chest. The sharp end of a shattered tibia protruded from it, surrounded by a splotch of blood that stood out darkly against the black T-shirt. Sangre stared at it, then raised his eyes and stared at Shane. There was no anger or hatred in his gaze—only astonishment. Then his eyes glazed and he slumped forward to sprawl across the supine body of the girl.

For a moment neither Shane nor Lia moved. Then: "Thank God!" Lia gasped as she ran forward,

"Lia, *wait!*" Shane shouted, but she either did not hear or ignored him. He followed, keeping a wary eye on the misty rift above the obelisk. Was it growing smaller, now that it did not have Sangre's energy to sustain it? The crackling colors within it seemed not as vivid. . . .

Lia had reached the altar; Shane was a dozen steps behind

her. She put her arms around Soukie, heedless of the ominous cloud that hovered above, and began to pull the girl out from under Sangre's body.

Sangre's hand grabbed her wrist.

K.D. stared at Dave's open eyes in disbelief. Another impossibility—there was no way he could have come out of the anesthesia so soon. But there was no way he could have had his gut stuffed full of bugs and spiders, either; they were far from the land of normal rules now. She clenched her teeth and moved forward, kicking aside a four-inch centipede as she reached his side. She grasped his hand and looked into his eyes.

He was awake; awake and aware. At least the pain seemed to have passed. He said nothing, simply stared at her in sorrow and intense puzzlement—then his eyes rolled up and set, and the lids slipped slowly, gently, down over them.

K.D. bent down, put her cheek next to his, and let the tears come.

PONTCHARTRAIN
CEMETERY,
NEW ORLEANS
MARCH 29, 1998

L ia shrieked, a scream of raw terror. The *bokor*, his face ghastly in the flickering crimson light, pushed himself up with his other hand until he was standing upright. He shoved Lia backward, away from the altar and Soukie, hard enough to make her stumble and fall. Then he seized the shaft of Anna Gautreau's leg bone and, his mouth twisting in a grimace of agony, pulled it through his body until it tore free of his chest.

Shane had stopped when he saw this. He raised the *asson* again, preparing to call upon another of the *loas*. But Sangre, eyes glaring, teeth bared, clenched his fist in a sudden, savage gesture, and the *asson* shattered in Shane's upraised hand.

Shane stared in shock at the stump of the gourd, still clenched in his hand. Then he looked up at Sangre, saw him raising the bloody length of bone over his head, saw him bring it down toward the girl's body—

Lia, sprawled in the clammy mist and wet grass at the altar's foot, saw Sangre raise the bone, preparing to impale Soukie with it. How could he still be alive? That bone must have skewered his heart, there was no way he could still be moving and breathing—

But he was. And in a matter of seconds Soukie would not be.

Lia saw Shane leap forward, even as she tried to rise, knew that neither of them would make it—

Lia felt time slow to a crawl. She'd experienced it before in emergencies, but never to this degree, and never with this level of clearheadedness. It was as if she saw with eyes that were more than human; although it was dark, everything seemed possessed of a luminous clarity. She felt as if she were a spectator in her own body, that it was rising, moving, under someone else's command. No—*something* else's command. For she knew that, whatever possessed her at this moment, it was something much more than human.

She spoke, and she did not recognize her own voice; it was feminine, yet no more human than the crash of breakers or the howling of a gale. *"Aida!"* It cried. *"Aida Wedo! Guardian of the Rainbow, goddess of many colors, sustainer of life! The girl is mine!"* And from her outstretched hands, from her body that now stood, tall and rigid, a band of rich and vibrant colors flowed, an arc that leapt from her to the altar, enfolding Soukie in its scintillating glow. Against that cocoon of multicolored light the bone struck and shattered as if against rock.

And then the rainbow was gone, and so was the power that had filled her. Lia collapsed to the fog-shrouded ground, sick and dizzy, and could do nothing but watch as Shane charged forward, coat rippling out behind him, to grapple with his enemy.

Even with the wound he had sustained, Sangre fought feverishly, fueled by hatred and fear. He shoved Shane backward across the altar and Soukie's body, raising the jagged stump of the bone like a knife again. Shane blocked the blow with his forearm. Their strength matched for a long moment, and they froze in tortured sculpture, the muscles of their arms and chests standing in sharp relief in the eerie light. Then, gradually, agonizingly, Shane pushed Sangre back, and with a burst of force hurled the sorcerer from him. Before Sangre could recover his balance or gather himself to use his power, Shane seized him about the waist, lifted him from his feet and, with an effort that distended the veins in his neck and arms, hurled the sorcerer upward toward the roiling, writhing cloud. Only a couple of feet in the air could Shane throw him, but it was enough. Down from the mist the red and purple beams licked and, like tentacles of light, wrapped eagerly around Sangre's struggling form.

Sangre screamed, a high, continuous sound of stark terror, as he was lifted swiftly into the cloud. His hands clawed the air in futile attempts to save himself. His screams faded and his body seemed to shrink, as though he were traveling an incredible distance in a matter of moments as the hungry light pulled him toward its source. Lia saw the billows of crimson and purple open at the heart, revealing a blackness that somehow burned with searing brightness, an anti-light into which the now tiny form of Sangre hurtled. And then the mists closed like curtains, and the rift soundlessly collapsed inward. After another moment it was gone.

There was another thunderclap, and from the skies a cleansing rain began to fall.

SISTERS OF GRACE
HOSPITAL AND
PONTCHARTRAIN
CEMETERY,
NEW ORLEANS
MARCH 29, 1998

A fter they had taken the body away Jerry came to sit down by K.D. The ward was relatively quiet for this time of night; at the moment the only real noise came from the orderlies moving equipment and gingerly searching for more vermin.

"I'm sorry, dawlin'," he said softly. "I know you was sweet on 'im." K.D. did not cry; she was all cried out. All that was left was a dull ache and an equally dull wonderment at what had happened. Dave had died a death that was as impossible as it was horrible. There was nothing in the books that even came close to this.

She kept going back to the warning St. Charles's companion had given him. *Sorcery. . . .*

"What the hell happened, Jerry?" she asked. "How did he get stuffed full of those bugs? I was with him all day; there was nothing that—"

"Dawlin', I don' know. I ain't never seen anything like dat before. I jus' pray Jesus I never see anything like it again."

He patted her hand and got up to go on his rounds. K.D. sat there, her back against the wall, her mask pulled down around her neck. She had barely had time to realize that she loved him before he was gone. Life could be cruel and fate capricious; someone in her line of work knew that better than anyone. She had seen the worst of what man and nature could do to the human body; now she knew there were other sources of horror out there, other ways to die that were even more painful and terrifying.

She thought about the coma case who had come in the night of Fat Tuesday, and the flatline who had gotten up and walked out of the ward. They had to have been connected with Dave's death—but how?

It had to have been retribution. Sangre's retribution. How he accomplished it she had no idea, but he had paid Dave back for killing his lieutenant. Paid him back big time.

Harmony. Homeostasis. Payback. Call it what you will; a strange equilibrium had been once more established.

She felt the tears starting again. No, she thought, wiping savagely at her eyes. I've cried enough for one day.

A familiar sound caught her attention: the big glass doors opening. Two paramedics were wheeling in a gurney with a pale form on it.

K.D. glanced around. There was no one else available to meet the newcomer.

She drew a deep breath, then stood and walked quickly toward him. The nearest medic gave her the rundown: bullet hole in the lower left quadrant, considerable loss of blood, deep shock.

"Put him in bay two," K.D. said. "Get him catheterized, I want his urine checked for blood." The ambulance guys wheeled the gurney past her and she turned to follow it.

Even surrounded by death, life goes on, she thought. As do clichés. She thought she saw something black and eight-legged scuttle across the white linoleum in front of her, and shuddered.

Eventually the pain would fade, the loss would grow abstract. But one thing had changed irrevocably for her.

For the rest of her life K.D. would know that, no matter how modern, bright, and clean the environment, no matter how controlled and comfortable her surroundings, always in the dark spaces and crannies poisonous things lurked and waited.

Lia St. Charles and Shane LaFitte stood in the middle of Pontchartrain Cemetery, neither feeling the slightest urge to seek shelter from the rain. Soukie Delaney huddled beside Lia, arms around her waist.

"What happened?" Lia asked finally. Shane looked at her and smiled.

"You called one of the *loas*," he said. "Aida Wedo, wife of Damballah. The Rainbow. The giver of life."

"But—*how?* I don't know the first thing about any of this stuff?"

"You know more than you think," he said. "In fact, I think Sangre was mistaken. I think *you* were the child of power, not Soukie."

"But you said *she* was. The one born after twins, you said. I wasn't born after twins; I was part of a pair. Only my sister died when she was born—"

She stopped when she saw the look of revelation on his face.

"Of course. *Manassa*—the sacred ones."

The word seemed to echo in her brain, the voice of an old woman in a dark room. . . . "What did you say?"

"*Manassa*—twins. Twins are consecrated to the *loa*. I did not sense your power because you did not know you possessed it."

Lia stared at him. For a brief vertiginous moment she believed him, believed all of it—and felt her reason totter on the edge of the abyss.

"Come on," she said faintly. "Let's get Soukie back to her mom."

They started toward the gate. The rain began to slacken. "What will you do now?" Lia asked Shane.

"Go back to Haiti, I think. Sangre was right about one thing—all I ever really wanted to be was the village *houngan*. There's still much good I can do there." He was quiet for a moment. "And maybe it will help me atone, to some degree, for what I did to Anisse."

"You couldn't help that. Sangre made you do it."

He didn't answer. They reached the cemetery's gate. Shane turned to Lia and put out his hand. "Good-bye, Lia St. Charles," he said.

"Good-bye?" The thought of never seeing him again shocked her. If what he had said was true—if she *was* somehow linked to all this—how could she face it alone?

"You don't need me to return the child to her mother. And it's probably best that I disappear before the police become involved."

"But . . ." Lia looked at him, at his eyes, saw the haunted

look still in them. It will always be there, she thought. He'll always be haunted by the ghost of his wife. Always trying to find a way to make reparation, to balance the scales.

She didn't care. There were worse things than grief to haunt someone. Regret, for example.

"You know," she said, "Haiti sounds like an interesting place to visit someday."

Shane looked surprised; then, after a second, he smiled. And for the briefest of moments, Lia thought, his eyes seemed free of ghosts.

"Oh, it is," he said. "It definitely is."